THE FLOATING MADHOUSE

Also by Alexander Fullerton

SURFACE!
BURY THE PAST
OLD MOKE
NO MAN'S MISTRESS
A WREN CALLED SMITH
THE WHITE MEN SANG
THE YELLOW FORD
SOLDIER FROM THE SEA
THE WAITING GAME
THE THUNDER AND THE FLAME
LIONHEART
CHIEF EXECUTIVE
THE PUBLISHER
STORE
THE ESCAPISTS
OTHER MEN'S WIVES
PIPER'S LEAVE
REGENESIS
THE APHRODITE CARGO
JOHNSON'S BIRD
BLOODY SUNSET
LOOK TO THE WOLVES
LOVE FOR AN ENEMY
NOT THINKING OF DEATH
BAND OF BROTHERS
FINAL DIVE
WAVE CRY

The Everard series of naval novels

THE BLOODING OF THE GUNS
SIXTY MINUTES FOR ST GEORGE
PATROL TO THE GOLDEN HORN
STORM FORCE TO NARVIK
LAST LIFT FROM CRETE
ALL THE DROWNING SEAS
A SHARE OF HONOUR
THE TORCH BEARERS
THE GATECRASHERS

The SBS Trilogy

SPECIAL DELIVERANCE
SPECIAL DYNAMIC
SPECIAL DECEPTION

The SOE Trilogy

INTO THE FIRE
RETURN TO THE FIELD
IN AT THE KILL

Alexander Fullerton

THE FLOATING MADHOUSE

LITTLE, BROWN AND COMPANY

A *Little, Brown* Book

First published in Great Britain in 2000
by Little, Brown and Company

A CIP catalogue record for this book
is available from the British Library.

ISBN 0 316 85544 8

Typeset in New Baskerville by
Palimpsest Book Production Limited,
Polmont, Stirlingshire
Printed and bound in Great Britain by
Biddles Ltd, *www.biddles.co.uk*

Little, Brown and Company (UK)
Brettenham House
Lancaster Place
London WC2E 7EN

THE FLOATING MADHOUSE

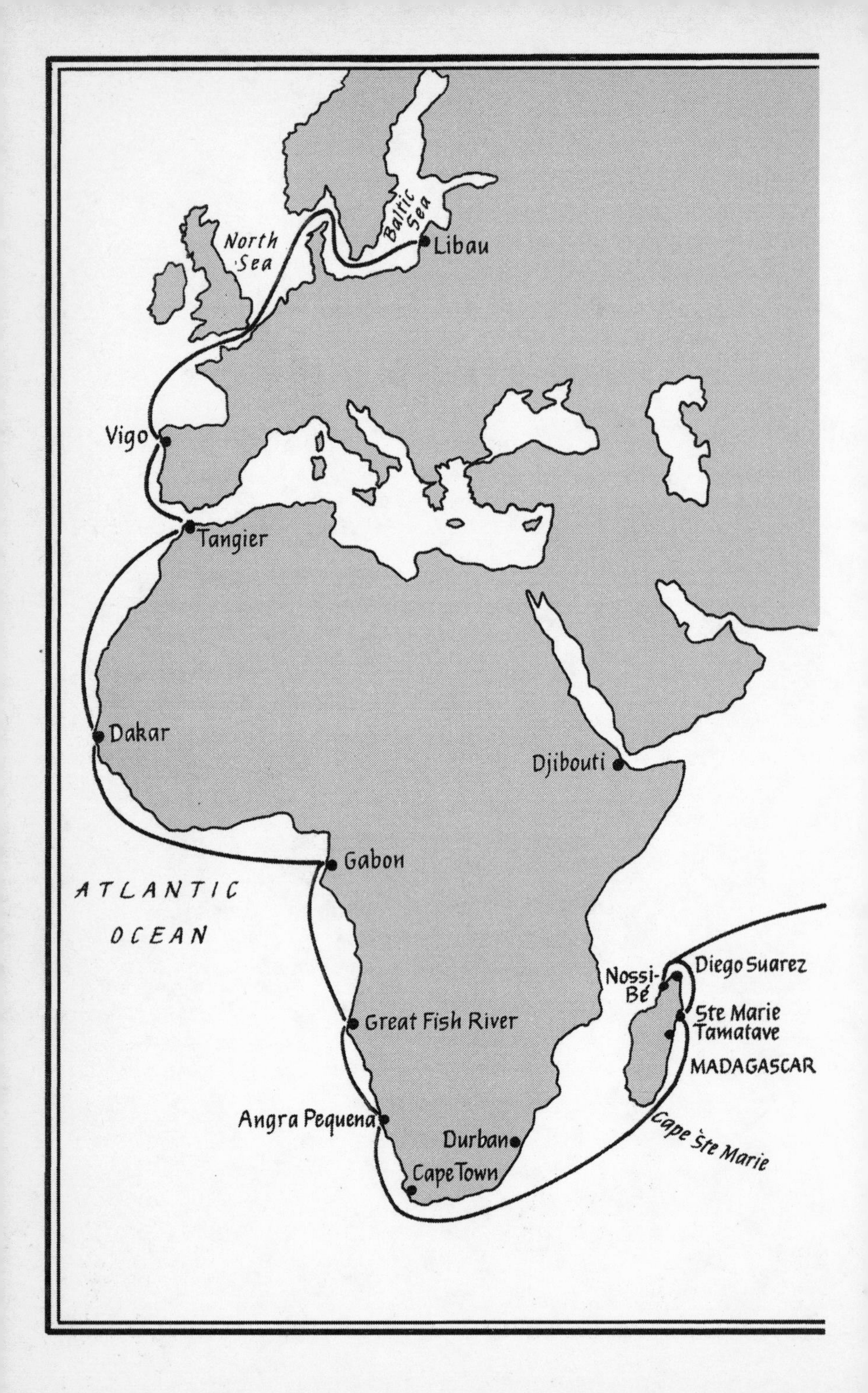

North Sea
Baltic Sea
Libau
Vigo
Tangier
Dakar
Djibouti
Gabon
ATLANTIC OCEAN
Nossi-Bé
Diego Suarez
Ste Marie
Tamatave
MADAGASCAR
Great Fish River
Angra Pequena
Durban
Cape Town
Cape Ste Marie

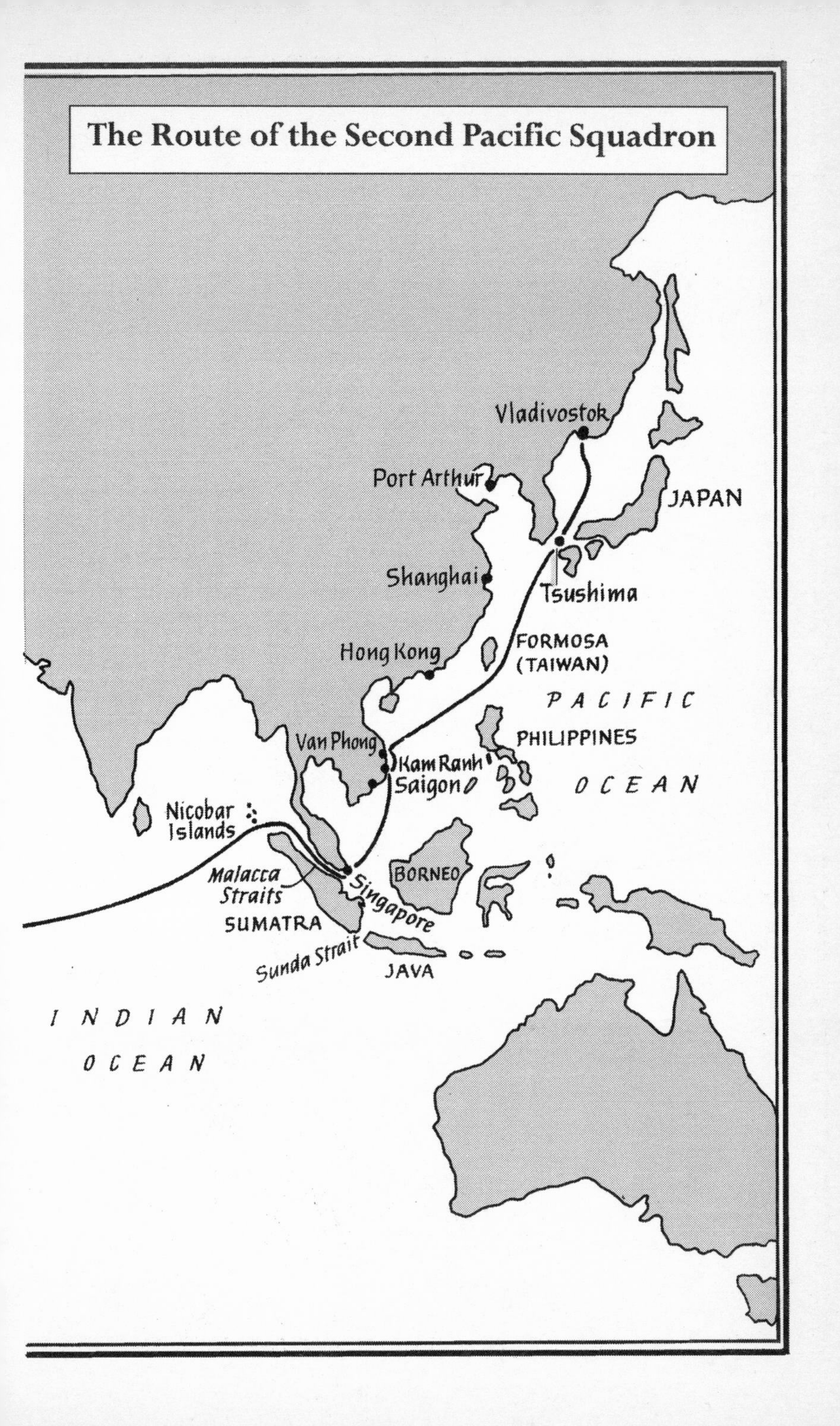
The Route of the Second Pacific Squadron
Vladivostok
Port Arthur
JAPAN
Shanghai
Tsushima
FORMOSA
(TAIWAN)
Hong Kong
PACIFIC
Van Phong
PHILIPPINES
Kam Ranh
Saigon
OCEAN
Nicobar
Islands
Malacca
Straits
BORNEO
Singapore
SUMATRA
Sunda Strait
JAVA
INDIAN
OCEAN

1

The train gushed steam as it clanked to a halt at Wirballen, the Russian frontier station where passengers were obliged to disembark and have their baggage checked. It was necessary to change trains here anyway – for the wider Russian gauge; wider and slower track. It was a dismal-looking place: grimy platform lit gloomily by oil-lamps and a fall-out of weak light from the train itself, railwaymen and porters sucking pipes and soldiers looking as if they'd been asleep on their feet like cattle. There was a lot of noise. Michael was glad he hadn't let Tasha come this far with him from Paris: she'd wanted to postpone their final goodbye to the last possible minute then continue her own journey to Petersburg – and eventually, Yalta – but he'd argued against it, and for the soundest of reasons her mother had supported him.

A headstrong girl, was Tasha. As well as beautiful. And not much more than half his own age. No sense of guilt in that now: only a kind of bewilderment mixed in with the exhilaration. He was out, on the Wirballen platform, Tasha still in his mind even while he was telling an old bent-backed *mujhik* of a porter, 'A metal trunk to come out of there.' His luggage consisted of that – one japanned-tin uniform trunk with *M.J. Henderson RN* lengthwise on its lid in Messrs Gieves' standard script, and this leather suitcase in a canvas, strapped-on cover; his name was stencilled on that too. He'd dumped it on the porter's handcart and was buttoning his covert coat against the chill of the autumn night when a voice on his other side demanded in a fruity, rounded tone, 'Might we share this contraption, sir?'

It was the rather comic-looking Russian whom he'd seen first in Paris and then in Berlin when changing trains. At the Gare du Nord he'd noticed him because he'd seemed to be taking a close interest in Tasha; Michael had been concerned that he might have been an agent of Prince Igor's, spying on them. Then some hours later in a ticket office in Berlin, the same individual had tried to strike up a conversation on the strength of having heard Michael ask the clerk for confirmation that the quickest route to Libau was to change at this Wirballen place rather than somewhere further along the line towards St Petersburg: the Russian had cut in excitedly, 'Oh, is that the case? *I'm* for Libau, and with not a moment to waste, so – why, great heavens, what luck that I heard you mention—'

Gobble gobble; decidedly turkey-like. Michael had pretended not to realize that it had been directed at him; he'd walked out on it and then made himself scarce, seen which part of the train the little man got into and taken care to put several coaches between them. For one thing he had plenty to think about – notably, of course, Tasha – and didn't want conversation, especially having to explain himself, and for another this fellow was odd-looking, his clothes neither fitting him nor matching his pompous manner of speech. The long black overcoat was tight on his shoulders and so long-skirted that it just about brushed the paving, and he had on a soft hat that was at least a size too large: despite which peculiarities he seemed to be aiming for a military look: shoulders braced, head back – to see upward under the hat's brim, no doubt; a comedy act it might well have been. But the destination of Libau – a port on the coast of Lithuania – gave one the clue: what the Russians were referring to as their Second Pacific Squadron had been assembling there, prior to its departure for the Far East, was in fact likely to be pushing off again in only a few hours – maybe at first light.

He'd nodded to this Russian about sharing the porter. After all, if he was going to be stuck with him on the next stage of the journey . . . 'If you like. Customs as I remember are in that building there.'

'Ah. Is that so? Well – thank you.' He was a lot shorter than Michael: round-faced, with a bushy brown moustache and small bulging eyes. Despite which it seemed probable that he was an officer in the Imperial Russian Navy – being in such a hurry to reach Libau, and travelling first class. Grasping the old porter's arm now, gesturing with the other hand towards a bulky, battered-looking portmanteau which he'd dumped a few feet away, urging the old man, 'This one too. Inside with it all – and double-quick, if you're expecting to be rewarded for performing no more than your duty – uh?' A bark of humourless mirth, and the peasant's face like grey pumice, slitted eyes sliding away so as not to show too clearly the resentment in the brain behind them: this would-be genial whatever-he-was either not registering it or so used to provoking hostility in his social inferiors that he took that reaction as standard and didn't give a damn. Asking Michael however in a contrastingly courteous tone, 'May I enquire the purpose of your travelling to Libau, sir?'

Michael gazed down at him for long enough to let him know that it was not his habit or inclination readily to satisfy a complete stranger's curiosity. Then shrugged: 'I'd guess much the same as your own.'

'Aren't you an Englishman? The name on your baggage – and if I may say so – without intending the least offence – your accent—'

'I'm as Russian as I am English, as it happens.' Remembering Tasha having put it more positively, about three years ago – in her mother's house at Yalta, this had been, Tasha just fifteen then, for God's sake – telling him, 'You're certainly more Russian than the Tsar, Michael!' Perfect truth at that, since the Tsar was only about one per cent Russian, with so many of his forebears having married Germans. And he – Tsar Nikolai II – had followed in the family tradition, marrying Queen Victoria's grand-daughter, the Princess Alix of Hesse-Darmstadt. Their progeny, indeed – if the truth were to be acknowledged, which it probably would not be, anyway not in much more than a murmur – could hardly claim to be Russian at all. Michael nodded to the porter: 'Yes – this gentleman's as well.' He added, unnecessarily but to make up for the other's boorishness, 'If you please.'

'Right away, your honour.'

'Get on with it then!' The Russian again – one contemptuous glance before turning back to Michael. 'Permit me to introduce myself – Selyeznov, Vladimir Petrovich, captain second rank. Delighted to make your acquaintance, sir.'

'Henderson – Mikhail Ivan'ich.' Meaning, 'Michael son of John'. He added, 'Senior lieutenant, Royal Navy.' In Russian, 'senior lieutenant' was *starshi leitnant*, whereas Selyeznov's 'captain second rank' would translate into English as commander, putting them in effect only one rank apart. At this time – 1904 – there was no such rank in the Royal Navy as lieutenant-commander. A lieutenant became a senior lieutenant after eight years in the rank, putting an extra half-stripe on his sleeve at that stage and *hoping* in as short a time as possible to make it to commander. Michael added, seeing the sharp interest – suspicion, even – in the piggy little eyes, 'You're wondering what I'm doing here – when my country's in alliance with Japan, with whom you're at war.'

'I confess – although I'm sure there's a perfectly good explanation—'

They were approaching the entrance to the customs shed – double doors, soldiers ostensibly on guard, passengers and porters squeezing in and out – the old man with their baggage on his cart waiting for an opening in the throng ahead of him, glancing apologetically back at Michael through the haze of cigarette and pipe smoke. Michael confirmed to the little Russian, 'I have papers that explain it – if you'd like to see them. The situation *is* somewhat bizarre.'

'May I ask by whom were the papers issued?'

'General Naval Staff at Petersburg – on the authority of Admiral Prince Ivan Volodnyakov. At Libau I'm to join the cruiser *Ryazan.*'

'Our newest and fastest, eh? Indeed, I envy you! But joining her as what? *Etranger de distinction,* evidently, but—'

'As an invited observer, might come closer to the mark.'

'And – well, what's this now?'

A whistle had shrilled. Blown, he saw, glancing towards the shed again, not by any railway guard – although they'd be shunting this train out soon enough – but by what looked like a colonel or lieutenant-colonel: a tallish man – about Michael's own height – booted and spurred, in a blue-grey overcoat with wide lapels, a gleam of highly polished boots below it and a silver Russian eagle in his cap-badge. Getting at least a degree of the silence he'd whistled for, he shouted, 'Selyeznov! Is there by any chance a Captain Selyeznov amongst you?'

'I'm Selyeznov.' Aside to Michael, 'Excuse me.' The little man strutted forward: 'I'm your man, Colonel! What's—'

'*You* are V.P. Selyeznov, Captain of the Second Rank?' The soldier's expression showed mild surprise, staring down at this diminutive, *outré* creature: creature explaining, 'My turnout, I'm very much aware, sir—'

'Never mind that – if you're V.P. Selyeznov and you can prove it—'

'I am, and naturally enough—'

'I've had a telegram about you. I command this frontier post – for my sins. My name is Abramov. You're on your way to join the Second Squadron, the flagship – the *Knyaz Suvarov* – correct?'

'Why, yes!'

'I have been told to ensure you're on the next train for Libau. Allows us a couple of hours. If you'll accompany me to our mess I'll see they give you a meal – and a chance to put your feet up for an hour or so. That suit you, Captain?'

'Extremely kind, sir! May I ask who sent the telegram?'

'The chief of staff to Admiral Rojhestvensky. They must be anxious to get hold of you – uh?'

'Most gratifying. I did telegraph to Rojhestvensky – several weeks ago, from Saigon, as it happens—'

'Saigon in French Indo-China?'

'Yes. I'll explain. But Colonel, I have a travelling companion here – an Englishman, an officer of the Royal Navy, extraordinarily enough – papers issued in Petersburg he tells me, by the General Naval Staff – he's for Libau too, apparently . . .'

Michael had shown them the papers, with Admiral Prince Ivan Volodnyakov's scrawled signature and the black wax seal: they'd been duly impressed but were obviously still puzzled. Suspicious, possibly: relationships between London and St Petersburg weren't at their best, for one reason and another. Meanwhile his luggage had been inspected, and the keys returned to him. Selyeznov had asked him whether his own British Admiralty were aware of his presence here, and Michael had told him of course they were; how would he be here if they hadn't been?

The truth was that their Lordships of the Admiralty in London, as represented by a Captain White of Naval Intelligence, and the Foreign Office in the person of Sir Robin Arbuthnot, had been tickled pink. The interview with White had taken place at the Admiralty, and that with the urbane, cigar-smoking Arbuthnot at the Athenaeum. In one day, all that business had been finished; all he'd had to do was get himself down to Wiltshire, organize his gear and then dash across to Paris.

To Tasha.

Selyeznov asked him, 'So your main purpose is – to "observe", you said?'

'To improve my spoken Russian is primarily what I came for. Taking advantage of an invitation to attend a Volodnyakov family occasion: first visit for several years, as it happens.'

'Are you in some way connected with the Volodnyakovs, then?'

'Connected, yes. Not related, now. But to cut the explanation short, out of the family get-together, there sprang this invitation to join the Second Squadron – an honour I'd hardly refuse, eh?'

'Only – ' Selyeznov hooped his eyebrows – 'if it occurred to you that such acceptance might cost you your life.'

'Indeed, it might.' Colonel Abramov nodded gloomily. 'They're no walk-over it seems, those monkeys!'

Makaki was this particular type of monkey. It was the Tsar's name for the Japanese, and therefore fashionable, in quite general use.

The officers' mess was only a brisk stroll from the railway station, and the catering was more than adequate, *zakuski* with vodka being followed by chicken *polonaise* and sweet Crimean champagne. This – the *champanskoye* – was a sudden extravagance of the colonel's, an emotional response to Selyeznov's explanation of how he'd just returned from the war in the East – nominally from Port Arthur in southern Manchuria, the naval base now under siege by the Japanese by land and sea – but more immediately from Saigon, where his battle-damaged cruiser, the *Diana*, had been interned by the neutral French and from where he'd taken passage in a Messageries Maritimes steamer via Suez to Marseilles; he'd arrived in Paris only a day or so ago. Disguise had been necessary throughout the journey, since effectively he'd been on the run, his parole having been agreed with the French authorities on the condition that he'd take no further part in the war. Not that they'd have cared: only wouldn't want to have been *seen* turning the blind eye. But that was how he'd come to be dressed as he was – they were the only 'civvies' he'd been able to get hold of; although by telegram from Marseilles he'd arranged for spare uniform and other personal gear to be delivered on board the flagship.

The colonel had queried, surprised, 'So you were – what, the best part of a year in Port Arthur?'

'Not quite that long. I travelled out on the Trans-Siberian railway, to join my ship which was already there – in the First Squadron, you understand.'

'And since then by the sound of it you've been knocked about to some extent?'

'Well – in the action on August tenth. And one or two other scraps. Yes, I suppose you might say—'

'Despite which you're now desperate to join the Second Squadron, get yourself knocked about some more?'

The little man had risen to his feet. 'Would a man sit twiddling his thumbs, while his comrades were still out there fighting for their lives?' He'd spread his rather short arms: 'Can there ever have been a more appropriate time, I ask you, to cry *For the Tsar, for the Faith, for the Motherland*?'

The colonel had swung round on his chair, pointed at an orderly and barked 'Champagne!' And now lifting their glasses for toasts both he and Selyeznov had tears in their eyes; Michael not able quite to manage that, but looking solemn enough while reflecting that from the Baltic to the Yellow Sea was roughly eighteen thousand miles, at – what, ten knots, if you were lucky? It certainly wasn't going to be a fast trip, with some of the old rust-buckets Admiral Rojhestvensky was said to be taking with him. Plain fact was, one was in for bloody months of it: and if one's messmates turned out to be anything like *this* idiot . . .

Perhaps they wouldn't be. This one at any rate – Selyeznov – was taking up an appointment on the flagship, the battleship *Knyaz Suvarov* – filling a job on Admiral Rojhestvensky's staff presumably, perhaps for the value of his recent experience of Far Eastern waters and of the Japanese; and one might hope to find a very different crowd of officers on board the new fast cruiser *Ryazan*.

Except for her captain – Tasha's dog-faced fiancé.

'I beg your pardon?'

Some question Selyeznov had put to him, and now repeated – on the face of it, an example of thought-transference. 'Do you by any chance know who has command of the *Ryazan*?'

'Yes. Zakharov. Nikolai Timofeyevich Zakharov. Captain Second Rank – a contemporary of yours, perhaps – d'you know him?'

'I've heard of him. His family are said to be rich. Merchants of some kind – bankers? Despite which he's said to be a hard-working and ambitious officer. He was recently in the Black Sea Fleet, I believe.'

Michael nodded. 'He was when Prince Ivan Volodnyakov was commander-in-chief down there.'

'Hah. One begins to see how two and two make four. Your own connections with the Volodnyakovs—'

'Quite.' There was no need to go into details. In fact good reason *not* to. 'Quite.'

'So Zakharov's evidently fallen on his feet. To have secured the patronage of Prince Ivan – he won't be a captain of the second rank for long, I'd guess!'

'Perhaps not.'

'You can be sure of it, my friend!'

'It's the same in the army.' Abramov shrugged. 'God knows it is. But – ' he raised his glass – 'to the ships and men of the Second Squadron, gentlemen! May you return in glory!'

Certainly the *First* Squadron, Michael reflected, the ships that had been out there from the start – Selyeznov's *Diana* being one of them – didn't have much glory going for them. Having been thrashed by the Japanese in what was now being referred to as the Battle of Round Island – the action of August 10th, Selyeznov had called it – the surviving battleships and cruisers were effectively locked up in the Port Arthur harbour, had even – according to Captain White – been landing their guns to be used in shore defences. Guns, and sailors too – sailors being put ashore to fight as artillerymen and infantry. And when the remorselessly advancing Japanese army gained certain heights in the vicinity of the port, those ships would be helpless targets for the besiegers' artillery.

He put his glass down again: having this time drunk to the

port's gallant defenders. The question was, could there be any realistic hope of Port Arthur being still in Russian hands when the Second Squadron did finally arrive out there?

Or *if* they did?

Tasha's urgent whisper: her mouth open under his, arms locked tight around his neck, naked loveliness, sweat-damp and sinuous. 'Damn well come *back*, Mikhail! Swear to God you will!'

2

The stone breakwaters surrounding the harbour at Libau – a recently constructed ice-free base also known as Port Emperor Alexander III – enclosed an area about two and a half miles from north to south and one and a half east–west: and the Second Pacific Squadron just about filled it. The landing and embarkation point where Michael was waiting was about two-thirds of the way up, on the Lithuanian shore; there were some port offices, a railway extension and two sizeable graving docks: he'd prowled around, inspected it all in the early morning light, was now back near the steps where he and Selyeznov had left their baggage. Selyeznov had taken himself off to the signal station to have their arrival reported and a boat or boats requested for their embarkation respectively in the flagship and the *Ryazan.* He'd been gone at least half an hour. Not a boat was moving out there amongst or around the mass of ships; in fact from this height and angle of view their overlapping density left virtually no unoccupied harbour surface visible. Out there one saw only a phalanx of massive dark-painted hulls and yellow, black-topped funnels – which in the earlier semi-dark had looked white – and inshore – to his right, northward – the low, slim, all-black shapes of torpedo-boats and destroyers. They'd be in shallower water there, probably two or three fathoms at most; the Baltic coast in this region was not by any means steep-to, and the battleships drawing as much as maybe thirty feet of water would need all the room there was further out, closer to the western mole.

He hadn't been able as yet to distinguish the outline or part-outline of Zakharov's cruiser. He knew pretty well what he was looking for, having been shown – in London – a photograph of her taken during her sea-trials off Kronstadt. She'd been completed only at the beginning of this year and Zakharov had only very recently been appointed to her – not, it had been only too evident, without considerable string-pulling by the Volodnyakovs – as Selyeznov had cynically but correctly guessed. That was exactly – and blatantly – how it had been. The purpose of the 'family occasion' at Injhavino had been for Tasha's father, General Prince Igor Volodnyakov, to announce her betrothal to this Captain Zakharov, who'd been guest of honour; on top of which he – Prince Igor, or more likely his nephew Admiral Prince Ivan, but that would have been at the old man's instigation anyway – had, as it were, iced the cake by arranging for the timely arrival of a telegram from St Petersburg appointing N.T. Zakharov to command the brand-new cruiser *Ryazan*.

'On this great enterprise –' Prince Igor had intoned, nearing the end of an hour-long speech – 'from which he and his fellow captains will undoubtedly return in triumph, having taught the monkeys a few sharp lessons and in so doing earned not only the nation's acclaim but his Imperial Majesty's undying gratitude!'

Pause for clapping and cries of 'Hurrah!' Tasha horror-struck, fighting to hold back her tears – clasped in her mother's arms, her dark eyes over Anna Feodorovna's shoulder pleading desperately to Michael. And twenty-four hours later, after certain other events and consequences, her father had got down to it again, pulling yet *more* strings and coming up with this invitation which he'd have known Michael as a professional naval officer wouldn't be able to resist – and which the British Admiralty wouldn't willingly have allowed him to.

As to the *Ryazan* though, Captain White at the Admiralty

had shown Michael a list of all the ships there was reason to believe might comprise this Second Squadron – details of armament, dimensions, speed, etc. – and the *Ryazan* was shown as having a displacement of six thousand, six hundred tons – length four hundred and forty feet, beam fifty-two, maximum draught twenty-four and a half, and allegedly a speed of twenty-six knots. He *still* couldn't see her. Looking for her three rather stubby funnels and raised fore and after parts with 6-inch guns on them, not especially tall masts – overall, a fairly distinctive profile – but seeing no such animal. Her sister-ships were allegedly the *Oleg* and the *Aurora* – both in this squadron – while a forerunner, first of the class and named the *Bogatyr*, was believed to have caught fire and been totally destroyed before even being launched. That was only one of scores of stories of sabotage by crews and shipyard workers – even of revolutionary activities by officers – and the Admiralty wanted every detail that could be gleaned – rumours, facts, fears, especially those held by the more senior commanders, as well as more routine intelligence, such as states of readiness and maintenance, weaponry, tactics, ships' and men's capabilities and performance.

It was fully daylight now: a fine morning with only the lightest of south-westerly breezes to stir the surface glitter – in which was reflected the whole mass of black-painted armour plate, patterned with the contrasting verticals of yellow.

'Hah! Lieutenant! Mikhail Ivan'ich!'

Selyeznov behind him, hurrying from the huddle of port offices – actually from the signal station of which the upper level was a timber deck on which were visible the revolving arms of semaphore machines, a signal lamp which earlier on had been flashing in red as well as white – Tabulevich, presumably, the Russian navy's equivalent of Morse – and masts carrying a festoon of aerials. Selyeznov hurrying, with his short, quick steps. He'd talked non-stop, all the way from Wirballen to Libau. Michael had dozed off at least once, woken that one time with a dream of Tasha in his semi-consciousness and become aware of the monologue still continuing – a dissertation on the origins of this Japanese war, Admiral Togo's treacherous torpedo-boat attack on the Russian fleet lying at anchor outside Port Arthur several days before any declaration of war – there'd been a Viceroy's ball in progress ashore, the Russian ships at anchor had been brightly illuminated and totally off-guard – oh, and a lot about the useless and pusillanimous Viceroy Alexeyev, and the disastrous death in action first of the highly respected Admiral Makarov, whose flagship the *Petropavlovsk* had been blown up and sunk in the space of sixty seconds, and then at the Battle of Round Island the even more sudden death of his successor Admiral Witheft, who'd been killed outright by the first shell of the engagement. All that and a great deal more, together with accounts of Selyeznov's own professional brilliance and steadiness under fire.

He called now as he approached, 'The *Ryazan* is not here, I have to tell you!'

'Not here?' Michael had stopped: while the statement and its possible implications churned in his skull. 'You mean—'

'She sailed yesterday in the afternoon. For the Great Belt or beyond – a scouting mission, so I was told. But you see, Mikhail Ivan'ich—'

A chance to call it off? Stay behind?

You'd have to contrive to have no option but to stay behind. For instance, Zakharov in his *Ryazan* was to have been his host only for personal, family reasons – well, persuasion by Prince Igor – and there wasn't much likelihood of any other ship's captain volunteering to take an Englishman, an ally of his enemies, to war with him. Zakharov having good reason for toadying to both Prince Igor and his nephew – although he couldn't have had any idea at all of Igor's real motive in sending Michael along with him. The old brute would have made damn sure he didn't have the least notion of it: and for Zakharov it would have been enough that there was this mutually advantageous understanding between them – the virtual *sale* of Tasha was what it came down to.

Michael could visualize Igor's old paw on the younger man's shoulder: 'See here now, Nikolai Timofeyevich . . .'

But if the *Ryazan* had sailed without him . . .

Get down to Yalta? Where Tasha and her mother would be arriving shortly?

To the utter fury of Prince Igor – of Prince Ivan too, if Igor had let him in on the truth of it. Which perhaps was unlikely: his daughter's reputation being, one might say, a vital part of his stock-in-trade, he probably would not have trusted even his damned nephew. So it would be only the old man who'd be after your blood and guts.

Very powerful and ruthless old man, at that. Which could make it a dangerous move not only for oneself but for Tasha too. Ducking out now wouldn't exactly delight their Lordships in London either: would hardly suit one's own hopes and prospects, therefore. Weakness of the flesh was primarily what had made the thought of giving up so attractive for a minute or so – desire for Tasha, and a positive interest in remaining alive – the truth being that this so-called 'great enterprise' was virtually certain to end disastrously . . . But drawing as it were a second breath, he was reminding himself that for him personally, taking that high degree of risk in one's stride, it happened also to be a marvellous opportunity. Captain White had even gone so far as to hint at a prospect of accelerated promotion if he pulled it off successfully. Which, God willing, he would: so in the long run it was in Tasha's best interests too: as long as she continued to feel as she did now – God willing *and* fingers crossed . . .

Selyeznov told him, 'Anyway, there'll be a boat coming for us in ten or fifteen minutes, from the flagship.'

'For *you*—'

'For us both. As soon as they've hoisted colours – at eight sharp – uh? I explained the situation, you see, and it's proposed that you should be temporarily accommodated in the *Suvarov*. Transferring at some later stage to the *Ryazan*, of course.'

* * *

The boat didn't come for them until after nine. At eight they heard a discordant wailing of bugles and saw colours hoisted, ensigns unfolding lazily on the still gentle but now steadier on-shore breeze. Ensigns white with the St Andrew's Cross in blue, and jacks – on the big ships' bows, vertically above the projections of their rams – deep red with the same blue cross. Boats were on the move then, but none coming this way. Selyeznov muttering angrily about the long wait as a symptom of perhaps more general inefficiency; he was obviously concerned as to how this foreigner would see it, his first impression of the squadron – as if the blame might lie on *his*, V.P. Selyeznov's, own shoulders. Michael had changed the subject: 'Do you know if your gear's arrived?'

'No. But it would I'm sure have been delivered on board when the squadron was at Reval. My own sister and brother-in-law were seeing to it.'

'And this – what you said – "scouting mission", by the *Ryazan*?'

'For Japanese lying in ambush, I imagine.'

'Japanese – here in the Baltic?'

He remembered, though: Captain White had mentioned that the Russians had a phobia of being waylaid in narrow seas by Japanese torpedo craft lying in wait for them even right outside their home ports. Michael had thought he was joking, but later Arbuthnot had confirmed it. 'It's preposterous, of course, but – the dickens, they're quite off their heads, you know. Even this fellow Rojhestvensky . . .'

Selyeznov was insisting, 'Anywhere at all. From the moment we leave this port. Well – those narrows down there – the Great Belt and the Skaw – ships obliged to pass through in single file, like a great brood of ducks! You may smile, but I tell you there's a general consensus of opinion that they *will* be trying something of the sort. Sneak attacks are their speciality – eh? Why, our attaché in Paris was telling me – showed me a newspaper article by a well-informed French authority – there've been literally dozens of reports of small craft sneaking into Danish and Swedish waters – disguised as trawlers and so forth, naturally. And as to that, look here – in certain British shipyards too, they're saying—'

'Then they're talking nonsense, Vladimir Petrovich!'

'Can you be so certain? It would have been arranged in the strictest secrecy, and no doubt at the highest levels – and after all – look, forgive my mentioning it, but Great Britain and Japan *are* – as you said yourself—'

'We are in a defensive alliance with them, that's all. Nothing new – an agreement signed in London the year before last. All it amounts to, as far as I recall, is we'd go to their assistance if they became involved in hostilities with more than one of the Great Powers at the same time. For instance, if France joined in with you against them now. Which you'll admit is hardly likely, is it!'

Sir Robin Arbuthnot had been concerned that Michael should have the facts of the Far Eastern situation straight in his mind; would be able to fight his own corner in any debates and disputes in which he might become involved during the months-long voyage that lay ahead of him. He'd explained, 'Wouldn't want to be putting chaps' backs up right, left and centre, would you? We'd much sooner have them confiding in you than – well, freezing you out, don't you know. Being as you say half Russian, nothing to stop you, as it were, blending into the background – if you worked at it a bit, eh?'

Briefing for a spy, he'd thought. From a man who claimed to be from the Foreign Office but would only meet him in his club.

Michael added – to Selyeznov – 'The only other provision in our agreement with the Japanese – as I remember it – was that we recognized their legitimate interests in Korea.'

'Their *legitimate* interests, you say!'

'Not *I* say – the treaty does. Words to that effect, anyway. So the basis of the differences between us – I'm only guessing, like you I'm a sailor, no great insight into diplomacy or politics – is that you see them as rivals and we don't – I suppose because we've no aims that conflict with theirs.

Whereas you *have*, with your Trans-Siberian railway and its extension right down to Port Arthur. Isn't that about the size of it?'

'But to offer an example of these so-called "legitimate" interests in Korea – so *legitimate* that on February ninth, the day after their sneak attack on us at Port Arthur, they did the same at Chemulpo and sank the two ships we'd had lying there until that moment quite peaceably!'

'That too before declaring war, was it?'

'Certainly! As I said – February the eighth at Port Arthur, the ninth at Chemulpo, and they finally went to the trouble of declaring war on the tenth!'

'Well. One should know what to expect of them, perhaps . . .'

'The behaviour of treacherous monkeys is what to expect! After those examples of duplicity, don't you see it's more than likely they'll attempt something of the same kind here – before we're even out of the Baltic?'

'I'd have thought they'd find it very difficult. However it may strike you in the light of our defensive alliance with them, *we* are certainly not your enemies, nor to the best of my knowledge are the Germans, French, Danes, Swedes or Norwegians. And think of the distance – eighteen or twenty thousand miles, for heaven's sake –' he jerked a thumb towards the inshore moorings, the torpedo-boats, little so-called destroyers – 'midgets like *those*, my friend!'

'Those will be coming with this squadron, presumably . . .'

'Will be starting with it, you mean. Haven't *got* there yet!'

'We'll have problems. Of course we will. But the Japanese – they could have built or converted vessels here. Minelaying craft, for instance – which can be of any shape or size, can look entirely innocent. As it was explained to me in our Paris embassy, newspapers all over Europe have been carrying such stories for weeks now – and it's known for certain that Japanese officers have come to Europe. What for – if they aren't up to their damn tricks again?'

'I don't know.' He shook his head. 'Except – one, as I

say, and assure you, Britain at any rate is not your enemy – and two – if I might offer some advice – don't believe all you read in newspapers. *I*'d say that an attack of any kind in European waters is highly improbable. I wonder what has happened to that boat they were sending, though . . .'

The answer was that it had been on some prior job which had taken longer than expected. It would have been a steam-pinnace or cutter, though why they couldn't have sent in an oared boat, for just two officers with this small amount of baggage . . . Selyeznov groused on about it, and the boat that did eventually take them out was not the *Suvarov*'s but a pinnace belonging to the port authority. In any case, it brought them out to the flagship's quarterdeck gangway at 0921 – Michael checking the time by the beautifully engraved silver half-hunter which Anna Feodorovna, Tasha's mother, had given him as a farewell present.

He slid it back into his pocket as the boat chugged in alongside. Remembering – like an echo in his brain, that voice which was almost indistinguishable from Tasha's: 'To remind you to come back to us, Mikhail Ivan'ich!'

'Imagine I'd need a reminder?'

Looking at Tasha – whose own impassioned pleas on the subject of his eventual return had been made during an afternoon of love in a borrowed apartment; the gift of the watch from her mother had come that same evening over a farewell dinner – Wednesday October 12th, the night before he'd left Paris. Anna – Princess Anna Feodorovna Volodnyakova – being Prince Igor's second wife, still young, vigorous and attractive; you could see Tasha almost duplicated in her: same dark eyes, creamy skin, hair like a tumble of black silk. She was herself young enough to be her husband's daughter, knew exactly what he was up to and hated it – hated *him* now – quite vitriolically.

Michael had promised her, 'I *will* come back.'

'Please God and all the saints!'

'A bit of help from them *would* be welcome.'

'And then – other matters being equal – forget everything

except to take this child with you out of Russia. Forget your preoccupation with becoming a commander. Which is worth more – a bit of gold braid, or *this* little creature?'

'Only that if one is to support the "little creature" in anything approaching the manner to which she is accustomed—'

'A few extra shillings a day would hardly do that, Micky. And fortunately it doesn't matter, since with Liza Andreyevna's help, on which we can surely count . . .'

Liza Andreyevna was his mother: better known in England as Lady Elizabeth Henderson. He'd temporized, 'Either way, I won't let you down.'

'If you haven't already.'

That reference was to the possibility of Tasha being pregnant. Which they wouldn't know about at any rate until the squadron was on its way. While the mention of Michael's mother being rich was a symptom of Anna Feodorovna's inability to comprehend that his future in the Navy might matter to him as much as anything did. Even Tasha herself. That it *had* to: not as a matter of wanting to have his cake and eat it, more that in practical terms the two weren't separable.

Wouldn't have to be – please God.

From the flagship's quarterdeck, where they were greeted by salutes to which he and Selyeznov responded by raising their hats, Selyeznov also halting and clicking his heels in the Prussian style, they were led by a rather heavy-set young *michman* – who'd introduced himself (Michael *thought* he'd heard) as von Kursel – along the upper deck, under the loom of the after-superstructure and then past the ship's two enormous funnels towards the towering forebridge. Up a level by this time – Michael having taken note of three twin 6-inch turrets as they passed them – secondary armament, three turrets each side, while the main armament of four 12-inch were in one twin turret up for'ard and one back aft. Seamen here and there taking gawping note of him and Selyeznov as they passed. Observing – noting

– smaller-calibre weaponry too, at differing levels. While two steam pinnaces, lashed in their cradles between the funnels, and other boats inboard as well, suggested that sailing might not be long deferred; although on the ship's other side there had to be a barge alongside – a derrick was bringing up crates of ammunition, its blocks squealing, guys and topping-lift manned by bluejackets and a petty officer bawling orders. Selyeznov was urging him to come on, and a moment later the *michman* ducked into an opening in the forebridge's lower-level superstructure: passing the foot of another up-ladder, from which a rotund, white-jacketed warrant officer came down like a ton of bricks, half-colliding with the *michman* and apologizing perfunctorily: a *michman* not being of much importance, only the equivalent of a sub-lieutenant – not midshipman, as one might have guessed from the similarity of the words. The badges of rank either side of this one's thick neck were yellow epaulettes with a black stripe down the centre and a single star halfway along the stripe. He'd halted now at a door marked CHIEF OF STAFF.

A double knock, and a reply of 'Enter!' Selyeznov edging up behind the *michman* and motioning to Michael to give him room to be first across the threshold.

3

The chief of staff, Captain First Rank Clapier de Colongue – in his early forties, of old French ancestry, tall and courteous, effusive in his welcome and even not doing a bad job, Michael thought, of masking his surprise at Selyeznov's 'turn-out' – had told them it was Admiral Rojhestvensky's intention to lead the squadron out of harbour at midday; but in fact it transpired during the course of the forenoon that the bigger ships were all aground and couldn't move. This had infuriated the admiral, who was said to be pacing about on the forebridge shouting abusive remarks about the port's designers and constructors.

Some cruisers – including *Oleg* and *Aurora*, and two others who were allegedly sister-ships to *Ryazan* but of which Michael until now hadn't heard – and destroyers and various other ships – several 'auxiliary cruisers', which were mostly large, former Hamburg-Amerika passenger vessels on which had been mounted a few small-calibre guns – and transports, store ships, old steamers of varying displacements – had up-anchored and found enough water under them to flounder out of harbour. They'd wait for the battleships outside, presumably.

'Anchor out there, I dare say. We'll get under way at about four, is the expectation.'

The speaker was Senior Lieutenant Count Nikolai Sollogub, the *Suvarov*'s assistant navigating officer, who after lunch had shown Michael around the ship and then brought him up to the signal platform at the back end of the after bridge – the emergency control position, Michael would have called it. He'd changed into uniform before lunch. They'd allotted him the spare berth in a cabin belonging to an engineer – actually an engineer-constructor, on the admiral's staff – a man by name of Narumov, who later had introduced him, in the wardroom over lunch, to this Count Sollogub, possessor of a name he felt sure he'd known from somewhere in the past – some reminiscence of his mother's, possibly – and with a friendly manner that contrasted with the frigid politeness most of them had shown him, in that wardroom. He'd met about twenty of them: mostly limp handshakes, cold eyes, formal words and practically no smiles. Their names and mustachioed faces were a jumble in his memory: Flag Lieutenant Leontiev, Captain Second Rank Semonov, Senior Lieutenant Sventorjhetsky – on the admiral's staff, number two of the gunnery department – and Lieutenants Bogdanov, Vladimirsky, Reydkin, Politovsky, Brakov, Ulyanov, Baylin, Guryenko, Grigoriev. And others: *Michmen* Fomin, Shishkin, Golovkin . . . All in those comic-opera knee-high boots with trousers tucked in and flopping baggily over their tops: the clown-like effect was only emphasized by a marked display of hauteur. Sollogub – ignoring the critical glances his messmates had been directing at him for consorting with the enemy – had expressed interest in improving his knowledge of the English language.

'Think you might find time to help?'

'Bags of time, I'd guess, and I'd be delighted – if it's possible, seeing I'll be in the *Ryazan*, you know. I'm aboard here only because she's already sailed, and I'd cut my arrival here so fine—'

'I heard about it. But now look at that.' Pointing at a dog – dachshund-shaped but with a coarse white coat – which was being given a fingerful of Beluga caviar by Sventorjhetsky, the tall and burly gunnery flag-lieutenant. Sollogub said, 'Flagmansky, they're calling it – because it came on board at the same time as most of Rojhestvensky's staff. But *Ryazan* – yes, we've been given all that background. Incidentally, I was intrigued to hear that you have connections with the esteemed Volodnyakov family. Had any of whom been aboard, incidentally –' he'd dropped his voice to a murmur – 'this rabble would be *grovelling* . . .'

'Do you know the Volodnyakovs?'

'I wouldn't say *know* them, quite. But might we discuss that later?' Lowering his tone again. 'Some of these chaps . . . Well, you've met a fairly typical selection, I suppose. They'll – oh, settle down, when they get to see which way the wind blows – but I wouldn't, I think, discuss – er – personalities, here and now . . . On the subject of moving between ships, though – whether for language practice or purely social visits – there'll be numerous stops *en route* – we'll be coaling in Danish waters, I'm told – Japanese permitting, of course – and stopping in the French port of Brest, and so on, and after that God knows where else, but we have somehow to get right round Africa, and we won't do that without frequent stops to take in coal. So there'll be boats to and fro, and the *Ryazan*'s wardroom might spare you for a few hours now and then.'

'Only too glad to get rid of me, I should think. But of course. Conversational practice, and vocabulary, that sort of thing? Mind you, I'm hoping to improve my spoken Russian too.'

'I should think there'd be quite a few who'd be keen to join in. It's going to be a long haul, I'm afraid, and with little to occupy one's mind . . . That is, if we ever get out of here!'

'You mean if we get off the mud?'

A shrug. 'That'll resolve itself in an hour or two – with a rising tide and an onshore wind to push some of it in here. The ships are over-loaded, that's the main trouble – nobody seems to have given a thought to it. More than over-loaded, some of them are positively unstable. No, what I meant was, out of the Baltic – with all the rumours of ambush by the Japanese—'

'I wouldn't believe any of that, Count.'

'Look – if you don't mind – I'm Nikolai Sergei'ich Sollogub, and despite our very brief acquaintance – also to make up to some small extent for my messmates' appalling manners—'

'Mikhail Ivan'ich Henderson.'

'Genderson . . .'

'If you like. In English it's Henderson – but that's tricky for you, of course.' Because of the absence of a letter 'H' in the Russian alphabet, they'd substitute a 'G'. 'But the talk of a sneak attack by torpedo craft, Nikolai Sergei'ich—'

'You don't believe in it?'

'Frankly, I do not.'

They were back then into much the same exchange of views as he'd had with Selyeznov – whom he hadn't seen since leaving him with Clapier de Colongue – de Colongue wanting to discuss what would be the little man's duties on the staff, but having changed his mind about taking him directly to meet the admiral – obviously because of his odd appearance and how the admiral might react to it. He'd told Selyeznov, 'A cabin has been allocated to you, of course – if you'd ask at the commander's office they'll show you. And I believe baggage was put on board for you at Reval. You'd feel more comfortable in uniform, my dear fellow – and *then* I'll present you to the admiral.'

'I have been keenly anticipating that honour, sir!'

Sycophantic little swine. Michael, after exchanging a few platitudes with de Colongue, had excused himself and left them to it, made his way back aft and found von Kursel, who'd directed him to Narumov's cabin, in which they'd already deposited his gear and where the engineer-constructor, a dark-complexioned man in his middle thirties, was crouched over a desk writing a letter to his wife.

'There'll be a last mail put ashore before we weigh. At least, I very much hope there will be . . . You're an Englishman, I was told?'

'Half English, half Russian.'

'Well, I might as well admit to you – in order to have it in the open and understood between us right from the start – that I dislike the English quite fundamentally. I think the reason you have been put into this cabin is that I shall be spending a lot of my time in other ships – supervising repairs of one kind and another – so often enough you'll have it entirely to yourself. I can't think of any other reason – except that with the number of staff officers we now have on board – that *is* the reason, of course—'

'In any case I'm only here until I can move to the *Ryazan*.'

'Yes. When the opportunity arises. I was assured of that.'

'But you're responsible for repairs in other ships? Don't they have engineers of their own?'

'Of course they do. And in each of the major vessels – our three sister-ships for instance – there's an engineer-constructor as well. But in the smaller ones the engineers are not up to dealing with constructional repairs – only with running their own machinery and routine maintenance. We do have a repair-ship coming with us – the *Kamchatka* – for as much as she may be worth – of which having taken a look around and spoken to some of her engineering staff I have some considerable doubts.'

Michael had unlocked his tin trunk. He said, 'You'll get it all in hand, I'm sure. Would it inconvenience you if I were to change now?'

'Not in the least. As a matter of fact I'd be glad to continue this letter to my wife.'

'I'm sorry to have interrupted in the first place. But tell me – if you would – why do you hate the English?'

'Because they are Russia's eternal enemy. Arrogant, cunning, with overpowering strength at sea and vicious in the use of it. *All* nations hate England – it only suits most of them to tolerate her, most of the time. Does that answer your question?'

'Very clearly.' He smiled, rather liking the man's directness. 'I can only hope you'll bear in mind I'm half Russian.'

'There's nothing personal in what I've said. You asked

me, so I told you, but none of it is directed in any sense at *you.* With that name there – Genderson – I take it that your father is English – *entirely* English?'

'Was. He died some years ago. My mother on the other hand is entirely Russian, and still very much alive. She was born Lizavyeta Andreyevna Sevasyeyeva.'

Blank look: and of course, this character had probably never heard of the Sevasyeyevs. He was nodding now, though. 'At least she brought you up to speak Russian. You're not married?'

'Not yet.'

Heavy sigh . . . 'At times such as these it's as well not to be.'

'Yes. I understand, how you must feel . . . And I'll shut up now, let you get on with your letter.'

'The worst of it is that I'm very much aware it could be the last I ever write. If the Japanese – your allies – *are* lurking out there . . .'

'It's highly unlikely. Really. Pretty well impossible.'

'That they'll attack us on our way out of the Baltic – through the narrow waters of the Great Belt and the Skaw, the Skaggerak – *that* you say is impossible?'

'Highly improbable anywhere at all in European waters. I assure you.'

'And when we turn the corner into the German Ocean?'

'The North Sea – *and* the English Channel – perfect safety.'

'Hm. I realize you'd have satisfied yourself on that before accepting the invitation to join us – logically, one might assume so. But are you an experienced seaman, may I ask?'

'I've been about ten years at sea.'

'Have you indeed. Well, I may as well tell you, you have the advantage of me there – this will be my first blue-water cruise. First, and I dare say last. I hope you're right in your views, obviously, but – well, the more general opinion seems to be to the contrary. However – excuse me now . . .'

Head down and scribbling. Michael pulled his reefer jacket out of the tin trunk and unfolded it. His sister-in-law Jane had helped him pack this lot. Coming to think of which – of Jane and Wiltshire, of the house and estate that had been his father's and was now his brother's; this was a Saturday – October 15th by the English calendar – and she and brother George would almost certainly be hunting. Allowing for time-difference, just about starting out, he guessed. He paused for a moment, first wishing to God he was with them and then reflecting that his sister-in-law and Tasha would be bound to get on well together, if and when they got to know each other. It was a very large 'if': to that extent Narumov's fatalism might be justifiable, in the long run. The Japanese did know their business, and their commander-in-chief Admiral Togo knew it very well – whereas from what one had seen here this far – as well as much of what Captain White had told him, which at the time had seemed far-fetched enough to be more like gossip or rumour than hard intelligence – what it boiled down to was that the Second Squadron's prospects weren't all that rosy. White had in fact made a point of it: 'We're assuming you'll have given serious thought to this, Henderson. Obviously it's in our interests to have you there, but – to put it mildly, it's not without its risks. If you did want to reconsider – be clear about this, nobody's *ordering* you to take it on.'

Thoughts of the past, present and future mingled and surged. His present situation, and events leading up to it – Injhavino, Paris, Tasha. Tasha as the mainspring of it all. It had all come up so fast, and he'd, as it were, been running with it. All very well for White to have talked about 'reconsidering' – there was time *now* for reflection, but there hadn't been before: really only for *reacting*. White hadn't meant that anyway, had said it because he'd felt he had to – putting on record that Their Lordships were *not* sending Senior Lieutenant Henderson either on a spying mission or to a watery grave.

Thoughts back again to Tasha, whose very existence was

of course unknown to either White or Arbuthnot, and whose huge importance to him was known only to her and her mother – oh, and to Prince Igor, damn him, and his spies; and to Jane now, since in eliciting her help in other matters he'd had to let her in on the situation. He'd asked her not to mention it to George, who was very much his father's son – loud-voiced, tended to adopt an authoritative manner and would have disapproved of Michael's pinching another man's fiancée – which as far as he was concerned would be all there was to it. Jane wouldn't tell him anyway, having promised not to, even though her own reaction had been somewhat equivocal: watching Michael as he explained it, attentive but expressionless and offering no comment. Jane was a ripping girl, everyone agreed – despite the puzzle of his mother's warning, years ago, 'Watch out for that one, Michael. She's charming, pretty, *very* capable, but—' But what? She'd cut herself short at that point, added a moment later, 'There's a lot of Russian in you, you know. None at all in George.' He'd guessed finally what she'd been getting at, the fact that George, her beloved first-born, wasn't exactly sparkling bright, that Jane had seemed at times to have a greater affinity with 'the Russian one'. Not that the old girl need have worried. Anyway he hadn't told *her* about Tasha yet. She – Mama – would have been on his and Tasha's side for sure, once she'd brought herself to face it, but she'd become scatterbrained of late, might have blurted it out to George or inadvertently put something dangerous in a letter – even to Prince Igor, with whom she still occasionally corresponded. Later of course she'd *have* to know – as indeed would George – but as a *fait accompli.*

Which brought one's thinking back again to Tasha and how she'd acclimatize – if such a dream could possibly come true, if one did (a) survive this expedition, (b) manage with Anna Feodorovna's help to extricate her. Well – forget that second 'if', if one was alive to do it one damn well *would.* But Tasha's only visit to England this far had been in '95, with her mother; George hadn't married Jane until the year after that, so the two girls had never met, and there'd be a good ten years between them. George had inherited the estate and the baronetcy on his and Michael's father's death – of a broken neck, in the hunting field, at the age of sixty-three – in 1893. Jane had been in the offing, of course, but not actually present during Anna Feodorovna's visit, and Tasha had been just nine years old, though already riding – brother George's description – 'like some drink-crazed Cossack'. Michael – then nineteen or twenty – nineteen, still a sub-lieutenant, hadn't acquired his second stripe until '96 – had taken the child cubbing, and conscious of his responsibility for her safety had tried at first to keep her on a leading-rein – at which she'd initially shown a degree of shock and disbelief, then refused absolutely to tolerate. She'd dismounted, 'cast off' (as it were, in naval terminology), flung herself back up into the saddle and left him standing; had then been in at the death, got herself ritually blooded and brought the cub's mask home with her – still seething at the indignity to which he'd tried to subject her. 'I should have realized,' he'd acknowledged later to her mother, 'I'm sorry – she'll probably never speak to me again.'

'Oh, she will – I promise you!' Laughing dark eyes. 'She *will*, my dear!' There was Georgian blood there in the background, Michael's mother had said. She was fond of Anna, and they'd had friends and acquaintances in common, despite the eighteen or twenty years' difference in their ages; and as for himself, it was Anna Feodorovna he'd been keen on then, he remembered – remembered now with slight embarrassment. She'd have been about thirty-five, dazzlingly attractive – and a mile beyond his reach, of course. While Tasha was only her somewhat wayward child – great fun, great character, but very much a child. He remembered his mother's description of her – Mama after his father's death having moved into the Wiltshire estate's dower house, where he, Michael, lived with her when he came home on leave – weekend leave, whatever, from Portsmouth; she'd likened Tasha to 'a beautiful kitten with wickedly sharp claws'. Smiling at that recollection, fitting a back-stud into a shirt to hold the starched collar in place, while Narumov's pen scratched on and on, he queried in his memory how it had happened that Anna and Tasha had come to England on their own – without Prince Igor – in '95 . . . To his surprise the solution came instantly: Tsar Alexander III had died at the end of '94, and Igor had had to call the trip off – *sine die*, since there'd been not only the State funeral to attend – indeed, probably to help arrange, at least the military side of it – but also the fact that Tsarevich Nikolai, who'd been in utter panic at the prospect of becoming Tsar, had needed support and guidance from all concerned and wouldn't have got much from his uncles the Grand Dukes – enormous men who'd terrified him right up to his coronation in May of '96; which of course was why no Volodnyakovs had been free to attend brother George's wedding in London to the Honourable Jane Pownall, in that particularly lovely spring.

Instead, they'd have attended the coronation in Moscow and taken part in the days and nights of banquets and balls after it: celebrations shockingly marred by a lemming-like stampede of people on Khodyinka Field, an army training ground outside Moscow where half a million of them had gathered to enjoy free beer and sausage, but when they didn't get enough of either went on a rampage that left nearly fifteen hundred of them dead, mostly by falling into open military trenches where they were crushed and suffocated by others piling in on top of them. The Tsar had shown his steel (or according to some, his bone-headedness) by continuing with the celebrations, that same night dancing at a ball given by the French ambassador. He was a good dancer, but the people were outraged and there were revolutionary rumblings all over Russia.

Still were. And more than just rumblings. Peasant riots in recent years had reached crisis proportions. And only three months ago Viacheslav Plehve, Minister of the Interior, had been assassinated. Anna Feodorovna saw only the bleakest of futures for her country. It was part of her reasoning in wanting Tasha out of it.

Engineer-Constructor Narumov had coughed, artificially, and his pen had stopped scratching. Michael, now in shirt and trousers and tightening his black tie, glanced at him across the cabin.

'I'll leave you in peace in a minute, don't worry.'

'I was wondering whether you might like to hear some words I have just written to my wife.'

'No, I wouldn't presume—'

'On the subject of yourself. Listen.' He looked down at the sheet of plain white paper which he'd been covering with an even, slanting script. '"I am about to surprise you, now, my dear. I have in my cabin with me at this moment an officer of the British Navy. Believe it or not – knowing as you do of my deep affection for the English! But you can believe it because I tell you so. Admittedly of partly Russian parentage, he is a guest temporarily accommodated in this vessel and making use of the spare berth in my cabin, but destined for another ship, a cruiser, at the invitation of some nobleman on the General Staff, and – I'm told – of that ship's commander. So here I have an ally of our enemies, if you please, dressing himself up in his British uniform and from time to time looking down his nose at me as I pen these words to you! Well, let me describe him to you. He's about six feet tall or perhaps an inch or so more than that, strongly built, has brown hair and blue eyes and a pleasant-enough smile. A pleasantly mannered individual, too; you, I'm sure, would take to him immediately. But what I was about to say – I referred in an earlier paragraph to the threat of Japanese covert action against us in the Narrows, but this Englishman – their ally – assures me that there cannot be any such Japanese presence in those waters, or in the 'North Sea' either – the 'North Sea' being what the English call the German Ocean. So join me please in hoping that he is right, and may such hopes relieve the anxieties that must be racking you on this score."'

Finished. Eyebrows raised queryingly as he held that page up close to a scuttle for the breeze to dry it. 'Do you think it may reassure her?'

'Easier not to alarm her in the first place, I'd have thought.'

'Everyone in Russia *knows* an attack is to be expected!'

'How long will your letter take to reach her?'

'Perhaps three, four days. She's in Petersburg – where I wish to heaven *I* was still!'

'In three or four days we'll be well past the Skaw. At least—'

'I wouldn't count on it.'

'You don't accept my assurance, then.'

'That's not it at all. What I'm saying is that some of the old vessels we have with us – frankly, they're barely seaworthy. And the crews no more than half trained – at least, most of them. This applies even in these modern and most powerful ships, the very core of our fighting force. I must ask you not to mention to anyone that I've told you this – it's only that I'm in the habit of speaking frankly.'

'Yes, I've noticed. But I promise you. Not a word.'

A shake of the head. 'The crews will become trained along the way – that's what our optimists will tell you. But listen again – something else I'll read to you . . .' He'd raised the lid of the desk, was rummaging inside it. 'Here we are.' A board, with a wad of signal-forms clipped to it; he riffled through them, then stopped. 'This one will do. Admiral Rojhestvensky's order number 69, which he put out during our sojourn at Reval. I quote: "Today at 0200 I ordered the officer of the watch to sound the alarm against torpedo attack. Eight minutes afterwards nothing whatsoever had been done. Everyone was sound asleep except the officers and men of the watch, and even they were by no means alert. The men detailed for countering attack were not at their posts, and no steps had been taken to illuminate the deck, although it is impossible to work guns in total darkness."'

Narumov tossed the log back into his desk. 'That describes

how it was – most likely still is – on his own flagship, this *Suvarov.* God knows how much worse it may be on others. I tell you, I'm no seaman, but I've got eyes and ears.'

'So you had a royal send-off from Reval?'

Talking to Nikolai Sollogub now, on the after-signal platform. Mid-afternoon, and men at work all over the ship – on the face of it at work, but looking more carefully one could see that a lot of them were just milling around. Sollogub nodding to Michael's question about Reval and Tsar Nikolai's visit to his Second Pacific Squadron. 'We did indeed have a dreadful day of it. His Majesty was accompanied by a whole team of admirals – including his ancient and elephantine uncle Grand Admiral Alexis – and your Volodnyakovs of course – the old one, the general, I suppose in the role of A.D.C. to his Majesty – but the younger, Admiral Prince Ivan, also well to the fore. He's General Prince Igor's nephew, isn't he? I'd forgotten, thought he was his son, but—'

'Nephew.'

'Wasn't he – Prince Ivan – with Tsar Nikolai when, as Tsarevich, there was an attempt to assassinate him during a tour of Japan?'

'Yes, he was. A tour of Japan, Indo-China and – oh, Egypt. Prince Ivan was a captain first rank at that time – aged only about thirty, mark you – senior naval aide in the royal entourage. I've heard him speak of it more than once. The date was 1890, and the place where some lunatic tried to kill him – not Tokyo—'

'Otsu?'

'You're right.' Michael offered the count a cigarette. 'Smoke?'

'Thank you. French, I see.'

'I passed through Paris recently. But – Otsu, yes. That was when he began to call them monkeys. Also, since that royal tour he's honoured Prince Ivan with his – well, "friendship" might be too strong a word for it—'

'Patronage.'

'Nearer the mark. At this rate, however it goes with your English, my spoken Russian will be improving fast. But as I imagine you're aware, Uncle Igor was a crony of Alexander III – which must have accounted for his nephew being given the world tour job in the first place – and then virtually instant elevation to Flag rank . . . Did you say that's the *Oryol* astern of us?'

'It is indeed. My God, has *she* had problems!'

She was a battleship of the same class as this. There were four of them: this *Knyaz Suvarov* – Knyaz meaning prince – the *Oryol*, the *Alexander III* and the *Borodino.* Michael said, 'Those further back on the quarter are the old brigade, obviously. The *Oslyabya*, the big one?'

'Twelve and a half thousand tons. Main armament ten-inch. That's Admiral Felkerzam's flag she's flying. He's Rojhestvensky's second-in-command. And in that crowd astern of her – hard to make out individually from this angle – the *Sissoy Veliki*, the *Navarin* – battleships – and the *Admiral Nakhimov*, armoured cruiser, eight thousand tons and twenty years old, main armament only six-inch and – well, antiquated. As are the *Navarin*'s. The ships themselves – not just their guns. Between you and me, and not to mince words, they're liabilities more than assets.

'But *Oryol* – as I was saying, she's had more than her share of problems. Almost capsized when they were launching her, then there was sabotage of her engines – steel scrap in one of the low-pressure cylinders, apparently – and at Kronstadt recently, when we were leaving port, heading for Reval, she ran solidly aground. They tried all the usual things, couldn't budge her, finally had three dredgers working for more than twenty-four hours before tugs could drag her off. But – forgive me, Mikhail Ivan'ich, changing the subject back again – the Volodnyakovs – I can't claim to have *known* any of them, but my family did, and I was a page – aged about twelve, you know – at Prince Igor's wedding to the ravishingly beautiful Countess Anna Feodorovna. Whose first husband –' he'd slapped his forehead, stirring memory – 'Boris Pavluchenkov – right? Wasn't he killed in a skirmish with rebels in Azherbaijan, or Chechnya, one of those places?'

'Yes. Although she herself doesn't talk about it. Hadn't been married long when it happened; she was very young and very much in love with him. In fact she was still too stricken with grief to think straight and take to her heels when that old goat Prince Igor began pestering her with his attentions.'

'I did hear – grown-up talk, you know, perhaps I should say did *over*hear – that Pavluchenkov left her with nothing but debts. You know her now, though, do you – I mean, you've seen her recently?'

'One could hardly know the Volodnyakovs *without*—'

'Is she still the eye-catcher she was?'

'Older than you'd remember her, of course – and married for some years now to Prince Igor – but yes . . .'

'He must be a *lot* older than her.'

'He's close on seventy, and she's – early forties. I tell you one thing, though, the daughter she had by him – Natasha – is certainly the most beautiful girl in Russia – probably in the world.'

'*Really?*'

Michael nodded. More or less poker-faced, he hoped. *Having* to mention her, although aware it might have been better if he hadn't. Sollogub asked him after a pause, 'What sort of age now?'

'Oh.' Frowning with the effort of working that out. 'Near enough eighteen, I suppose.'

'How is it that one has never seen her, I wonder?'

'Well, Natasha was at school in Petersburg, but Anna Feodorovna moved her a year or eighteen months ago to a *lycée* in Paris. She's finished there now. And although Prince Igor has a house in St Petersburg – which he doesn't need, still spends all his Petersburg time out at *Tsarskoye Syelo,* at His Majesty's beck and call – well, Natasha and her mother are hardly ever there either. Anna has a house at Yalta, which they both adore, and there's the family estate at Injhavino, of course.'

'Ah, Injhavino. Have there been riots around there? That awful time the year before last, for instance?'

'No. They seem to have been lucky in that respect. But – what I was telling you – there's also a house in Paris which belongs to Prince Ivan's mother, the widow of Prince Sergei, who died about ten years ago. She was the Countess Tatiana Zurin – name ring a bell?'

'Why, yes – looking back, childhood memories again . . . Sergei was Igor's brother – right?'

'Right.'

'And the Zurins were very rich?'

'Right again. Tatiana inherited the Paris house from a Zurin uncle and she's managed to hang on to it. She's getting on now – well into her sixties – but she and Anna Feodorovna are firm friends. So one way and another – this is still answering your question – they do move around a bit.'

'No lack of money, by the sound of it!'

'You might think not, but Prince Igor considers himself hard up. Prince Ivan too, I'm sure. Injhavino does swallow money by the bucketful, of course, and a lot of the great estates *have* been sold, you know – well, of course you know. In the case of Injhavino they're trying hard to make a go of it – Ivan's sons Stepan and Pyotr doing all the hard work, living really like peasants.'

'And may I put a more personal question – your own connection with them? I've been racking what pass for brains, ever since Narumov introduced us, but I'm *damned* if I remember . . .'

'Prince Igor's first wife was my aunt Varvara – Varvara Sevasyeyeva.'

'The Sevasyeyevs. Yes . . . And Igor Volodnyakov's first wife – the Princess Varvara – she was your—'

'My father met the younger sister at Varvara's wedding to Prince Igor, and married her – Elizavyeta, my mother –

a couple of years later. By the way – your leadsman's in the chains again . . .'

'The chains' being a platform projecting from the ship's side just below the forebridge; the platform had chains around it against which the man could lean while he heaved his 'lead' – a leg-of-mutton-shaped weight on the end of a line marked in fathoms. When the ship was under way he'd heave it in a soaring arc to drop into the sea ahead and with skilful management to be 'up and down' with the line taut as it passed below him. Lying stopped now, of course, he had only to lower it until it touched bottom and the weight came off the line. Michael heard his bawled report: 'By the mark five!'

'Thirty feet.' Sollogub nodded. 'We should be clear. When the *Oryol* got herself stuck at Kronstadt she was drawing twenty-eight and a half – there again, overloaded, *should* draw twenty-six.'

A bugle sounded and moments later was being echoed from other ships. Sollogub pushed himself off the rail. 'That's "Men to their stations for leaving harbour". I'd better get for'ard.' He patted Michael's arm. 'Great fun, reviving old memories. I hope we don't rendezvous with your *Ryazan* too soon.'

From this after bridge, which was still comparatively unpopulated, he could hear the cable clanking in, the regular metallic thumps as each link was dragged up through the hawse and crashed over its lip. Wind still in the west, but stronger, and grey cloud thickening. Sailors swarming like bluebottles all over the big ships' foc'sls: and a grey-painted steam pinnace coming up from astern – from the far side of the *Oryol* – slewing in to stop a few feet clear of the *Suvarov*'s side amidships. Collecting mail, sacks of it being lobbed down to be caught and dumped on the heap already almost filling the boat's stern. On his own account, while in England and Paris Michael had made what he thought should be effective arrangements for his mail: he'd be sending all his letters to Jane in Wiltshire, and so would Tasha. Jane would forward his to Tasha at the Yalta address, and enclose her missives to him in envelopes which she'd address to him in care of a ship's agent in Odessa by name of Gunsburg – an agency of which, oddly enough, Prince Ivan had told him. Gunsburg would be forwarding supplies of all kinds to the squadron as it made its way around the world, and would be as well informed as anyone of its whereabouts from week to week. Prince Ivan had provided this useful tip in ignorance of the fact that the only letters Michael cared a hoot about would be those between himself and Tasha. Touch wood, no mail addressed in her handwriting or even seeming to have originated in Russia would be coming to him in the *Ryazan*, nor would his missives to her be posted on board with her name on them.

Vibrations through the deck under his feet and a swirl of mud-coloured water astern told him that the *Knyaz Suvarov* was now under way. *Oryol* too – her starboard bower anchor hanging a-cockbill while a hose gushed down at it, dislodging mud. Profiles of other black-painted, yellow-funnelled ships beyond alternately opening or closing as angles of sight changed; *Suvarov* slowly gathering way, and the rest of them manoeuvring to follow her out: a herd of mastodons lumbering ponderously out of their stone pen, filing slowly and clumsily into the dredged channel leading westward.

4

The battleship *Sissoy Veliky* in the course of weighing had managed to lose her anchor: then near the outer end of the dredged channel the torpedo-boat *Buistry* had collided with the *Oslyabya.* Admiral Rojhestvensky was leaving the *Sissoy* to recover that anchor – by grappling for it from a pinnace, presumably – and then follow on her own. Rojhestvensky had shouted at his chief of staff, 'Teach the swine to take more care!' Because following alone, unescorted, was reckoned to be a highly dangerous proceeding – the Baltic being thick with Japanese torpedo-craft and minelayers, as everyone knew it was. As to the *Buistry*, she'd been approaching the *Oslyabya* to deliver some message and her captain had either misjudged his distance or put his wheel the wrong way; Narumov, whose job it would be to organize repairs, probably when the squadron anchored off Bornholm some time tomorrow, expressed the view that if the man was typical of his kind he'd almost certainly been drunk.

The weather was worsening, visibility considerably reduced by rain and drizzle sweeping grey across a now choppy sea. At about six o'clock Michael was in the wardroom, hearing from Narumov that he'd been the assistant constructor on the *Borodino* throughout her building and consequently knew this class of ship intimately – which had to be why they'd decided to send him in the flagship despite his having no previous sea experience – and watching a game which involved the dog Flagmansky and a champagne cork on a string – when his former travelling companion, Selyeznov, came down with a message from the chief of staff: Admiral Rojhestvensky could spare a few minutes now, if he'd be so good as to come up to the bridge.

'Right!'

He stood up. Selyeznov said, 'I'll take you up there, Mikhail Ivan'ich.'

'All right. Thank you. But I'd find my way—'

'Hah!' Narumov grinning up at them. 'When Boyarin Zenovy snaps his fingers, even the proud English jump!'

'I suggest you refrain from referring to your commander-in-chief in terms of such familiarity!' Selyeznov puffing himself up like a frog, glaring down at the engineer, adding, 'Especially in front of an outsider!' Michael aware that Zenovy was Rojhestvensky's christian name, and 'Boyarin' meant 'Lord'. Facetious, certainly, but not so terrible an insult. Narumov shrugging, telling the little man that he himself was an outsider: 'A constructor, I build ships, I shouldn't be called upon to sail on the accursed things. If Boyarin Zenovy would care to put me ashore somewhere I'd be only too gratified!'

Up to the forebridge then, where Clapier de Colongue first introduced Michael to the ship's captain – Ignatzius, a tubby, cheerful man, who evinced no noticeable hatred of the English, in fact seemed entirely friendly. The battlefleet, Michael had noticed, was pushing along at nine or ten knots, steaming in two separate divisions. Felkerzam's second division – the *Oslyabya* and company – was a mile astern of this one, while the black smudges of another group of large ships visible ahead through now heavy drizzle and under a cloud of their own funnel-smoke were – Ignatzius informed him – 'auxiliary cruisers', those former German liners, in company with the transports, some of which were at least as big as the so-called 'cruisers'. Michael had commented, 'No destroyers with us, then,' and Ignatzius told him, 'Destroyers and the first-class cruisers have gone ahead. Mines are therefore of no particular concern to *us* – as long as those fellows draw enough water to explode them for us. What?' Laughing heartily, swinging his arms and stamping his feet, presumably to warm them. Then: 'Tell me, lieutenant – are you a big-ship man?'

'Not really, sir. My last job was navigator of a cruiser – on the West Indies station – but I've served mostly in destroyers. Only spent a few months in a battleship – as a midshipman, that was.'

'So the *Ryazan* will suit you better than this – if, or when, we happen to come across her – eh?'

Another roar of laughter finalized that interview – suggesting perhaps that the *Ryazan* had got lost. Otherwise, what was the joke? Perhaps he didn't need one. The chief of staff, guiding Michael around the superstructure's more sheltered side to the admiral's quarters – at the after end of this bridge level, behind the chartroom, wireless office and what was probably Ignatzius's sea-cabin – had only smiled thinly, shaking his head as if it puzzled him too. Halting now, raising a fist to knock on another black-painted door.

Rojhestvensky – the name was pronounced 'Rojh *est*v'nski' – was a very large man: taller than Michael, and broader, with a squarish face, strong jaw, neatly trimmed beard and moustache and wide-apart, glaring eyes under jutting brows which gave him a ferocious look. Michael had placed his cap under his left arm on entering the cabin; at attention, he bowed slightly.

'An honour, sir.'

'I've heard about you from Captain Selyeznov.' Loud voice, fierce expression. 'You have close connections with the Princes Volodnyakov, I understand. I'm bound therefore to welcome you to my squadron.'

'Thank you, sir. Most kind . . .'

'Despite the fact that Great Britain is in alliance with our enemies!'

He'd shouted that. Michael told him, 'I'm half Russian as well as half English, sir.'

'You're an officer of the Royal Navy! Answers *that* conclusively enough – eh?' The eyes blazed at him. 'Why you'd have *wanted* to come with us I find puzzling! Explain it, can you?'

He nodded. Not having been invited to sit down: in any case the chairs around the table were heaped with files, signal-logs, rolled charts ... There was nowhere Rojhestvensky himself could have sat, even on his own, only presumably in his sleeping-cabin, which would be through that door in the port for'ard corner. Michael began – soothingly – 'I'd say first that it was not my idea or proposal, sir. To start with I was only invited to the Volodnyakov estate for a family occasion – the announcement of a betrothal.'

'Whose?'

'Prince Igor's daughter's to Captain Zakharov of the *Ryazan*, sir.'

'Oh, yes.' To Colongue: 'You mentioned something of the sort.' A hard look at Michael then: 'But you had no difficulty in obtaining leave for this "family occasion" – eh?'

'I was due for some saved-up leave, sir. I've just completed a two-year commission on the West Indies station, and had none in all that time. But in fact, owing to my mother being Russian – she was a Sevasyeyev—'

'*Was*, was she?'

'—and having been brought up speaking at least *some* Russian, and there being a need for officers who can serve as interpreters when necessary—'

'They've sent you to practise your Russian on us – that it?'

'Initially, yes – as far as visiting the Volodnyakovs was concerned. Although as I said, I had leave due to me in any case – and I've been granted periods of leave in past years for that same purpose. But there's a lot more to it than that, sir – as I'm sure you'll have guessed. A chance to get seagoing war experience, very likely experience of action – especially because since steam replaced sail, wooden decks and hulls are now armour-plated and guns immensely more powerful as well as being mounted in trainable turrets with telescopic sights, and so forth. It's an entirely novel situation in which we've had no major war or battle experience and tactics as taught now can only be based on theory and supposition – at least, until your own very recent engagements with the Japanese—'

'Of which the less said, the better!'

'Well . . .'

'You agree, do you, less said the better?'

'Well. As one's heard – regrettably . . . There's no doubt your First Squadron did have dreadfully bad luck. The loss of Admirals Makarov *and* Witheft—'

'You're not totally uninformed, then!'

'I hope not, sir. But I'm sure that with this powerful reinforcement now—'

'We'll turn the tables on them, have no fear of that!' He'd slammed one fist into the other palm, and glanced for confirmation at Clapier de Colongue; the chief of staff spreading his hands, murmuring, 'No doubt at all, Excellency . . .'

'Despite enormous handicaps they've forced on me . . . But we're your Admiralty's guinea-pigs, are we? It's to hear from you how we handle things that they sanctioned your coming with us?'

'I wouldn't put it *quite* like that, sir. But if I may say this – I'm not here as a spy, either.'

'*Why* say it? Did anyone suggest—'

'I had the impression, sir – from the line of this interrogation—'

'*Interrogation?*'

'The questions as to my reasons for accepting this invitation, sir.'

'Oh – that . . .' A glance at de Colongue: then back again. 'They'll be expecting detailed reports from you all the same – eh?'

'Not in the interim, sir. No question of sending reports back *en route*, for instance.'

'For example, then . . . Hasn't it occurred to you or to your superiors that I'm facing the most immense problems over coaling? Where and how to coal, when since we're belligerents – through *having been attacked*, mind you – neutrals won't let us into their damned harbours virtually anywhere at all, despite the need to replenish bunkers after every few days' steaming?'

'I had wondered, yes . . .'

'Won't your Admiralty be wondering too? Wouldn't you like me to tell you how I'm going to do it, so you can tip them off – enabling them to forestall us somehow?'

'They're not expecting to hear from me at all, sir.'

'Are they not?' A snort – derision, disbelief. 'In their position, *I'd* certainly be expecting it.' The admiral's eyes were narrowed, crafty. Enjoying the role of interrogator, perhaps. A shrug, then: 'All right, I'll take your word for it.' Another sideways glance at Clapier de Colongue: 'The conclusion's simple, if that *is* the case. They don't need reports from him, because we'll have their ships trailing us every mile of the way – snooping and reporting back, and their government threatening anyone who even *thinks* of letting us in. Because the Japanese would expect nothing less.' To Michael again: 'You realize that's what your people will be doing? Exerting pressure right across the world – France, Germany, Spain, Portugal, all the territories they've grabbed like marauding dogs along the African seaboard – and in the East as well?' He'd turned to de Colongue, throwing his arms up in a gesture of despair: 'Isn't that exactly what we'll be contending with?' Swinging back now, pointing with a forefinger the size of a banana: 'We *will* damn well contend with it! I'll beat the whole damn lot of them!'

Michael nodded. 'I'm sure you will, sir.' Rojhestvensky staring at him, taking long, deep breaths, presumably to calm himself. And changing the subject now: 'Have you known Captain Zakharov long?'

'Only weeks. In fact we met about – yes, three weeks

ago, over a period of two days at the Volodnyakov estate at Injhavino.'

'Was it Prince Ivan's notion, to ask him if he'd take you?'

'General Prince Igor's, I think. But since it's a naval matter he'd have given it to Prince Ivan to arrange.'

'I still wonder *why* . . . Look here – you might think this rather a personal question—'

'Perfectly all right, sir.'

'Simply this – how did your connection with the Volodnyakovs come about originally? That's to say, we know your father married a Russian – of the Sevasyeyev family – but how did that come about?'

'He met the Countess Elizavyeta Andreyevna at her sister Varvara's wedding to Prince Igor. Prince Igor had invited him. So that was the start of it – two years later my father married the younger sister.'

'The *start*, surely, must be wherever your father and Prince Igor first met.'

'Oh – of course. In the war we and the French fought against you – in the Crimea, fifty years ago. My father was a captain in a regiment of dragoons, and he happened to save Prince Igor's life.'

'Saved his enemy?'

'Prince Igor was a lieutenant at the time – he was five or six years younger than my father – in one of your Guards regiments. Might have been the Preobrazhenskis . . . Anyway he'd got lost somehow behind our lines and had the bad luck to be cornered by a troop of mounted French who were –' he glanced at de Colongue – 'this is unpalatable, I know; they had no officers with them, must have been running wild – were about to make *him* run – on foot, to ride him down then with their lances – for sport, as it were. Well—'

'Your father intervened?'

Michael nodded. 'Charged them with his sabre drawn, they scattered, he recovered Prince Igor's horse for him and rode some distance towards the Russian lines with him – pointed him towards home, and that was that.'

'Having I suppose exchanged cards.'

'At least identities and regiments. Leading – some five years later – to the wedding invitation.' He looked again at Clapier de Colongue. 'Sorry to tell such a story, sir. Not a pleasing one to French ears.'

'As it happens my ears are well and truly Russian. But we all have our miscreants, in whom war often brings out the worst, as well as sometimes the best.'

Rojhestvensky had turned away – striding to the door of his sleeping-cabin and then back again. Halting, nodding, fists on his hips: 'No wonder Prince Igor was pleased to bestow such an exceptional mark of favour on that man's son.' Pointing again suddenly: 'And as you remarked, Genderson, that was fifty years ago – *exactly* fifty years, surely! Wasn't it in the middle of October of that year – fifty-four – that you laid siege to us in Sevastopol?'

'You're absolutely right, sir!'

The admiral liked that. Nodding, happy with it. 'So there you are. The anniversary – the debt he's owed your father for so long. Never mentioned that aspect of it, eh?'

'No, sir. Until this moment it hadn't occurred to me.'

Because it was plain coincidence, irrelevant.

'Satisfying his own conscience – sense of obligation, memory of your father. Becomes much easier to understand, doesn't it? But I want to get on with this now. Tell me, Genderson – man to man: what do you know of the Japanese threat here in the Baltic and the Skaggerak?'

'I don't believe there's any such threat, sir. Not anywhere in European waters.'

'That's what you maintained to Selyeznov. Who, as an adviser on my staff, with very recent first-hand experience of Japanese monkey-tricks, is convinced there's a definite and immediate threat – every likelihood of our being attacked – with mines if not torpedoes, especially in the confined waters of the Belts, the Kattegat and the Skaw. How do you answer that?'

'Can't see it as a possibility, sir. The Japanese might wish they *could*, but they'd have colossal dificulties to overcome. Operating so far from their own bases and knowing there's no chance at all we or any other European power would help them in any way. Britain's alliance with Japan is purely defensive, not *off*ensive; and for the same reason that the French and Germans won't let you coal in their ports, neither they nor we would allow Japanese into ours.'

'Strange – considering you've built most of their ships for them!'

'We build ships for half the world, sir.'

'*And* train their officers. Not excluding their Admiral Togo.'

'So I've heard, sir. But there again—'

'What about small steamers – or fishing vessels, say – adapted for minelaying? Hiding in recent weeks in the Scandinavian fjords perhaps?'

'They'd need a fitting-out base to start with, sir, wouldn't they? And shoreside support and supplies – and such total secrecy as in present circumstances – well, with all the newspaper speculation, and all of us intent on guarding our neutrality—'

'Now you're just babbling, lieutenant. The fact is that to adapt small vessels for minelaying would be as easy as falling off a log. Some launching arrangement, that's all – such as many trawlers might have already, I dare say. And the supply of mines, of course – but they'd be brought by – oh, anything at all, even sailing ships. Nobody'd have to know a thing about it.' Sardonic grin directed at his chief of staff: 'While they're busy "guarding their neutrality" – eh?' Back to Michael: 'What could be easier than to sneak out ostensibly to fish but actually to plant mines – in those narrow, shallow waters – conveniently shallow, seldom more than ten fathoms and often less – correct? – in the Belts and the Kattegat?'

He was right about the depths, and in laying moored mines from small craft it would help, obviously. But – he shook his head again. 'I can't see how they'd be in a position to do any of those things, sir. Captain Selyeznov I know has been persuaded that Europe's crawling with Japanese naval officers, but I very much doubt it. After all, when you see a Japanese you *know* he's Japanese, don't you?'

'Well – hear *this.* But just a minute . . . De Colongue – clear the rubbish off these.' Off the chairs. Chief of staff as clearer-upper, Michael thought. Rojhestvensky leaving him to it, striding to the door and wrenching it open, his bulk filling it for a moment as he passed through. Glimpse of wet, black-painted steel, slanting rain, grey sea heaving: Rojhestvensky standing for a few moments gazing around, then disappearing towards the starboard side – for a view ahead, no doubt – but within a minute back again, hunching through the low door, brushing the wet off his frock coat. 'Sit down.' He grabbed a chair for himself, turned it to sit astride it. Bearded jaw jutting . . . 'Genderson, some facts now – but quickly, I didn't expect to take this long. Listen. Weeks ago we anticipated the dangers we'd be facing here, and an officer of our Secret Service, by name of – well, never mind – was sent to Copenhagen to set up a network of agents – in Sweden, Norway and Germany as well as Denmark. And I tell you, the reports have been flooding in! Unidentifiable vessels in hidden coves, comings and goings by steamers on apparently legitimate business but calling in by night at those same places – *there,* see that?' Pointing at a signal log. 'A whole series of such reports, none of which can be ignored. Have you wondered what your *Ryazan*'s doing, so far ahead of us? I'll tell you: Zakharov's investigating localities of special danger. He's a good man, I wish I had a dozen more like him – in place of some of the riff-raff I *have* been given. Decrepit ships and rotten officers.' He glared at de Colongue: 'Eh?' A courtly inclination of the fair head: 'Indeed, Excellency.' De Colongue was about the same height as Rojhestvensky, but slimmer – in fact willowy. Michael didn't envy him his job. The admiral swung back to him: 'So there it is, Genderson. As from sunset all ships will be mounting doubled watches, guns will be manned night and day with twice the normal quantity of ready-use ammunition close at hand, and searchlights manned of course throughout the hours of darkness. Nobody'll be turning in, officers and men will sleep at their action stations fully dressed.'

'Ah. Well . . .'

'What are your thoughts on the subject now?'

'Well, sir – with the greatest respect – if you feel such precautions are necessary—'

'Great God in heaven!' A bellow, from a distance of about four feet. 'After getting these reports, should I be doing *nothing*?'

'Not if you believe them, sir. As I can see you have to . . . May I ask – will we be anchoring off Bornholm tomorrow, as I heard?'

'No, we will not! We'll be anchoring tomorrow evening, off Langeland – where we have a rendezvous with colliers. Know what or where Langeland is?'

'Danish island, in the southern approaches to the Great Belt. The fairway leads slightly east of north between Langeland and Lolland.'

'You're familiar with these waters then.' The admiral was levering himself up. 'And I respect deeply what you've told me about your father. But as to your view of the dangers we're facing, I have to conclude that you have a naïve quality about you, a defensive attitude towards your country's alliance with our enemies, and more than a streak of obstinacy. Well, we'll see, we'll see . . .'

Telling Count Sollogub later that evening about his interview with Rojhestvensky, Michael asked him what highlights in the man's career had won him the Tsar's approbation and hence this appointment as c-in-c.

'Did *he* tell you he's a favourite of His Majesty's?'

'No. Someone, in the last day or so. Selyeznov, perhaps.' Glancing round the crowded wardroom. But no Selyeznov, of course – senior members of the staff messed with their lord and master, and he would presumably be dining with him now. In any case the source of that information had been Captain White of the Admiralty in London. White hadn't in fact known much else about him, except that he was a gunnery specialist. Sollogub drained his wine-glass and put it down: 'Did you hear the shooting this afternoon?'

'Two practice rounds from one of the for'ard six-inch, was it?'

'Our admiral firing blanks at the poor old *Oryol*, who'd failed to acknowledge a flag-hoist telling her to pay better attention to her steering. She'd been weaving all over the place, that's a fact. Narumov thinks her steering gear's probably defective. But Zenovy Petrovich has been known to fire *live* rounds on such occasions. Not directly *at* ships but close enough to them, so one's heard. Answering your question, however, he made himself a reputation as a fire-eater in the Turkish war. He's brave, no doubt of that – as well as forceful and – well, intemperate, at times. But there was a scandal from which he emerged – strangely enough – triumphant: his captain – the ship's name I forget, but our man was its second-in-command – claimed to have sunk a Turkish battleship when actually he'd run away from it. Zenovy Petrovich kept his mouth shut for a while but then blew the gaff before the truth became public knowledge – he wrote a letter to *Novoye Vremya*, confessing all – and as I say survived, with a reputation for fearless adherence to the truth, while his former C.O. received the order of the boot, of course. Rojhestvensky had been caught in an awkward situation, and it was seen as a brave act – you know, facing the music. Even if it might also be called saving his own bacon. He came out of it well, in any case.

'And then – oh, the year before last, this was – we were honoured with a visit by Kaiser Wilhelm and his Grand Admiral Tirpitz – invited by Tsar Nikolai to Reval to witness a gunnery demonstration under the aegis of the then *Captain* Rojhestvensky – and the shooting was absolutely top-hole. So impressive that the Kaiser said he only wished he had a few commanders of such brilliance in *his* fleet. Which the

Tsar loved, of course. God knows how Zenovy Petrovich had done it: must have had his gunners practising day and night for months. He can go days and nights without sleep himself, and he drives his underlings just as hard. He's a harsh disciplinarian, you know. Can be brutal. Fact remains, every shot struck its target – moving targets too, floats towed by torpedo-boats – whereas this lot with us now can't even hit static ones. Result of that success, however, Z.P. Rojhestvensky promoted to chief of naval staff in the rank of rear-admiral.' Sollogub beckoned to a steward: 'Another bottle, please.' He turned back to Michael. 'What a man needs, to get to the top in our navy, Mikhail Ivan'ich, is either powerful family connections, or some fluke chance that attracts the notice of His Majesty. But whether this adventure now won't be the end of the road for him: whether in the first place he'll get us there, or in the second be any match for Togo – which I suppose is tantamount to saying it may well be the end of the road for all of us – huh?'

'Togo may be a little over-rated. He won the battle at Round Island, but going by what I've heard he should have made a much more thorough job of it. Had the most amazing luck – which if he'd taken full advantage of—'

'Didn't he, though? Sent 'em all scuttling back into Port Arthur, surely?'

'Not all of them, Some got clean away. Only to Chinese ports, admittedly – where they're interned, of course. But in any case, if he'd really seized his opportunity—'

'Look – talk about it another time, perhaps. Getting a bit crowded in here.' Shake of the head. 'He beat us hollow, anyway. To say he might have done it more completely still—'

'All right.' Glancing round . . . 'I'm surprised there *is* such a crowd. The admiral said you'd all be at action stations from sunset on.'

'Guns are manned, for sure. And searchlights, and extra lookouts posted. Any alarm, we'd all be up there within seconds. But a lot of these are staff, not ship's officers. In any case, one does have to eat – and if one is not a gunnery man . . . And they seek each other's company, you know. Lonely up there – *and* nothing to drink, unless they have a brandy or two sent up – keep the chill out, or sharpen the Dutch courage.'

'I've noticed there *is* a – well, a degree of anxiety, here and there.'

'Blue funk, you mean. What a diplomat you are.' Sollogub chuckled, fiddling with his empty glass. 'High degree of anxiety, indeed – they're mostly shivering in their boots! They *are* – literally – and for all sorts of reasons, not only this expectation of attack . . . Ah, good!' The wine: a Tokay, also from the Crimea. Sollogub resumed. 'The men know as well as we do that they're at best half-trained, that quite a few of the ships are really fit only for breakers' yards, and – for instance – even in these modern battleships the gunnery-control equipment is out-dated. As you saw, they're only now cutting holes in gunshields in order to fit telescopes. Our Russian gunlayers have never *had* telescopes. Oh, and the guns are fired by jerking lanyards – with consequent delay between the order or resolve to fire and the implementation of it – whereas in your ships and I'll bet the Japanese too, the triggering is by electric impulse. Isn't that the case?'

'In *our* ships, has been for some years.'

'Crews, again.' The count glanced around for eavesdroppers: but there was a high level of sound, and no one all that close. He said quietly, 'Some are straight off the streets or fields, virtually shanghai'd, while a significant number of them are revolutionists – who of course don't want us to win this war. Perhaps when the time comes – if it does – they'll fight as best they can, simply because they'll see that the alternative is to be blown up or drowned; but if for instance we were stuck in some hell-hole on the coast of Africa – for lack of coal for instance, which is quite a possibility – or arrive out East too late to be of any use . . . Well, wars that are lost tend to promote or assist revolution, while victory has the opposite effect – cheers for the Tsar, the *last* thing those fellows want!'

'You paint a black picture, Nikolai Sergei'ich.'

'Wishing you hadn't come?'

'Not really . . .'

'Well, here's to you. Although you must be crazy.'

'And to you. But I *had* to come. Couldn't have turned down such an invitation – especially from Prince Igor.'

'Although he's only one of the two thousand princes we have in Russia?'

'He does happen to be an old friend of my father's. *And* still at the top of things – having the ear of the Tsar, for instance.'

'Does that really concern *you* so much?'

'Well – all right. I suppose the truth is I *wanted* to come. To see modern fleets in action, as much as anything.'

'That's another thing entirely. Only yourself to blame, you might say. Incidentally – regarding that statistic of two thousand princes, I should quickly admit there are roughly the same number of counts littering our fair land. Returning however to the more serious topic, and to give you the full flavour of our national predicament, I'll tell you another thing – very much between ourselves.' Glancing round again, as he sipped at his wine. 'You'll have heard, I imagine, that our army out there – Generak Kuropatkin's, in the Liaotang Peninsula – is on the run?'

'In retreat at the moment – one's gathered from newspaper reports.'

'Well, yes, it's true he's waiting for his reinforcements to build up – reaching him by way of the Trans-Siberian railway, of course, but not fast enough. There's still a gap in that line at Lake Baikal, which has to be crossed by steamer, or in winter on the ice in sleds. And meanwhile although Kuropatkin is commander-in-chief, he has the deadweight of Viceroy Alexeyev on his shoulders – interfering, countermanding orders and so forth. But this other thing, Mikhail Ivan'ich – I happen to know for a certainty that the best of our troops, the ones who *should* be going to Kuropatkin, are being kept at home, mainly around St Petersburg and Moscow where they may be needed sooner or later to quell riots. That's God's truth – but don't say I told you . . .'

5

He'd written a letter to Tasha – in Russian – and enclosed it with one in English to Jane; telling Tasha that she was in his mind night and day, and a lot more that was much more intimate, emotions and images that had interrupted his sleep night after night, set his brain and body on fire even to think about, let alone put down on paper; but also prosaically informing both of them that the squadron was at sea and on its way. Which it was again now, after spending two days at anchor off Langeland, the mass of ships then filing up through the Belts and into the Kattegat. Sea calm, rain still about but with fine spells in between, barometer happily a bit higher than it had been.

On arrival off Langeland the whole squadron had coaled, from colliers of the Hamburg-Amerika Line who'd been waiting for them. Sollogub, who as assistant navigator heard a lot of what was going on or being planned, had said he thought this would be the shape of it all the way round the world, rendezvous after rendezvous with German colliers under no doubt highly lucrative contract to St Petersburg and in constant wireless contact with this flagship.

If the wireless worked. That was German too, and there were doubts about it, apparently.

After coaling, a day and a half had been spent trying to set up a minesweeping operation. Selyeznov had persuaded Rojhestvensky to give him his head on this, since the danger from mines was so obvious, and he, Selyeznov, had apparently organized sweeping off Port Arthur with great success. In the Great Belt, however, it hadn't worked. For one thing the ships allocated to it were of such disparate size and power; the large ice-breaker *Yermak* and the small tug *Roland* were required to drag between them a considerable length of chain cable with small grapnels trailing from it on lighter chains. Each of the major vessels in the squadron had been told to have their engineers work all night forging grapnels, but only a few had filled their quota, and the fleet repair ship *Kamchatka* which should have supplied fifty had made none at all. Asked by semaphore from Selyeznov *Why not?* the reply had been *Because no written order was received.* Eventually Selyeznov, fuming, had embarked in the tug to take command of the sweep, which of course was intended to precede the squadron all the way through the danger area, but he ended up being towed into the Great Belt stern-first, signalling in panic to the *Yermak Stop your engines. What are you doing?* At about the same time the chain cable snapped, while the looming mass of the squadron under a pall of black funnel-smoke was closing up remorselessly astern. Rojhestvensky then saved the day by signalling *The passage is to be considered as having been swept,* and the Second Pacific Squadron ploughed on by, ancient battleships dwarfing the two small craft and collision after collision being narrowly avoided, tug and ice-breaker pitching and rolling helplessly in the great ships' spreading wakes and bow-waves.

'Zenovy Petrovich was spitting blood,' Sollogub had remarked later, joining Michael in the after bridge. 'And I'd guess your friend Selyeznov might have been in tears.'

Michael had had his own binoculars up there with him – a pair of Messrs Heath's Prism Binocular Glasses which had been an extravagant present years ago from brother George – and although with the restricted view forward from this after bridge he hadn't been able to see it all, he'd had a fair notion of what had been going on. Even in the Royal Navy one had on occasion been privileged to witness snarl-ups, and seeing some of it, one could guess at underlying causes; although a disadvantage from which Michael suffered was that he couldn't read Russian semaphore, let alone Tabulevich.

What he had been able to do while in that anchorage was sort out some ship detail, especially in regard to the cruisers and to the still absent *Ryazan*. The *Oleg* was apparently *Ryazan*'s only sister-ship, and theoretically belonged in this squadron but had been left behind in Reval or Kronstadt for the repair or replacement of machinery that was thought to have been sabotaged. She was expected to overtake and rejoin at some later stage. The *Aurora* on the other hand was a sister to the *Diana* - the ship Selyeznov had left in a wrecked condition in Saigon – while the other two 'first-class' cruisers, *Zemchug* and *Izumrud*, were of only half that displacement, definitely light-cruisers and accordingly more lightly armed – with 4.7-inch instead of the others' 6-inch – and slower.

Most of this information came from Captain Ignatzius who, to Michael's surprise, in contrast to the ancient RN tradition of captains messing in solitary grandeur, had all his meals in the wardroom and was a most relaxed and companionable messmate: from Michael's point of view in fact he had been helping to break the social ice. *Suvarov*'s executive officer or second-in-command, for instance – Captain Second Rank Makedomsky – was a contrastingly morose individual with whom it was virtually impossible to have any sort of conversation. Whereas even on the evening after the minesweeping debacle, when there were also serious worries about the squadron's wireless communications, Ignatzius wasn't letting anything get him down. He'd been making fun of Selyeznov and his slapstick performance in the tug, and from this the chat had turned to the *Oryol*'s breakdown: her steering had failed, she'd had to drop astern and anchor in the middle of the Great Belt, and the admiral had found he couldn't communicate with her by wireless and had had to contrive a way of doing so through the tug *Roland*, which having been left astern of the main body, with Selyeznov still on board, had gone to stand by the *Oryol*. Wireless messages were then sent via the tug, which passed them to and from the *Oryol* by semaphore. Ignatzius had found this screamingly funny too – that the much-vaunted Second Squadron should have been sent on its way with ships unable to communicate with each other, let alone with the outside world.

'Some German system, they were saying?'

Sollogub had nodded. 'Bogdanov and Leontiev have been grousing about it day and night.'

Bogdanov was the torpedo lieutenant, also the ship's wireless expert. The two jobs went together, apparently. Leontiev was the flag torpedo lieutenant – and wireless expert – on Rojhestvensky's staff. Michael asked them, 'Why couldn't you have had Marconi?'

'*Much* too simple. The Marconi system *works*!' Ignatzius threw a crust of bread for Flagmansky to chase. Two other dogs seemed to have been adopted by the wardroom now, one a smaller edition of Flagmansky, dachshund-shaped, and the other a smooth fox-terrier puppy. Sollogub told Michael, 'This German gear is called Slaby-Arco. Untried, experimental and, according to Bogdanov, bloody useless. Just happens the technical committee in Petersburg plumped for it – for the entire squadron. It's the Central Administration who issue the contract – and of course one asks oneself who's paying out how much to whom!'

'But couldn't the admiral—'

'He'd have had no say in it at all. We're talking about the *Central Administration* for heaven's sake!'

'But to be steaming halfway round the world, and unable to communicate—'

'They may yet get the hang of it.' Ignatzius crossed his thick fingers. 'We have German technicians with us, square-head bastards must be capable of *something*.'

The next anchorage – to coal again, also to wait for the *Oryol* to catch up – was south-southwest of the Skaw. In fact the squadron sailed again without fully completing the coaling, in order to forestall the Japanese, who it was assumed would be expecting Rojhestvensky to take his squadron around the top of Scotland and coal at the Faroe Islands. There'd been reports of strange vessels and suspicious movements on the southwest coast of Norway and off northeast Britain. What the Japanese would not be expecting, therefore, would be for the squadron to take the 'obvious' route, the shorter way – moving out sooner than expected into the 'German Ocean' and there turning sharp left to make a dash – at least, the Second Pacific Squadron's equivalent of a dash – southward through the English Channel. This was October 21st, Michael noted – Trafalgar Day. The *Oryol* had arrived on the 20th; it was her steering engine that had given trouble – and according to Narumov was likely to give a lot more. In the same breath the constructor had mentioned that the destroyer *Prosorlivy* was being sent back to Libau with condenser trouble.

'One thing after another, isn't it?'

'Or teething troubles – getting the worst of it over right at the start?'

'The general view – which I believe I share, despite your English complacency – is that the worst is likely to hit us on this next stage. That damned English Channel – if they're going to hit us anywhere . . .'

'East China Sea or Yellow Sea is where they'll hit us. Why would they bother to flog all the way over here?'

He added to himself mentally, *When all they need do is sit and wait for us . . .*

It didn't really bear thinking about. The state this squadron might be in by that time – and Togo's fleet in mint condition – fighting-fit, highly trained, experienced in battle and high in morale, and for maintenance purposes close to their own ports and dockyards!

At three in the afternoon the destroyers, fleet auxiliaries and transports including the *Anadyr, Sibir, Irtysh,* repair-ship

Kamchatka, and the *Yermak*–which had been into Fredrikshavn to land mail, land also the binocular-sight artisans, who'd return to Kronstadt by rail – weighed anchor and set course to round the Skaw. Then the first division of cruisers: *Oleg*, *Aurora* and the little *Svetlana*, and the old *Dmitry Donskoi* which had been built to carry sails – and might have got along better, Ignatzius had remarked, if she'd still had some. Behind them, the second division: *Zemchug* and *Izumrud*, and the *Almaz* – which looked more like a yacht than a cruiser. The cruisers were under the command of a Rear-Admiral Enqvist, of whom up to this time Michael hadn't heard. He had a straggly white beard like an Old Testament prophet, Sollugub said. 'Weighing and proceeding' was a slow process: at about seven p.m. the second division of battleships got under way, to be followed an hour and a half later by these four – *Suvarov*, *Alexander III*, *Borodino*, *Oryol* – accompanied for some reason by the transports *Anadyr* and *Sibir*.

At dinner in the wardroom there was talk of omens, of which during the day there'd apparently been a number, all of them scary. Michael observed to the chaplain, Rasschakovsky, who'd been advising them all to place their trust in Almighty God, that by morning they'd have rounded the Skaw and be safely out in the open sea.

'So they'll strike at us before dawn. First light's the time to watch out for.' This advice came from Guryenko, the paymaster – who knew rather less about fighting tactics, Lieutenant Danchik was heard to murmur, than Flagmansky did. A *michman* by name of Shishkin added, 'But it could come at any hour. Any moment. Turn in wearing a lifebelt, Padre, if I were you.' They believed it, weren't just teasing him. Michael had expected that once they were out of the narrows and through the Kattegat – up here rounding the Skaw in fact – they'd have pulled themselves together, but not a bit of it.

Trafalgar night, he remembered. The ninety-ninth anniversary. Should have ordered some decent wine and toasted the Immortal Memory. Too late now, anyway. He said goodnight and went to his cabin, where Narumov, who'd eaten early, was once again writing to his wife.

'I write every day if I have the time. A series of notes, thoughts, observations, more than letters of an ordinary kind. Keeping it up to date; when I hear there's a mail about to be landed all I need do is add a line of farewell, and off it goes. Still a clear sky up there, is there?'

'Moonlit, clear and calm.'

'Would moonlight be more in our favour, or the enemy's?'

'Depends on the direction from which an attack was being made. The attacker would want to have us in silhouette with the moon behind us – while we'd do better to have *him* in that position.'

'So he – the attacker – since he's the one who chooses his line of approach, would be invisible to us, at least until the attack developed – and if it was torpedo-fire, as one imagines it would be—'

'It's *all* imagination, my dear chap. Don't go frightening your poor wife with that nonsense!'

Next evening while Michael was smartening himself up for dinner, Narumov insisted on reading out aloud some further extracts from his long-running letter.

'This I wrote yesterday at eight p.m. I would like your opinion of the literary style: as you'll have realized, my education has been largely technical, vocational. Listen: "Panic has us by the throat. Disturbances in the sea are watched fearfully. The weather is good – it is warm and there is moonlight – but our nerves are stretched taut. The guns are loaded, the turrets' crews are standing about on deck. Half of them will sleep at their guns fully dressed, the other half – and their officers – will keep watch. It is strange, to be so far from the theatre of war and yet so conscious of the dangers surrounding us."'

'Well, *that*'s the truth!'

'But the style?'

'Oh, you put it down very well, I think. But your poor wife—'

'The fact she'll have received the letter –' flipping the pages – 'with these later additions, incidentally—'

'Should reassure her that those fears were all imaginary.'

'Well, hear *this*. I offer it as proof that I'm telling her nothing but the truth. I wrote this during the forenoon. Listen, just this once more?'

'If you like.' He'd fixed his bow tie. With his better uniform suit on it was as far as he could go towards changing for dinner; he'd saved packing-space – to his sister-in-law's consternation although it had made the job easier for her – by not bringing Mess Undress uniform with him.

Narumov cleared his throat, and began: '"What a night it has been – racked with constant anxiety. Earlier on in the evening there was nervous tension, then barely concealed panic when news was received that four suspicious craft showing no lights had been spotted from the leading ships. Vigilance was redoubled – but thank God the night passed uneventfully. At present we are in fog. Nothing is visible all round and the sirens are shrieking. I went to bed fully dressed last night and awoke quite freezing. The rats – of which there are hundreds in this ship – can be heard moving about all night. We are now in the German Ocean, which they say will be rough. At present it is calm under the fog. We will be calling in at Brest, in France, and although it is said there will be no communication with the shore I very much hope it will be possible to land mail."'

Head up again: 'None of that would frighten her, would it?'

'I'd guess she's beyond being frightened, by this time. But are you coming along to the wardroom? Oh, the style's excellent, by the way.'

The fog had lifted at about midday, a wind coming up to clear it, and there'd been relief as the blare of 'sirens' – fog-horns – died away. The noise had been tremendous, *Suvarov* and her sisters like monsters trying to roar each other down. Afternoon and early evening passed without incident, but with very few of the squadron's forty-odd ships in sight, despite good visibility. One could see only the battleships and the *Anadyr*; even the four *Suvarov* class quite widely separated now, and no one bothering about it, and the second division – *Oslyabya* and company – discernible but a very long way astern. Discernible in fact mainly by the smoke they were making. The cruisers were all miles ahead – according to Sollogub when he joined Michael in the wardroom – while the transports with the auxiliaries escorting them were somewhere in between. Nobody seemed to have heard anything of the *Ryazan*; perhaps she was down there with other cruisers. The repair-ship *Kamchatka* though had reported a breakdown during the dark hours and hadn't been heard of since; Enqvist, the cruiser admiral, who should have had her under his wing, had told Rojhestvensky that he had no idea at all where she might be. Narumov commented, when he joined Michael and some others in the wardroom, arriving neck-and-neck with Sollogub coming from the forebridge – the count's stint having finished at eight p.m. – that in his opinion it mightn't be a bad thing if the *Kamchatka* did get lost. He'd spent time on board her, of course, in connection with various repairs – the *Buistry*'s, for instance.

Michael had ordered a round of vodka, signalled now to the steward to bring glasses for Sollogub and Narumov too. Asking Sollogub, 'All the same up top?'

'Wind's come up a little, sea's getting a bit bumpy. Well, you can feel it, can't you? Apart from that, guns and search-lights manned, lookouts' eyes on stalks.' He took his vodka. 'Best not to drink too many of these, in case we suddenly find ourselves fending off the entire Royal Navy. How far's Portsmouth from here?'

'It's you who's just come from the chart. But a long, long way.' Michael smiled. 'No need to be frightened.' He picked up his glass: 'To the bottom!'

'The bottom!'

Heads back, vodka sluicing down, grimaces for a moment

and watering eyes. Michael thinking that the battleships' present position would be roughly halfway down the length of Denmark, but in aiming for the Strait of Dover their course would be fairly well out – before long in fact would be skirting the Dogger Bank.

Michman von Kursel stumbled into the wardroom, looked around in his dumb-ox way, then spotted Sollogub and came lurching over. He was a Courlander, apparently – came from somewhere near Libau – and although he spoke Russian fluently his home language was German. Murmuring in Sollogub's ear now: Sollogub looking surprised, jerking his head round to stare up at him: 'This some leg-pull?'

'No, sir, not at all. Captain Sidorenko wants you back up there.' He told them all, then: 'The *Kamchatka* is under attack by torpedo-boats.'

'Where?'

'Don't know. Nobody does. That's half the problem.'

'Christ Almighty!'

There was a rush for the door – almost as if he'd said *this* ship was under attack. Sollogub suprised Michael with, 'Want to come up?'

'To the forebridge?'

'Well, chartroom. After all – this close to British waters—'

Narumov cut in with a hand on Michael's arm. 'Nothing in it, eh? Not possible anywhere in European waters, did you say?'

In the chartroom, Sollogub's superior – the senior navigator, Captain Second Rank Sidorenko – stout, with sparse grey hair and a contrastingly black moustache – stared at Michael in surprise. They'd met a couple of times in the wardroom. Sollogub explained, 'Lieutenant Genderson is here at my request – being himself a navigator, and seeing as we're on the edge of British waters – well, if one had questions—'

'Take a look at these.'

Signals, scrawled in blacklead pencil. Sidorenko handed them over one at a time and watched their faces as they read them. The first one was to the *Suvarov* from *Kamchatka*: *I am being pursued by torpedo-boats.*

Next, to *Kamchatka* from *Suvarov*: *How many? From which side?*

Kamchatka had replied: *From all directions.*

Michael thinking, I don't believe this . . .

A messenger came in, put another signal form in front of Sidorenko, who turned it so the others could read it too. To *Kamchatka* from *Suvarov*: *How many torpedo-boats? Give details.*

Michael said – since both Russians were staring at him, seemingly wanting his reactions – 'I'd guess the *Kamchatka*'s skipper's had a few too many. He'll tell us next he's being chased by pink elephants.' Actually he didn't think Rojhestvensky's questions were all that pertinent, either. Sidorenko murmured, fingering his moustache, 'He'd have to be raving mad as well as drunk – if it *isn't* really happening!'

Michael checked the dead-reckoning position on the chart. It was about where he'd expected, but being so spread out the squadron would of course be covering a very large area of sea. The cruisers for instance might be fifty or more miles ahead. He shook his head: 'If there *were* Japanese torpedo-boats in these waters – which there can't be – why would they be wasting their time on the *Kamchatka*? An old steamer of no distinction whatsoever – virtually unarmed, slow, and in any case with nothing to link her to this squadron.'

'Very much what's been puzzling me.' Sidorenko nodded. 'Why indeed? On the other hand, why would he *say* he's under attack by torpedo-boats?'

The messenger came back in and handed him two more signals.

Kamchatka to *Suvarov*: *About eight torpedo-boats.* And *Suvarov* to *Kamchatka*: *What distance are they from you?*

Sollogub muttered, 'What a useless question.' He took out his cigarette-case, offered it to his chief, who declined, and to Michael, who took one. Sidorenko explaining to Sollogub, 'I sent for you because once a panic starts the admiral seems to want me at his side – for some reason—'

'But the Flag navigating officer—'

'Exactly. Where does *he* get to? Anyway, that being the case, I need to have you in here.'

'I understand, sir.'

'You two can't have dined yet, I suppose.'

'I doubt anyone has. Imagine it – Flagmansky's dream of heaven: wardroom table spread with dishes and nobody there to beat him off. Him *or* his Flag lieutenants.' Sollogub laughed. 'Don't worry, they'll be keeping it hot for us. Oh, here we go again . . .'

The signals received and transmitted during the next twenty minutes were: first, the repair-ship's reply to the *What distance* question, which was *About a cable's length.* A cable's length being only two hundred yards, it was a case of a silly question getting a silly answer.

And then – from *Suvarov*: *Have they fired torpedoes?*

From *Kamchatka*: *We haven't seen any.*

From *Suvarov*: *What course are you steering?*

From *Kamchatka*: *South seventy east. Please give position of squadron.*

A peculiar course to be steering, Michael thought. Unless she was in the approaches to the Firth of Forth, say. More likely perhaps somewhere off Jutland and they'd meant south seventy *west.* But neither of the others had commented; and Rojhestvensky wasn't giving away *his* position, replying instead with, *Are torpedo-boats still chasing you? Evade the danger. Change your course. Indicate your position and we will send further instructions.*

From *Kamchatka* then: *Fear messages will be intercepted.*

Sidorenko thumped the chart-table: 'You're right, this is a farce! I'm sorry to have dragged you up here. Please, go on down and have your meal.'

Sollogub said, shrugging, 'If Flagmansky's left us any . . .'

It was about ten-thirty when he went to turn in. Narumov

was already asleep and snoring. Michael had decided that the solution to the *Kamchatka* mystery might be that her skipper had been given a mistaken, panicky report by a lookout, sent off the first signal in a rush of panic of his own, then realized it was a false alarm but felt stuck with it, tried to bluff his way through. His judgement might also have been clouded by drink, of course.

That probably was the answer. Rather more alarming therefore was Rojhestvensky having taken it seriously and for so long continued with that gibberish. *Michman* von Kursel, who'd returned to the wardroom while Michael and Sollogub had been eating, had told them there'd been further exchanges and that some of the senior officers including Selyeznov had thought it might be a Japanese torpedo-boat flotilla commander impersonating the *Kamchatka* in the hope of being given the battleships' position. Sollogub had exclaimed, 'Isn't it remarkable what stark terror can do to the human brain?'

Michael turned in quietly, taking care not to disturb Narumov, pulled a blanket over himself and encouraged his thoughts to drift to Tasha. Who by this time would be in Yalta: and with whom he could have been, if he'd rejected Prince Igor's invitation. Not in Yalta – in those circumstances he'd have had to have got her quickly out of Russia: maybe via Paris. But he could not have kept from the Admiralty that he'd had the invitation and declined it: Prince Igor had made sure of that, told him he intended writing to them – as he had done, in the event addressing his letter to Admiral Sir John Fisher whom as it happened both Prince Ivan and Rojhestvensky had had the honour of meeting, when the latter had been naval attaché in London some years earlier, and who it was no secret was about to be appointed First Sea Lord. In his letter Prince Igor had explained that he'd issued the invitation only out of his considerable regard for Lieutenant Henderson and his late father, and very much hoped the young man would be granted an appropriate extension to his leave. Igor had of course foreseen that

Naval Intelligence, to whom his letter would be passed, would be very keen to have their own observer in the Russian squadron – as they had already with the Japanese – and that if Michael had turned down the opportunity he'd have been sabotaging his own prospects even of *eventual* promotion, let alone hopes of the 'accelerated' variety.

If he *had* refused the invitation, at Injhavino that crisis morning, he'd have had to have eloped with Tasha immediately, there and then: and it would have been in Prince Igor's power to have them stopped – physically stopped and detained at the frontier, if not sooner. Ignominious return home for Tasha then, and perhaps a rushed, early marriage to Zakharov; plus – you could bet on it – a follow-up communication to Jackie Fisher referring to Lieutenant Henderson's disreputable conduct in attempting to make off with the Princess Natasha Igorovna Volodnyakova, who'd only recently left school and in any case had been 'promised' to a certain distinguished officer in the Imperial Russian Navy.

Michael knew that if he'd run off with her he'd never have got beyond Senior Lieutenant. Hard up, and with a failed marriage almost inevitably to follow. In fact, not necessarily all *that* hard up, since his mother had become rich in her own right, following the deaths of her parents and subsequent sale of the Sevasyeyev estate, to which she'd been sole heiress. But if he wasn't standing on his own feet it would still amount to failure, which was what Anna Feodorovna hadn't understood.

He'd sworn to Tasha he'd come back to her. Sworn it in the dark and in daylight (in Paris) too, and repeated it on the platform at the Gare du Nord. All right, so in this shambles of a squadron he could end up being drowned. Could, but would not. Please God, would not. Whatever happened, there'd be *some* survivors, and – again, please God – he'd be one of them.

While Zakharov might not be?

Alternatively, if they both survived – well, he'd have to get to her and get her away before Prince Igor knew he was back in Russia. Or telegraph, have Anna Feodorovna take her to Wiltshire where he'd join them when he could. As far as their Lordships were concerned he'd have done this job, might hope they'd turn blind eyes or at least non-censorious ones on his private life. The dream-picture though was of Tasha beside him in a troika racing to the frontier. Tasha in close-up, lovely in her furs, the three horses' pounding hooves, and somewhere ahead the sanctuary where he'd divest her of those furs and every damn thing else.

Drifting off. Behind his closed eyelids, Tasha's body emerging from fur and silk. Tasha's scent, her touch . . .

Crash of gunfire. He felt it as well as heard it: even in half-sleep still. Bugle-call, then. Action stations? And the guns again – starboard for'ard 6-inch, he thought. The light was on, and Narumov was shouting from close range, 'Genderson! *Genderson*, wake up!'

6

Searchlights blindingly bright, sweeping the sea and probing distance, dispelling mist as well as darkness but lighting no enemy that *he* could see: gunfire again – from ships astern as well, but from this one the 3-pounders and 3-inch with flickering spurts of flame overhead and along the starboard side. Intermittent flashes of brilliance, and the crashing noise an assault on one's eardrums. The starboard after 6-inch turret was trained out on the beam, he'd seen – but needing some excuse or order before it could join in, presumably. Shooting at *what,* though? He was on the external ladderway leading past that turret, up the side of the superstructure to the after bridge, with Narumov close behind him. Or *had* been – seemed not to be there now. Astern – roughly, not in line-astern formation, in fact dispersed raggedly on the quarters – the dark masses of the other three – *Borodino, Alexander III,* and *Oryol* outlined in the whitish glitter of broken sea – were giving similar firework displays. He kept his eyes down as he reached bridge level: searchlights here were on the upper bridge and higher, on the mainmast above the after gunnery-control position, and if you'd looked at one of them directly you'd *really* be blinded. Gunfire from this end of the ship had slackened, he realized, but was still brisk from her forepart – 3-pounders on the for'ard upper bridge especially hard at it, the sea on that bow as a searchlight beam traversed it leaping from fall of shot – to no obvious purpose, and the searchlights' continuing search surely an admission of no target or targets having been found; if they had found one they'd be holding it. He had a premonition that whatever was happening might well be a prelude to disaster. Glancing round again for Narumov – worried that as a landsman who hadn't acquired his sea-legs yet he might have fallen off the ladder – Michael found himself face to face with Selyeznov, and with him the doctor, Nyedozorov, and the junior torpedo lieutenant, Baylin. Michael yelled in Selyeznov's ear, 'What are they shooting at?'

'Torpedo-boats!' Ducking as a shell passed close – from astern, one of the other battleships – startling enough, but that was all it could have been; the tearing, rushing sound had been unmistakable, and there was nowhere else it could have come from . . . A scream from Baylin then – his arm out, hand as white as a corpse's in the searchlights' milky fallout: 'There! See? They've *hit* it!'

A fishing-boat – trawler, about a hundred tons – pin-pointed in a searchlight beam but showing no lights of its own. There should have been a tricolour light above a fixed white one on its foremast – which he saw now was only a stump, its upper part shot away. The boat was half over in a heavy list to port, and its little shed-like wheelhouse had been stove in and was burning. Hit again – wreckage flying and flames spreading; on fire aft as well. With about forty guns belting away at it at very close range, there were bound to be *some* hits – and deaths and maiming as well as destruction. And now again – the upper part of that narrow, upright funnel disintegrating in an orange flash. Range at the most two hundred yards – less than two hundred yards, although lengthening now for the for'ard guns as the trawler fell abaft the beam. Red-painted hull and upperworks, black at and below the boot-topping, the lower hull's planking so exposed to view because of the list to port. She'd be half full, he guessed, wouldn't float long. Searchlights meanwhile had found another one and the for'ard guns were shifting to it – at least, plastering the sea in its vicinity. Even if only one shot in fifty hit, the little craft was doomed. Selyeznov open-mouthed, stupefied: Michael grabbed his arm, bawled into that same ear, 'Fishing-boats, not torpedo-boats! British fishing-fleet – Christ's sake have them *cease fire*!'

Explosion – another hit – on this nearer boat, at a range of about *one* hundred yards. The other was astern by this time. This one, on fire and with steam gushing from the wreckage of its funnel, gushing white like ectoplasm – that shellburst had been internal, perhaps the boiler gone. There'd be dead men in there too. But some – two – were fighting their way out of the smashed and smouldering wheelhouse. One of them – surprisingly – holding up a fish. Proof of identity – telling these stupid, murderous bastards what he was – *all* he was. Waving the other hand as well – with something glowing red in it. Red lantern? Burning timber? The man beside him in the next moment lost his head – literally had his head blown off his shoulders, an explosive decapitation under floodlights as the boat either under full helm or with its wheel shot away passed out of sight on a curving track that would take it under the *Suvarov*'s stern. Twelve-pounders meanwhile still flaming and crashing although not from this immediate vicinity. Selyeznov had disappeared and Michael thought young Baylin might have gone up one level to order at least a localized cease-fire. Michael himself back on the external ladder now – had only been on that bridge about two minutes – getting down it as fast as he could, destination the forebridge and Rojhestvensky – with the sight of the headless trawlerman still vivid in his memory. The other trawlerman had gone reeling at the same moment, might have been killed in that blast. Murder at point-blank range was what this was, the thought at the back of his mind as he ran forward – switching to the port side because of a crowd of men milling around on this side – spectators, *cheering*, for God's sake! An extension of the immediate shock was that what was happening here might easily – even *probably* – lead to war between Russia and Great Britain. Innocent fishermen slain while going about their legitimate business – fathers and husbands cut down by these heartily disliked Russians, the cruel bear slavering with blooded fangs and claws in a dozen newspaper cartoons each week – well, this was the *reality*, and the desperate, immediate need was to have Rojhestvensky call a halt to it. Even if he was half-mad too, which seemed not unlikely. And beyond the distinct possibility of war, the thought *Go ashore at Brest? Telegraph to them at Yalta from there?* Panting as he hauled himself up the port-side ladder – having *en route* to climb around a seaman who was frantic to get down – bawling, 'Let me by! Let me by! Oh, Christ Jesus, let me by!' A lunatic – Michael swinging out sideways from the ladder, getting the reek of long-unwashed peasant as he passed, and starting to climb again just as the for'ard port-side 6-inch opened up – this turret immediately below him – and then the midships one: and the 12-inch were in it too now: deafening, night-shattering crashes from the turrets for'ard *and* aft – employing the main armament against fishing-boats, perhaps? He'd got there, anyway – slinging himself via the ladder-head platform into the after end of the bridge – where a tall, bearded officer by name of Klado, who was a captain first rank and an exceedingly self-important member of the admiral's staff, was standing with binoculars levelled out to port, shouting to those behind him in the bridge, '*Undoubtedly* Japanese cruisers!'

Out of *his* senses too. If he'd ever been in them. Michael shouldered past him into the bridge's forepart, saw Selyeznov, and Makedonsky, and the navigator, Sidorenko: then the skipper, Ignatzius, close to whom was a bugler-boy with a bugle at his lips but no sound coming from it. The boy's face was as white as paper in the radiance from searchlights overhead; he was shaking, witless in his terror, probably incapable of pursing his lips or mustering enough lung-power to produce whatever bugle-call Ignatzius wanted. Cease fire? Abandon ship? Engage the enemy more closely? Hands to dinner? Madness started from scratch, here. Thunder from the 12-inch again – firing to port, as were the 6-inch on that side – while on the starboard side the 12- and 3-pounders were engaging yet another batch of fishing-boats, shot and shell lashing the sea's surface to a frenzy. Big guns were firing from the battleships astern as well, their flashes vivid in the night sky and the sound of them a pounding, thumping background to the nearer bedlam. Some of the action astern was at a distance suggesting that the second division of battleships – Felkerzam's old crocks back there – was also loosing off. Michael reached Ignatzius: 'Captain, sir—'

'Out of my way!'

Rojhestvensky, arriving at a trot, at his heels one of the Flag lieutenants and *Michman* Prince Tsereteli, the admiral's hurtling bulk sending Ignatzius staggering and fetching up against the forefront of the bridge, swinging a telescope like a club then at the bugler's head and roaring, 'Sound the cease fire, damn you for a swine! *Sound* it!' The boy had more or less dodged the blow, which might have cracked his skull if it had landed squarely, but still caught some of it glancingly on one shoulder. He was backing away with terrified eyes on his admiral, but also with the bugle coming back up to his lips: and then making the call – or *a* call . . . Rojhestvensky pointing the telescope at Michael now: 'What do *you* want?'

'Came to tell you those are harmless fishermen, sir!'

'What of it? Torpedo-craft amongst them, weren't there? Or did you have your eyes shut? Any case I've ordered cease fire. Hear it?' A gesture towards the bugler. Then to Makedonsky, 'What are you waiting for? One beam up, damn you!'

Meaning one searchlight to shine its beam vertically, as an order to all ships to cease fire. Sidorenko was considerately murmuring this explanation in Michael's ear while Makedonsky passed the order to *Michman* von Kursel – who was now rushing aloft. They'd use the searchlight on the upper bridge here. But Captain Klado was intervening: 'Your Excellency – with respect, and with your Excellency's permission—'

'Respect be damned! Not granted!'

Rojhestvensky glaring, roaring like a maddened bull. Should have pawed the deck, Michael felt, then charged, swinging at that pompous idiot with the telescope. *Might* have, if he'd thought of it, and Klado, perhaps aware of it, was retreating, looking haughtily offended. Sollogub had mentioned that the admiral hated Klado, Michael remembered. Bellowing at him now, 'Can you read Tabulevich when it's made on foreyard signal lights?'

'Why, yes, I expect I'd—'

'Take a harder look, then! Those are our *own* cruisers you've had us firing at, you infernal ninny!'

The searchlight was vertical, a bright pillar in the night sky, and others were switching off, the beams seemingly dying back into their silver roots. Still some desultory firing, but not much. Ignatzius was covertly but urgently gesturing to Michael to clear off, and it was probably good advice. He went down the internal ladder this time – inside, there was one for up and one for down – and at its foot was stopped by Selyeznov, who'd come scooting down the wrong one in order to intercept him.

'Mikhail Ivan'ich – a moment, please. I want you to know it was I who persuaded the admiral to have the action stopped: but also that there *were* torpedo-boats among those trawlers – yes, there *were*, they were using them for cover – typical of their tricks, eh? Thank God we were on to them as smartly as we were, so our gunners were able to catch *them* on the hop! As for what you were saying – and saw – well, naturally I sympathize, but their own fault, surely. If, when they saw us coming, they'd simply cut free of their nets and run for it – huh?'

Sailors, notably guns' crews, were all over the ship in shouting, dancing groups – on the gundecks to start with, while clearing away and ditching empty shellcases – but then below decks as well, rollicking in relief and delight at having driven off the Japanese attackers. They'd seen dozens of torpedo-boats; had seen some blow up, others founder, the rest turn tail and save themselves. The gunners' skill had been well and truly demonstrated, the monkeys taught a lesson they wouldn't forget in a hurry, huh?

An answering shout from another of them as Michael passed through, heading aft: 'Not just the monkeys either! Won't the news of how we dealt with them flash clear around the world now?'

He felt sure it would. Initially, and most importantly, to London. When the survivors of the fishing-fleet got back to port with dead and wounded on board and damaged boats in tow, the telegrams would start flying. In Brest, presumably, one would get the first repercussions: if after this the French took the risk of letting the squadron go in there, which if they'd any sense they wouldn't. Jackie Fisher, who'd been due to take over as First Sea Lord on Trafalgar Day, wouldn't be taking it lying down, he thought: Fisher was about as resolute as they came.

He went on down to the cabin, found Narumov pulling on overalls over a thick jersey. Explaining, 'To be ready if I'm sent for. Those were our own cruisers we were firing on – did you know?'

'Yes. Incredible as it seems . . .'

'Lieutenant Vladimirsky assured me he saw several hits. Although the powder in our shells doesn't show up much – it's Pyroxyline, you know, the smokeless stuff – but he explained that at night the flash is visible.'

'Did he also explain that they were trying to tell us who they were?'

'It was their own fault entirely! He said that they shouldn't have been within miles of where they were, or approaching from that direction, or have switched the lights off on their ships, or then directed searchlights at us. Perhaps you know better, but as he said we *had* to assume we were being attacked – and he's sure we scored hits. From where he was in the gunnery control position up there above the bridge—'

'I'm going along for a drink. Frankly, I can't believe this has happened.'

'What d'you mean, "can't believe"?'

'Innocent fishermen run down and blasted by gunfire in the middle of the night? It's – a nightmare!'

'But they were acting as cover for the torpedo-boats!'

'What torpedo-boats? How many did *you* see?'

'Well – I personally saw none, but—'

'There weren't any. As I've been telling you for days, there couldn't posssibly have been. Fishing-boats, engaged in fishing, and that's all. Boats out of English east-coast ports such as – well, Hull, probably. And wherever they came from, there are widows and orphans who don't know it yet.' Narumov was standing stock-still, staring at him; Michael shook his head as he turned away. 'Come along and have a drink, Pavel Vasil'ich.'

'But if what you say is true—'

'I saw it, so did you. Did you see that man's head blown off? I saw one boat on the point of sinking and another so badly damaged it couldn't have floated long. There'll be hell to pay. Believe me, we could be at war within days, d'you realize? Come on – if they need you they'll find you . . .'

In the wardroom, Flag Gunnery Lieutenant Sventorjhetsky – he was number two to Colonel Bersenev of the Marine Artillery, Michael had learnt – towering head and shoulders above the group surrounding him, was insisting that of *course* there'd been Japanese torpedo-boats using the fishing-fleet as cover – and then saving themselves double-quick, leaving their allies to face the music!

'Pretty damned effective music – uh? But there you are. If the English lend themselves to such deceit . . .'

He'd seen Michael, and shut his mouth. He was quite a decent fellow, Michael thought; these people collectively – or Rojhestvensky perhaps – had made a colossal blunder, and he happened to be the Flag 'G' lieutenant, that was all. *Michman* Shishkin was audible suddenly – his voice high with excitement – telling Rasschakovsky, 'Morale among the ship's company is amazingly high now, Padre. Done us a world of good, that spot of bother!' Michael tried to hear the chaplain's reply, but Sollogub joined him at that moment: 'Brandy, Mikhail Ivan'ich?'

'Yes, please.'

'We all need some lubrication.' A glance at Narumov: 'Brandy for his excellency the constructor too? Costumed for a boat-trip, are you?'

'To be ready if I'm sent for. It may be that we hit the cruisers. But – thank you, I'd prefer a glass of tea.'

'Why not. I can tell you, we did score hits – on the *Aurora* anyway. Or someone did. A fair number of ships were firing in that direction, I believe. But before I left the bridge the *Aurora* had signalled that her engineers were assessing damage, and she'd had two men wounded, one seriously. Here, steward . . .'

Selyeznov had dropped in, was holding forth authoritatively in the Sventorjhetsky group now. *Of course* there'd been torpedo-boats. Was anyone suggesting that Admiral Rojhestvensky would order fire to be opened on mere fishing trawlers that actually were fishing and nothing else?

Michael called to him, 'It's what happened, Vladimir Petrovich. I'm sorry to insist on it – it puts me in an invidious position to have to do so – but as you know I was on the after bridge when you were—'

'I do recall that, yes, but as I was explaining to you—'

'There were no torpedo-boats. *You*'d seen none.'

'With that I must take issue—'

'Excuse me.' The doctor, Nyedozorov, tapped Selyeznov on the shoulder. 'I too was with you at that stage, Vladimir Petrovich, I had my binoculars with me, and having no duties until men are injured I was in a position to give my full attention to what was happening. What's more, I've been at sea as long as any of you and longer than most, and I assure you I know at a glance the difference between a torpedo-boat and a steam-trawler. I positively *swear*—'

'The answer is they'd gone by that time. We'd driven them

off.' Sventorjhetsky again. 'Regrettably some of the gunners in their enthusiasm continued firing for longer than was necessary. Many of them are less skilled in ship-recognition than is our greatly respected quack here. Eh?'

'Your brandy, Mikhail Ivan'ich. And your tea, er—'

Michael told Sollogub quietly, 'His christian name is Pavel and his patronymic is Vasil'ich.'

'But don't bother, please—'

'Pavel Vasil'ich, I should have known it by this time without being told. Your health!'

'And yours. You're very kind. You too, Mikhail Ivan'ich. But my God, *could* this result in war?'

There was an immediate lull in the hubbub of conversation; faces turning, startled eyes on Michael. From Sventorjhetsky, an incredulous '*War?*'

'No, surely—'

Selyeznov cut across Sollogub: 'You aren't seriously postulating—'

'Listen.' Michael addressed Selyeznov, who was the most senior officer present. 'As I said, it puts me in a difficult position. And I must say I'm, frankly, bemused by what's occurred. So I'll answer that question now – simply as *I* see the probabilities – but I'd be grateful if I might be excused from discussing it further, after this. As long as I'm your guest on board here—'

'Here.' Sollogub handed him another tot of brandy. 'Here. I've told him to put this round on *your* chit.'

'Thank you, Nikolai Sergei'ich. But listen: ask yourselves how the Russian people – you yourselves – would feel if a Royal Navy squadron steamed up the Baltic and started blowing the heads off Russian fishermen. On top of that it's an unfortunate truth that our governments haven't been getting along all that well in recent years. Now, the British people – and parliament – are going to ask, aren't we going to *do* anything about it?' He shrugged. 'We do have a very large and powerful fleet – as you must know, of course – and – well, putting two and two together, Vladimir

Petrovich, that's my assessment of the situation we're in now.'

Snatches of overheard conversation then, while he with Narumov and Sollogub remained slightly apart from the main throng, included, 'But several of our lads actually saw torpedo tracks fizzing by!' and, 'Great heavens, man, they are in alliance – isn't it what's been expected of them all along?'

Nyedozorov paused briefly beside Michael. 'You are, of course, absolutely right, lieutenant.'

'Thank you, doctor.'

'A matter of facing facts, that's all. Goodnight.'

Sollogub put down an empty glass. 'Time we *all* turned in.' Sventorjhetsky's voice again then: 'However that may be, gentlemen, foremost in my own mind is satisfaction that our shooting was so good.'

7

The shooting had in fact been rotten – quite apart from having been directed at their own ships. Not that Captain Ignatzius, over breakfast, seemed at all depressed about it. Not only was he a naturally ebullient character, half a dozen hits in a night engagement lasting only a few minutes didn't sound too bad – if you overlooked minor details such as that fire had been opened at fairly close range, for big guns – four thousand yards, two nautical miles, or as Russian naval gunners liked to call it, twenty cables – and that there'd been no fewer than seven battleships contributing to the barrage. *Suvarov* herself had loosed off twelve rounds of 6-inch and five of 12-inch; in all there'd have been something in the region of a hundred large-calibre shells fired.

The last-minute fitting of telescopic gun-sights seemed not to have done them much good. Michael refrained from comment, even to Sollogub, but he felt that if he'd been in Admiral Togo's shoes he wouldn't be losing any sleep.

The vital question, of course, was what was happening in England, and between London and St Petersburg. The survivors of the fishing-fleet would be getting into port during the forenoon, he supposed – into Hull, or Grimsby – so one might reckon on the news being received in London by, say, midday. And if Rojhestvensky had telegraphed his account of the night's action to St Petersburg – getting his version in first – which he would have done, if the Slaby-Arco wireless equipment had had the range for it . . .

'Our destroyers and the transport *Korea* are to put in at Cherbourg, Mikhail Ivan'ich.'

Sollogub, who'd spent the morning watch, 0400 to 0800, on the bridge, had told him this. Michael queried, 'Will the French allow it?'

'That is a question, of course. But the chief of staff seems to expect they will.' He shrugged. 'One doesn't get to see every signal or telegram that comes in or goes out, mind you.'

Ignatzius chuckled, over his sour milk and raisins. 'You could say that, indeed!'

'Even you don't, sir?'

Amiable smile. 'As flag captain, you mean.' Shake of the head. 'I'm here just to drive the ship around, my dear count. On wider issues the admiral decides, either on his own or in conjunction with those members of his staff in whom he chooses to confide; I then receive my instructions. Whether in the final outcome we float or sink, therefore, is not on my slop-chit – as the saying goes. D'you have such an expression in your navy, lieutenant?'

'Precisely the same – oddly enough.'

'And speaking of your fleet, here in your home waters, how many battleships could be mustered – that's to say, would be available at a few hours' notice, here on your south coast?'

'Off-hand, I'd guess, perhaps a dozen.'

'Modern, well-found ships, we're speaking of?'

'Oh, yes.'

'And first-class cruisers?'

'Captain – with apologies, as your guest—'

'All right. I'm only looking for an approximation of relative strengths. Say twenty cruisers?'

'If you like. But then out of the Mediterranean by way of Gibraltar – if it was decided such strength was called for – you might double those numbers.'

'Twenty-four battleships?'

'At least.'

'And forty cruisers?'

'Rather more than forty, probably.'

Sollogub murmured, with milk running down his chin, 'We'd be completely overwhelmed, of course.' Others were staring from all around the long table, looking shocked. Engineer Captain Bernander had uttered a croaking sound – open-mouthed, words failing him. Michael spooned sugar into his coffee. He thought it would add up to something like thirty powerful, well-crewed battleships – each of which on her own could take on this whole squadron – and up to fifty cruisers. Ignatzius was murmuring to Sollogub, 'As well as God knows how many torpedo-boat destroyers . . .'

There was some motion on the ship, this Sunday morning, a rhythmic pitching as she stemmed a long swell funnelling up-Channel from the Atlantic. Sound-effects to match: groaning, and creaking, the rattle of gear on the upper deck and the regular slam of the sea as she drove her ram and forepart into it.

'So let's pray to God –' Chaplain Rasschakovsky munching a rusk, crumbs of it decorating his beard – 'that diplomacy may prevail.'

'Amen.' Thinking *perhaps* it would. If Balfour and his Foreign Secretary, Lansdowne, were so minded – depending on what other irons they might have in the fire, internally and/or internationally. Rasschakovsky was telling him that he'd be conducting a mass on the seamen's messdeck in half an hour's time, and vespers this evening. In harbour, he added, the morning service was always held on the upper deck – following, Michael gathered, some kind of ritual equivalent to the RN's Sunday 'Divisions'. He added, 'You're Church of England, I know, but you'd be welcome at either or both.'

'Very kind. Thank you.' He'd attended Russian Orthodox services on occasion; with his mother in London a few times, and on earlier visits to Injhavino and to his grandparents the Sevasyeyevs. The difference, to him, was only a matter of outward form: at home there'd been the village church where he and brother George had often enough played marbles on the floor of the family box-pew while their father read the lesson – thumping the lectern with a fist when the Lord had reason to be displeased – then the Navy where Divine Service was very much an extension of 'Divisions'. *Stand at – ease! Stand – easy! Off – caps!* Then shout the Lord's Prayer and a few others, bellow *Oh God Our Help in Ages Past,* and invariably a prayer one had known by heart since cadet days, referring to those who passed on the seas upon their lawful occasions – in terms of which, come to think of it, there might be some doubt as to whether this lot would qualify, in God's eyes. They wouldn't in Jackie Fisher's, you could be damn sure.

He said to Rasschakovsky, 'I'm very sorry to hear that your colleague in the *Aurora* was wounded last night, Padre.'

'Indeed. The mass will be said for his early recovery.'

A priest by name of Afanasy: he'd had most of one arm torn off when a shell, possibly but not necessarily from this ship, had passed through his cabin when he'd been in it. Probably hadn't exploded in there, or he'd have been dead, but he was in a bad way in any case and they were worried for him. Michael had heard of it from Narumov, who'd arrived in their cabin – waking him – at about six, having stayed up all night in case of being required to cope with action damage. He'd sat here in the wardroom, he'd told Michael, with Flagmansky snoring in his lap; the squadron steering southwest at its best speed, cruisers three miles ahead of the battleships, visibility much reduced by fog, and at one stage passing through an even larger fleet of trawlers than they'd been involved with earlier. The violent alteration in course to avoid collision with them had alarmed Narumov, who – to Flagmansky's annoyance, he'd said – had rushed up on deck to see what was happening.

'Some we passed very close indeed. In fact we carried away some of their nets – trawls, if that's what they're called. I met von Kursel up there, he was telling me there's a danger of nets and such becoming wound around a ship's propellers. As of course you'd know. We were in luck, though.'

'But the trawlers weren't.'

'You mean losing their nets?'

'At least they weren't shot at. You might say *that* was lucky.'

He wondered where the *Ryazan* might be, where she'd join the rest of them. Whether he'd ever get to transfer to her now – or might indeed disembark at Brest. If last night's blundering did lead to war, he'd *have* to. Another possibility was that the squadron might be recalled to the Baltic: if the admirals in St Petersburg reacted quickly enough, facing up to the fact that if war did break out now it hadn't a dog's chance of getting past Cape Finisterre – let alone around Africa, across the Indian Ocean and up to the Yellow Sea.

The fog was lifting: pale patches on the beam to starboard were the white cliffs of Dover. Michael had come up to the after bridge again, bringing Sollogub for his first sight of England – also, by intention, for some English language practice, which turned out to be mostly Russian with a few English words or phrases injected from time to time.

'Not very impressive, I'm afraid.'

'A pity we're not a little closer. Although we do seem to be cutting the corner rather, don't we? What's worth looking at to the west of Dover?'

'Nothing much. Seaside towns. A biggish one called Brighton – in a couple of hours or so. Then Portsmouth and the Isle of Wight – which as a navigator you'll know is just about opposite Cherbourg, where you tell me the destroyers have gone. We won't be that far west until the afternoon, of course. What are we doing now – fifteen knots?'

'Aiming for that, but making good more like thirteen. Well behind schedule. For one thing we had to stop for a while – just after four, the start of my watch – the *Oryol* again, more steering problems.'

'Which must be why the second division's ahead of us. I

was going to ask you. But *Oryol* – at this stage, with so far to go . . . Anyway, more work for poor Narumov!'

'Not necessarily. She has her own engineer-constructor on board. Narumov's a nice fellow though, isn't he? Very good at his job too, they say. A rough diamond, of course . . .'

'I like him. Even if he does hate England and the English.'

'*Does* he?'

'So he says. He maintains that everyone on earth hates us. We're cunning and arrogant – and "Russia's eternal enemy". Despite which I find him entirely friendly – amusing, too.'

'Perhaps he's accepting you as part-Russian.'

'I did suggest he might. How do *you* feel about the English, Nikolai Sergei'ich?'

'Oh, I take 'em as they come – the same as Russians. One can't love all one's fellow men. I've never been to England, as it happens, but I've spent a lot of time in Paris, where as you know one meets the whole world – including English. Same in Biarritz, always lots of you in Biarritz. I used to go there with my parents, they loved the place . . . Do you think England *will* go to war over this?'

'I don't know. There'll be an outcry – political *and* popular – to avenge those trawlermen. And when one has a Navy such as ours – to which Narumov objects, incidentally – and one's citizens are assaulted on the high seas, what's it *for*?'

They'd moved aft to the signal deck, the rearmost part of this bridge level. Michael filling his pipe, gazing astern at the rolling, out-spreading wake: and at the *Borodino*, their next-astern, for once exactly in station, although the two astern of her were wandering somewhat. The four astern; the transports *Sibir* and *Anadyr* were still there – in sight, anyway. He went on, 'The Japanese are another factor, or they might be. The image of your war with them, in our newspapers, is the huge Russian bear looming over a midget in a loincloth who's valiantly standing his ground. "Plucky little Jap" is the phrase. Last night's business, I'm afraid, will match that – huge battleships blasting away at fishermen in cockleshells, who tend to be national heroes anyway, defying foul weather and all the dangers of the seas in order to feed their countrymen. Not all that far off the truth, as a matter of fact.' He'd got his pipe going. 'Not a promising outlook, I'm afraid.'

'You'd leave us, I imagine.'

'I'd have to. Perhaps in Brest – if we get that far . . . Changing the subject, though, tell me about Captain Klado? On the bridge last night he and the admiral almost came to blows!'

'I heard about it. And I may say it's not at all unusual. Klado's a poseur and a schemer, more politician than naval officer. He writes articles on naval matters – in *Novoye Vremya* especially – and he's somehow managed to convince our most senior admirals that he knows more about – oh, strategy, in particular – than anyone else. Shows how much *they* know! But it's said that the Tsar himself reads his rubbish. It was the naval staff – headed by that great heap of lard Grand Duke Admiral Alexis Alexandrovich, the Tsar's uncle – who forced Rojhestvensky to accept Klado on this staff. Old Zenovy'd throw him overboard if he thought he could get away with it. The root of it is that Klado's responsible for our having with us the oldest, least seaworthy, let alone *battle*worthy ships. Rojhestvensky fought tooth and nail against taking any of them – and we'd have had a lot more and worse encumbrances if he hadn't. Some ancient coastal-defence vessels for instance they threatened to send with us, he absolutely refused, and Klado hates him for having won even that much of the battle.'

'Your Petersburg administration isn't quite the finest in the world, is it?'

'How nicely you put it. But Klado's last employment was at Port Arthur, as naval advisor to Viceroy Alexeyev – which by association damns him for a start – and although neither he nor Alexeyev was ever anywhere near any action whatsoever he's now accepted by Petersburg as *the* authority on all matters relating to the naval war. Extraordinary, but true. Listen: the way he argues that particular nonsense is that the more old crocks you can take along, the more targets the enemy has to shoot at – ignoring the facts that they slow the entire squadron to their own crawl, burn thousands of tons of precious coal and constantly break down, that their guns are museum-pieces, and that the enemy will shoot not at old wrecks but at the head of the line – the flagship, first and foremost – which is precisely how they defeated us at the Round Island battle – uh?'

'Yes. Admiral and staff wiped out – confusion, no alternative command structure—'

'You were advancing a theory the other day that Togo missed his chance?'

'He did. Admiral Witheft's orders were to break through to Vladivostok – and as you know, a lucky or astonishingly well-aimed salvo killed him and his staff and wrecked the flagship's steering. Well, Togo had them at his mercy then – admittedly did a lot of damage and sent them running – but if he'd followed through as he should have, he could have wiped up the whole damn lot.'

'That's the British view, is it?'

'Well – yes . . .'

'You have observers with the Jap fleet, one's heard.'

'I've heard so, too.'

'Well.' A hand up, rubbing his bony, clean-shaven face. 'About Klado and his nonsensical theories, anyway – you can imagine how your friend Selyeznov reacts to them. He's a know-all himself, of course, but at least he did see action, out there. While on the subject of wiping out an admiral's staff, it would be one way of dealing with the overcrowding in our wardroom, wouldn't it – but imagine what it must be like in that senior officer's mess. Klado pontificating, Selyeznov snarling and biting his moustache, Zenovy Petrovich shouting them all down—'

'And Clapier de Colongue pouring oil?'

'Oozing charm. Yes, that's *his* job . . .'

He was up there again in the afternoon with Narumov, the

engineer-constructor having expressed interest in seeing something of England's southern coastline, especially having one of its denizens on hand to tell him whatever it might be he was looking at. As it happened, Beachy Head's high chalk promontory was abeam at that time, the South Downs humped greenish against a patchy sky to the left of it.

'There are people all over that headland, Mikhail Ivan'ich!'

'They'll be English. Sets your teeth on edge, does it?'

He borrowed his binoculars back, and there *were* a lot of people on the Head. Sunday, he remembered – families taking the air.

Or flocking to watch the Russian bullies pass?

Time – by Anna Feodorovna's extravagant present – coming up for two-thirty. The general populace could hardly have heard the news this soon. In London they might have, but in the wilds of Sussex?

He passed the glasses back. 'Family outings, Sunday picnics. It's a favourite spot. Not only for relaxing, but also for suicides.'

'Are you serious?'

'Entirely. Dramatically high cliffs – close on six hundred feet, as far as I remember.'

'You see some place that's high, you want to jump off it?'

'Well – if circumstances have given you the inclination—'

'Meanwhile they're getting a free show, those people, seeing us pass by. Do you truly believe war is brewing in what passes for the English heart?' A gesture towards Beachy Head: 'In *their* hearts?'

'They aren't likely to have had the news yet. Although I expect it'll be known in London by this time. It's *possible* they've heard, I suppose. If so, they're watching us steam by filling the sky with smoke and telling their children, "There go the monsters who go around murdering fishermen!" I dare say the newspapers will have got the story – not that any are published on Sunday afternoons or evenings – but the news agencies – Reuters, for instance – will have telegraphed it, oh, world-wide.'

'Reuters and also Havas.'

'Havas putting out the Russian version – the lies about torpedo-boats. How's your own despatch going?'

'My letter to my wife? Well, recent events I've not touched on yet. I'm concerned to tell the truth – since these *are* despatches, in a way, and may become part of a full-length narrative, in the course of time – and there *is* an element of doubt – in private as we are I can admit it. Dr Nyedozorov's view for instance contradicts just about all others – except yours, obviously: but how to describe it all with certainty—'

'I hadn't realized you had doubts, Pavel Vasil'ich.'

'Well, in the wardroom for instance – you should bear in mind that since I'm neither a sailor nor a nobleman I'm in any case somewhat isolated . . .'

'Best keep the doubts to yourself.'

'Exactly. About my letter, though, I'd better get down to it. I'll tell her the facts as I see them now, that's all. I must have it ready for when we reach Brest – since between now and then I might be busy with some new emergency. And there's plenty to write about, other than last night's action – this sight of England, for instance . . . From the other side, is France in view as well?'

'Barely. All of forty miles away. But later, Barfleur and Cherbourg, on the Cotentin Peninsula.' Anna's watch again: 'Two-thirty now. About a hundred miles – at thirteen knots, seven and a half hours. No – we'll be passing it in darkness.'

'And Brest?'

'Fifteen to seventeen hours after that – if all goes well. About this time tomorrow, say.'

'Do you have a chart and all the distances in your head?'

'Sort of. Familiar waters, these. But it's guesswork, isn't it – the *Oryol* might break down again, for instance.'

'She never completed her trials, you know.' Shrugging, lowering the glasses. 'Effectively, went straight from the builders' yard to join us in Reval. What a muddled business it's been . . . Look, I think I will go down now, but first let's just see if France is visible at all?'

Over to the port side: and both of them surprised at the sight not of France, but of a warship that was already close and steering as if to intercept. Or ram, even – all things being possible, as one was learning ... He focussed the glasses on her.

Cruiser – black with three yellow funnels. Russian ensign. Coming fast, high bow-wave creaming, doing twenty or twenty-five knots, he guessed. Helm over now, beginning a turn to port – either to turn away or to fall in on this same course – close on this flagship's beam, perhaps. He'd guessed right, too – she was heeling hard over in executing the fast, sharp turn: was easing her helm now and cutting her speed suddenly, dramatically: you saw the rapidly diminishing bow-wave and her own rolling wake overtaking her as she fell into station a cable's length on the beam and a string of signal-flags broke at her starboard upper yard.

Rather stylishly done, he thought. Looking for'ard then, seeing what could only be Rojhestvensky's immensity leaning out from the port side of the forebridge, waving his cap – and the cruiser's captain doing the same.

Zakharov?

'What is it? A cruiser, I can see *that*, but—'

'I think –' studying details of this and that, mainly her armament –' it *might* be the *Ryazan*.'

Jane Henderson wrote, sitting at the small Sheraton writing-table in her sitting-room on the manor's first floor,

> Have had no news from you yet, but I dare say there may be a letter in the post from somewhere or other – at least one for Let's Not Say Whom, and I dare hope you would have put in a little note to me too, while you were at it. You might have written before you set off from wherever it was, which I forget – oh, Libau, which is in Lithuania, I looked it up in the big atlas – but from there I suppose you might have written in the ordinary post direct to Yalta. In any case, there's one for

you from her, and I'm really only writing now to enclose it. Her hand-writing in English on the envelope is very copperplate, is it not? I was going to say 'copybook' but you might take that to mean 'schoolgirlish' and take serious offence. All right, I'll admit, she can write in English, that much anyway, and I certainly could not in Russian: so she's one up on me there too. Changing the subject back again, however, we read in *The Times* a week ago that your squadron under its Admiral Rogersvoski (?) had sailed from Libau for Port Arthur; and where you may be now, heaven knows. I will be most interested to hear from you, and all about whatever you're doing, so I repeat, dear Michael, please don't only send me letters to HER.

But what else now? Well, your mother's in good health, would surely send you her love if she had any idea that I might be writing to you; and George is in his usual boisterous health and

She started at a knock on the door. Less a knock in fact than a bang. Murmuring to herself as she slid the letter into the blotter and checked that Tasha's was out of sight, 'Speak of the devil . . .'

'Come in, George!'

'Hah.' He'd been on his way in before she'd invited him. 'Writing home?'

'On the point of doing so. For the life of me, though, my brain's addled – can't think of a single interesting thing to say!'

'I'm sure *I* can't help. Except perhaps your sister having yet another baby?'

'They'll know about that, George.'

'Well – Johnny swotting away for his entrance examination? And that capital run we had yesterday? Eh? Like to hear about *that,* wouldn't they?'

'Doubt it – but I dare say I could fill a page with it. Yes, thank you, that is a help.'

'Not what I came up for though. About quite another

letter. From old Igor Volodnyakov – *didn't* mention it, did I?'

'No, George, you didn't.'

'It came yesterday and I put it aside, but I've just taken a gander at it – a surprise, you know, not having heard from the old boy in, oh, God knows how long. Mama does, once in a blue moon don't you know, but—'

'Did he write to you about anything special?'

'About Michael, partly. Primarily though about young Tasha, who's become engaged to some Russian naval fellow – who, reading between the lines, either Igor or his nephew the admiral found for her.'

'Isn't she rather young to be engaged?'

'I suppose she is. But the fellow's as rich as Croesus, apparently. Going to bring a mint of money into that run-down estate, he hints – as though it were just fortuitous. I'm probably not supposed to tell you that – keep it under your hat, eh? He's as pleased as Punch, of course!'

'It sounds to me like an unpleasantly mercenary transaction. What does it have to do with Michael?'

'Well, there's the rub, as they say. What he says is – more or less, you can see the letter if you like – silly of me, should have brought it up with me – he seems to be suggesting that Michael's nose may have been put out of joint, that *he* had hopes concerning Tasha. Huh? Dash it, she's still a child, isn't she? Well – as you said . . . If he had any such thought in mind, it's the first *I've* heard of it. Did he ever come out with anything of that sort in *your* hearing?'

'There's no reason he would have, George.'

'No. He'd have told me though, I'd have thought . . . Anyway – Prince Igor felt he needed taking out of himself, and that's why he gave him the chance of going on this extraordinary voyage. He admits it might be a risky business – says he hadn't given a thought to that when he issued the invitation – and Michael being a sailor anyway—'

'Dreadfully risky, I thought as soon as I heard of it. Your mother's *extremely* concerned for him too. She tried to persuade him against it in fact – when he was here the other week—'

'Didn't mention the girl then, did he?'

'Not to me – as I just told you.'

'Or seem down in the dumps at all?'

'Michael? Down in the *dumps*?'

'I suppose I'd better write to him. Tell him if he did have any such ideas he'd do best to put 'em out of mind double-quick. That's what Igor's hoping I'll do – or so I deduce . . . See what *you* make of it. But I'll do that anyway. Although where one would send a letter with any hope of it reaching him—'

'I've no idea, George.'

When he'd gone, she added to her letter:

> STOP PRESS. George has just been up to tell me he's had a letter from Prince Igor V. telling him of T's engagement and that he (Igor) suspected it might have 'put Michael's nose out of joint', which is why he offered you the chance of going out East with their precious squadron. George thinks the purpose of the letter was to get him to write to you and advise you to drop any ideas you may have had about You Know Who. I, of course, am no less surprised than George that you should have had any such feelings, or intentions. Joking apart, Michael dear, I feel deep down that no good at all can come of it: as I said when you were here – and you poo-poo'd it, but since then there have been several newspaper articles expressing the same view – the expedition you're embarked on is virtually suicidal, while on this other issue – which must be blinding you to *that* reality – Michael my dearest, the girl *is* only just out of school, how could anyone of her age and lack of worldly experience even guess at how she'll feel about anything at all in, say, a year's time? I'm sorry, I wasn't going to nag you about any of this – although it's spoiled my sleep more than a few

times recently. Anyway – it's said. And you'll probably be hearing from your concerned elder brother in due course – *if* he finds an address to write to, on which question of course I couldn't help . . .

8

The *Ryazan* had steamed alongside the flagship for about twenty minutes, during which time Michael had gone up to the forebridge in the hope of finding out what was going on. He'd visited the navigator, Sidorenko, in his chartroom, and Sidorenko had considerately offered to go and find the chief of staff – leaving Michael waiting on the port side of the signal deck, in sight and earshot of Rojhestvensky and Zakharov bawling at each other through megaphones – which distorted their voices to such an extent that he couldn't pick up enough consecutive words to make sense of any of it. Meanwhile Zakharov was conning his ship in even closer – to no more than a hundred yards or slightly less, Michael, even without glasses, recognizing the face he'd last seen at Injhavino – wide, heavy jaw, face narrowing upwards to deep-sunk eyes crowding a large, straight nose: Nikolai Timofeyevich Zakharov, whose presence at Injhavino and whose manipulation by Tasha's father had effectively flung her and Michael into each other's arms.

Should be grateful to him, perhaps? Might otherwise have held back too long – out of sensitivity over the age business – and missed the boat? But – listening again, at this closer range picking up more of the shouted megaphone exchanges. There'd been talk of coaling, and of the destroyers leaving Cherbourg – and the admiral had now congratulated Zakharov on his promotion to Captain

First Rank. Which in itself was news – another strand in the deal of course. A reflection, then: wasn't Prince Igor going to expect his quid pro quo? Or one might say roubles pro quo . . . Speculation – and megaphone conversation – interrupted then by the firing of a line from the *Ryazan*'s foc'sl break; from what might have been a Coston gun, as used in the Royal Navy – the same bark of the hand-held gun's discharge, then a Turk's Head weight on the end of the soaring line lodging itself over the receiving ship's guardrail, sailors down there grabbing it and hauling it in, with a stronger line following it and after that a steel-wire rope which, rigged tautly between jackstays, had a mailbag slung from it on a 'traveller', which was rapidly pulled over.

Mail? One to him from Jane/Tasha, even? This soon? Brought to him, at that, virtually by the hand of her damn 'betrothed'.

Clapier de Colongue was with him then: murmuring as they followed Sidorenko back to the chartroom, 'Of course – it was in the *Ryazan* you were supposed to have embarked. To tell you the truth, it had slipped my mind. One hears you've made many friends on board, we've come to think of you as one of ourselves.'

'Kind of you to say so, sir. It's true I've come to know some of them quite well – they're all most hospitable. But in the present circumstances – knowing nothing of what's going on between London and St Petersburg—'

'You're thinking of your position here not simply in terms of transferring to the *Ryazan*, then. No, I understand. Although in Brest, perhaps – if we do call there—'

'Is there some doubt?'

'There's no certainty. As you say, the outcome of any dialogue between Petersburg and London – and of course, if as neutrals the French insisted on strict observance of the legalities – in which with the world's eyes on them they might feel they had no option— '

'So where would we coal?'

' – but even if we do go into Brest – forgive me – there's

no certainty the *Ryazan* would join us there. Her immediate destination, as you may have heard— '

'No—'

' – the vicinity of Cherbourg. She'll rendezvous off Barfleur with a collier, then escort our destroyers and the *Korea* – who should be leaving Cherbourg this evening – to – oh, Vigo, possibly, otherwise—'

'Will the Spaniards let them in?'

'Lieutenant—'

'I'm sorry. One question after another . . .'

'The questions are fully justified, the problem is providing answers. It's all very much in the air. Your own people's reactions to recent events – which in turn might well influence the attitudes taken by France and Spain . . . I'll tell you what, Genderson – I'll ask Captain Selyeznov to keep you informed. When we ourselves know anything that might affect your own situation . . .'

'That would be very kind. Meanwhile may I ask one more question?'

'Please.'

'If we don't put into Brest, where do we coal?'

'*Where* – on the English coast here. *When* – in not much more than an hour's time. Colliers are there already, the second division's taking coal from them at this moment.'

Michael said – smiling, *almost* disbelieving – 'But that's – surely, in the circumstances—'

'Extraordinary, isn't it? *Quite* extraordinary. But none the less . . . What's pre-arranged, I suppose – with the Hamburg-Amerika Line of course—'

'There.' Sidorenko stretching across the chart, pointed with a pencil-tip: 'That's the rendezvous position.'

Off Brighton: three miles south of the New Palace Pier.

In international waters – just – but still twisting the lion's tail. At least, as the lion would see it . . .

The *Ryazan* had dwindled and vanished southeastward, while *Suvarov,* hugging the coast, altered by a few degrees to starboard. The swell had subsided, leaving the sea only slightly crumpled – just as well, since the intention was to anchor and have the colliers berth alongside. It was only a partial replenishment, a couple of hundred tons for each ship, and the work was completed well before sunset, all hands being then employed washing-down decks and gear. In a full-scale coaling every man on board including officers would have taken part – as was the custom also in the Royal Navy – and Michael, although a passenger, would have felt obliged to join in. He was glad there was no such obligation this time, since he wanted to have his gear more or less packed and ready prior to the possible call at Brest tomorrow – either to transfer to the *Ryazan* or to disembark for return to England – and it wouldn't have helped to have it black with embedded coaldust. Narumov's sailor-servant, Dombrovsky, was already sucking his teeth at having to wash and iron some shirts; Michael had told him at the outset that he'd give him a few roubles for the extra work, but it hadn't seemed to cheer him up at all. He took on this surly look even when Narumov gave him dirty overalls to wash.

'He's a revolutionist, is what's at the heart of it.' Narumov winked at Michael. 'Am I not right, Dombrovsky?'

'It's not for me to dispute with his worship the engineer-constructor.' Sneering, gathering up shirts, socks and drawers. He had a thin, pale face and a narrow head, black hair which he plastered down with oil. Asking Michael – taking a chance on it, since this was a foreigner and the other only a technician, really, but his eyes and manner shifty: he was aware that from many officers the answer to such questioning might come as a punch in the face – 'Will your English fleet be coming at us, then?'

'Coming at you?'

'On account of us sinking the trawlers, your honour.'

Michael shrugged. It was the question they were all asking; even though most of them were still proud at having seen off the monkeys in the torpedo-boats. 'It could happen, I suppose. But it's up to the politicians, isn't it?'

'Might be ordered back, d'you reckon?'

'Back?' Narumov showed surprise. 'You mean to the Baltic?'

'Have a *few* ships left then, wouldn't they, your worship? I mean, might have. Won't if they leave us to the English.'

Narumov nodded to Michael, 'He'd *love* it if we were recalled. His Majesty and the government and the General Staff disgraced, riots all over the country, protest meetings – even mutinies.'

Dombrovsky stock-still, arms full of dhobi, staring at Narumov across the cabin. Shrugging, then: 'It's you saying that, not me.'

'But it's the truth, you insolent swine! More to it than that too – this squadron's the only hope we have of pulling our chestnuts out of the fire at Port Arthur and Liaotang. Recall it to Kronstadt, we've lost the war. Port Arthur and Vladivostok too, like as not. Greatest disaster ever for Russian arms. Match your wildest dreams – eh?'

'What makes you think I'm of that mind, your worship?'

'Go on with you.' Narumov chuckling, winking again at Michael. 'I don't think it, I bloody *know* it. You're one of hundreds in this ship, thousands in the squadron. We *all* know it, Dombrovsky. Cut along now – and cut out the dirty looks, eh – before someone takes you seriously . . .'

No letter. Those must have been despatches of some kind the *Ryazan* had brought. But Tasha would have written to him via Jane by this time, he felt sure she would have. The question was, if Jane had sent it on to the agent in Odessa – Gunsburg, the man Prince Ivan had told him about – how could Gunsburg know (or have known) where to forward it, when Rojhestvensky himself didn't know where he'd be calling next?

Michael attended the evening service, and after dinner played dominoes in the wardroom with Trafilin. Narumov was writing his letter and Sollogub was on the bridge. Officers and men were to sleep fully dressed at their action stations again, but most of the officers were in the wardroom until getting on for midnight. According to Padre Rasschakovsky, the captain of the *Aurora* had wirelessed for permission to put in to some convenient port – he'd suggested Plymouth – to put his wounded priest Afanasy into hospital, but Rojhestvensky had refused. Rasschakovsky, who'd heard of it from the torpedo lieutenant, had requested an interview to discuss the matter, but the admiral wouldn't even see him, only sent a message by von Kursel that there were no ports they *could* put in at. Michael guessed at the reasoning behind what Rasschakovsky was condemning as callousness, and suggested it to him: that whether or not a war was on the cards, any Russian ship that had taken part in the Dogger Bank fracas and now entered a British port would almost certainly be arrested and held against settlement of future claims.

Where *Aurora* and *Donskoi* had got to now, nobody seemed to know. Except presumably the admiral and Clapier de Colongue.

Narumov wrote in his letter that night a concluding paragraph which he insisted on reading aloud to Michael. '"Today we were close to England's southern shores. Involuntarily I pondered over this clod of earth – so powerful, so rich, so proud and so ill-disposed towards us. I am depressed – fearfully depressed. Anxiety presses on my soul! What would I not give to be with you now! In so many ways, not simply in order not to be where I *am*. But how exhausting it all is! Lying on my bed last night I watched the rats making themselves at home in my cabin. I used to sleep with my feet towards the door, but have now put my pillow there because of the rats. They can jump from the writing-table on to the settee, and from there could easily have jumped on my head. The Englishman who is still occupying the spare bunk does not appear to notice them."'

The division would not be calling in at Brest. This emerged at breakfast, Ignatzius explaining that there were reports of heavy coastal fog in that area and that the approaches in such conditions were especially hazardous. Where they were at that moment there was rain, no fog at all – somewhere off Ushant, Michael guessed, going by his own estimates of speed and distance; in which case there'd be an alteration to port very shortly, to head southwest across Biscay. Vigo, Ignatzius confirmed, was now their destination. Michael guessed, and Sollogub agreed with him, that the story of fog on the French northwest coast was a fabrication, that Rojhestvensky had probably decided not to take his chances with the French, might have had some advice or warning in the despatches Zakharov had brought. But whatever the reason, it meant a lost chance of landing and/or receiving mail. Brest, Sollogub told him, had been on their itinerary right from the start.

From Vigo, send a letter straight to her at Yalta?

There'd be no risk in it. As far as he knew, no one in this ship knew anything about Tasha. Prince Igor (or Ivan) might conceivably have arranged for his correspondence to be monitored on board the *Ryazan* – on a pretext of security, perhaps, of their English guest passing intelligence to the Japanese – but until departure-day from Libau nobody could have known he'd be joining the *Suvarov.* And Igor would have played it very carefully, wouldn't have risked arousing Zakharov's suspicions of the truth, Zakharov then backing out of their squalid deal. In fact, even from *Ryazan* the despatch of letters should be safe enough: and completely so in any port of call where landing was permitted and one could post them ashore. Except if there *were* suspicions of communicating with the enemy – or with the British Admiralty even, in which case one might be watched even on Zakharov's initiative. Therefore, direct to Yalta now, but from the *Ryazan* play safe, use Jane.

Selyeznov came to find him during the forenoon, ostensibly to confirm that they were by-passing Brest – the chief of staff wanted to make sure he knew it – but also to tell him in confidence that they'd been shadowed during the night by three of four ships, certainly warships and probably cruisers, which had overtaken the division from astern, showing lights when first sighted but then dousing them, passing darkened up the division's starboard side, later reappearing ahead and on the landward side, maintaining that position until shortly before dawn.

'Assumption is they were British, I suppose. Could they have been French?'

'The admiral is assuming British. Circumstances being as they are.'

Whether it augured well or badly one could hardly guess. Well, on second thoughts, one could. Political cut and thrust in progress, threats and bargaining and so forth, and Jackie Fisher meanwhile ensuring that the hour by hour positions, courses and speeds of all the squadron's separate divisions – two of battleships, probably two of cruisers, plus transports and auxiliaries, some of which would be accompanying the destroyers – were precisely known, so there'd be minimal delay in implementing whatever orders might eventually be forthcoming.

There were no ships trailing them now. In the whole grey lumpy circle of visibility there were only the four *Suvarov* class vessels, the *Anadyr* and *Sibir* and another transport, the *Malay*, which had joined them either last night or earlier this morning. Both she and the *Anadyr* were laden with coal, Selyeznov informed him: although German colliers would be awaiting them at Vigo. The *Sibir*, bigger than the others, was carrying field-guns and ammunition to be landed at Port Arthur.

'Any indications yet whether the Spaniards will let us in?'

A plump hand to the newly trimmed moustache: 'My impression is that the admiral intends to take us in in any case. There's really no good reason we should not expect to be treated with normal courtesy.'

On the 25th, it was rougher, and Narumov was seasick. He had been since the previous evening, and noisily so during the night. He had a bucket on the deck beside his bunk and frequently apologized. But after Michael had assured him they'd be out of the dreaded Biscay by evening and that having suffered this initiation he'd be all right thereafter, he began to recover, even to the extent of coming on deck for a look at Spain – Cape Torinana and the Spanish Finisterre – after which he felt well enough to resume work on his letter, Dombrovsky having peevishly taken the bucket away and this time not brought it back.

Michael wrote to Tasha:

> My own darling. I think of you all the time I'm awake and dream of you when I sleep. That is not just a turn of phrase or said to advance my cause with you, it is simply a statement of the truth: I long for you, physically and mentally, day and night. This letter will be posted in Vigo in northwest Spain, where we should be tomorrow – our first port of call I may say since leaving Libau – if the Spaniards will allow us to lie at anchor there and replenish with coal and so forth. Long before you receive this you will have heard about the trouble we ran into in the North Sea, resulting in some fishing-boats being sunk: in the mind of the admiral (and others) there was an erroneous belief that there were Japanese amongst them. We have not heard yet what's to come of it, but there's bound to be a tremendous fuss and possibly – at the very worst – even war between Russia and Britain. If it comes to that I shall have no option but to disembark, at Vigo or wherever else we may happen to be, and in such event, Tasha darling girl, I will telegraph to your mother suggesting that the two of you should travel to England, to my mother's house – where you stayed when you were eight years old and the cook referred to you as 'a limb of Satan' – remember? I hope enormously that in the circumstances you and your mother will agree that in our personal situation the sooner you're out of Russia the better: if there is

a war I could understand your feeling that it might be your patriotic duty to remain, but the fact is that once your father heard I had left the squadron he would undoubtedly have you brought to Injhavino, or St Petersburg, even, if necessary, by force – well, you know it, and I can only beg you and your mother to anticipate any such move on his part by doing as I suggest. Naturally I would join you in England as soon as I was able, although I would have to report to our Admiralty first, making myself available for sea duty. So – I'd telegraph to your mother and also to mine, who at present knows nothing about you and me; once I tell her she'll do all she can to help us. Of this I've no doubt at all, only it's best that for the time being she shouldn't know, simply because she and your father do from time to time exchange letters, and she might let something slip or even try to plead our case for us – which she might not realize would be like tapping a stone for blood, as well as dangerous. Tasha, my love, I believe I can safely address this to you at Yalta, but you must not send letters to me to any address except Jane's in England. At this time of writing I am still not yet on board the *Ryazan*, still in the flagship, *Suvarov*. It's conceivable that the *Ryazan* may join us in Vigo in the next day or two: but that's why I can post this to you in Yalta quite safely, and may in fact be able to do so – posting them ashore that is, even after I move into Z's ship – I must add *if* I do, if I don't have to leave the squadron altogether – in the event of war. Forgive me, I realize this letter is becoming somewhat convoluted: when I sat down to write to you I did not have in mind all these practical details, I had – and have – only the most urgent desire to talk to you, my head teeming with thoughts of your sweetness, of your lips and eyes, the cloud of soft dark hair framing the loveliness of your face – oh, and your voice, my darling, your whispers in my ear, the whole slim beauty of you in my arms.

I have only to close my eyes and I have all that – in a sense I have, what I suppose I mean is that I *long* for it – long for *you*, my Tasha. But now burn this, please – at once, *don't* risk keeping it no matter how secure you may think it is; as we both know, your father is not above employing spies. I'm endangering you by putting even that much on paper, I only have to because it's the most important thing in the world for you to know that my heart and soul are exactly as they were when we were together – and will *never* change . . .

Morning, October 26th, approaching Vigo; sea only a little choppy now, and a promise of warmth in the southerly breeze. They'd be anchoring at about ten-thirty, Sollugub told Michael, but an hour or more before that entering completely sheltered water – Ria Vigo – with the town about ten miles inland on the starboard hand. Breakfast in the wardroom was consumed hurriedly, everyone being keen to see this landfall and heartened by the prospect of fine weather ahead. Baylin took Flagmansky up on deck with him, insisting that there was no point in a dog being well-travelled if it had no visual memory of the places it had passed through.

They'd been shadowed again last night, Selyeznov told Michael, joining him and Narumov briefly on the after compass-platform. As before, the shadowers had vanished before the light came, but by that time it would have been obvious to them that the division was shaping a course for Vigo.

'So your compatriots know where we'll be now – and no doubt the authorities in Madrid will have been advised.'

'I suppose that's not unlikely.'

'And requested not to accommodate us beyond some minimal length of time.'

'You sound as if you believe war really might be imminent.'

'Well.' The silly moustache receiving more attention. All three of them gazing out ahead and to port at the rocky coastline, the wide mouth of the inlet – and inland, distantly, snow on mountain peaks glittering in the early sun. Selyeznov said portentously, 'We *are* at war, with those who are your allies. From that as the starting-point, and what one might call logical progression – and sorry as I am to say this . . .'

What was really irking *him*, Michael realized – only half listening, and Selyeznov then departing for'ard – was how Tasha would react, if it did come to war now. It hadn't really hit him until he'd finished his letter and then read through it: that she was in her heart and bones essentially Russian: and that if England went to war against her country . . .

Face the truth, Mikhail Ivan'ich. *You* wouldn't rat on it – if you'd been brought up in Russia, the Russian half then naturally predominating. Nor would Anna Feodorovna – or Tasha, for God's sake: remembering her for instance on the subject of Russian-ness just a few years ago – 1900, when he'd been twenty-four. He had been promised the command of an old destroyer – a *command*, for God's sake, at that age! – but had been obliged to apply for leave in order to escort his mother to Russia and the sickbed of *her* mother, who was then over eighty and had been given only weeks or months to live. In being granted the 'compassionate' leave, he'd lost the promised command: another man had got it, and Michael had been left where he was; he'd return from leave to the same job – a more modern, larger destroyer certainly, but only as second in command.

So the start of that trip had not been exactly joyous; but after a few days in the huge and gloomy old Sevasyeyev place – palace, virtually – at his mother's suggestion he'd left her there and travelled on alone to Injhavino, not having seen any of the Volodnyakovs in the five years since Anna had brought her little girl to stay in Wiltshire. Anna he'd found just as alluring, despite her forty years, which one would never have guessed at; but Tasha, now fourteen, had looked and behaved more like seventeen – which wasn't all *that* much younger than twenty-four. In any case hadn't seemed to be: and his visit got off to a flying start through his having brought with him the mounted mask of the fox-cub from the hunt at which she'd been blooded: a complete surprise to her, since he'd never told her he'd had a taxidermist in Salisbury fix it up, with her name and that date on its wooden shield. She'd been first astonished, then wild with joy: 'wild' indeed being a word that tended to enter one's thoughts and memories in respect of Tasha. In any case, being bound to get back to the Sevasyeyev place by a certain date, he'd had only a few days with her and her mother and a few other assorted Volodnyakovs – old Princess Olga for instance, Igor's spinster sister who was well into her seventies and ran the household, and Ivan's sons Stepan and Pyotr who with half a dozen paid retainers did all the work of the estate on which several hundred 'souls' had at one time laboured – but neither Igor nor Ivan had been there. And how that visit had come to mind now was from the concept of Russian-ness not only in Tasha but also in *him* – as she, aged fourteen, had put it to him so challengingly, on their way home from a day-long excursion, leaning from her saddle to grasp his arm: 'How long before I see you again, Mikhail? Why not more often? Why don't you come to Yalta this very next summer? You're Russian, you know: your brother got all the English blood, you got all the Russian, you *belong* here!'

Almost his mother's words. With truth in them too; even as a child he'd been aware that George was more obviously English than he was himself. Like a litter of puppies of diverse parentage – this in fact had been George's simile, 'One comes out this way, the other that way. No choice in the matter – eh?' George had actually been commiserating with him, Michael had realized, saying in effect, 'Bad luck, old chap, but never mind, we can't all be four-square British!'

Back to the Injhavino memory, though – on the day he'd been leaving, Anna Feodorovna, obviously prompted by Tasha, had come out with the same invitation: 'Yalta next summer, Micky? *Could* you?'

The thought was nagging him as the division steamed up towards the town of Vigo. Nagging and depressing: even in terms of physical reaction – a sick feeling, and sweat – really, panicking . . . The fear – real enough, a contingency that seemed entirely possible – was that if there was war now he might well lose her: to Zakharov if Zakharov survived – Prince Igor would see to that – but otherwise to some other Russian – a rich one, naturally.

Could be the old swine might even find her one she'd *like*? And in circumstances entirely changed by war – as they might well be . . .

You wouldn't blame her. *Couldn't.*

The colliers were there – five of them, at anchor and displaying their Hamburg-Amerika Line house-flags; Narumov expressing satisfaction that it wouldn't be necessary – yet – to use the coal that was in the *Anadyr* and the *Malay*. Rojhestvensky led his battleships past them, to anchor in clear water where there'd be room enough for the Germans presently to move up and berth alongside.

Closer to the town two warships were lying: Michael put his glasses on them quickly. He didn't say anything to Narumov, but the larger of the two was British. Cruiser – *Monmouth* class, he thought. Technically, an 'armoured cruiser': about ten thousand tons with a dozen or so 6-inch guns in turrets and barbettes, and a speed of – well, better than twenty knots.

The other, much smaller, was Spanish.

Roar of *Suvarov*'s cable rushing out . . . He was thinking that if he was allowed – or required – to land here, he'd wear civvies; and do his best not to run into some fellow RN officer whom he might know. Primarily to avoid the need for explanations, but also not to arouse Russian suspicions of a surreptitious rendezvous, passing intelligence to the Japanese.

What intelligence, heaven knew. One knew about Russian paranoia now, that was all.

'This boat's coming to us I believe, Mikhail Ivan'ich.'

Narumov was pointing at a steam cutter which had what looked like port officials in its stern; while below them here on the starboard side of the quarterdeck a white-jacketed bosun was chivvying a party of bluejackets into getting the gangway down. *Michman* von Kursel joining them now. In the wardroom last night von Kursel had mentioned that he spoke a little Spanish and hoped it might come in useful, especially if there were to be any welcoming celebrations ashore at which the admiral might like to have an interpreter at his side. He'd added, winking at Golovnin, that the Spanish girls tended to be raving beauties. Looking back towards the town and the British cruiser then, Michael saw two other cutters on their way, with men in uniform in them: black uniforms and peculiar headgear. Police? The nearer boat was meanwhile still lying off, waiting for the gangway. He was wondering whether he might not re-draft his letter, find some way to word it that would not seem to be taking it for granted she'd turn her back on her country and rush to his side no matter what.

9

On *Suvarov*'s bridge the port officials had told Rojhestvensky, with the port commandant's compliments and apologies, that the Russian ships might remain here for twenty-four hours, but in accordance with international conventions concerning belligerents in neutral harbours, not one hour longer. Nor could there be any embarkation or transfer between ships of stores or fuel; under no circumstances would coaling be permitted. Two Spanish harbour policemen were being put on board each of the ships to ensure that these regulations were observed.

Rojhestvensky, flushed with anger, had pointed with his telescope at the *Anadyr* and the *Malay*, both of which were flying the Russian ensign: those were Russian ships carrying Russian coal – Cardiff coal, to be precise, but paid for with Russian roubles: how the devil could these battleships be prevented from filling their bunkers with coal that was their own? Alternatively, how could they sail in twenty-four hours – or for that matter twenty-four days – without coal to drive them?

The Spaniards expressed regret: those were the orders as passed from Madrid to the port commandant. There was nothing to be said or done about it. Beyond those unfortunate restrictions, of course, as the admiral must know, Russians were always welcome guests in Spain. It was hoped that their stay here would be a congenial one;

and if there was any way in which it could be made more so . . .

They'd trooped down to their cutter and pushed off. Rojhestvensky pointed at the two policemen in their funny hats, and shouted at a warrant officer to take them below and give them what they wanted: 'See how much the swine can hold!' In other words, get them drunk. Then to Torpedo Lieutenant Leontiev: 'Signal the German colliers to come alongside. One to each battleship, the fifth can suckle the transports. Coaling is not to be commenced however until further orders. But –' turning to Ignatzius – 'once they're alongside, I want armed sentries on the securing hawsers. Pass this order to the others too: sentries are authorized to shoot if necessary.' To Clapier de Colongue then: 'You and I will call on this commandant after we've had lunch. Have a message sent ashore to that effect.'

'That the commander-in-chief of his Russian Majesty's Second Pacific Squadron hopes to have the honour of—'

'– of twisting his arm until he screams! Put it any way you like. We've no consulate here, have we?'

'No, sir, but the French have, and in certain ports including this one we have a reciprocal agreement—'

'Good. I want lunch served as soon as possible.'

Within minutes the colliers were shortening-in their cables and weighing anchor; by the time Nick Sollogub was describing Rojhestvensky's interview with the officials to Michael and others in the wardroom, a berthing-party up top was taking the first collier's lines and securing her alongside. Sollogub telling Michael, 'I have to admit that Boyarin Zenovy was marvellous. One could see he was practically exploding with fury, but perfectly self-controlled. By his standards, anyway. Though what'll happen now . . .'

What had happened *already*? Michael was wondering. So far one had nothing to go on, except for the Spaniards' uncompromising manner. Meanwhile a steam pinnace had been launched, using the main derrick, and after it had fired-up its boiler von Kursel was sent inshore in it with the admiral's message to the commandant – in writing, Clapier de Colongue having a command of most European languages – and taking also some sacks of mail, amongst which were Michael's and Narumov's letters, in the charge of a petty officer steward to whom paymaster Guryenko had entrusted a sum of pesetas for the purchase of Spanish stamps. Von Kursel's orders from the chief of staff were to wait for a reply from the commandant, and to bring the steward back with any mail that might have been waiting here for this and/or other ships. He'd seen to all that, and was back on board – joining them in the wardroom now and accepting the glass of vodka that Michael offered him.

'No mail for us, eh?'

'Nothing. Health, Mikhail Ivan'ich!' Tossing it back, then shaking his head. 'Because we were never supposed to be calling here, I suppose. My God, that English lot – the armoured cruiser, I mean. I made a note of its name, not sure how you'd pronounce it—'

'Let me see?'

'Here.' He'd printed it in capitals but with the 'N' reversed: LAИCASTER.

Michael nodded. He'd been right, she was one of the *Monmouths*. Off-hand he couldn't think of anyone he knew who was serving in her. Von Kursel telling them all, 'You'd think *we* were monkeys – or wild beasts of some kind – the way they gawped at us when we were passing the ship, then at the landing-place where others were hanging about.'

Trafilin shrugged: 'Such is fame . . . What we should do, though, is give these dogs a run ashore. Flagmansky'd love it – weeks since he's seen a tree.'

'What about the admiral's visit to this fellow?'

'The commandant will be honoured to receive him, and is notifying the French consul that his Excellency will be requesting facilities for telegraphing to St Petersburg.'

'That's fine, then.' Sventorjhetsky stubbed out a cigarette. 'Petersburg will surely make the Spaniards change their tune. Look, I'm ready for lunch now . . .'

Michael had added to his letter:

> Re-reading this, I can see I may have expressed myself badly. I want you to know I fully realize that if war comes now neither you nor your mother would be inclined to leave Russia – especially to come to England, if we had become your country's enemy – which God forbid. All I can do is implore you, my darling, first, to come as soon as you and Anna Feodorovna can bear to leave, and second, to take whatever steps you can in the meantime to avoid your father's machinations. Another thing – *if* war comes and mails are interrupted, don't doubt that I will be *trying* to write, as well as longing for letters from you, and living every single day and night with you in my heart. I love you, Tasha . . .

That was as good as on its way to her now. But he was uneasy about it again, wasn't sure he hadn't overdone the valedictory angle – as if one knew war *was* coming, and was too phlegmatically prepared to accept a long separation.

Which he was not. The very thought of it – and of Prince Igor up to his tricks . . . 'Hey, where did *this* come from?'

Champagne . . .

Sollogub explained, 'If the news, when it reaches us, is as bad as it may be, chances are we'll be losing you. So while we still can drink together . . .'

The admiral and his chief of staff, and for some reason Selyeznov, went ashore in the pinnace at about two o'clock and were received with a military guard and band. Part of this ceremonial was visible to those with telescopes and binoculars in the flagship's superstructure: and it was taking place under the very noses of the British in that cruiser, Narumov pointed out. How would they react to *that*?

'With interest, I'd imagine.' Michael had shrugged. 'As I've said before, we are *not* your enemies.'

'May become so at any minute, however!'

'Let's pray not.'

He was praying not. For his own good reasons as expressed in the letter to Tasha. Which, if the war-clouds had vanished by the time she got it, she'd dismiss as fussing about nothing. She herself being anything but fussy.

Girl of action, he thought, longingly. Of sudden passions and compensating calms. Beauty *far* more than skin deep. Bit of a harum-scarum, really, despite her noble birth. An *exquisite* harum-scarum!

It was evening, the light beginning to fade and shoreside colours change, when the pinnace was reported to be coming out from shore and most off-duty officers went up on deck to witness the admiral's return. There'd been speculation that the Spaniards would have given them a skinful – toasts to each other's monarchs and so forth – but although Rojhestvensky was flushed and bright-eyed and by the look of him in high spirits, there was no sign of unsteadiness in any of them. They had newspapers on board, and a stack of others had been dumped at the head of the gangway.

Flag Captain Ignatzius, receiving his admiral at the gangway's head, asked matter-of-factly, 'Start coaling, Excellency?'

'Not yet.' A bark of mirth, and waving a rolled newspaper, 'Hell's breaking loose all over the world – thanks to these newspaper swine and the damned English throwing their weight about – confound them . . .'

Selyeznov told Michael that they'd been courteously received, but that the news-coverage and foreign reactions certainly were alarming – although the admiral seemed to be treating it all with contempt. From the commandant's reception – where toasts *had* been drunk, accompanying warm expressions of friendship, and gratitude for Rojhestvensky's assurance that he wouldn't for a moment consider fuelling his ships until the commandant received Madrid's instructions to permit it – they'd trooped along to the consulate of France, where facilities were provided for the despatch and receipt of telegrams to and from St Petersburg. Selyeznov had no details, had not been shown the several long telegrams, but Clapier de Colongue had told him the general naval staff were backing Rojhestvensky, accepting that in all the circumstances his actions had been fully justified, in line with his responsibility as commander-in-chief for ensuring the squadron's safety; and he – the admiral – had remarked to de Colongue that they'd 'soon have it squared away, all this hysteria'. Although the newspapers, French and German as well as British, were uncompromising in their view that war was inevitable, their only doubt being whether France and Germany would remain neutral. London had demanded, apparently, that Rojhestvensky himself and the captains of all the ships that had been involved should be tried by courts-martial, and that the battleships should return immediately to Reval. A leading German paper expressed the view that the admirals and captains 'must be permanently in an abnormal state of mind', and this carefully worded allegation was echoed in an English cartoon showing a sodden-looking Russian admiral on his knees with one arm up clinging to his ship's rail, the other hand clutching a bottle, a litter of empties on the deck around him. While the *Daily Express*'s three-day-old front-page offering had been:

BRITISH SHIPS FIRED ON BY RUSSIAN FLEET
EXTRAORDINARY OUTRAGE IN THE NORTH SEA

HULL FISHING STEAMERS RAKED BY THE BALTIC
FLEET WITH SHOT AND SHELL WITHOUT WARNING

One Trawler Sunk. another Missing, and others Damaged with Loss of Life – Many Wounded – Amazing Action apparently Due to Fear of Attack by Japanese – Riddled Fleet Returns to Hull with its Dead – Statements by Eye-witnesses of the Attack – Baltic Fleet now in British Waters. Killed: Capt. Geo. H. Smith and John Leggatt. Wounded: About 30 men.

Michael translated this and the detailed account which

followed for the benefit of Narumov and several others. He did not show them the drunken admiral cartoon, although Ignatzius later came across it and laughed so uncontrollably and for so long that Nyedozorov came hurrying from the other end of the wardroom thinking he was having an apoplectic fit. By and large, though, the fact that hostility and derision were general and world-wide was received with shocked surprise.

Vladimirsky, for instance: 'This is the blackest day in the whole of my naval service . . .'

And Sollogub, white-faced: 'It's not good, is it, Mikhail Ivan'ich? To my mind the worst aspect of all, oddly enough, is that one can understand the calumnies!'

It began to look worse next morning, when Selyeznov came along to the wardroom to give Michael a piece of information which he'd forgotten to mention the day before. It was that in expressing gratification at Rojhestvensky's abiding by Madrid's rules on fuelling, the port commandant had added rather slyly that it was probably a wise decision since there was now a squadron of British cruisers at anchor in the Pontevedra estuary.

'Pontevedra?'

'An inlet about ten miles north of here. I had a look at it on the chart.'

'They'd be our former shadowers, I dare say.'

They were outside the wardroom, which was on the main deck – one down from the open-air upper deck. Selyeznov had beckoned to Michael to come out to hear this, since while it was his brief from de Colongue to keep Michael informed, especially of British moves, this wasn't an item for general consumption in the prevailing atmosphere of uncertainty. Michael offered, 'They're probably only here for show. Satisfy parliament, press and public that our government's on its toes.'

'Or to ensure we turn back to Reval. For that we might even be permitted to coal. But – strictly between ourselves, Mikhail Ivan'ich—'

Bugle-call.

'What's this about?'

'All hands to muster on the upper deck. The admiral was, I know, intending to address us. There was a boat from shore at first light with despatches of some kind. Perhaps we'll have some questions answered now.'

He could hear the crew pounding up from their messdecks. They'd pack the quarterdeck, while Rojhestvensky would make his way aft along the main deck and go up the ladderway right aft. Michael, with several others now including Narumov and Sollogub, headed for an internal ladderway leading up into the after superstructure; to the signal deck up there, from where one would be looking down on the crowd of about eight hundred officers and men – ship's company normally seven hundred and fifty, but with the admiral's staff embarked, plus extra cooks and stewards, slightly over eight hundred, the paymaster had told him.

Out into the daylight then, between the after bridge and the signal deck, and turning aft. *Suvarov*'s collier lay secured on the port side, with a haze of smoke drifting from her small galley funnel and some of her German crew gathering on her stern to see what was going on. The sea was mill-pond flat, dark blue, glossy-looking under the rising sun. There was activity of a similar kind to this taking place on the other battleships as well – certainly on the *Alexander*, the nearest.

Sollogub beckoned to him: 'The man himself.'

Rojhestvensky – towering above the officers and men surrounding him. Head and shoulders over them even when standing on the deck, but positively gigantic when he'd leapt up on to the stern capstan. He was getting a few cheers, but silencing them easily enough – nothing persistent about it, only what was expected of them. Rojhestvensky bellowing then: 'Men of the Second Pacific Squadron! Fellow Russians! Comrades! I've called you together to hear a message received this morning from His Majesty the Emperor. His Majesty has been graciously pleased to send me the following telegram:

'"In my thoughts I am with you and my beloved squadron with all my heart. I feel confident that the misunderstanding will soon be settled. The whole of Russia looks upon you in confidence and in resolute hope".'

Glaring round at the crowd of upturned faces . . .

'The message is signed "Nikolai". And I have replied, "The squadron is with your Imperial Majesty with all its heart".' Pause . . . 'Is that not so, comrades? What the Emperor orders, we carry out – eh?' Great arms spread: 'Hurrah!'

Cheers rolled away across the harbour, joining with those from the other ships, whose captains were reading out the same 'Order of the Day'. Sollogub said, after *Suvarov*'s crew had been dismissed to carry on with their forenoon's work, 'Rather suggests no war – eh? Hope of the so-called misunderstanding being settled?'

'Let's hope and pray so.'

Vasiliev, an engineer lieutenant – his shoulder-boards white with red rank-stripes instead of yellow with black ones – muttered, 'Or it might suggest that His Imperial Majesty doesn't know his royal arse from his elbow.'

Sollogub turned on him quickly, scowling: 'Look here—'

'Please.' Narumov intervened, standing up for his own kind: 'He was joking. A crude way of expressing a thought which I must say had occurred to me – that whether or not it's settled must depend more on the British, who see themselves as the aggrieved party, than on Tsar Nikolai – who may well *feel* confident, but—'

'Exactly,' Vasiliev agreed. 'I'd add however that while obviously our own people will be doing all they can to avoid war, in my view that's a pity.'

'Why, what—'

'Your Royal Navy, lieutenant, would scatter us to the four winds, as soon as we poked our noses outside there – eh? If we sailed without their honours' permission to do so? Whereas if they decide to let us off that hook, we're faced with dragging ourselves across a couple of oceans so that the Japanese can smash us up no less effectively. I for one would as soon have it done with here and now.'

Very similar to sailor-servant Dombrovsky's sentiments, Michael reflected – at least, as attributed to him by Narumov.

In the afternoon a message came from shore that each battleship was to be allowed to embark four hundred tons of coal from the Hamburg-Amerika ships. Cheers went up, and a start was made at once. Ignatzius politely but firmly refused Michael's offer to take part: he was a passenger, a guest, it was out of the question – although the offer was very much appreciated.

By eight o'clock next morning, after a whole night's strenuous work, each ship had embarked *eight* hundred tons. Michael had written another letter to Tasha, and slept much better for it. There did seem to be a chance of war being averted. Selyeznov told him that at the request of the general naval staff Rojhestvensky had telegraphed a further, more elaborate justification of his defensive North Sea action, together with an expression of personal regret for the lives that had been lost. Meanwhile St Petersburg had agreed to British demands that compensation should be paid and an international commission set up to investigate the incident. Officers with first-hand knowledge of the action and what had led up to it were to be landed here at Vigo to return home overland and take part in it: one officer respectively from the *Oryol*, *Borodino* and *Alexander III*; and from the *Suvarov* – Selyeznov challenged Michael – 'Guess who?'

'You?'

'Certainly not.' He snorted. 'Klado. It was the admiral's own idea, and he's fairly dancing with delight!'

'Klado also dancing?'

'Who knows – or cares. The admiral's selected him, and that's that. But as I told you, the bastard never got a whiff of powder, he took care not to. Remember the stories of rats and sinking ships?'

* * *

The division weighed anchor at first light on November 1st, and *Suvarov* led her consorts seaward – clearance having been received by telegram from St Petersburg the night before. The day before that – Sunday – Klado and the other 'delegates' had been sent off by train: the three others were said to have been hand-picked by their captains as those most easily dispensed with. Which meant, Michael thought privately, they'd be serious liabilities in any ship at all.

He'd written again to Tasha; also to his sister-in-law, Jane, mainly to let her know that he was alive and well and that so far he'd been sending letters directly to Yalta, which however he could only do until he transferred to the *Ryazan* and/or the squadron left European waters.

> As I'm sure you will have been made well aware by the newspapers, there's been a lot of fuss and bother caused by the Dogger Bank incident – which one day I'll tell you all about – but matters seem now to have calmed down, thank heavens. War with Russia is of course the last thing we'd want – Germany poses the threat we have to prepare for, and I'd guess this may be what's saved us; but the popular outcry might well have forced us into it, which for me and T would have been *extremely* difficult. While I think of it, Jane dear, if you can spare the time and effort, would you include in your letters (I mean when forwarding T's) any cuttings of news reports concerning this squadron and its doings? Or news of the war in the East, for that matter?

He'd landed, to post these letters, with a group which had included Sollogub and Bogdanov, who'd brought Flagmansky along on a lead of plaited spunyarn. They'd only stayed ashore a couple of hours – seen the town, of which there was very little, stretched their own legs and the dog's and drunk a few glasses of Spanish wine.

This was a lovely early morning. Hazy blue sky, the sun burning its way up through layers of inland mist, a light southerly breeze barely ruffling the water. On the flagship's bow to starboard the Spanish light cruiser *Estramadura*, which had lain at anchor off the town all the time they'd been here, was courteously escorting them out of territorial waters – in which they'd initially been told they could stay for twenty-four hours and had in fact remained five days. Land was falling back fast on either hand as the Ria Vigo broadened: they'd be back in the Atlantic soon, and turning south; two days' steaming then – all going well – to Tangier. The thought of finding a letter from Tasha waiting there was exciting, although the fact that it would have had to have gone by way of England and Odessa in a comparatively short time seemed to make the the chances slim. Although according to Selyeznov, Tangier, like Brest, had been an intended port of call all along, so Gunsberg might have been forwarding mail there. If he'd been shipping other supplies as well, for instance. Hope alternated with pessimism – or realism – according to one's mood. Another concern was that unless his own first letter, sent ashore in Denmark, had reached Jane quickly and she'd sent it on to Yalta very promptly, Tasha couldn't know that he wasn't on board the *Ryazan*: where mail might therefore be awaiting him, in the personal care of N.T. Zakharov.

But Jane would know by this time. Would have forwarded them to him in *Suvarov*, surely. And Tasha would not have tried to cut corners – as he had himself, admittedly, but only because it had clearly been safe to do so.

Impetuous, she might be. Idiotic, she was not.

Narumov pointed with his head: 'Flag signal going up.'

For the turn to port, no doubt. It was an irritant that one couldn't read the Russian flags – or semaphore, or lights. But there, on the starboard bow – a warship, a couple of miles beyond the *Estramadura* but on roughly the same bearing and coming south – this direction. He took his glasses back from Narumov: already guessing it would be the British cruiser – *Lancaster* – who'd slipped out of Vigo between sunset Sunday and dawn Monday – or one of the others who'd allegedly been anchored in that inlet . . . This one was the same class as *Lancaster*, all right. While astern of *Suvarov*, the *Alexander* had the equivalent of an answering pendant close-up, doubtless signifying 'signal understood'; it would be the same with the *Borodino* and *Oryol*, he guessed. You'd see it now in any case: from *Suvarov*'s foreyard that hoist fluttering down, giving the order 'execute' – as it would in a *real* navy. Helm over, and a curve developing in the wake as the flagship's rudder hauled her round. He put his glasses back on the British cruiser, who'd timed it well to witness the Russians' departure – and would no doubt be wirelessing a report of their course and speed. Course a few degrees west of south, it would have to be to clear the Buelengas islands and Capes Cervoeiro and Roca, two hundred and fifty miles or so south; also to gain sea-room against the possibility of further breakdowns – by the *Oryol*, for instance, who might choose to do it next time in a westerly gale, with Spanish rocks to leeward.

The *Lancaster*, if that was what she was, seemed to have replaced the Spanish ship as their escort, but had taken station on the division's starboard quarter. Then in the evening, approaching sundown, she moved in closer and increased speed, gradually overhauling, passing on the starboard side at a range of about fifteen hundred yards. In the *Suvarov* all hands were on deck and at points of vantage in the superstructure; there was a long swell from the west and the battleships were rolling ponderously. The coast of Spain had long since been lost to sight. The cruiser had cracked on another knot or two, and when she was about two miles ahead, in gathering dusk and with lights burning on all ships by this time, crossed the division's bows from starboard to port and came back on an opposite course, as close on that side as she'd been on the other.

Then she'd gone, disappearing astern. Comment in the wardroom was that it had been a crude display of hostility and contempt: another phrase used was 'deliberate provocation'. Sollogub, who'd been noticeably silent, leaving the expression of indignation to others, murmured as he leant over to top up Michael's glass, 'They're right, aren't they? Sorry to say it, Mikhail Ivan'ich—'

'Say what you like. But don't forget what happened to those trawlermen.'

He could imagine how they'd be feeling in that cruiser. British fishermen killed and their boats sunk – by this ugly, lumbering circus that was now getting away scot-free. The fleet would have been told to prepare for action: then the politicians had backed off. But Jackie Fisher would still want to know of every movement the potential enemy made, to be in a position to move swiftly and decisively if they cut loose again or if there was a politico-diplomatic change of mind.

Down from his watch on the bridge, von Kursel announced, 'We have five of them with us now. Five cruisers. Playing games with us, coming up close astern or up one side of us or the other, criss-crossing ahead . . .'

'Showing lights?'

'Heavens, yes. They're not trying to be discreet about it!'

'It's intolerable!'

Vladimirsky, glaring at Bogdanov, who shrugged. 'What can we do about it – except get hot under the collar?'

'Will they keep it up, d'you think?'

Michael thought they probably would – at least as far as Tangier, which after all was only spitting-distance from Gibraltar, where you could bet a sizeable force would have been assembled and until a day or two ago would have been expecting action. He went to turn in early, spent several hours on and off thinking about Tasha, seemed to have only just fallen asleep when he was woken at about seven by Narumov, who was clattering around throwing on his clothes – and overalls – and muttering angrily to himself. The ship's engines had stopped, Michael noticed. The roll was of course more pronounced now she'd lost steerage-way.

'Have we broken down?'

No – but the *Oryol* had, Narumov told him. Not her steering this time, some other machinery defect, and the engineer-constructor on board her had asked for Narumov to be sent over to advise him. All ships were lying stopped, and *Suvarov* was lowering a whaler. 'I'm to be *rowed* across to her – would you believe it?'

'Easier than swimming.'

'Oh, very funny!'

'If you put a steam-pinnace over you'd have to wait for it to raise steam, wouldn't you? There's a lot to be said for oars.'

'In these conditions?'

Meaning, with the ship rolling as she was. Michael told him, 'Doesn't feel like much. Only because we've stopped.' He was on deck in time to see him shin down a dangling ship's-side ladder, then be bounced across a hundred yards of heaving, blue-black sea and, alongside the *Oryol*'s towering black side, there receiving instructions from the boat's coxswain in how to jump for the ladder as the boat rose to its highest – jump and grab hold and start climbing in the half-second's pause before it plummeted again.

He'd done it – was clambering up, then being lugged over the side. Michael, who had watched this from the spar-deck, went on up to the after bridge then and found Dr Nyedozorov and Lieutenant Reydkin there. Nyedozorov pointing: 'A bit much, isn't it?'

The cruiser squadron was exercising around them. Here in the centre the funereal-black battleships and transports rolling like disabled whales, while manoeuvring around them at distances varying between about three and twelve thousand yards were five lean, grey ships. At this moment in line-astern, but making – *now* – a ninety-degree turn in succession, followed by a turn 'together' – simultaneous – that brought them into a perfect line-abreast, back on their previous course: and then splitting – two to port, two to starboard, the centre ship reversing her course and the two pairs sweeping in to reform on her in quarter-line port and starboard – an arrow formation. All at something like twenty-five knots, and executed very smartly indeed, not one of them even a yard out of station, and all of it to orders passed by flags.

'It's *too* much.' Nyedozorov quizzing Michael. 'Don't you agree?'

'Not entirely. They're shadowing us – for reasons you and I can both guess at – and we've stopped, so what would you have them do?'

Reydkin – lieutenant in charge of the starboard after 6-inch turret – muttered with glasses at his eyes, 'I have to admit it's – impressive . . .'

Michael heard later in the day from Selyeznov that Rojhestvensky had also been watching the drill display and had asked him – Selyeznov – 'Well, d'you admire it? You damn well *should*! That's really something. They're seamen, those! My God, if only I had such . . .'

He'd cut himself short, and continued down some ladder. Selyeznov said he'd had tears in his eyes. And you could understand that he might well have had, was Sollogub's opinion. His analysis of Rojhestvensky's situation was that although he was inclined to be overbearing, even at times savage – well, hysterical – he was utterly devoted to the service of the Tsar and would never shirk any responsibility that was placed on him or offered to him. Here and now the responsibility he'd accepted was to get the Second Squadron out to the Pacific to relieve Port Arthur: so, while very much aware that his ships weren't up to it, that he had untrained and potentially mutinous ships' companies and some appallingly bad officers, this was what he intended to do.

'Or die in the attempt.'

'He probably expects to.'

'While praying for miracles.'

'That, of course. Who doesn't? Don't you?'

Narumov had evidently performed *his* miracle: by eight o'clock the *Oryol* was ready to proceed, and after re-embarking her constructor the *Suvarov* led off again. The five cruisers stayed with them all day and before sunset were joined by five others – from the south, presumably Gibraltar – the ten ships combining to form a closely encircling escort. They were still in close company at first light, but had redisposed themselves into two columns of five ships on each side. They looked magnificent, Michael thought: and in mid-forenoon he had the luck to be on the after flag-deck again to see them reverse course in succession and reform astern into a single compact formation which shaped a course eastward – for Gibraltar, obviously. This division's estimated time of arrival at Tangier was three p.m.

10

Tangier, November 3rd.

Zakharov shook Michael's hand and more or less smiled – a twist of the lips, nothing more – at Michael's congratulation on his promotion. At Injhavino he'd been clean-shaven, but since then had grown a beard, close-trimmed around the heavy jawline, a dark frame enclosing straight, thin lips, large nose and deep-sunk eyes. Michael had thought of him, at Injhavino and since, as dog-faced, but the truth was that there was more expression in Flagmansky's furry visage than in N.T. Zakharov's. All right, so a man couldn't be blamed for the face he'd been born with, or the way the facial muscles worked or didn't, but the blue eyes were sharp enough – and if the brain smiled, why didn't they?

Presumably the brain didn't. Ergo, his true feelings were hostile. But why, if he didn't at least suspect Michael's involvement with Tasha? Well – easy answer – this was an Englishman he was not smiling at, was accepting as his guest only because he'd felt he had to oblige Prince Igor. Nothing to do with one's relationship with Tasha – perhaps. Telling the Englishman guardedly out of that wooden face, 'I regretted having to sail from Libau without you, Mikhail Ivan'ich. But if you'd left Paris a day or two earlier – eh?'

Close to the mark: could have been only his imagination, but the tone of it implied 'if you could have *torn yourself away* from Paris'. Or 'from Tasha', even. Imagination arising from the fact that that was what was on one's own mind, what actually *mattered.* Keeping one's own expression friendly in a way that one was uncomfortably aware of as being duplicitous, while reassuring oneself that even if Prince Igor did know that his wife and daughter had spent a few days with him in Paris before going on down to Yalta, he would surely not have tipped-off his future son-in-law. Explaining casually, 'I thought I had several days in hand. And was amongst friends there, of course. Gave me a shock, when I heard from the embassy . . .'

'No accident either.' Rojhestvensky shook his massive head. 'I wasn't telling the world – especially the monkey-world . . .'

They were in the admiral's sea-cabin, behind the fore-bridge. Had there been no admiral on board, Michael had learnt from Sollogub, it would have been the ship's captain's; the little cupboard into which Ignatzius had had to move would normally have been the navigating officer's sea-cabin, and he – Sidorenko, the navigator, alternatively Sollogub his assistant – was having to make-do with the settee in the chart-room. Not ideal arrangements, in a battleship that obviously had to be prepared to embark an admiral and his staff. The architect would have insisted that this *was* a flag officer's accommodation, only happened to be useable by less exalted persons when the ship was 'private', i.e. *not* a flagship; but it would also account for Ignatzius taking his meals in the wardroom – his own preference obviously, since as flag captain he should have messed with the admiral and his senior staff.

They'd anchored at nearer three p.m. than three-thirty, and it was now about four-thirty. Outside and on the decks below was bedlam – gun-salutes, boats queuing to get to the quarterdeck gangway, bringing other ships' captains and shore officials in gaudy clothing and tarbooshes: a few top-hats even. Russians were welcome here, apparently; although Morocco was a French protectorate the Sultan had decreed that the Second Squadron could stay as long as it liked. Twelve colliers had been waiting for them; coaling was to commence this evening – in an hour or two – and be finished by daylight. The hope was to put out to sea some time tomorrow.

Rojhestvensky, in full-dress uniform decorated with stars and orders, was going ashore presently to pay an official call on the Sultan.

'Well, Captain . . .'

Glancing at the time . . . Zakharov got up quickly: 'Yes, Excellency. I'll be off – I'll take Genderson with me. Good of you to see me, when you have so much pressing business.'

'Genderson was half-expecting to be landed here, I gather.' The admiral heaved himself to his feet. 'Or was it at Vigo? Expecting a declaration of war – a night attack by the cruisers that have been following us about, I dare say. Mind you, they can handle their ships, those fellows, one has to admit it. But I'm glad, Genderson, it won't be up to *me* to hang you or shoot you.'

'I'm relieved for *your* sake, Excellency.'

'I believe they're right for once, those dolts in the wardroom. For an Englishman, you're not such a bad fellow.' The hand was extended: 'We'll meet again, no doubt.'

'Thank you for your hospitality, sir.'

'My regards to Prince Ivan, should you be writing.'

Zakharov asked him on their way down to the upper deck, 'Were they celebrating, on your way in here?'

'The Tsar's accession. Yes.'

There'd been a lot of vodka around, during the forenoon and at lunch-time, on the messdecks as well as in the wardroom. It was the tenth anniversary of Tsar Nikolai's accession – accession as distinct from coronation. When they'd been anchoring here he'd seen foc'sl hands actually staggering, and several officers in no better state. Zakharov must have noticed something of that sort too; his tone of voice made it plain he didn't like it. Telling Michael,

'We'll be having our own quiet celebration on board this evening.'

'Have you already coaled?'

'Yesterday. Felkerzam's ships the same, including the destroyers. They'll be off early in the morning, the admiral was telling me.'

'And we follow?'

'No. He's sending them with the destroyers through the Mediterranean and the Suez Canal. The rest of us he's taking round the Cape, to rendezvous with Felkerzam at Diego Suarez – Madagascar.'

Madagascar. You'd be about two-thirds of the way, there. Have only to cross the Indian Ocean and the southwest Pacific. *Only* . . .

The *Ryazan*'s steam cutter had been lying off, and was called alongside now by von Kursel, who was officer of the watch. Michael excused himself for a moment and went below to the wardroom to say goodbye to the twenty or so officers who were there – some less inebriated than others – but neither Flagmansky nor Narumov was present. The puppy was there, fast asleep – had had a few too many, it was alleged – and Flagmansky, they said, was getting himself slicked up to go ashore. He was after girls, was so desperate for them that he was ignoring warnings he'd been given about dogs being trapped and eaten in such places as this. Rasschakovsky at this point pushed through, grasped Michael's hand and wrung it, muttered, 'Go with God, my friend,' and shuffled away, leaving Michael surprised, staring after him. Sollogub explained, 'Afanasy – *Aurora*'s chaplain – died on the way down here. They buried him at sea. Listen, Mikhail Ivan'ich, when there's a chance to come visiting . . .' He came up to the quarterdeck with him: Michael checking that his tin trunk and suitcase were already in the boat, then joining Zakharov who was chatting with – or being chattered at by – Selyeznov, who remarked as Michael and Sollogub joined them, 'This Englishman and I met at the frontier post at Wirballen, both of us on our way to Libau. In fact we'd seen each other on the railway station in Paris and then again in Berlin. Then end up *here.* Extraordinary, really!'

'What had you been up to in Paris?'

Asking Selyeznov, not Michael . . . Selyeznov looking at him in surprise – as if Zakharov should have known that he was addressing the hero of Round Island, back from internment in Saigon and thirsting for yet more action. While Michael was thinking that if that question had been addressed to him he might have answered, 'Oh, making love to your fiancée . . .' Her image would be in his mind every time he saw or spoke with Zakharov. In Zakharov's too, mightn't it be – irrespective of the subject of their exchanges? Hearing Selyeznov's grudging explanation – addressing this man who was probably younger than himself but now senior in rank – the sort of thing Selyeznov would be very conscious of – telling Zakharov stiffly, 'I had arrived from Saigon via Marseilles. The cruiser *Diana,* of which I had the honour to be second-in-command—'

'Oh, the *Diana.*' Zakharov glanced away: at von Kursel waiting for him at the gangway's head. 'Yes, of course. A casualty of Round Island. You did well to get her away.'

'Our achievement, actually, was to keep her afloat. The worst action damage I ever saw. And of course as executive officer it fell on *my* shoulders—'

'I'll tell him all about it. Cutter's alongside, bit of a rush.' Michael put his hand out: 'Thanks for all your help, Vladimir Petrovich. See you from time to time, I hope.' Turning to shake hands quickly and warmly with Nick Sollogub then, asking him to say goodbye to Narumov for him; then preceding Zakharov down into the boat's sternsheets. As in the Royal Navy, the more senior officer, in this case Zakharov, got into a boat last and disembarked from it first. He was glad of the swiftness of this escape though – Selyeznov's starting to talk about Paris and their having seen each other at the Gare du Nord; the truth of it being that the little man's eyes had been focussed exclusively on Tasha at that time, and garrulous as he was he might well have come out with some arch comment – as indeed he had once to Michael, referring to 'the beautiful young lady who seemed close to tears at your imminent departure'.

Michael had ignored it: had decided that if the subject came up again he'd say it had been his sister-in-law who'd come over from England to see him off. In a conventional sort of way Jane wasn't bad to look at, as it happened. He asked Zakharov as the boat pushed off and got going towards the cruiser anchorage, beyond the transports and auxiliaries, 'Would you happen to know if there's been any mail for me?'

'Uh?' He'd been studying the ships they were passing. There was a bit of a swell running, which Michael hadn't noticed until they'd embarked. There was no shelter to speak of, in this huge stretch of water; in fact if it blew up at all, coaling might become impossible, although some of the colliers back there had already begun shortening-in their cables in preparation for going alongside the *Suvarov*s. Zakharov had glanced round at him in surprise – even slight irritation – at the question about mail. A shake of the head: 'Not as far as I know.'

'I'm sorry. I thought they'd have brought them to you, if there were any. Letters from England, you know.'

'Ah. Well, in that case, no.'

He hardly moved his lips when he spoke. This was what gave him the wooden look. The thin lips just parted slightly, and the words came out. He was pointing ahead now towards the transports: 'See that?'

A rusty old steamer with what looked like a chicken-house on her well-deck. She was flying a Russian naval ensign though, was evidently a unit of this squadron. He looked queryingly at Zakharov, who told him, 'The *Kamchatka*. Repair-ship, so-called. God knows how her skipper found his way here. Did you hear that stream of cock-and-bull the night your fishermen attacked us?'

Michael smiled, acknowledging the joke, which was also a surprising admission of the squadron's colossal blunder –

and a first hint of any irony or humour in the man. 'But you weren't—'

'We were close enough to listen-in. Even on the erratic German wireless. But then I was also investigating. What that fellow was shooting at was a Swedish cargo vessel, a German trawler and a French schooner. Liberal with his favours you see – especially when drunk.'

'Incredible.' Studying the broad-beamed, rust-streaked hull as the cutter chuffed close under the *Kamchatka*'s stern. 'You say you investigated?'

'There was a theory about minelayers in the squadron's path, foreign vessels of diverse types chartered by the Japanese. I personally considered this was more likely than the torpedo-boat stories, and I chose to interpret my briefing in that way – took a close look at all of 'em and boarded several. We may well be at the same game in the later stages, too. Now *there*, Mikhail Ivan'ich, is my *Ryazan*. Not a bad looker – eh?'

She was anchored at the end of a line comprising the *Aurora*, *Nakhimov* and *Donskoi*. *Nakhimov* flying the cruiser admiral's – Enqvist's – flag. Beyond were the light cruisers – *Svetlana*, *Zhemchug* and *Almaz*. But *Ryazan* was indeed not a bad looking ship: in comparison with her elderly neighbours, in fact, she looked positively stylish. Michael remembered that he'd liked the look of her when Zakharov had come visiting off Brighton.

'Very fine, Nikolai Timofeyevich. Incidentally, I hadn't realized the only other ship in her class is the *Oleg*.'

'It's not. There are two others – in the Black Sea fleet. The *Otchakov* and the *Kagoul*. I had the *Otchakov* from the day she was launched, at Sevastopol in nineteen hundred and two.' Nodding towards *Ryazan*. 'So this one I couldn't know better if she were my sister. There's not a ship afloat I'd rather have.'

Michael nodded. 'You're a lucky man.'

'In more ways than one, I might add. But you need more than luck. In this navy, in any case. More even than luck plus ability.' Following the direction in which Michael was then looking – at a handsome white-painted ship – passenger transport of some kind – anchored on her own beyond the *Ryazan*, her whiteness an eye-catching contrast to so much sombre black. Definitely a passenger-ship – with what they'd call a promenade deck – and similarly right aft, that raised, railed poop. Looking back at Zakharov, waiting for him to continue, to tell him what it was a man needed as well as luck plus professional ability: because it could only be influence and connections, in Zakharov's own case the patronage of the Volodnyakovs which had already led to his getting this command and promotion to captain first rank. Although, if his abilities were outstanding – as Prince Ivan had asserted they were – by the age of forty-four you'd have expected him to have achieved that rank at least.

He wasn't developing the theme, though. Nor following-up on the 'lucky man in more ways than one' remark. Not yet, anyway. But forty-four, for God's sake, to Tasha's just eighteen: Michael asking himself for the umpteenth time *So what are* you *worrying about?* Forty-four-year-old hand meanwhile gesturing towards the white-painted ship – five or six thousand tons, clipper bow, two slighty raked funnels, two masts raked to exactly the same degree. Those masts had carried yards and sails not so many years ago; she'd have been conned from that poop where her wheel and binnacle would have been.

'Know what she is?'

Not exactly difficult – with a green band around the white hull and red crosses on her funnels. And as well as the Russian merchant-navy ensign, a Red Cross flag at the mizzen. Glancing at Zakharov: 'Hospital-ship. She coming with us?'

'Indeed she is. The *Orel.* Arrived this morning, from the Black Sea. One hundred volunteer nurses on board – some of them the daughters of noblemen, I'm told.'

'Well, good for them!'

'Could lead to problems, though. The admiral has asked

me to keep an eye on her – when we have her in company, that is. Now listen: the first thing I'll do is introduce you to my officers. Several of them are men I've had with me before. Even some of my NCOs – the chief quartermaster and chief bosun for instance – I was able to have drafted from the Black Sea. You'll notice white caps here and there – not cap *covers*, the caps themselves. That's Black Sea gear; some of 'em didn't have time to re-equip. But as far as you're concerned, Mikhail Ivan'ich – a word in your ear, privately, while we have the chance – I would not have chosen to bring you with us, but since I agreed to and you're here, my inclination is to treat you, as far as possible, as one of ourselves.'

'I'd like that.'

The boat was slowing as it chuffed in to pass around the *Ryazan*'s high, black-painted stern. There were men up there on the quarterdeck, others at work around the stern 6-inch turret and the casement – another pair of 6-inch – on this quarter. There wasn't much superstructure aft here: a fairly low after conning position built around the mainmast-step, with a searchlight and 3-pounder deck above it. The boat chugging slowly now, under helm, bowman and sternsheetman standing by with boathooks, having slung rope fenders over. Zakharov was saying, 'We'll find employment for you. You're a navigator, as I recollect. Probably of greater experience than my own pilot – whom I don't know well but seems competent enough, a senior lieutenant by name Radzianko. He was an applicant to join the squadron – in fact to the admiral's chief of staff, who passed him on to me when my own choice for the job had his knee smashed by a cab-horse. Yes, can you believe it . . . Understand me, I wouldn't want you to seem to be treading on the fellow's heels, but you might – assist him. We'll get you settled in, then see how it goes. Agreed?'

Yet another batch of new faces and names to memorize: hard work initially, as it had been on the *Suvarov*. So far he'd met only the officer of the watch, a *michman* by name of Dukhonin – visual-mental note of wispy blond beard, Adam's apple – and the ship's second-in-command, Captain Second Rank Burmin – balding, with a wide head and broad, strong jaw, brown moustache and sideboards, gruffly reserved manner. Zakharov led the way down to the main deck and turned forward, passing what he said was the wardroom on the port side and continuing past rows of cabins to one on the starboard side with its door latched open. 'Here you are.' Tapping a card that was pasted on it: *Starshi Leitnant Genderson.*

'All right?'

'Splendid.' In fact, much as one would have expected – room to swing a *small* cat round, a high bunk with drawers under it, narrow wardrobe cupboard, hand-basin, a wooden flap that hinged down to make a desk, and a chair to sit on. The desk-top was folded up against the bulkhead: his eyes had gone to it and the top of the bunk in search of letters, and drawn blank. All spick and span though – as from the moment of stepping on to the gangway out there he'd noticed the ship herself was externally, despite having put in a lot of sea-time recently. Through the brass-rimmed scuttle above the bunk he saw again the white-painted hospital-ship, the *Orel*, the *Ryazan*'s nearest neighbour in this wide anchorage. He turned back: 'Very decent of you, giving me a cabin to myself.'

'Two *michmen* doubled-up, elsewhere. But wardroom now, for introductions. They'll be waiting for us.' He led back the way they'd come. 'I'll be dining in the wardroom tonight – by invitation, a celebratory dinner. I dare say we'll have a chance to discuss more private matters, sometime during the evening.'

'Fine . . .'

'As routine, I have meals in my own day-cabin –' a wave of the hand – 'back aft there. Or at sea, on the bridge. As I'm sure it would be in your own navy. From time to time I'll invite you to share a meal, of course. Now, here we are . . .'

Pushing into the wardroom – a space about forty feet by twenty, with the dining-table and sideboard and hatch to the pantry and galley at the for'ard end, this part furnished with chairs and settees; very much as in the *Suvarov*, only smaller. A number of officers were getting to their feet to meet their C.O. and his guest: and Burmin, the commander, who had come down from the quarterdeck, was arriving now behind them. Zakharov told Michael, 'Pyotr Fedorovich here, whom you've met, as my second-in-command is of course president of this mess.' He raised his voice: 'Gentlemen, I present to you Mikhail Ivan'ich Genderson, who is a senior lieutenant in the British navy but in mitigation of that has as much Russian as English blood in his veins and as you already know is joining us on board as my personal guest. I expect we'll find him some work to do – he speaks reasonably good Russian, and I'm anxious he should not be regarded simply as a foreign passenger. I hope to have your co-operation in this – strange as it may seem, in the circumstances –' a wave of one hand – 'such as English cruisers following us around . . . So, Mikhail Ivan'ich – introducing one navigating officer to another, this is Victor Vasil'ich Radzianko.' A tallish but also fattish man of about Michael's own age – dark-haired, clean-shaven except for a small moustache – offering him his hand: 'Delighted, Lieutenant.' Overweight, with a soft look about him and a weak handshake. Russians in fact didn't go in much for firm ones, but it was the softness of the hand itself that one noticed in this case. Torpedo Lieutenant Galikovsky then: full moustache, pointed beard, anxious-looking eyes: but he'd stand up under pressure better than Radzianko would, Michael guessed. Now Senior Lieutenant Murayev, the gunnery lieutenant – black moustache, squarish face, bulbous nose. And – in contrast – the paymaster, Lyalin. As an *aide-mémoire*, 'pay' matching 'pale' – also some resemblance to a ferret. Two engineer officers now – Arkoleyev and Skalinin, the first red-headed and the second bald; and in rapid succession thereafter watch-keeping and gunnery-department lieutenants and *michmen*, lieutenants Milyukov, Konyev, Tselinyev – hooked nose and long chin, resemblance to Mr Punch – Karasyov, Abramsky; and *michmen* Count Provatorov, Rimsky, Pepelyayev, Denisov, Vortzin, Egorov . . . As well as that one on the quarterdeck, of course, Dukhonin. They'd become established in one's mind soon enough, names attaching themselves to faces and functions, surnames linking as if inevitably to Christian names and patronymics. One had only to give it time and let it happen; try too hard and the memory would seize up. He was shaking hands with the doctor now – Baranov, a small man with shrewd black eyes and jug ears, asking Michael about his Russian parentage, and where he'd served during his Royal Navy service this far, and why had he wanted to risk his neck by coming along on this ill-fated voyage.

'Who says it's ill-fated?' Zakharov, cutting in sharply. Baranov spread his hands: 'Only a flippancy, sir – to see what answer I might get.'

'You'll get an extremely sharp one from me if I hear further talk of that kind, doctor – *you'll* be the one who's ill-fated!'

'I regret the ill-chosen word, sir.'

Zakharov had turned his back on him, was saying to Burmin, 'I'm joining you for dinner, aren't I, Pyotr Fedorovich? Invitation greatly appreciated. The champagne can go down to my account. Meanwhile Radzianko – Viktor Vasil'ich, you might give our guest a tour of the ship – as one navigator to another. The sooner he can find his way about, the better. Although he'll want to unpack his gear first, I imagine. Mikhail Ivan'ich, I'll see you later.'

He'd decided to make the guided tour first, since Radzianko had been available there and then, and left unpacking to the sailor-servant whom he'd found waiting for him outside the cabin. His name was Shikhin. Short, thickset, with a wide face and thick features, on which was a look of relief when Michael spoke to him in Russian, then surprise at having his hand shaken. Michael gave him the keys of his luggage and asked him to hang up what needed hanging and stow the rest in the drawers.

'Papers and so forth in that one with a key in it.'

'Your honour speaks Russian well.'

'Did you think you might have to learn English?'

'Your honour, I simply didn't know!'

Straight off the land, Michael guessed. From behind a plough or even possibly in front of one. He'd seen that more than once – a team of peasants doing a horse's work.

Radzianko had waited for him in the wardroom, and they started on their tour. Up to the quarterdeck first, which was in fact a raised deck with the after 6-inch turret on it, then past the small after superstructure and down a ladder to the spar-deck. Talking as they went along: abreast the ladder was the port-quarter 6-inch mounting in its casement – there was a pair on each quarter, so that taking the for'ard and after turrets into account *Ryazan* would have a broadside – either side, not both sides simultaneously – of eight 6-inch. And a dozen 12-pounders: 'Up there below the searchlight mounting, d'you see? – and between the funnels and each side of the bridge – each side of the conning-tower, to be more accurate. Torpedo tubes by the way are above-water for'ard and aft and a submerged tube each side here amidships. Might be better if I left it to Galikovsky to show you his tubes though – and Murayev I'm sure would be delighted to lecture you about his guns and control circuits, so forth. If we make it a tour just of the general layout now?'

'If you have the time to spare.'

'My dear fellow, of course I have.' A pudgy hand on his shoulder. 'I have also my skipper's orders.' He chuckled; pointed then at the white ship anchored a few cables' lengths to starboard: 'How about *that*?'

'Hospital-ship, I'm told. With a hundred volunteer nurses on board.'

'Well, exactly!' Crossing to that side for a clearer view. 'Some are the daughters of noblemen, one hears. How are they going to stand up to being dragged through the tropics and back up the other side!'

'I suppose if they've volunteered they must know what's ahead of them.'

'Bless 'em, I'm sure they do. They're lay assistants of course, not *religiosos.* The sisters provide them with some training and they perform the most menial tasks. But the proof's in the eating, isn't it? Might be glad of a little diversion now and then. Why, heavens, a few of them one might even know! In fact a young cousin of mine – here, smoke?'

'Thank you.'

Women *might* find him attractive, Michael thought. Doubting it, though. And if they didn't it might account for his apparently rather strong interest in them. A smirk lingered as he cupped his hands to shield the match: then lit his own. Straightening, exhaling smoke . . .

'Our skipper's just got engaged – as you'd know as well as anyone – to a girl half his age, a cousin of Admiral Prince Ivan Volodnyakov – and as you're in some way connected with that family, can you tell me the background to it, the *inside* story?'

'What an extraordinary—'

'Why? Isn't it natural that one should have a keen interest in one's own skipper's doings? On top of which now – arrival of a foreigner who by all accounts is related to those self-same Volodnyakovs—'

'A tenuous relationship, and very much in the past. All it amounts to is that my mother was the younger sister of General Prince Igor's first wife. Prince Igor as you may know being Prince Ivan's uncle.'

'His first wife – was your aunt, therefore.'

'Except that she died before I was born.'

Raising his eyebrows, blinking, thinking about it . . . A shrug, then. 'Complicates the relationship no end, that, doesn't it.' Thick shoulders shrugging. 'But it's true that our Nikolai Timofey'ich is to marry this *little* Volodnyakova – huh? And that she's very pretty?'

'Is this your wardroom gossip?'

'I have to admit I brought it on board with me – at Reval. Nobody'd heard a whisper of it until then. Guards his secrets well – eh?'

'Entitled to, wouldn't you say?'

'I should mind my own business, you mean?'

'Where did you scrape up the information?'

'Oh, in Petersburg. In the officers' appointments section. A friend of mine who's working there was telling me what I was in for, sort of thing. Normal enough, surely. But perhaps we should push along with our tour.'

'Yes. Please. Chartroom and bridge, to start with?'

'As you say. Chartroom and bridge.' Another glance at the hospital-ship as he prised his bulk off the rail. An assessing, re-appraising glance at Michael as he did so. A man to be careful of, Michael thought; understanding Zakharov having his own doubts of him.

Moving on, meanwhile, past massive ventilators – half funnel-height – abaft and between the funnels: and the tallest of all just for'ard of them. Five of them: a huge amount of draught. But of course, with steam-power for twenty-five knots or more . . . The height of the foremost one, he realized, would be for its intake to stand clear of the raised foredeck which might otherwise impede the flow of air. Stopping, looking around at this and that: Radzianko had gone on ahead. There was another searchlight here, between the second and third funnels, mounted above a platform with 12-pounders port and starboard: seaboats in davits where there was room for them along the ship's sides, and a steam-pinnace chained into its timber cradle amidships: and the cutter's stowage was on the other side to balance that; the main derrick would be used for launching and hoisting them, of course. A call from Radzianko now – 'Lieutenant Genderson – Mikhail Ivanich – are you coming?' He was on a ladder that led up to the foc'sl deck, with a screen door into the bridge superstructure at the head of it. Would be duplicated on the other side, no doubt. The port for'ard 6-inch turret was here, its armoured roof on a level with the higher deck, twin barrels trained for'ard. Michael ran up the ladder and ducked inside – into a lobby with iron stairs leading both up and down and Radzianko pointing with his head: 'Ship's ikon – a minor one. Big one's below, main deck amidships. You haven't met our priest yet, he's gone over to the *Aurora.* I suppose you heard—'

'Afanasy. Yes.'

'Well – these things happen . . . Now then, my chartroom. In action it'll be noisy, with a twelve-pounder on the bridge gundeck right above here. But – voicepipes to the bridge and to the skipper's sea-cabin.' Touching each of them as he spoke. 'And this one to the wireless room – up there. And that's about it – as much space as I need, chart folios in these drawers, instruments in the rack there, chronometer inset here, deck-watches and sextant in that cupboard. Electric distance-run register: there's another on the chart-table in the bridge. So – what more could you want? Oh – the settee of course – on which to rest my weary bones when necessary. Bridge now?'

'Yes. And conning-tower.' The conning-tower being the action control position – circular, enclosed in 5-inch armour plating. For the moment though he was still leaning over the chart. 'If you please . . . But – next port of call –' finger hovering, then descending – 'this one?'

'Dakar – yes, that's the guess. As yet unconfirmed. Ever been there?'

'Oh, yes. You haven't?'

Shake of the head. 'Never this far south. You might help me find it, eh?'

'It's straight-forward enough. Don't hit the Canaries *en route,* that's all.'

11

He'd written to Tasha, and a covering note to Jane; there'd be a landing of mail before they sailed, and he'd be ready for it. His letter to Tasha was of course in Russian, but hidden in the envelope with Jane's, and left in the drawer that had a key. He'd more than enough time then to take a salt-water bath and smarten himself up for the evening's festivities. Smoking a pipe up top before going down to the wardroom he'd heard the distant battleships' bands playing on their decks – less as part of the accession celebrations, he guessed, than to jolly the crews along in their coaling operations, which Rojhestvensky would be anxious to have finished before the deteriorating weather obliged the colliers to sheer off and anchor. This did in fact happen within the hour; a signal was brought down to Zakharov just as they were starting their meal, announcing the postponement of the Cape squadron's departure by twenty-four hours.

'Cape squadron?' Burmin, from the table's other end. 'That what we're calling ourselves now?'

'Why not?' Zakharov shrugged. 'As distinct from Admiral Felkerzam's Suez detachment. The purpose of which must be to take the destroyers by that calmer route, of course. The Cape of Good Hope's also the Cape of damn great seas – or can be.'

Burmin had put Michael on Zakharov's right, and the

priest, name of Myakishev, back from his visit to the *Aurora,* on his left. On Michael's other side was the chief engineer, Arkoleyev – tall, red-haired, small eyes rather close together. Zakharov was saying, about Felkerzam, 'He's transferring his flag to the *Sissoy,* and taking with him *Navarin, Svetlana, Jemchug, Izumrud* and *Almaz.* Several of the auxiliaries as well. The *Oslyabya,* however, remains with us.'

Radzianko asked, in the lazy tone of voice that matched his sleekness, 'For us, sir, the next stop is Dakar?'

'I can't see there's much alternative.' Zakharov speared a meat-ball, tasted it appreciatively. 'Any port at any appropriate distance worth stopping at or large enough to accommodate us all. Not this side of Cape Verde. And the distance – Mikhail Ivan'ich, how far to Dakar, would you say?'

'About fifteen hundred miles.' A glance at Radzianko: 'Wouldn't you say?'

'Or a little more.'

'I suppose the admiral keeps his intentions to himself as he does because of the English putting pressure on – well, in this case on the French, but on the Germans, Portuguese, anyone – to shut us out of any port we want to make use of.' Burmin stared down the table at his captain, seemingly taking care not to look at Michael. 'Isn't that the reason?'

'It's how he chooses to handle it. He confers with his chief of staff, they reach a decision and when they see fit they tell us about it. Who needs to know before that – except the Japanese, and the world's press, who *think* they need to . . . Come on, let's have some more champagne!'

Later – after the formal toasts to the Tsar and every member of his family, and to Russia, and the Second Pacific Squadron and the gallant defenders of Port Arthur – he drew Michael aside. 'A personal question, Mikhail Ivan'ich. Not of any great consequence now, only to satisfy my curiosity. Why did Prince Igor want me to bring you along with us?'

'Didn't he give *you* a reason?'

'Several. And this afternoon the admiral trotted out the story of your father saving the old man's life – which of course

I'd heard before, but frankly I don't believe has much to do with this. Prince Igor never even mentioned it. One of the things he said was it would be a fine opportunity for you – oh, and generalities such as that diplomatic complications – your country's alliance with our enemies, he was referring to – shouldn't be allowed to interfere with long-standing friendships. And that you and I should get to know each other, to our mutual advantage – both of us being what he called "rising stars" in our respective navies. Well – whatever maggots were or are working in that old brain, I'd rather please him than annoy him – seeing his closeness to His Majesty, and that in purely naval matters Prince Ivan has great influence – *and* that Igor is my prospective father-in-law. It won't have escaped you that these aspects are important to me personally; in fact, that I'm taking advantage of a system of which I strongly disapprove – which I admit I'd fight tooth and nail if ever I found myself, well, in Prince Ivan's position, for instance. Not that one's ambitions could reach quite *that* far. I'm being completely frank with you, you see. But there was another thing he mentioned, Mikhail Ivan'ich – that he suspected my betrothal to his daughter might have come as a shock to you – your little cousin throwing herself away on a man so much older than herself.'

'Little cousin?'

'No – not cousins, are you, but—'

'And throwing herself away?'

A hard stare: then a nod. 'Point taken. A manner of speech, was all. If I may continue, though: according to her father, you and she have been virtually older brother and baby sister – despite having seen each other quite infrequently over the years? I was treated to an account of some fox-hunt in England when she was still a child, and – oh, some reminiscence reflecting your concern for her, to which she took exception, for some reason. Well, she's still very young, of course, I realize that; whereas I – I'm in my forties, as is fairly obvious—'

'Never considered marriage before this?'

'No. One reason and another . . . Well – I *have*, but circumstances were not – conducive . . .' A shrug. 'Neither here nor there, however. The fact is that I will marry Natasha – she looks like her mother, and isn't *she* a handsome woman?'

'Anna Feodorovna. Oh, yes . . .'

'Closer to one's own age-group, too. In fact almost *precisely* one's own age. But there you are – and it allows one a glimpse of how the years will treat Natasha. As I said to you earlier, I'm a *very* lucky man. And I can assure you I won't let her down. I say this because of your own brotherly concern for her, as remarked on by her father: which brings us back to the main point, that I very much hope you *will* be able to reconcile yourself to the difference in our ages.'

'What matters, surely, is how *she* reconciles herself to it.'

A quick stare: with surprise in it. A new concept to him, that *her* feelings might be of consequence? Or that she might not be overjoyed? He let it go anyway, with a shrug and an expression of having missed some point. Continuing, 'I heard that you set off from Injhavino rather abruptly on the day after the announcement. And I of course left even earlier – to assume command of this ship, no less. Everything was happening at once, eh – right, left and centre. Natasha, I was informed, was indisposed – meaning still fast asleep, I dare say. In any case it would have been indelicate, to have insisted on seeing her there and then. I'm very conscious that in what is known as an "arranged" marriage, a wise man treads softly – at least, until all positions are made clear. Hasn't she written to you since then?'

'To *me*?'

'I thought perhaps in the circumstances she might have.'

'Must have made her reactions clear at least to her mother and father, surely?'

'One would have thought so. But Prince Igor is not the most communicative of men. As he'd see it there'd be no great urgency in any case – in view of where she is and where I am. One can only – naturally – assume that everything is as – as was agreed: and it would be reassuring to hear from you that your own reservations – if they exist at all—'

'Will you be writing to her? Or have you already written?'

'I'll have to, of course. But there again . . .'

Pausing, turning away to put down an empty glass: glancing around the room, at this face and that – and the steward with the brandy decanter starting over towards him. Michael wondering whether he could be as blind to the truth as he seemed to be, could possibly have not seen the look on her face as she'd hurried out of the room, or her mother's anxiety as she followed her. All right, so in the very brief interval since then he wouldn't have had a spare minute – getting himself to Petersburg then Kronstadt, taking over this ship and crewing her, working her up into shape to the remarkable extent that he had done, in just weeks – was therefore only *now* beginning to think about his personal situation . . .

'What's this deputation now?'

Paymaster Lyalin – looking healthier, with a bottle or two of wine inside him – lurching up in a dead-heat with the steward and his decanter, and the square-cut figure of Captain Burmin bringing a box of cigars. All of them having seen the obviously private conversation in progress and tactfully leaving them alone for those few minutes. Lyalin already giving tongue now though, telling Zakharov excitedly that he'd had word – by signal, presumably – of a French-flagged refrigerated cargo-ship, the *Espérance*, expected tomorrow from Odessa with a thousand tons of fresh meat on board.

'Save us having to start on the salted stuff for quite a while yet. That really is something, sir, isn't it?'

'Could be a mail in her too. If she's come directly from Odessa.'

'Let's hope so indeed.' Chaplain Myakishev, joining them, nodding to Burmin, who was proffering cigars. 'That would do us all a world of good!'

* * *

In the morning the weather was still foul, precluding any possibility of colliers lying alongside the battleships. Michael was on deck early, wanting fresh air to clear the cigar taste from his throat; and before that he'd added a paragraph to his letter to Tasha, telling her about Zakharov's sensitivity to his own feelings about the difference in their ages: and that he honestly didn't know why Prince Igor had been so keen to send him – Michael – along with him.

> That it might have been to get me out of the way for the duration of Z's own absence obviously hasn't occurred to him. He also asked me whether you'd written to me since Injhavino. I'm sure you must have, my darling, but being a better actor (or dissimulator) than I ever dreamt I might be, I was able to express surprise at the question. His belief, imparted to him by your father, is that you and I have over the years enjoyed an entirely 'family' relationship, with me in the role of 'big brother' taking care of you. Even the story about the leading-rein came into it! As far as I could make out though he's completely in the dark as to your own feelings. He said 'I'm aware that in an "arranged" marriage a wise man treads softly'. He's heard nothing, incidentally, from your father, and this seems to be of some concern to him. Perhaps he'd have expected a report from him on your reactions – compliance, naturally – and I dare say that even if he'd seen your shock and revulsion he'd have expected you to have become reconciled to the situation by this time. It might have been a part of the bargain that your father would see to it that you *were.*

Last night after Zakharov had left to turn in, Michael had been asked the now familiar question as to what on earth had persuaded him to come on this voyage; whether he'd really thought his highly placed friends the Volodnyakovs had been doing him any kind of favour. He'd told them yes: because of the British Admiralty's very keen interest in having an observer present – in the context of dramatically new conditions of naval warfare, especially fighting tactics, and because it was virtually certain this expedition *would* end in battle.

'Each and every one of the naval powers will be agog to learn valuable lessons – and I'll have been right there, *in* it with you, in a position to produce a detailed, first-hand report. Which, frankly, can't do my career prospects anything but good.'

'There speaks an honest man!'

'Or a fool. To assume he'll have prospects of any mortal kind!'

'Exactly. *If* you reckon you'll live to tell the tale, Mikhail Ivan'ich.'

Arkoleyev, the engineer. Ginger hair standing on end, and gimlet eyes somewhat reddened by this stage. Michael had postulated, 'Why shouldn't we all? All of us here, I mean. All right, so the Japanese have had all the luck out there, but no run of luck ever lasted for ever – and this is a fine, modern ship, perhaps better manned and officered than any other in the squadron.'

'Oh, listen to him!'

'How much brandy has he had?'

'It's a fact – as far as my observation goes. You have a first-rate captain—'

'Protegé of the man's own relations, he's *bound* to say that sort of—'

'I mean it – it's my immediate, clear impression. I can tell you, if I'd been stuck in the *Suvarov* I mightn't have rated my chances very highly, but here, in *this* ship—'

'You're flattering us, sir!'

'No, I'm not. Not "sir", either – Mikhail Ivan'ich, if you please. And yes, Pyotr Davidovich, I *do* expect to live to tell the tale.'

Not all of them did. The doctor, Baranov, wasn't saying much – possibly the result of having been shut up by Zakharov earlier – but there were some, including Arkoleyev, who in their captain's absence were deeply pessimistic. He'd murmured privately to Michael at one stage, 'The admiral, for a start, is a maniac. I have private information on the subject, as it happens. But you've met him – seen him in action, haven't you?'

'Well – in very peculiar circumstances—'

'It's the admiral who decides on the manner in which he commits his fleet to action. Dispositions, tactics to be followed, everything. The fact this cruiser is beginning to respond to our man's hard driving can hardly render her immune from the crass mishandling of the entire squadron by a blundering incompetent!'

'I think you're overstating it. Certainly hope you are. As I see it, Rojhestvensky's under great pressure at the moment. Not least, the coaling problem – especially from Dakar southward. I was checking distances, and it must be a nightmare for him. And he keeps it all to himself – even now, for instance, although our next port of call must be Dakar—'

'He trusts nobody, one's heard. A buffoon, if you want my opinion. A man who gives no trust earns none. And Togo's far from a buffoon – he's a very clever monkey. Incidentally, who taught him his business?'

'Oh, Lord . . .'

'Yes – exactly. You British did. Listen, Mikhail Ivan'ich – don't quote me to our captain, but he knows all this as well as I do!'

The weather had eased surprisingly by noon; bets were being placed that coaling might be resumed by late afternoon or evening. The refrigerated store-ship had arrived, and anchored near the other transports. Michael hadn't seen her come in. He *had* seen a pinnace which had looked to him like *Suvarov*'s call at the hospital-ship and embark two white-clad figures, presumably nurses – perhaps the head ones – and an officer who might have been the *Orel*'s merchant-navy captain, and steam off back towards the battleship anchorage. Rojhestvensky and Clapier de Colongue doing a bit of entertaining, no doubt. The nurses, Zakharov had mentioned last night, were of the order known as Sisters of Mercy.

Another topic of conversation at lunchtime came from the previous day's *Gibraltar Chronicle*, a copy of which had found its way into the wardroom and included a report, which at the chaplain's request Michael translated, that Viceroy Alekseyev was leaving Port Arthur to return to Russia, and that General Stossell the land commander had telegraphed St Petersburg saying Port Arthur would be his grave.

Radzianko asked, shrugging, 'Who gives a toss where they bury him?'

'Who indeed!' Murayev – Aleksandr Aleksei'ich, the gunnery lieutenant: 'As long as they dig him in deep enough, eh?'

'Oh, I beg you . . .' Chaplain Myakishev – grey-bearded, with droopy eyes like a spaniel's – turned away. 'Please, my children . . .'

'I've splendid news!' *Michman* Pepelyayev bursting in, looking excited. 'There's a mail coming! From *Suvarov*, where it's being sorted. Dozens of sacks, they say – arrived in that French transport from Odessa!'

There could be one from her, Michael thought. Pacing the quarterdeck with Radzianko and Galikovsky the torpedo lieutenant, after hurrying through lunch. *Could* be. Coming directly from Odessa, where the Gunsburg agency was. It was definitely *possible*.

It would be silly to count on it, though. Seeing that it had to depend on the posts between Yalta and Wiltshire, and how quickly or otherwise Jane might have re-addressed it and re-posted it – wasting time in writing one of her own to send with it, no doubt – and how long it might then take from England to the Ukraine. And lastly this French ship. From Odessa to Tangier – more than two thousand miles. At eighteen knots, say? No – play safe, say fifteen. Although a refrigerated cargo-vessel was likely to be modern and quite speedy. But then again, with the Bosporus and the Dardanelles to negotiate . . . Anyway, say fifteen knots – three hundred and fifty miles a day . . .

One week?

They'd paused to light fresh cigarettes.

'The letter or letters you're hoping for, Mikahil Ivan'ich – from England, obviously – from family?'

'Oh, yes.'

'Not from girls?'

'Well . . .'

'How many of them?'

'Oh, Lord . . .'

'A dozen, say?'

'Why not say fifty? Especially as I've been out of England for most of the past three years.'

The boat with the sorted mail would be calling at every ship in turn, presumably. Could be on its way round already: in which case there might not be more than say half an hour to wait. Time might have been saved by telling ships to send their own boats; but that would have led to congestion around the flagship's gangways. And if the colliers *were* on the move, the last thing you'd want would be a whole regatta . . .

'Listen – I'm going down for a cup of coffee.'

When the mail did arrive, an hour or more later, there was another sorting before the officers' letters were brought along by paymaster Lyalin and dumped on the wardroom table, where everyone flocked round like vultures to claw through them. Michael recognized one of Jane's almost at once – re-addressed in a Russian hand, doubtless in the Gunsburg office – and was then handed another that was identical except for being fatter. *Two* letters, not one! But the thin one could hardly have more than a single sheet of paper in it.

Might be from Tasha, though. If Jane had simply forwarded it on its own?

'Here – Mikhail Ivan'ich—'

Another?

Addressed by Tasha in Russian and posted in Yalta, for God's sake!

'Thanks.' Michael slid the Russian-addressed one into his pocket – in the circumstances, it felt rather like handling dynamite – and flopped into an armchair that had its back against the cream-painted ship's side. As if any of them would look over his shoulder . . . He opened Jane's fatter envelope, extracted her own two sheets of writing paper, the first one headed with the Wiltshire address, and another two – no, three, and larger sheets than Jane's – that Tasha had covered, bless her, in her angular Cyrillic. Those went into his pocket too, while he scanned Jane's first . . .

Written on October 24th and starting, *Michael dearest – have had no news from you yet, but I dare say there may be a letter in the post from somewhere or other – at least one for Let's Not Say Whom . . .*

Waffle. Simply covering Tasha's. Which, of course, was all one wanted, had any real interest in at all. But now – postscript: about brother George having heard from Prince Igor – wanting George to write and say drop any ideas one might have had about – oh, Jane's joke of the week, referring to Tasha as You Know Who.

Devious old bastard, though. Aiming to stop that bolt-hole: but revealing in so doing that he knew he might still have trouble on his hands. Otherwise, why bother? And anyway, thank you, Jane. In fact bless you, for this help.

Tasha had spent the first half-page telling him how much she loved him. Which certainly wasn't any waste of space or effort; he'd needed to be asssured of it as much as she'd have needed to express it, and he felt better instantly. His eye raced over the lines and over some words that weren't easy to make out: he'd go over it more slowly in his cabin presently, make sure of getting every word. But this one, for instance . . .

Got it. *Nightmares.* She'd been having nightmares about his having drowned.

> It's my father who comes to tell me every time, and it's as if he's enjoying the telling and my horror at it. If it did happen, I can tell you here and now I'd die. Mama tells me that's nonsense, that women all through the ages have had to face such things and steel themselves against the shock and deprivation: I realize, of course, that she's talking of her own experience, but the truth is I wouldn't *want* to. I'll tell you this, too: if my father tried to force me into *any* marriage, I'd refuse utterly, I'd tell him that if he persisted I'd kill myself – which would give him a real jolt, seeing that that would mean my commercial value going down the drain! In fact he's been trying to persuade Mama to bring me back to Injhavino – although he himself is in Petersburg with no expectation of getting away as long as the war lasts – no more than Ivan has, apparently. The reasons Mama gives for remaining here in Yalta are that this is where we've always felt happy and secure, and there have been disturbances recently in the Tambov-Saratov districts. The poor Djhenskinovs for instance, only eighty or ninety versts from Injhavino, had their farm buildings burnt down and their horses slashed with billhooks: can you imagine the mentality, the beastliness of such creatures? The Djhenskinovs were never cruel to their people either – in fact others have criticized them for spoiling them, thus encouraging theirs to expect too much . . . But it's – you know, the ill-wind, that we have that reason to stay away. Mama is determined we should remain here.
>
> If you could only be here too, my darling! Oh, just wouldn't it be paradise! I could faint from the longing I feel for you. And at times, I admit, with *fear* for

you. I wake with my mouth dry and pulses drumming, wondering where you are and what's happening. It is a crazy situation, isn't it, that you should be with Z – who is the primary threat to our happiness but whose survival must be a precondition of your own? It's baffling as well as harrowing. I ask myself why you agreed to accept my greedy, treacherous father's scheme; why it seemed inevitable (anyway, unarguable) at the time that you should; and Mama's answer is that your career is what comes first with you – as it has to be, I know, and as you explained and when I can get my thinking out of its customary muddle I do understand – that a successful outcome to this venture will advance your prospects of early promotion, which in turn will make it easier for you to marry me. Mama's attitude – though she remains rock-like in her support of me and of all that you and I both long for – is rather different . . .

The business about his own mother now being rich, so that he could afford to marry anyway. The background to this was that grandmother Sevasyeyeva had died in the winter after their visit to her. Brother George had been prevailed upon to attend the funeral with his mother; Michael couldn't posssibly have applied for leave again so soon in any case – especially as he was hoping to use his annual leave that next summer for the planned Yalta visit. The disposal of the estate – vast house and lands about the size of an English county – had been left in lawyers' hands and was now finally complete, enriching Elizavyeta Andreyevna considerably, though not as stupendously as it might have done twelve or twenty years earlier. Not that Michael had any thought of sponging on her anyway: that was *all* in Anna Feodorovna's mind.

I know we've said it all, over and over – but I still *think* of it over and over too, and shiver with longing and excitement when I recall surroundings, sights and sounds and certain hours and moments, whispers mouth to mouth which in the end amount more to tastings – of each other's souls? – than to exchanges of any articulated kind – that *need* articulation . . . Well, there's been fright and desperation to contend with – may be again, I often remind myself, so as to be ready and able to withstand whatever temporary vicissitudes may arise – but there's been – and *is* – oh, so much delight and glory too, all of it so *good* and so *right* that in these still warm, quiet nights I can look out at the stars and know for certain that in the end we *will* break through to lasting happiness!

Pray for it, Mikhail. I do, all the time, and perhaps our prayers might unite, become twice as strong . . .

Reminiscence followed: semi-coded reminiscences of Paris, references to the night at Injhavino too – the hectic, convulsive hours that had effectively been a process of committal. Remembering it as he folded the letter into Jane's – and *Michman* Count Provatorov asked him, glancing up from a letter of his own, 'Good news from England, I hope?'

Radzianko's bulging neck half-turning: 'Still loves you, does she?'

He ignored that. And Provatorov hadn't finished: 'What I'm really asking – when that was written, had they – or, excuse me, had *she* – had news of the action at the Dogger Bank?'

'No.' Folding it; he was going to read the other two letters in his cabin. He pushed himself up. 'This one was written at just about that time. But I've others to read, I'll let you know.'

'Study those in peace and quiet, eh?'

Baranov, the doctor, squinting – a letter in his hands and a cigarette wagging between his lips, its smoke in his eyes. Michael agreed: 'Exactly.'

'These are the ones that will really tell you does she love you, therefore. Amateur psychologist at work, you see. But good luck . . .'

Jane's second letter, dated October 26th and written in a hurry, was all in one scrawled paragraph.

> Michael – honestly, what do you people think you're doing, savaging our poor fishermen? There's a rumour now, to crown all that, that a lot of great ugly-looking leviathans are parading off our own south coast! There's talk of going to WAR, Michael! If it happens, what will they do with you – make you walk the plank? George has been over to Billy Selkirk's place to use his telephone but he'd already heard a great deal about it last night at the Armitages, whose other guests had just arrived from London. Trafalgar Square has been jammed solid with protesters – a mob of them in Downing Street too – and we hear the fleet's being mobilized. I daren't cut this out of *The Times* because it would drive George mad, but they're saying things like 'The mind of the Government, like the mind of the nation, is made up', and describing your Admiral Rogersvosky – who must be a homidal maniac? – as 'the ham in a strategic sandwich' – whatever that means. I suppose that he'll be eaten up – by Lord Fisher perhaps. Really, Michael, what *have* you done? I must rush now anyway – the trap is as you might say 'alongside' and I have duty calls to make, will drop this off at the P.O. on my way through the village. I suppose – seriously – if there is a war they'll put you ashore somewhere or other, so we might have you back with us much sooner than we'd expected – but then might it not be difficult getting You Know Who out of Russia?

The letter that mattered, now: from Yalta, addressed to *Leitnant Genderson* on board the *Knyaz Suvarov*, care of the Gunsburg agency in Odessa.

> Mikhail my darling
> I've had your sweet letter that you posted somewhere

in Denmark, telling me that you are (or were) in the flagship, not in Z's ship, and in view of this I'm taking a chance and writing to you through Gunsburg's instead of that long way round. You'll say I'm naughty to take such a chance, but anyway, here's the good news – *I am very well.* Aren't you relieved to hear it? *(He was. Had closed his eyes and thanked God. It meant she wasn't pregnant.)* But Michael, you've been in the thick of it now – fighting off Japanese torpedo-boats in the English Channel! There are some asserting that it was a mistake, that the English are right and there were no torpedo-boats, only fishing smacks – you wrote only a day or so before that there were 'silly rumours' going around which could not possibly be true, so perhaps that's it. Now we hear that His Majesty has apologized and that our government will be paying thousands of roubles in compensation, despite which England is still threatening to go to war! Well, I'll hear from you again soon, and you'll tell me how it looks from wherever you are now; if it did come to war, you'd be landed, wouldn't you? In such a case, will you telegraph us? Mama feels that in the event of war, leaving Russia might be difficult, since frontiers would be closed: all I can say is that nothing on earth – war, closed frontiers, anything – could change my love for you or my *need* to be back in your arms, my precious darling, at the earliest moment – in fact *now,* this minute! God, if it were only possible! Telegraph, my darling, and I'll come to you – no matter where you are or how many frontiers are closed against me! Now I live for your next letter. We know your squadron did not stop in Brest, so heaven knows where you may have posted it or whether you'd have sent it to me here or via England. I say 'it', but perhaps you've written several times! War wouldn't halt the postal services, would it? What a ghastly prospect that would be! My darling, I love you and I long for you. How many more times will we say this to each other? I suppose continually, until we are back where we belong, in each other's arms. For me my love for you is in the air I breathe, in every thought that passes through my head, it possesses me absolutely. What I could have thought I was alive for – whether I *was* alive even – before that night at Injhavino, I can't imagine. Except that – yes, I *can* – it started here in Yalta, didn't it – truly, didn't it? Unless it might have been the year before. Well, *I* could say I've been mad about you since I was quite a little girl; but for you, my lover, wasn't this really the time and place?

12

A thin cry from down for'ard of 'Clear anchor!' was repeated to Zakharov by Burmin; would have originated with Lieutenant Vetrov, foc'sl officer. Zakharov responded through rigid-seeming lips, 'Slow ahead both engines,' and a petty officer rang that order down on the engine-room telegraph. Zakharov stooping to the funnel-shaped copper top of a voicepipe to tell the helmsman in the steering position four decks lower, 'Port ten. Steer northeast by north.' Aiming to take them out clear of what looked like a rapidly worsening mess about a mile ahead of the *Ryazan* – trembling all through her iron frame as engines and screws began to churn. At higher revs you wouldn't get that vibration effect, Michael guessed. He'd been here only about five minutes, Zakharov having sent him a message please to come on up – which had come as a surprise, especially as one hadn't given the reassurance Z had been asking for last night on the subject of the gap between his age and Tasha's; Z then dropping the subject, seemingly giving Michael up as useless. This in any case was how he recalled or reconstructed it – in one sleepless period during the night wondering whether he shouldn't have been more diplomatic; having months to spend now in this man's ship, no option but to get along with him: but rejecting that, finally, for the plain fact that in discussing Tasha there could be no compromise.

Here on the bridge, Zakharov had greeted him with a nod:

Michael then keeping out of the way, watching and listening, mentally translating and comparing the Russian orders and acknowledgements with their equivalents in English. He'd borrowed a Russian seamanship manual for reference and study, and there was very little difference in approach, once translated; if he'd been in Zakharov's place at the binnacle his own orders in imperfect Russian would almost from scratch have produced the desired results. The port helm order now producing a slow swing of the ship's head to starboard – slow because she was only moving very slowly, this far, and the quartermaster would in any case be easing the degree of wheel as she approached the ordered course. Which *would* take her reasonably well clear of the melée of transports and Enqvist's three cruisers, who'd made the mistake of moving up astern of the old *Oslyabya*, who for some reason – aberration – had broken her anchor out before the *Suvarov* and begun forging ahead as if to lead them westward. Had now stopped, however: by the look of it she might have her engines running astern. Her captain fearful of Rojhestvensky's wrath, no doubt – and more than likely receiving clear indications of it by semaphore or wireless. Lucky perhaps not to have been shot at – yet. The transports too were all over the place – wallowing hulks pointing in every direction and all of them on the move, making things worse minute by minute and pretty well surrounding the battleships, impeding *their* movements. Rojhestvensky, Michael thought – adjusting his binoculars' focus on that slowly shifting area of confusion – Jane's 'homicidal maniac' would not be at his sunniest, right at this moment.

The telegraph clanged. Stopping again, he guessed. Time, seven-thirty. Weighing had been scheduled for seven, and the *Ryazan*'s capstan had begun dragging her up to her anchor precisely on the hour. Coaling of the battleships had been completed at two a.m. And Felkerzam's Suez-bound division had sailed last evening at nine, in heavy rain which in the dying light had rendered even their lights invisible within minutes – and which would not have made the *Suvarov* division's coaling operation very pleasant: must in fact have resulted in vast quantities of wet coal pounding down the chutes, creating a risk – later on, especially, when the squadron would be getting into the tropics and those internal spaces became ovens – of bunker fires.

The engines had stopped, and she was losing way. Zakharov swinging his glasses to the hospital-ship – also lying stopped, evidently following this ship's movements, having been told, as her master would have been by Rojhestvensy or his chief of staff, that the *Ryazan* would be his ship's individual escort. Burmin had explained over breakfast that while the *Ryazan* came under Rear-Admiral Enqvist for general administrative purposes, she was in fact at Rojhestvensky's immediate beck and call, no reference to Enqvist being necessary even as a matter of courtesy: Rojhestvensky might, at a minute's notice, send her ahead on a scouting mission, or to close-in off some port for purposes of communication, i.e. to send a telegram to St Petersburg through shoreside facilities – the German wireless system having proved to have a range of no more than thirty or forty miles at best. The rest of the time she'd be nursemaid – or chaperone – to the *Orel*.

Zakharov glanced round, saw Michael and beckoned. Michael joined him and Burmin in the bridge's forefront.

'What you see going on there, Mikhail Ivan'ich, is not typical of Russian fleet manoeuvres. The battleships haven't exercised together to anything like the extent they should have, and the *Oslyabya*, of course – well, words fail one. The transports I won't even mention. My concern is that perhaps you *will* – you'll be sending despatches from time to time, I imagine?'

'No, sir. Only a full report of conclusions after – well, after we've relieved Port Arthur.'

Another hard stare: as if wondering whether to believe him. Or to believe that *he* believed in the relief of Port Arthur being even on the cards. There were advantages in that complete lack of facial expression, Michael thought.

Glasses up again now anyway, on the slow-moving circus under its pall of black smoke. Arkoleyev and Skalinin had been critical of the soft German coal last evening: even when it was embarked dry, for heaven's sake. Zakharov nodding in the direction of the battleships: 'There are some good men there, believe me. Ignatzius, for one, but also – well, all of them – Bukhvostov of the *Alexander*, Serebryanikov of the *Borodino* – and Jung who has the *Oryol*. Snag is, the older men were trained in sail and some of 'em still *think* in sail . . . Ah –' muttering to himself now – '*Oslyabya*'s out of the way at last. So the transports now – yes, getting them sorted out – to *some* extent—'

'Captain, sir.' Galikovsky – torpedo lieutenant, therefore also wireless-telegraphy lieutenant – worried-looking, hovering . . .

'Well?'

'They're using their wireless almost continually, sir, and it seems the *Anadyr*'s got her anchor snagged in a sea-bed cable. *The* sea-bed cable—'

'This one linking Tangier and all the rest of Morocco to Gibraltar and points north, sir. It's shown clearly on the chart.' Radzianko had brought the chart with him from the table – there was a chart-table here on the bridge, with a sheltering canopy over it. Radzianko looking rather pleased about the *Anadyr*'s mishap. Winking at Michael: back to Zakharov then, who'd sighed, shaken his head: growling, 'They'll have to wait for divers. Either that or lose the anchor and a shackle or two of cable. In which case it's likely *we*'ll be told to wait for the divers and bring it along – since we have the speed . . .'

'Beg pardon, your honour.' A petty officer telegraphist – although they were actually called torpedo-machinists. But he was a *chief* P.O. – chief yeoman of signals, in RN terminology – grey-headed, with a school-masterly look about him – except for tattooings of whales and mermaids on his forearms. He was offering a sheet of signal-pad to Galikovsky, who motioned to him to give it to Zakharov. The chief yeoman muttered, 'Told 'em cut the cable, your honour. Order from the admiral to *Anadyr*.'

'*What* cable?'

'The sea-bed telegraph cable, sir. *Anadyr*'s to haul it up and cut it.'

'The reason I invited you up here – ' Zakharov, tired from half an hour spent watching the miserable performance up ahead, had lowered his binoculars and beckoned to Michael to join him – 'is to have you accustom yourself to the running of the ship. Spend as much time as you like on this bridge. Assist with the navigation: well, play that softly of course, but – just use your head . . . As I was explaining yesterday, or began to, rather than spend your days as a passenger – foreigner at that – it would be in the interests of the ship – your own too, probably – for you to become part of the – community. Morale's of the highest importance, and in this long haul there are going to be strains enough – although I've done my best to weed out potential trouble-makers it's something we must all remain alert to . . . On the political front, are you aware of the state of affairs in Russia?'

'To some extent, yes. Not a happy state of affairs at all.'

Might have blurted, *Oh yes, Tasha says* . . . Thinking of that passage in her letter about revolutionary activity in the Tambov-Saratov districts: Injhavino lying about midway between the two – and the Volodnyakov estate actually a dozen versts outside Injhavino . . . Zakharov saying, 'It's a bad time that will pass, please God. Defeats tend to sap morale. We need a victory now – better still a whole string of 'em, the Japanese sent reeling . . . How would you feel about that, incidentally?'

'You mean as an Englishman, when my country is—'

'Well?'

'It's a political thing, isn't it – and Britain's alliance with the Japanese is only defensive. And obviously, being with this squadron – and since I'd rather return alive than drown—'

'That's it, then. When you feel up to it you might even stand a watch. When you've got the hang of our systems.'

'Only snags are – one, I'm at a loss over signals in Russian, either by light or semaphore, let alone flags. So if I was on the bridge alone—'

'You won't be, you'll have the signalmen of the watch to rely on, and a junior officer of the watch to assist you. Never less than that. If you wanted to study the Tabulevich system – I'd guess you'd be the first non-Russian ever to do so.'

'Intriguing. *And* pass the time.'

'A second point?'

'The political angle – I'd suggest that when or if it comes to action—'

'You'll be an observer, nothing more.'

'I could help your doctor, of course – stretcher-bearing, first aid . . .'

'Indeed, why not?' He put his glasses up again, studied the black smoke-covered confusion of ships on the bow to port. 'He *is* getting them sorted out – I think . . . But thank God there's some way to go before we meet the enemy. No "if" about it, incidentally, you can be sure we *will*, Mikhail Ivan'ich – in the Yellow Sea if not before. Togo isn't going to sit in port and watch us steam past him to Port Arthur, is he! Even if Port Arthur's still holding out by that time . . . Anyway – about covers all we had to discuss, doesn't it?' He raised his voice: 'Half ahead together.' The telegraph clanged: Zakharov glanced round to check on the position of the hospital-ship – still lying there waiting – and Michael, accepting dismissal, moved away, making room up front for Burmin and/or Radzianko – or *Michman* Egorov, who was also now in attendance.

Propping himself against the side of the bridge he put his glasses up, focussed on the squadron which under its drifting canopy of black smoke was at last getting into the formation ordered by Rojhestvensky. Roughly so, anyway – the port column by no means straight as yet, but – getting there. The *Anadyr*'s adventure with the cable would have been the main cause of delay: but in fact she must have made short work of severing Morocco from communication with the outside world. Perhaps that *had* been the quickest way out of it. Rojhestvensky's ruthlessness therefore, more than actual lunacy: but another heavy bill, no doubt, for St Petersburg to settle, this time with the French. In any event, that lot was on the move at last: the starboard column led by the *Suvarov*, with her consorts in line-astern, and only the older battleship *Oslyabya* noticeably out of station, as well as emitting twice as much smoke as any other. The port column still snaking or zigzagging across each other's wakes – led, peculiarly enough, by the *Kamchatka*. Radzianko had shown Michael the formation-diagram, over breakfast, and in that column the repair-ship was to lead the *Anadyr*, *Sibir*, *Meteor*, *Korea*, *Malaya*, *Rus*, and the refrigerated storeship *Espérance* – presumably on charter from French owners. The *Rus* was the tug, formerly *Roland*, in which Selyeznov had disported himself so spectacularly in the Great Belt; she'd been on charter then from civilian owners but had since been purchased and re-named.

It was a pleasant morning. Getting on for nine-thirty now and the sun well up out of the coastal mists, climbing into a clear sky while a small breeze from the east no more than wrinkled the sea's surface. And the transports *had* got themselves into a single column.

Radzianko joined him, gesturing towards the now comparatively well-ordered squadron, 'Progress, eh?' That rather oily smile. 'But look at this.' Producing a sheet of signal-pad from his pocket. 'Specimens of the flagship's signals over the past hour. I'm keeping it for my scrap-book.'

In an educated hand: doubtless copied from the signal-log by himself . . .

Where do you think you're going?
Increase your speed!
Stop engines immediately!
Do not continue in that direction!
Steer more to port!

Get out of my way, you idiot!

Are you intentionally forcing me to run aground?

Michael handed it back. 'Priceless.' Zakharov had put on more revs: *Ryazan* was up to ten or twelve knots now, steering to close up on the other cruisers, which were in a double quarterline formation – *Nakhimov* in the lead flying Enqvist's flag and with *Aurora* and *Dmitry Donskoi* more or less on her quarters, cutting across from the deep-field where they'd been playing safe, moving now to take station astern of the main body. Neither *Ryazan* nor the hospital-ship had been shown on that formation diagram: presumably they'd be tagging on astern.

Start a new letter to her today, Michael thought, have it ready for posting at Dakar. If they let us into Dakar of course – which they might not, if they'd heard of Rojhestvensky's cable-cutting. Perhaps he *is* mad . . . He was leaning out over the rail now with his glasses trained astern, seeing the white hospital-ship following at a distance of about two cables, silvered water curling away from that elegant clipper bow. As elegant as a swan – and, extraordinarily, full of Russian girls of noble parentage, following this lumbering herd to God knows what.

Switch of mind to Tasha, then: the switch being less plain escapism than the thought of returning or not returning to her. And from there to the question in her letter: *it started here in Yalta, didn't it? For you, my lover, wasn't this really the time and place?*

In the sense of having finally realized how he felt about her, yes, it had been. *And* in going to the brink – starting what they'd finished or rather continued at Injhavino. As in answering that letter – starting this evening, maybe – he'd admit. But not admit to the state of frustration he'd been in at an earlier stage, resulting in an attempt at flirting instead with her mother – with whom the age-gap though even wider applied in the reverse direction, the thought being – if you could call it 'thought' – that in fooling with an older woman one couldn't be accused or even accuse oneself of *taking advantage*, or *trifling with* – or whatever. Anna had been alone – Tasha supposed to have joined them on the terrace, for tea or it might have been for wine, but she hadn't and he'd made his move really without any thought at all – a spur of the moment, unpremeditated blunder. It had been Tasha, not her mother, about whom he had been – well, meditating. If that could be the word for not being able to keep his eyes off her.

Eyes or before long – God help us – hands. Which he'd reason to suspect might have been welcomed. By this *schoolgirl*!

Anna had pushed herself out of his embrace. '*Silly*, Micky! Aren't you forgetting I'm married to Methuselah?'

'Well – exactly—'

'What's *that* mean? Unless the thought's insulting . . . But never mind – don't look so hangdog . . . Just tell me though, don't you find Tasha sufficiently attractive?'

'Of course I do!'

'Well, then?'

'Anna, she's fifteen years old! *Fifteen*, for God's sake! I know, to look at her or talk to her she could be nineteen. But – in fact, a *child*!'

'If you really think that, take another look!'

'What?'

That soft laugh of hers. 'I knew you were right for her when she was *nine*, you silly man! Don't you remember? You'd made her angry, and you came to me moaning that she'd probably never speak to you again? You were still *very* young at that time, of course—'

'Very much attracted to you, as it happens.'

'D'you think I was unaware of it?'

'Amused you, I dare say.'

'No, not *amused*, but already then wondering if, in the distant future, you and Tasha might not—'

'You told my mother that I bore a close resemblance to your first husband.'

'And she promised not to mention it to you. I'll tell her

off for that. But – yes, as a boy to the man – as you might have been his little brother – it's true – and still is now. Extraordinary. But we won't discuss Boris, please. Except I might tell you it's not Methuselah to whom I'm faithful unto death, it's him, the memory of him. That's all I'll say on *that* subject. But you and Tasha, Micky – no, wait, I'll tell you, even though it may sound to you like nonsense – I'm certain Boris knows what a fool I was, how as soon as his mortal back was turned, so to speak—'

'My mother told me that you'd been left in a dreadful situation.'

'A mine of information, is Lizavyeta Andreyevna. Anyway we have to learn to emerge from dreadful situations. And let me tell you, Micky; Tasha won't make any such errors. All right, so she's that old devil's daughter—'

'Prince Igor's—'

'Technically, poor lamb. What I'm telling you though – strictly between us, please – is that I think of her as Boris's. As the child I *would* have had from him. It's a way of thinking that I find – comforting, that's all. I'm a very practical woman, Micky – *now*, I am – and – listen, I'd like nothing better than for you and Tasha to get to really know and love each other. Listen to me – she may be down at any moment; and then we have the Krylovs coming . . . Micky, I'm thinking of the future, and very seriously. While the conclusions to which you were fairly leaping – I am *not* offering you my child now as a plaything, to satisfy your – cravings – or hers, for that matter—'

'Please – I never suggested—'

'You didn't have to, did you. And never mind that anyway. As I say, it's the future I'm looking to. *Her* future. I want you two to become in your hearts entirely committed to each other. What you do together – today, tomorrow or the day after or next week – that's for her to say. She's had my advice and reasoning, be sure of it – and we're close, as you'll have realized, she takes notice. In any case, you're a man of honour – genuinely fond of her, wouldn't do anything that might bring harm to her – if I didn't know it I wouldn't be talking to you like this. You following me, Micky?'

'I miss words when you talk so fast, but by letting them go I get the rest – most of it. But if you've given me the reasoning behind what you're saying, Anna – which I *don't* altogether understand—'

'The reason is that Methuselah has plans for her. For himself, I should say, but *using* her – which is anathema to me and would be hateful to her. So, being warned of his intentions this far in advance, since she still has years of schooling ahead of her, it's his *ultimate* intention I have to keep in mind and guard against. He sees her as a saleable – oh, *asset.* A bargaining chip to win some rich man's support for that crumbling, barely workable estate. Rich *old* man's, if necessary. It's the answer he sees to a great weight of financial problems – and quite natural to him as a solution; he's mentioned it several times, and to *him* it's normal, proper.' Her dark eyes intent on his, again querying his understanding; he'd nodded, and she'd continued, 'I have *not* told Tasha. I don't want her frightened and unsure – or at this stage set against her father. He'd guess at once. Keep it to yourself, please. Nothing's required of you, Micky – you're going to be away a long time, half a world away, and Tasha'll be at school, where, for the time being, she's safe from anything of that kind. Well – I said that nothing's required, I should have said nothing beyond convincing Tasha – please, *please* – of your love. Which I'm assuming exists, *believe* it does – or will – because as far as she's concerned – at least, as she feels *now* . . .'

Not all that clear, in the emotional flood of fast Russian. He'd got about three words out of five, maybe. Was not expected to commit himself, only to be what she called 'open-hearted' with Tasha – and to be around, if he and Tasha both felt that way about each other, in a few years' time. To stand as an alternative candidate, more or less, the candidate her mother had had in mind – she *said* – for years.

Blue sea, hot sky, and the scent of flowers. The house, which they called a *dacha*, suggesting that it was smaller than it was, was white-plastered, had its foundations on rock and nestled in acres of roses, wistaria, oleander, magnolia, bougainvillea. He'd been there about a week, had a fortnight left of his leave, and that had been the first time in several days that he'd found Anna Feodorovna on her own. It was June, the month of cherries, pears and peaches, and the sea already warm enough for lazy swimming. Steps were cut into the rock leading down to their own private swimming place. Swimming from rock, not sand; there were sandy beaches all along that coast, but this was out to the northeast, closer to Mount Kastel than to the more populated centre of the coastal strip – between mountains and sea – which in the course of the past hundred years had become built up with the palaces and summer houses of the immensely rich, as well as more modest places such as this. Well – not all *that* modest . . .

No more than Tasha was. Practically naked on that rock, within arm's length of him. Acting as if she didn't know the effect it had on him: as if she *were* a child, baring herself in innocence. And that place entirely private, rocks all round and no sight of it from the overhang above. Other situations too, other moments. Although they weren't by any means always alone; there were other families close by, friends of long standing, with young sons and daughters. Tasha was extremely popular – so bright, such fun, such marvellous company. He'd found himself wishing she *was* nineteeen. Which she truly might have been, and as many of these others were – all older than her in any case. Nobody seeing her out, either in that crowd or alone with him – that last day for instance, in Yalta itself, lunching on their own in Vernet's café – nobody could have thought, 'Oh, what a pretty child with that young man!' They'd have murmured, 'Don't look at once, but have you noticed that absolutely stunning girl?'

It had been such a lovely day, that last one, for all the

element of sadness in it. He remembered the sea as blue and the air at least as warm as this through which the *Ryazan* was now ploughing westward – soon, southwestward – with the mass of the squadron out to port, clear of the roads by this time; *Ryazan* with the *Orel* following astern of her overhauling the others, following some signalled order from the flagship. Michael remembering, assembling the memories ready for inclusion in the letter he'd start this evening; how from the village that afternoon they'd taken a cab out to Oreanda, and walked and walked, and in the evening sat together on a bench beside the church, looking down at the sea: behind them the mountains, and trees all round, and the chorus of cicadas' voices. There was an open-air restaurant out there at which they'd decided to have a lobster supper. He'd told her, answering a question about the cruiser he'd be joining shortly as navigator – 'big ship time', and a break in his service in destroyers – 'I'll be gone about three years. As a matter of fact I don't care how long – since you'll be slaving away at school.'

'Finishing school, when that's over. By the time you're back I'll be – oh, heavens, seventeen, *eighteen* even—'

'Almost past it. On the shelf. Unless I take you off it?'

'Will you be a commander by then?'

'No fear. Only a senior lieutenant. That *is* a snag, I admit. Be getting a bit long in the tooth, too – twenty-seven, twenty-eight. Tasha, I want *streams* of letters from you – and I swear I'll write every week – or thereabouts—'

'In all that time, what'll you do for girls?'

'Do for them?'

'You know what I mean.'

'There's only one girl, Tasha. I'll be writing to her, and getting letters from her – if that's what you mean?'

'Have you had many girls, Mikhail?'

'Hundreds.'

'Seriously!'

'Dozens, then.'

'Truly?'

'No, of course not!'

'But *some* . . . Mikhail, put your lips—'

He told her a little later, 'No difference anyway, one simply does not reveal, or discuss—'

'If we did it – if I'd allowed myself—'

'Tasha—'

'Could I count on that, that you'd keep it a total secret? God, this is so *huge*, I doubt I could *possibly*—'

'One day.' Kissing. Could have swallowed her whole. One hand where his lips had been; and kissing. Up for air then: 'And we'll remember *this* . . .'

In the event, in all the time he'd been away there hadn't been many weeks in which they hadn't heard from each other. But in the letter tonight he'd remind her of that last Yalta evening: the lobster and the wine, and the cab-drive home in scented, gathering darkness, kissing, loving – as a man of honour, naturally . . .

A howl from a petty officer – that yeoman of signals, the tattoo'd one – 'Your honour – the flagship's—'

Other shouts confused it: but from the head of the starboard column, the *Suvarov* had turned sharply to port, was charging at the wallowing *Kamchatka*: who had now put *her* helm over – which you would, with fifteen thousand tons of battleship coming at you like a charging elephant from a distance of about a hundred yards.

'Stop both engines. Yeoman, hoist . . .'

Hoist *something*. And stopping engines. Michael glancing aloft, seeing a black sphere rushing up *Ryazan*'s mizzenmast: that was the hoist Zakharov had ordered, telling the hospital-ship astern *My engines are stopped.* Total confusion in that port column though: the *Kamchatka* seemed to have saved herself all right; had acted fast enough to be more or less stern-on to her crazed attacker, and the other transports were scattering or stopping or both while the *Alexander* was leading the other three battleships out to starboard. The cruisers were also turning away – northward – making their escape. Enqvist on his toes, Michael thought – as well he might be, knowing the state of affairs in general and having some instinct for self-preservation . . . *Suvarov* by the look of it more just drifting on now than driven – passing between the *Kamchatka* and the *Anadyr* with so little room to spare that it had been either sheer luck she hadn't hit one or other of them or creditable ship-handling in a very quick reaction to emergency.

Galikovsky produced the answer then: bawling from the after end of the bridge, 'Signal from *Knyaz Suvarov,* sir: steering engine failed . . .'

13

Dakar looked attractive enough, after a week at sea, but from two previous visits Michael knew it would be hardly worth setting foot on shore. Except just to stretch the legs, breathe tepid air with jungle fragrance in it instead of funnel-smoke. Following the rest of the squadron one had had plenty of that – in mostly windless or near-windless conditions, there'd been fringes of the smoke trailing virtually to sea-level. And when you got your *own* funnel effluent, through a gust of wind overtaking from astern, when you were steaming at the best speed the squadron as a whole could make – eight knots was how it averaged out, after two thousand miles interspersed with breakdowns – it could be choking, nauseous.

For the past few days they'd been rocking over a heavy swell, but that was gone now, in the shelter of Cape Verde. November 12th, this was: Dakar in the lenses of his binoculars a cluster of whitish buildings amongst palms, with a forefront of light-coloured, sea-washed foreshore, background of dark forest and inland heat-haze. Sea flat as a skating-rink, air treacle-ish. They'd be in there and anchored, he reckoned – checking the time by the beautiful little watch Anna Feodorovna had given him – by about eight p.m. Zakharov had warned his officers and ship's company that the admiral would probably want coaling to commence immediately.

The *Orel* still glided swan-like in this ship's wake. As far as Michael knew there'd been no communication with her; but he'd heard Radzianko telling Zakharov that he thought a young cousin of his was quite likely to be on board – she had volunteered as a nursing trainee with that order and her family home was in the southern Ukraine. So if there should be any opportunities for socializing with the sisters . . .

'It's not likely,' was Zakharov's response.

Zakharov's bleak look. Graven-image look. Radzianko seemingly not discouraged, smiling as if that was exactly what he'd hoped to hear: or perhaps as if he knew better. It was a thickness of skin, Michael suspected, enabling him not to give a damn how others saw him. Plus a degree of interest in those nurses as compulsive as Rojhestvensky's determination to get this assembly of old wrecks out to the Yellow Sea.

Even knowing – as Rojhestvensky must have – that the odds were he'd end up leaving it there. One could see it in imagination: black hulls embedded in the silt, fishes and crabs exploring . . .

Tasha or Anna Feodorovna getting the news how, then? By telegram from Prince Ivan in Petersburg? It would be news of Zakharov's demise of course, not of one's own.

The battleships were dropping their anchors shortly before eight p.m. This close inshore the scent of rotting vegetation was overpowering. There'd be mosquitoes by the million: Michael was reminded of them by that stink. Smoking was the best defence against them: preferably a pipe. Zakharov had taken over the conning of the ship from his navigator and was leading the *Orel* off to port, where the two of them would anchor on their own – Enqvist having taken his cruisers the other way, to drop their hooks inshore of a waiting crowd of German colliers. Ten of them: and in fact not all that much waiting going on: activity already discernible on several of those foc'sls, with colliers weighing anchor before the customers had even secured their own.

Pre-arranged by Rojhestvensky, of course – doubtless to get coaling under way before the French told him he couldn't. Nothing here to stop him, anyway – nothing visible, certainly no warships. The last sight of those British cruisers had been north of the Canaries four days ago.

Ryazan stopped engines. *Orel* diverting further out to port – to anchor with the *Ryazan* between her and the rest of the squadron. *Ryazan*'s engines churning astern for a few seconds, taking some of the way off her, then stopping again. Silence, and cessation of that vibration. Only a slow forward drift, and the *distant* sounds of other ships' cables rattling out. Zakharov's quiet order then to Burmin, and Burmin's yell of 'Let go!' through the megaphone he'd had ready, and from the foc'sl the crash of a hammer knocking the slip off. A splash, roar of chain cable rushing out; by the time it had slowed and quietened the *Orel* had let hers go too – no more than half a cable's length on *Ryazan*'s beam. Voices in this bridge were audible again by then: Zakharov moving to leave the bridge, telling Burmin, 'Both – the cutter and a whaler. Whaler to take me to the flagship, cutter to raise steam and stand by at the boom. Rig the boom and the gangway starboard side. If we're to start coaling now, tonight . . .'

'Signal from the admiral, sir!'

The chief yeoman, with what looked like rather a long message, on his clipboard. Zakharov was already on the down-ladder from the bridge – on his way to his main-deck cabin, no doubt to get himself ready to be rowed over to the *Suvarov.* He stopped where he was, gazing up: the message might have been something with which Burmin or others could deal, whereas he'd be wanting to get over to the flagship before other ships' captains beat him to it.

'Read it to me!'

'Aye aye, sir.' The chief yeoman read out loudly, '"To all ships, from Flag. Coaling is to commence immediately. with ships' companies in two watches. Allocations, which are to be embarked in toto, as follows . . ."'

Then came the shock – tonnages of coal to be embarked by each ship. The battleships, to start with, were each to take on board twenty-two hundred tons: 'normal' bunker capacity being eleven hundred. The figure was staggering, surely unachievable: as were the others now being read out. Zakharov was climbing slowly back up into the bridge, growling to Burmin, 'Some mistake . . .'

And worse to come. *Ryazan* was allocated fifteen hundred tons. Her normal full capacity was seven hundred and fifty.

'Travkov.' Addressing the chief yeoman. 'This wasn't taken in by some clown who can't read figures?'

'By no means, sir!'

'Very well.' It was certainly *not* 'very well': but he'd absorbed the shock, was squaring up to deal with the cause of it. Glasses up first, checking that colliers were already on the move. Calling to Burmin then: 'Pyotr Fedor'ich!'

'Sir!'

'Start as soon as we have a collier alongside. We'll coal to capacity in any case, I'll see about the rest of it. In two watches – right?'

'Starboard watch from the start to midnight, say—'

'First get that whaler in the water and a crew in it. And tell Arkoleyev I want a word with him – in my cabin, *now*.' On his way down again. Burmin yelling for the bosun – Feklyenko – to get a whaler lowered and manned, gangway lowered and boom rigged, main derrick cleared away for hoisting-out the steam cutter. Then yelling into the engineroom voicepipe, getting the message to Senior Engineer Lieutenant Arkoleyev – with whom Zakharov obviously wanted to discuss the extraordinary inundation of coal that almost certainly *would* be coming. This was like a disturbed ants' nest now in the failing light; lights indeed were coming on here and there. And Zakharov did have a reasonably well-run ship, Michael thought. It was surprising to find, after a week at sea with the man, that he respected him, actually quite liked him. Nothing to do with Injhavino, Petersburg, Yalta, Paris – *this* was the man's true habitat. One's own, too? But what on earth could they do about this vast tonnage of coal – except fill the messdecks and any other spaces, not only filthying the ship up but also endangering her stability? That would be a particularly serious consideration for the battleships who, according to Narumov, were already top-heavy due to overloading, and thus in danger of capsizing in a heavy sea or under too much rudder.

Of course, Rojhestvensky's biggest anxiety all along had been coal – the question of access to neutral ports where he could or couldn't get it. Maybe he had reason to anticipate a hardening of anti-Russian attitudes further south.

Michael went into the chartroom – Radzianko was at the binnacle taking anchor bearings, sensibly enough, the weather *could* go to pieces and blow up suddenly – and pulled out the large, small-scale chart, spread it on top of the one in use. On the way down here Zakharov and others including Radzianko and Michael himself had speculated on the admiral's most likely intentions and/or best bets in regards to future ports of call, and the consensus had been (1) Libreville, (2) Great Fish Bay, (3) Angra Pequena. British-occupied territory had to be ruled out, maybe Portuguese as well, and there could be no certainty about the French – which, of course, applied to this place, Dakar, as well. The need was for harbours big enough to accommodate the squadron plus colliers: could be harbours or could be sheltered bays. So, Libreville, say – meaning the Gabon River. About two thousand miles south from here, and French-controlled. Measuring that distance: yes, two thousand, as near as, dammit. But if the French were uncooperative – as they might still be *here*, for all one knew – then you'd be facing about another thousand miles to reach Great Fish Bay. Lobito, as the Portuguese were now calling it. And if *they* decided to be nasty – Michael realized that he was thinking like a Russian – if the Portugese wouldn't let you in, your last hope would be another thousand miles south – Angra Pequena. Also known – to the Germans – as Luderitz Bay.

Angra Pequena was in fact the one safe bet. The colliers and the coal itself were German, after all – they'd hardly shut *them* out. But – four thousand miles, roughly, if you tried the other two places first. Alternatively, if Rojhestvensky took the bit between his teeth and made straight from here to Angra Pequena . . .

Using dividers again, measuring: and finding it would only save about five hundred miles. If that. And coaling in the open sea could be ruled out – might be feasible in some empty, sheltered bay, but out there, in the southeast trades, and as likely as not a gale or two . . .

Zakharov got back from the flagship at about ten, was met at the gangway by Burmin and brought down to the wardroom, where those who hadn't eaten earlier were finishing a late supper. It was very hot and mosquitoes were already a problem. A collier was berthed on the port side and coaling had been in progress for some time: Michael had offered to join in but Burmin had told him it wasn't necessary, working in two watches as they were. Tomorrow, maybe: it would be going on all day and would be worse in the midday heat. Bad enough now even just sitting around. Zakharov, in his shirt-sleeves – rolling them up – inviting the attentions of mosquitoes – took the chair he was offered at the head of the table and swallowed about a quart of water before accepting wine.

'Thank you. Although I'm not here to cadge drinks, only to tell you what's going on. I spoke with the chief of staff and some others, but with the admiral only for a few minutes before we were interrupted . . .'

The flagship had been coaling when the French captain of the port – a rear-admiral as it happened – had arrived by steam pinnace to inform Rojhestvensky that coaling would not be permitted. He had orders from Paris to that effect: also to request the Russian admiral to remove his squadron forthwith from French West African waters. He personally regretted having to insist on compliance, and explained that

Japan had protested against belligerents who were on their way to attack her being allowed the use of neutrals' harbours, that England had supported the monkeys' protest and Paris felt some obligation to accede to it. On the other hand the governor of Senegal – this territory – was prepared to assist the squadron and its admiral in any way he could, including the supply to them of fresh provisions, and the port captain was suggesting they might find it just as convenient to coal off the Cape Verde islands, a stone's throw away, where shallow water would allow them to anchor more than three miles offshore, thus outside Portuguese territorial waters.

Rojhestvensky had turned this down. In the swell that was running out there coaling would be impossible. Nor could his squadron leave Dakar without coaling, and the French government in trying to prevent them from doing so were in fact acting not as neutrals but as allies of the Japanese.

The port captain had left, to report by telegram to Paris, also took with him one from Rojhestvensky to be transmitted to St Petersburg.

'And we're coaling, anyway. It's not unlike the situation we had in Vigo. But as you'll all know by now, we'll be taking in twice as much as we have room for. I'm sorry to tell you that it's unavoidable. First I'll explain why – if you haven't guessed already. In a nutshell, we may have to steam the devil of a long way before we find any place where we *can* coal. Libreville was to have been the next stop, but we're not to be let in there – in the Gabon River, that is. It's hoped we may instead be able to meet colliers in that vicinity and three miles offshore: that's what we'll aim for. Snag may be the weather, which is unpredictable. Depth's fine for anchoring – ten or twelve fathoms – and the French are prepared to help in any way they can – which shows you, doesn't it, they're only playing a diplomatic game, don't actually give a damn – jumping through hoops simply to please – well, we know who, too.' Eyes were on Michael: not Zakharov's, but just about all others'. Michael ignoring them, watching Zakharov, who added, 'We'd be safe as houses in the river, but on that coast the weather's unpredictable, can be hellish – sudden violent storms followed by long periods of disturbance.'

He'd paused, was drinking down his glass of pale amber Tokai. In one steady draught – all of it. Nodding then, and licking his lips. Close resemblance to a tortoise, Michael realized, a tortoise who's just devoured a leaf of lettuce. Mental note: put that in the current letter to Tasha, amuse her. Or perhaps not. Think about it . . . Zakharov meanwhile pausing, watching his glass being refilled.

'So, although that's where we're going next, it's a toss-up. And the next best chance –' his glance covered both Radzianko and Michael – 'as we discussed, a day or two ago, would logically be Great Fish Bay. Very extensive, well sheltered, surrounded by nothing but desert. Snag there too, though – it's Portuguese and they do what the English tell them. If they knew in advance we were coming, might even have a British squadron there.'

Shrugging, lifting his wine-glass hand and crossing his fingers. 'Again, therefore, it's uncertain.' Glancing at Michael: 'You have a lot to answer for, you English.'

'Well . . .'

'Shouldn't have sunk your fishing-boats, should we.'

'No.' His turn to shrug. 'It won't have helped.'

'But –' tortoise eyes flickering around the table – 'on board this ship Mikhail Ivan'ich is half Russian – and one of us, an honorary *Ryazan*. He's nothing to do with politics.'

'French should know better. Supposed to be our friends, aren't they?'

Lyalin, the paymaster. Others were agreeing with him: 'Fine-weather friends, is what they are. And if things go any *worse* for us—'

'That's the truth. The principle of kicking a man when he's down!'

'To be on the winning side's what matters to them. At least not associated with losers, eh?'

'Calling *us* losers, you garbage?'

'My dear fellow, up to this stage, in Manchuria – which as far as I know is what we're discussing—'

Burmin cut in: 'How *are* we expected to stow the coal?'

'Yes, I'm coming to that. I'll finish first on the subject of ports of call. Here again, we guessed right – that German place, Angra Pequena. You were right, Viktor Vasil'ich.'

'That we'll be made welcome there?'

A nod to Radzianko: 'So the admiral expects. Well – *knows.* But there again – at Pequena we'll need to cram in every ton of coal we can, because from there on there's only Cape Town, Durban and Delagoa Bay – no place anywhere around that entire coast that isn't either British or Portuguese.'

'Non-stop Pequena to Madagascar, then.'

Radzianko again. Zakharov nodded. 'Where, of course, we meet the others. But now – storage of coal. I have some notes here compiled by the engineer-constructor on the staff, a man by name of Narumov. He'll be visiting us tomorrow – mainly to check various points with you, Pyotr Davidovich –' looking round for Arkoleyev, who nodded grimly – 'but in the meantime he let me have these notes.' Three pages of them, which he held up for all to see: it looked to Michael like the same paper Narumov used for those letters to his wife. Zakharov tapping page one: 'I'm not going to read it all to you. Headed – see – Instructions For Storing Coal. I'll leave it with you, Pyotr Fedor'ich. What it comes down to is there's no part of the ship we *won't* stack coal in. In this wardroom for instance – you might rig some boards across that end perhaps, and get rid of the armchairs. Officers' cabins are not excluded either. I'll evacuate mine completely, move up to the bridge lock, stock and barrel, and in harbour I'll mess with you in here. The messdecks, of course – washplaces, lobbies, engine-room auxiliary spaces, wing passages, torpedo flats – wherever there's any space that can be used without impairing the fighting efficiency of the ship. That's the *only* consideration, nobody's comfort is of the least concern. He's noted here,

"Rigging windsails through skylights for ventilation – since all ports and deadlights must be kept shut, in view of the dangers arising from instability".'

He slid the pages across to Burmin. 'You're thinking it couldn't be worse, aren't you?'

'Well, sir – at first sight, I must admit—'

'Of course. You *all* are. So am I. But you can also see there's no alternative. It's going to be hellish – especially while passing through the tropics. Bite on the bullet, that's all.'

The racket of coaling went on all night. The collier was on the *Ryazan*'s port side, of course, so it was less noisy than it might have been, in this oven of a cabin, but it was still a powerful challenge to anything more than fitful sleep. Coal-bags filled in the German steamer's holds had still to be winched on board – by means of an apparatus called a Temperley – and dumped, then dragged to the chutes and emptied into them: and there were chutes on this starboard side as well as that one. Coal didn't slide noiselessly down iron chutes, either. When he dozed off he dreamt of the cabin door bursting open inwards and the coal flooding in like a black fast-moving tide up the level of the mattress on which in the dream he could see his own sleeping body, prone like one of those stone effigies in the Abbey and as white as the coal was black, the coal mounting swiftly to surround and bury it. His sleeping brain had forgotten the choking black dust, which in reality would rise suffocating above the coal itself; but then waking, in the momentarily happy discovery that it had been no more than a dream, despite continuing sound-effects – fully awake, happiness dissolving in sweaty heat, fetid air and recognition that the dream might soon become reality or damn near it; he could almost see and definitely smell the dust-cloud like a black sandstorm filling all this space, obscuring light and replacing what passed now for air. How it *would* be. Except – well, wind-funnels, as prescribed by Narumov in those notes.

But there were no fanlights, for God's sake – might be in *Suvarov*-class battleships, but—

Sleep on the upper deck henceforth. *Simple* answer!

He had nothing on except a pair of drawers. They, and the sheet under him, were soaking wet. The mattress would be too. Wouldn't dry out in a hurry either – in this humidity, absence of any breeze, fans that turned too slowly to be shifting any air . . .

It would be good to see Narumov – Pavel Vasil'ich. Thinking of whom turned one's thoughts to letter-writing – his own unfinished screed to Tasha, and the need for a covering note to Jane. Might turn out now, in fact, get that done before breakfast. And use the chartroom? Well, why not? As quasi assistant or additional navigating officer – why not indeed? Cooler up there, and lighter: much better than in this fug . . .

Looking around the small, stuffy space, early light spearing in pinkly through the open scuttle that would soon have to be clamped shut: thinking about the coal invasion, the form it was likely to take. Up to three or four feet of it say: and how one might dispose one's gear so as to have access to it without the use of a pick and shovel . . . Seeing only one way – have Shikhin bring the tin trunk back from wherever he'd taken it, keep it here on top of the bunk and use it as a clothes-safe. Wouldn't be needing the bunk *as* a bunk – and only reachable by clambering over the coal-heap – in heat which even here, fifteen degrees north of the Equator, had one lying in what felt like a puddle of warm water, and could only get worse as the squadron laboured southward – a puddle by that time hot and black . . . So – tin trunk on the bunk; and one might be able to use the bunk's top drawer. Probably not any lower ones – nor the wardrobe cupboard, which would have its door jammed shut by the weight and bulk of coal against it. You'd have no hanging-space for uniforms. The top drawer wouldn't be anything like proof against coal-dust either: might therefore use it for shoes and other items that could easily be dusted-off. The trunk should remain pretty well dust-free, if one opened its lid only briefly and when absolutely necessary. Here and now, anyway – transfer whatever one was likely to need out of the wardrobe to the bunk: ditto the contents of the lower drawers. Do that *now.* Then send for Shikhin, get the trunk. The suitcase too for ready-use stuff? Not as air-tight as the trunk, but – yes, that too. *Then* wash, shave and dress and get down to Tasha's letter.

He wrote, in the chartroom, in reasonable comfort despite the reek of coal and its dust hanging to masthead height or higher, and the racket of the non-stop work down there – in which one should certainly take a hand oneself before much longer.

> It's going to be uncomfortable, to say the least, but there you are. I'm only telling you about it because it's something new and peculiar, whereas in the tedium of shipboard life on a long voyage like this, there's little of interest to write about, and I know my letters must be frightfully dull. Simply being in communication with you is the aim – *some* sort of answer to the ennui of separation as well as continuing concern for you and your mother under the threat of your father's machinations. The worst of it is being cut off from you, unable to help in any way. I think you're very wise to remain in Yalta, to refuse absolutely to be budged. Anyway – I'll be sleeping in the open air from now on – that's about as far as this coal business is likely to affect me personally – but my dreams will still be of you and of our future together, of my love for you, longing for you, and oh, Tasha darling –

There'd been a hail from somewhere down on the starboard side. He got up, went out to see. Could have been some visitor arriving, a challenge to a boat from the watchkeepers down aft. One of the *Suvarov*'s boats bringing Narumov, for instance. Or infinitely better, a mail. All right – hope springing eternal: but if some steamer had arrived from – wherever, Tangier perhaps, making twice this squadron's speed . . .

A swimmer, was all. Twenty yards out from the ship, treading water, with a hand cupped to an ear: 'What?'

''Ware *sharks*!' That yell had come from the quarterdeck – officer of the watch, probably. And the swimmer, for heaven's sake – Radzianko. Out of character, one would have thought – sharks or no sharks. The man down aft assuring him, '*Are* sharks around, we *seen* 'em!'

Radzianko put himself into motion – a clumsy trudgeon stroke, thick white arms thrashing, fat legs flailing. Heading for the gangway. Beyond him, all over the wide harbour, black ships with yellow funnels lay cocooned in their individual clouds of coal-dust. As here too: the sun lifting out of that jungle swelter was an orange fireball seen through the filter of *Ryazan*'s own shroud of muck. You weren't just smelling it, you were *breathing* it. Radzianko meanwhile floundering up to the gangway. Shouting up, 'Made a full circuit of the ship! Where were you when I set off, Vortzin?'

Vortzin was a *michman* – as squat and dark-complexioned as a Tartar. He'd sent his quartermaster down to give Radzianko a hand up. Michael heard, 'Fact, your honour, sharks *have* been seen!'

'Never mind.' Puffing and blowing: bulgy in a black costume, brushing water off his arms and shoulders and fat thighs. 'What matters is they didn't see *me*, eh?' Laughing, on his way up. 'Eh? Didn't see *me*, that's what counts!'

If he hung around now, wet, he'd very soon be coated with the black stuff – as were the fellows down there, dragging their sacks to the chutes and tipping them in: labouring and enduring like so many slaves. Coal-dust in their sweat running in streaks and streams: and in their eyes – which you couldn't wipe without rubbing more in, You'd almost think there would be men with whips down there, driving them on. They were stripped to scraps of clothing and had cotton-waste clamped between their teeth and plugging their nostrils: all wet black, bodies and rags and the waste. Every hour or so they'd be allowed a break, to sluice themselves off under a hose, take a few breaths of coal-scented, humid ozone before returning grimly to their labour.

Michael returned to his own. Asking himself as he picked up his pen: writing to Tasha – *labour*?

At breakfast in the wardroom Radzianko was immaculate in his whites. He'd enjoyed his swim, he said. First rate, nothing like it!

'Not scared of sharks?'

'Tell you the truth, I never thought of sharks. But no . . .'

'Any shark meeting *you* – ' Galikovsky poked him – 'would hardly believe its luck!'

The word 'coal' came into practically every sentence, every utterance. During the night's work apparently, several men had passed out down below; they'd been dragged up on deck by their mates, resuscitated under hoses and sent back to work. It was accepted that if you allowed a man more than a couple of minutes to get himself together you'd be encouraging malingering. None of them last night had sustained any lasting harm, according to the doctor. The worst job of all was that inside the bunkers, where the coal had to be raked level as it came in to ensure completely filling the compartment with no blockages under the chutes. Burmin admitted that the temperature in those spaces, even at this comparatively cool time of day, was about one hundred and twenty degrees. By noon, with the decks so hot a man couldn't go barefoot on them, working down there would be unbearable even in shifts of at most ten or fifteen minutes; men only saw *those* through because it entitled them to extra tots of vodka when they finished.

The bunkers would be full well before noon, Burmin predicted, and from then on they'd be carrying the sacks down through hatches instead of emptying them into chutes. In fact this stage was reached about an hour after Michael started work at the after Temperley. There were two, one for'ard and one aft, plumbing the collier's forward and after holds: sacks filled by men working with shovels in those deep, superheated, airless pits were slung up through the uncovered hatches and their hooks transferred by a mechanical contrivance there to a 'traveller' which, running on sheaves on overhead rails, slid them over to the *Ryazan*'s iron deck, where they were taken charge of manually. A close eye on the operation was essential, and taking the weight of a sackful of coal at shoulder height three or four times a minute wasn't child's play. Like all the others, Michael worked stripped to the waist, was still hard at it when Narumov arrived on board and Burmin sent a message that the staff engineer-constructor was asking for him. He handed his job over to a warrant officer who'd just had a stand-off period, crossed over to the starboard side amidships to get himself hosed down, and was then agreeably surprised to find that his cabin hadn't yet been filled with coal. None of the cabins had been at that stage, they were filling spaces at lower levels first and, as he was shortly to discover, there were preparations to be made up here in any case. He put on the whites he'd been wearing earlier – with an open-necked shirt instead of the (Royal Navy) regulation Number Six jacket – and went to the wardroom to see Narumov.

Burmin was there, and Arkoleyev. Zakharov had been with them but had apparently just left to check on the transfer of his gear from large day-cabin to small sea-cabin. Narumov and Arkoleyev had sheets of signal-pad in front of them covered in pencilled mathematical calculations. They – and Zakharov – would have been considering the extra tonnage of coal and its distribution internally, being concerned to put as much of it as possible as low in the ship as could be managed, so as not to reduce her metacentric height to such an extent that her stability would be seriously threatened – as well as its distribution fore and aft, in the hope of retaining at least *some* degree of trim.

Michael and Narumov greeted each other enthusiastically,

and he'd brought messages from other members of the flagship's wardroom. From Nick Sollogub especially, but from Captain Ignatzius and the chaplain too – and even from the Hero of Round Island.

'And how's Flagmansky?'

'A trifle subdued by this heat, I'm afraid. Having spent his youth in the more equitable climate of Latvia, of course.'

Burmin queried, 'Who's Flagmansky?'

'A dog. Came on board at Reval, you see, with the rest of the staff, so—'

'Yes. Well.' A brusque nod as he pushed his chair back. 'I'll see you before you leave us, perhaps. At least, if anything else occurs . . .'

A carpenter was at work at the after end of the room, raising a timber coal-barrier. The door at that end would be out of use, obviously. And the pantry was going to be filled with coal. Food from the galley, which henceforth would serve the warrant officers' mess as well – since they were losing their own – would be brought round through the remaining door and dished-up on the sideboard against that forward bulkhead. God only knew where all the mess-traps would be stowed, but arrangements were in hand for the safeguarding of wine and spirit stocks, and for unimpeded access to them. Michael asked Narumov to what height the coal was to be piled in cabins, and the answer was to a maximum of three feet. The constructor explained, 'At the level of this deck we have to be especially careful. Down below – well, the seamen's messdecks will be filled to a height of four feet – safe enough at that level. Up here is a different matter. Another factor of course is the use of smaller spaces wherever possible – such as cabins – rather than wider areas where in heavy weather we might get the equivalent of cargo shifting. The messdecks are a case in point, and there the solution we've arrived at—'

'How does one open a cabin door with a three-foot depth of coal inside it?' Michael had only just hit on this: that cabin doors opened inward. There was a corollary to the question, too: 'How do you shut the door on the coal in the first place?'

'I asked the same question.' Engineer Arkoleyev's gimlet eyes shifted from Michael to Narumov. 'Don't think much of his answer to it, either.'

'Well, I'd venture to say it's not bad. The doors have to be removed – a start is being made on it now – and planking put in at the bottom to a height from the deck of a little more than three feet. A timber sill, in effect. The beauty of it is that when the coal's required for use all they have to do is pull that up and the stuff flows out – to be bagged in the companionway then carried up to the bunker-chutes. Since the coal reserves on this deck will be the highest in the ship, that procedure will commence as soon as there's space in the bunkers for it.'

'So to enter the cabin one climbs or leaps over this sill—'

'Captain Burmin is considering the provision of a plank which would serve as a bridge between the doorway and the bunk. At the door end it would, of course, rest on the sill, and at the other it could be fixed – perhaps nailed where a drawer at the appropriate height would have been removed. But whether there'd be enough timber, after subdividing the messdecks and so forth—'

'Send a party ashore to fell some trees and saw them up, perhaps.' Arkoleyev winked at Michael. 'Shake a few coconuts down while you're at it . . . Oh, I'm sorry, I know it's not your fault, Narumov, you're doing the best you can. Christ, let's have a drink . . .'

14

Narumov had drunk two bottles of lemonade before leaving for the *Dmitry Donskoi.* His next call after that would be at the *Nakhimov*, where he expected to be lunching. He was obviously a very busy man: despite which he'd invited Michael, on behalf of Nick Sollogub as well as himself, to dine on board the *Suvarov* on the 15th. This was the 13th, of course – a Sunday, not that you'd have known it. Narumov had also brought news that the port captain had received authority by telegram from Paris to permit coaling, provided it was completed in twenty-four hours and the Russians then quit French West African territorial waters. Rojhestvensky had accepted these conditions, without mentioning that his ships had been hard at it all night and would be most of the day, or that the transports would be getting theirs in tomorrow, Monday, or that Tuesday, after all ships had washed-down, would be devoted to rest, recreation and further cleaning-up, so that the earliest he could sail would be Wednesday – sailing then, incidentally, for the Gabon River, another territory under French administration. Narumov had heard this on board the *Alexander III*; he'd started his tour of the squadron early and was hoping to have visited all the ironclads by sundown.

Michael had asked him on their way up on deck, 'Straight answer to a straight question, Pavel Vasil'ich?'

'When have I given any other kind?'

'You'd know that better than I could. But what I'm asking – just between ourselves – are you confident that all the ships will be reasonably stable when we leave here?'

'Mikhail Ivan'ich – ' the constructor was frowning – 'the very purpose of my visit – the whole point of these discussions—'

'You're hedging, aren't you?'

'You're trying to force me to answer categorically, when in fact the situation is unprecedented – beyond even your own considerable experience – whereas I'm a technician, not a seaman at all!'

'With that amount of prevarication, the truth has to be that it's a toss-up.'

'No. Figures are figures, definitive, and metacentric heights are precisely calculable!'

'Of course. And you're as good as saying they aren't what they should be but it can't be helped, we've got to chance it.'

'The only chance we're taking is on the weather. If we have good conditions, we'll be perfectly all right.'

'And if we have rotten weather?'

'Then one or two might be in trouble. There you are, your straight answer. Please *don't* raise this subject on Tuesday night.'

At three p.m. an officer on board the *Oslyabya* dropped dead from heatstroke while engaged in coaling. His name was Nelidov and he was a son of the Russian ambassador in Paris. Radzianko claimed to have been a friend of his, and immediately went off to write a letter of condolence to the father. Galikovsky's comment when this was mentioned in the wardroom was, 'I doubt he'd ever exchanged a word with him. Sees a chance to strike up acquaintance with that family, is all.'

'He'd better do some homework, if that's the case.' Murayev, the gunnery lieutenant – grubby and sweat-soaked, from hours spent prowling above and below decks ensuring that no coal was dumped where it might impede the working of his guns or ammunition-supply. 'He's a sly one, if you ask me. Looks it, doesn't he ? Despite the name, I'd say he had Armenian blood. That oily look.'

Paymaster Lyalin agreed. 'You may well be right. As for the name, an Armenian streak could come from his mother's side. Goes to show, doesn't it, how careful one should be?'

'Damn right! But clever, you see – psychologically – catch people who've just lost a beloved son. Depending on what other family there may be, emotionally almost step into the dead one's shoes.'

'But with what advantage?'

'Well – who knows. But until you cast a line in, who knows what fish there may be . . . A pretty sister, perhaps?'

'Ah – now *there*, yes . . .'

Radzianko had also got himself an invitation to dine on board the hospital ship on Tuesday. Zakharov had mentioned at lunch (cold soup, and cold mutton with beans and raspberry sauce) that he'd been invited by the *Orel*'s captain to accompany the admiral and Clapier de Colongue to this dinner, bringing with him one other officer of his own choice. He'd said apologetically to Michael, 'I'd have taken you, Mikhail Ivan'ich, since you're my official guest, but—'

'They'd expect a Russian officer, surely. In any case – Tuesday; as it happens I've already accepted—'

'May I propose myself, sir?' Radzianko – eyes fairly glittering with enthusiasm. 'If you remember – I mentioned it the other day – I have a cousin who's a lay assistant with that order and really quite *likely* to be among them.'

The choice would probably have fallen either on him or Galikovsky or Murayev, as they were the three senior lieutenants, and Burmin as second-in-command couldn't be out of the ship when his captain was. Zakharov had thrown a questioning glance at the other two – who weren't contesting it, Galikovsky only murmuring, 'Spends half his time gazing at 'em through binoculars—'

'For a sight of my cousin, damn you!'

'If you truly believed any such person might be on board,

wouldn't you have enquired when the ship first joined us?'

'Shut up, Vladimir Aleksand'ich.' Zakharov, expressionless as ever, had raised a hand with its palm towards his torpedo officer. He nodded to Radzianko: 'It might as well be you, Viktor Vasil'ich.'

'*Most* kind, sir!'

'You can introduce me to your cousin.'

'Sir, if she's on board, I should be *delighted*—'

'But one thing – you've been cluttering up the chartroom with your personal gear, I've noticed. I want it cleared away. I've no objection to your sleeping up there if you want to, but I use that chartroom at least as much as you do – Mikhail Ivan'ich too, for that matter.'

'I'm very sorry.' Radzianko's jowls wobbled slightly as he shook his head. 'In fact I was only – well, trying it out, you might say, prior to requesting your permission—'

'As I say, clear it all out.'

In fact Michael had had a slight contretemps with him on that issue when he'd gone up there after Narumov's departure to start a new letter to Tasha, for posting before they sailed on Wednesday. He'd sent this last one to Jane in Wiltshire, in a mail that had been landed this morning, and there was bound to be another – possibly using a home-bound collier – before they sailed. In the chartroom though, he'd found Radzianko pulling chart-folios out of the specially fitted drawers to make way for shirts and uniform white trousers. The doors of the sextant cupboard had been open too, with footwear visible inside. There'd been gear all over the chart-table itself, while Radzianko crouched at the folio drawers with his great rump stuck out – filling about half the space just on its own.

Peering round: panting and sweating and annoyed at being disturbed.

'Want something?'

'I came up to write a letter.'

'What – in my chartroom?'

'I've been given to understand I have the run of it too. But don't worry – since you seem to have other uses for the place.'

'Yes. If you wouldn't mind, dear fellow. Circumstances *have* changed somewhat, have they not? Why not write your letter in the wardroom?'

The cabins were doorless, fitted with the timber sills and full of coal, by sunset. Coal-dust everywhere: at *least* as penetrative as a sandstorm. Wherever you looked, whatever you touched: and the reek and – when eating or drinking – taste of it and grittiness between the teeth. In the cabin the plank bridge didn't work, the plank being a couple of feet too short. You could toss it over against the bunk and use it to stand on after clambering over the coal, but that was all the use it was.

Lieutenant Nelidov was given a military-style burial ashore on the Monday afternoon. The governor of the territory attended in a feathered hat and had provided a guard and band, supplementing that from the *Oslyabya.* The French band played their version of the Russian national anthem and the *Oslyabya*'s ground out the funeral march *Kol Slaven*; volleys of rifle-shots were fired over the grave, and photographs were taken for sending to Ambassador Nelidov in Paris. The French in fact seemed to have been making a bit of a meal of it. Michael heard all of this from others, didn't himself attend. Nor strangely enough did Rojhestvensky, although Clapier de Colongue and a few other members of the staff turned up. It must have been quite an impressive turnout: from *Ryazan* the chaplain had gone, of course, and Burmin, Radzianko and Murayev, as well as several of the junior lieutenants and *michmen*, and the largest contingent came, obviously, from the *Oslyabya* – most of her officers and several hundred of the ship's company.

Michael asked Murayev, 'Sisters of Mercy?'

'None. Odd, that.'

'Disappointing for Radzianko.'

'Indeed. But I tell you, in the cutter coming off from shore I saw him making notes.' Murayev nodding, fingering his black moustache. 'Notebook and pencil with him expressly for that purpose. Nelidov's Christian name and patronymic and perhaps other bits and pieces he'd have got from the priest's and the *Oslyabya*'s skipper's eulogies. Might have dug up even better stuff from former brother officers.'

'Justifying his enquiries how, though?'

'Well – what about, "I think I may have run across him. Tall, good-looking fellow, wasn't he?" Might get the answer "Certainly not! Miserable little runt . . ." Huh?'

They'd laughed. Michael pointing out, 'But you've no evidence whatsoever—'

'Not a scrap. Instinct, that's all.'

Michael slept on deck from that Sunday night onwards – on the quarterdeck under the jutting barrels of the stern 6-inch, on his damp mattress and wearing pyjamas with a sheet over him for protection against mosquitoes. On both the Monday and Tuesday mornings he'd heard the splash of Radzianko flopping in for his early swim; the man was curiously insensitive to the shark danger, and Michael found himself waiting almost hopefully for sudden screams. But on Wednesday, after a late night with his friends in the *Suvarov*'s wardroom, almost without thinking about it he went in himself. Partly perhaps because Radzianko had been getting away with it, but mostly from an irresistible desire to cool off. Cool his head. It had been a *very* late night; he'd been given a lift back to the ship in the *Suvarov*'s guard-boat, a steam-pinnace, and the officer of the watch at *Ryazan*'s gangway-head had told him that the captain and Radzianko had returned from the *Orel* hours earlier.

He'd felt better for the swim – for a while. In *Suvarov* they'd played cards after dinner – chemin de fer – Michael at first doing well but then losing a few roubles, and in the course of it drinking too much brandy.

Radzianko came into breakfast with his black hair still gleaming wet from his own swim, and patted Michael approvingly on the shoulder as he sat down beside him. 'I hear you've been following my good example, Mikhail Ivan'ich.'

'Well – I stayed within a few strokes of the gangway – and I was only in for about two minutes. How was your dinner party?'

'Excellent. And as it turned out, most interesting. Really, fascinating!'

'Your alleged cousin on board then, is she?' Galikovsky, with his mouth full and an expression of derision on his face. Radzianko told him, 'Regrettably, she is not. But after I'd enquired for her – as you may recall, Nikolai Timofey'ich had said he'd like to meet her – they routed out this other young lady – Nadyejhda her name is, Nadyejhda Prostnyekova – who happens to be my cousin's dearest friend! A sweetheart, absolutely, and –' he was telling Michael this – 'so interesting in what she told me – heavens, I could scarcely believe my ears!'

'So let's hear it!' Burmin, glaring at him down the table. He rarely spoke at breakfast, and when addressed directly tended to respond only with a kind of angry stare. Radzianko favoured him with a smile of regret: it was rather a personal matter, he told the second-in-command, personal and private.

'Why jabber about it, then?'

'Ah – well – if I may point this out – Vladimir Aleksand'ich asked me a certain question, and the fact of having found my cousin's friend there did seem quite relevant. That was all I set out to tell him – him and Mikhail Ivan'ich here, that is.'

In other words, wasn't talking to *you*, you swine. Which in the circumstances seemed fair enough. But Burmin had pushed his chair back and was already halfway to the door, hadn't bothered to listen to any of it. Radzianko murmuring to Michael, '*Rather* ill-mannered, don't you agree? But Mikhail Ivan'ich, I'll tell you the rest of it – what the Prostnyekova girl told me – a bombshell, really – later, when we're on our own.'

'Not if it's private and personal.'

'Not to *you*. You'll be spellbound!'

'Well. Have it your own way, then.' He wasn't eating, only drinking coffee. Feeling a bit like Burmin might, he thought. Radzianko asking him, 'Did you have a good evening in the flagship?'

The mail was landed at noon and Michael's second letter to Tasha went in it. He'd also written to his mother, having been meaning to for weeks. He'd thought of addressing Tasha's to Yalta and asking Narumov to post it with his own in *Suvarov*'s mail, but then remembered having mentioned Tasha to Sollogub, who might happen to see it, read her name on it; and it wouldn't have been sensible to let Narumov think there was anything to be kept secret. Better to play safe, accept delay and make use of Jane. (Whom he'd told in his covering note that his cabin was full of coal – which would mystify her – and that it was high time he heard from her, and had not as yet, incidentally, received the promised admonitory letter from brother George.) Not that Nick Sollogub would have spread such a thing around; he'd *know*, that was all – and the only safety lay in nobody knowing anything at all. Gossip *did* fly. Inadvertently even – for instance, Nick S. tapping the letter which he might have been taking from Narumov to post with his own – 'Why, isn't that the girl the *Ryazan*'s skipper's—'

Then a need for lies or other subterfuge – which might make matters worse, since one wasn't at all good at it.

As Radzianko on the other hand probably *was*. That oily grin . . . And what on earth *that* was about: which in any case one would take with a large pinch of salt. At sailing time – a bugle-call sent the hands to anchor-stations at two-thirty – he – Radzianko – was in the bridge's port wing with his glasses up, looking across at the *Orel* yet again: hoping for a sight of the girl, no doubt – if she existed, if he hadn't invented her as a smokescreen to his having invented the cousin in the first place. In fact couldn't have, if she'd been presented to Zakharov. But Murayev was right, one *did* instinctively distrust him. As, Michael suspected, did Zakharov – who'd just arrived in the bridge with Burmin at his heels, Radzianko and *michmen* Count Provatorov and Pepelyaev saluting, Zakharov cursorily acknowledging the formality and telling Burmin he could start shortening-in the cable.

'Shorten in!' A bull-like bellow through the megaphone, then Vetrov's echo from the foc'sl, where the electric capstan would now take the cable's weight – and the ship's too, hauling her up to lie directly above the anchor. There was no need to inform the *Orel* that they were weighing – they'd see it happening and hear the steady clanking of the cable coming in. They'd be hearing it on shore by now – a considerable racket from all over the wide anchorage – battleships, cruisers, transports, all at it. To the port captain's ears it would be music: he could telegraph Paris now that he'd finally driven the Russians out, and from the Quai d'Orsay word to that effect might find its way to London.

Michael was at the back of the bridge beside the chart-table, out of the way of those who had jobs to do. Thinking about the letter-writing problem – he hadn't found writing these recent ones at all easy. One factor was not having heard from her for so long, and suspecting that her father wouldn't leave her and her mother alone indefinitely. While at the same time one didn't want to express one's anxieties over and over, setting *her* nerves on edge, perhaps unnecessarily. There was also the possibility of letters having been intercepted: a dire but real possibility, knowing Prince Igor and his use of servants as spies. Another angle on that danger – which was particularly frightening because of that old man's ruthlessness and the fact that when the chips were down they'd be entirely at his mercy – was that any blunder or carelessness of one's own might put their necks on that block. Having risked writing direct to Yalta, for instance. Although if her mail *was* being monitored, why not Jane's mail from Wiltshire too?

But one had to be in touch *some*how – take *some* risks.

God knew, they'd taken plenty earlier on. At Injhavino first, then Paris: both times, as it had happened, on *her* initiative. Whereas now, in isolation and practically nothing to do but think – and with her far more at risk than he was himself, but powerless to help, no matter what was going on . . .

So shut your mind to it. Since here and now there's not a damn thing you can do . . .

He'd had his eyes on the *Orel*, a handful of seamen at work on her foc'sl, but turned inboard now on hearing a yell from down for'ard of, 'Cable's up and down!' and then Zakharov's order, 'Weigh.' Start heaving in again, in other words, to break the anchor out of the sand. One other thing, though, which he found inhibiting in his letter-writing was what to say or not say about Zakharov. In the letter he'd started a day or two after leaving Tangier, he'd referred again to his having asked him whether it was true that he, Michael, in his 'big brother' role disapproved of Z as a husband for her on account of the difference in their ages, and that his non-committal answer had led to a coldness in Z's manner and no further mention of the subject. He'd added:

> He's a cold man altogether. No facial expression ever – his face could be made of wood, and when he speaks his lips don't visibly move. On the other hand he's friendly and hospitable, had even gone to the length of giving me a cabin to myself – in which I'm writing this to you now . . .

But could one say to her, for instance, What's more he's a competent seaman and an excellent commanding officer and with neither of us mentioning you or your family or the damned 'betrothal' he and I seem to get on very well?

How might she take that? Conclude that he was chumming-up to Public Enemy Number One, in some sense ratting on her?

A howl from for'ard: 'Anchor's aweigh!'

Had been broken out of the sand. Leaning over the

bow, looking down from above the starboard hawse, they'd have seen through the clear water that it was about to happen, wouldn't see now because the water would have been muddied by the disturbance, all they'd see would be a slight swing on the cable, telling the same story. Another call then: 'Clear anchor!' So all right, it *was* visible – the sand having settled quickly – and was not fouling any other ship's mooring, or wreckage – or sea-bed cable, *Anadyr*-style. The telegraphs had clanged and you felt the vibration as her screws churned – one ahead and one astern, to turn her more or less on the spot. A small pendant had fluttered down from the yard – for anyone's information, but most usefully for the *Orel*'s. As the ship turned, giving him a view across the harbour now, he saw that the battleships were on the move – and beyond them, Enqvist's cruisers. The *Donskoi* anyway – that high, stubby profile and twin funnels . . .

And here in *Ryazan*'s bridge, Radzianko insinuating himself up beside the binnacle, close to Zakharov – making himself available to con the ship out, which was a navigating officer's job if his skipper felt inclined to leave it to him – which in this instance he evidently did not, and must have told him so, in that quick turn of the head. Remembering the chaotic departure from Tangier, no doubt, keeping matters in his own hands until that circus had got itself sorted out. Burmin meanwhile passing the order by voicepipe and telephone for the ship's company to fall out from anchor stations: relaxing to cruising stations therefore, probably in four watches.

Telegraphs again – stopping engines. The hospital-ship had also turned, and was lying stopped on that quarter. Gleaming as white as ever, evidently having made a thorough job of their washing-down. Here around the *Ryazan*, on the other hand, just those brief spells of vibration from the engines had sent up a haze of coal-dust which then settled on every surface. Radzianko, coming aft, grimaced as he tried to dislodge some of it from the chart-table's canvas hood by reaching in and slapping the inside of it.

'Might blow clean when we get outside.' Cocking an eyebrow at Michael then: 'Like to hear what it was she told me?'

'What *who*—'

'The Prostnyekova girl.' Jerking a thumb towards the *Orel*. 'Last night. I was telling you—'

'And I told *you* I wasn't interested. Stuff to do with your cousin, you said. Did you introduce this other one to the skipper?'

'As it happens, yes. But in any case . . .'

They were on the move again, engines thrumming at low revs, sand-coloured water swirling astern, vibration stirring up the dirt again. Michael asked Radzianko, gesturing towards the *Orel*, 'She stuffed full of coal too?'

'Oh, yes. The girls' cabins, all low down in the ship, and they – the girls – have been moved up into two of the wards – on cots, dormitory-fashion – which they don't like at all!'

'I'm surprised she still looks so white.'

'Well, if you were to go on board, you'd see . . .' Radzianko broke off, and changed the subject. 'I'll tell you this anyway. This young lady, my cousin's close friend, by name Nadyejhda Prostnyekova – auburn hair, blue eyes, and – really quite a looker – I'd never met her, but I *had* heard of her from my cousin, as it so happens, and she knew of me, knew at *once* who I was. My cousin must have given me a favourable reference in that quarter!'

'Nice for you, I'm sure.'

'It's an important point because it meant she could talk to me confidentially right away. In fact she was dying to pour it all out. His nibs being there as well – she was fairly stunned, you see!'

'No, I don't see at all.'

'Coming straight to the point then, Mikhail Ivan'ich – she happens to know Natasha Volodnyakova rather well.'

He didn't *think* he'd shown any sharp reaction – despite a tightening of the gut and a sudden, powerful inclination to punch Radzianko in his smirking face. Glasses up though

– unhurriedly – to study the movements of the battleships instead. Radzianko murmuring on, 'Must know her *very* well, in fact. She drew me aside to ask me – this fellow with me – you know, *there*, talking to your admiral – is he not the officer of that same name to whom Natasha Volodnyakova is said to have become betrothed? Yes, I said, he is indeed, and she whispered to me that – oh, I think she said a year or more ago – this Natasha – they were in Petersburg – Natasha swore to her in the course of a chat about some mutual friend who was getting married or engaged that *she*'d never marry any Russian, for the reason that – great secret, it was supposed to be – there was an Englishman she was mad about and who'd promised he'd wait for her. I should have mentioned, she was only fifteen or so at that time, and he was an English naval officer – Royal Navy – huh? Away then on some distant posting. Well, Natasha didn't divulge his name, but – heavens, d'you remember the talk we had when you'd just come aboard and I was showing you around?'

'I remember you asked a lot of questions.'

'Won't you admit it all adds up, Nikolai Ivan'ich?'

'To what?'

'Well, surely, my dear fellow—'

'No, I'm not your dear fellow.' Speaking quietly: lowering the glasses, turning to look at him and let him see his contempt. He'd got the hang of it too, knew how to handle it. Telling him as the smirk faded, 'You may find amusement in what may have been a young girl's dream – which you say was told to this friend of yours as a *secret*. Certainly none of your business, nor even of mine – but the skipper might see it as his – if you felt brave enough to talk to *him* about it.'

15

November 21st: five days out from Dakar, a thousand miles of this leg covered, another thousand or twelve hundred to go. Michael had the morning watch, the four to eight, with a *michman* – Egorov – as assistant officer of the watch. The sun was up, a blaze of fire rising over what traders called the Grain Coast – although with Cape Palmas coming up on the beam to port, you'd be swapping that by about midday for the Ivory Coast, and adjusting course from southeast to east after rounding it. Not that it would look any different – coastline hidden in a heat-haze shimmering like a mirage, where at the moment you couldn't look without being blinded and from where there was already a positive radiation of heat. By mid-forenoon heat would be striking upward as well, from armoured decks hot enough to fry eggs on. But although one might have been thankful for some wind or breeze other than that of the squadron's progress at nine and a half knots through warm, coal-stinking air, you had only to look at the ships ahead to see how lucky you were with the continuing calm – the battleships especially, wallowing so deep that the *Suvarov*s for instance, the core and main strength of the force, had their lower decks awash even with no wind, no movement whatsoever on the sea, other than their own disturbance of it. On those lower decks were 3-inch guns, ten each side, and although all the ports at that level were being kept shut they still leaked all round, as did whole rows and sections of loose rivets that were normally above water. Pumps were being kept running, of course; but with the increased draught and altered trim – evidently it hadn't been possible to distribute the weight better, they'd simply had to use every cubic foot that could be allocated as bunker-space – the ships were practically uncontrollable, needing all their captains' skills to handle them even in the open sea.

Ryazan was all right, anyway. Zakharov had stipulated that no more than ten degrees of rudder should be used in any circumstances, and Michael, who'd been keeping watches since departure from Dakar, had found she responded well enough to half that much. Not that anyone was performing fleet or squadron manoeuvres at that stage: only altering when necessary to remain in station on the crowd of ships ahead of her, or to stay clear when they all stopped for breakdowns. The *Borodino* had had a lot of trouble. The eccentric strap on one engine had broken on the second day out; she'd stopped for a while, then got going on her other engine at seven and a half knots, which perforce became the speed of the whole squadron until early yesterday when the damage had been made good and speed increased to the squadron's standard nine and a half – for a few hours, until *Borodino*'s other engine packed up. An overheated bearing was said to have been the cause. Narumov to the rescue, yet again: and why not, since he'd overseen her building and fitting-out. Then the old transport *Malay* – with her holds full of Cardiff coal although she was now bunkered with the German rubbish – had temporarily given up the ghost. Something had gone wrong with her engine during the arrival at Dakar, it was remembered, and Narumov's verdict had been that she'd be able to stagger on – no more than half joking, in using the word 'stagger' – as long as they kept her air-pump running. Which no doubt they would have been doing, so something else must have gone skew-whiff. Whatever it was, they'd fixed it, after a few more lost hours, and she was plugging along all right now, somewhere ahead there under the pall of smoke.

One didn't trust her, though. Didn't trust any of them. Michael, lighting a cigarette, looked round at Egorov. 'Smoke?'

'No – thank you—'

'No breakdowns today, please God.'

'Please God.' Crossing himself, and really meaning it. A gangly young man with a toothy grin and a dry, harsh cackle. His father was a colonel of engineers on General Kuropatkin's staff in Manchuria, so he had this added personal anxiety – desperation, it looked like sometimes – to reach Port Arthur before its defences collapsed. All the obvious reasons – the squadron's *raison d'être* in fact – but on top of that, fears for his father's safety, because rumours of the land war situation were all bad – and on the other side of the coin a daydream of steaming into Port Arthur with bands playing and Papa delirious with happiness on the quayside. He'd talked about it one night in the wardroom – brandy playing its part of course, but oddly enough as a foreigner one did now and again find oneself the recipient of confidences.

'Perhaps we'll get news soon, Gavril Ivan'ich.' Michael added a warning, 'Not at this next stop, mind you.'

Egorov had his glasses up. 'Why *not* at—'

'Well – as you know, we'll be coaling outside. Probably won't have any contact with the shore. Anchoring three miles out – *if* weather conditions are right.'

'Look good enough now.'

'Yes, but—'

'Mikhail Ivan'ich – fresh trouble ahead, I think they're—'

'Stop both engines!'

The telegraphs clanged. Ahead, Enqvist's ships were under helm and starring – *Nachimov* and *Aurora* to port, *Donskoi* to starboard – and there was confusion in the left-hand column, the transports. The signal yeoman of the watch had been howled at by Egorov to hoist the black ball as warning to the *Orel*, and Zakharov was in the bridge, coming at a trot from his sea-cabin – in pyjama trousers only, perching himself on his high stool in the starboard for'ard corner and snatching up binoculars.

'What's it this time?'

'One of the transports – don't yet know which, sir.' Michael looking astern to make sure the *Orel* was staying clear. As she was. Her merchant navy officers did seem to know their onions – at any rate hadn't been caught napping yet.

'Could be the *Malay* again, sir.' He gave Zakharov a 'sir' occasionally – *always* when he was on watch with others in earshot – although more frequently of late he'd been addressing him as 'skipper', acknowledging the fact that he was this ship's commanding officer, but not wanting to overdo it. Especially as in Russian naval usage a 'sir' to one's captain involved not just one syllable but six.

'It *is* the *Malay*.' Zakharov glanced round at Egorov. 'Don't worry, Gavril Ivan'ich. Remember the tortoise and the hare.'

'Signal to the *Malay* from Flag, sir: *What is the matter?*'

'Same as last time, probably.'

'Could be anything. Steering, or her engine – or her bottom's fallen out—'

'Reply from the *Malay*, sir: *Cross-head pin of the air-pump broken. Regret this necessitates lengthy repair. Would be glad of attendance by engineer-constructor.*'

'Meaning that fellow Narumov.'

'Further signal to the *Malay* from Flag, sir: *Engineer-constructor will transfer to you immediately. If repair is to take more than an hour or two the* Rus *will take you in tow.*'

'Scared of the weather breaking, no doubt.'

'Oh God, yes . . .'

Two reasons for praying that wouldn't happen. One, the fact that many of these ships weren't seaworthy, and two, the physical impossibility of coaling in the open sea if the wind did get up.

It took the *Rus*, whose crew were either new to the job or badly out of practice, almost two hours to pass the tow to the *Malay*. They got her moving then at about four and a half knots, and there were six hours of this slow crawl before the repair was completed. Tow cast off then, Narumov back in the flagship, and the great caravan lumbering on at nine and a half knots again. Shaping an eastward course by then, heading for the Gulf of Biafra, Cape Palmas abaft the beam to port.

In *Ryazan*, Zakharov kept them busy with internal exercises: gunnery drill, night alarms, steering breakdowns – switching at a moment's notice to emergency rudder controls – battle and battle-damage simulations of all kinds. For some of them Michael tagged on to the doctor, Baranov, and his stretcher-bearing parties, familiarizing himself with the organization for getting wounded men to the sickbay, and so forth. He and Radzianko were steering clear of each other; Radzianko obviously humiliated that his ploy with the Prostnyekova girl's story had failed in whatever its purpose might have been – blackmail of sorts, presumably – and Michael aware there might still be some threat in it: if the girl knew *more* than that, for instance. As it was, the story amounted virtually to nothing – partly because one had had the presence of mind not to react guiltily – but if it got to Zakharov it might start him thinking. Being no fool: and already in doubt of Prince Igor's motive in sending this Englishman to sea with him.

Would it *matter*?

Yes, it would: for Tasha's sake, if it even hinted at their affair. That was what mattered: very much less so the possibility of some constraint developing between Zakharov and oneself – on the lines for instance of that already existing *vis-à-vis* Radzianko. Which in fact looked like being worsened when on the night of the 23rd Michael's starsight put them a dozen miles closer inshore than Radzianko's dead-reckoning position, which had been based on his moon-run-sun observations of the previous morning – and Zakharov had chosen to accept Michael's result rather than his navigator's. Radzianko had not unnaturally been aggrieved. 'I'm sure you'll find we're near enough *exactly* on the track I've laid off there. Of course, it's your decision—'

'Yes.' Hard eyes on Radzianko – and as expressionless as always. 'Two good reasons for it too. One, Mikhail Ivan'ich puts us twelve miles closer to danger and for that reason alone can't be disregarded. Two, look at the particularly small dimensions of his cocked hat there. Doesn't that tell you anything?'

'Well – it *might*, sir—'

'Easy enough to settle, anyway. I'll take morning stars myself.'

And later, to Michael, 'You don't like him, do you?'

He shrugged: 'Mutual, probably. Usually is, isn't it?' Getting his cigarettes out – Russian ones now, which he'd bought through Paymaster Lyalin. He offered Zakharov one. 'Smoke?'

'No – thank you. Listen – it's of concern to me that he seems to be quite generally disliked. Can you put a finger on what's wrong?'

'Well – do *you* like him?'

'As commanding officer I have to be impartial. As long as an officer behaves in an officer-like manner and does his job. Come on, what is it?'

'I don't know. Except one doesn't trust him. Someone – I forget who – remarked that he's sly; I'd agree with that. Also he's addicted to gossip.'

'About what?'

Flicking ash from his cigarette . . . 'Anything. Any*one.* I never listen, but – there it is.' Looking back at the sharply alert eyes. No facial expression, but eyes like probes. One wondered what was in the brain behind them: speculation that some of the gossip might be about himself and the Volodnyakov connection? Michael said, 'As a foreigner and newcomer I'm very much on the sidelines. If you were to put the same questions to Murayev or Galikovsky—'

'It's *because* you're an outsider that we can have this kind of discussion, Mikhail Ivan'ich.'

He was feeling a bit sorry for Radzianko, as it happened. Being *generally* disliked couldn't improve things, exactly. He felt it didn't help either when Zakharov's morning stars gave a precise run-on position from Michael's six hours earlier. Neither Zakharov nor Radzianko commented – at least, not in Michael's hearing – but there it was on the chart, plain to see. They'd had a straight run during the night, no breakdowns that held them up at all, only the flagship at about two a.m. losing all her electric power. She kept going but went dark, causing the *Alexander*, her next astern, and the *Kamchatka* on her beam to spout frantic signals – effectively she'd disappeared, might have sunk. The failure lasted only a few minutes: long enough for Lieutenant Tselinyev as officer of the watch to send his messenger running to shake Zakharov: the squadron meanwhile thundering on through the blackness of the night – there was no moon – and Zakharov almost before he had his eyes open passing a light signal to the *Orel* that he expected to be stopping engines shortly, at the same time passing orders for calling away both the whaler and the gig, also to searchlight crews to stand by – his entirely reasonable notion being that there might be survivors in the water, even though the rest of the squadron would have ploughed through them by that time. In the event, the *Suvarov*'s lights came on suddenly and the news was passed swiftly through the fleet, Zakharov's warning to the *Orel* being promptly cancelled. Michael and the others heard about this at breakfast, from Tselinyev; the general view of the wardroom officers was that their skipper might be the only one in the entire squadron who had his head screwed on.

'Doesn't look good, Mikhail Ivan'ich.'

Referring to the swell. Ahead, all the black monsters cavorting like drunken elephants, and astern the *Orel*'s fine white clipper bow soaring and plunging. This was November 25th, one day short of expected arrival south of the Gabon River, Michael had the afternoon watch, with Egorov as his number two again, and Zakharov had just come into the bridge from his sea-cabin where he'd been taking a post-prandial nap. Adding now, with his glasses focussed on the old *Donskoi*'s gyrations, 'Could have been much worse. If we'd run into this four or five days ago. For one thing we'd have had it on the beam, and for another we're now lighter by five days' steaming, all that weight shifted down. Are you using your cabin now?'

'Not to sleep in. Sleeping in the wardroom – mattress on the deck. Hot enough in there but worse in the cabin with the scuttle shut. Do you think we might get a mail—' He checked himself. 'No – of course not, silly question. If we're to have no contact with the shore—'

'It's possible, if some steamer had brought it. Not likely – the settlement doesn't even have a telegraph. Have to wait until we make Great Fish Bay perhaps. Expecting to hear from home, are you? From England?'

'*Hoping* . . .'

'Big family there?'

'Very small. My mother, elder brother and his wife. She's the one who writes – and I've asked her to send me news-cuttings of anything about this squadron or the war in the East.'

'That's all the family you have, eh?'

'I have a sister – older than me and married. Otherwise – yes.'

'A sister is all *I* have, as it happens . . . If you do receive any such news cuttings, I'd like to see them.'

'With pleasure, Nikolai Timofey'ich.'

'Even if they're hostile to us. You needn't be shy of that. You'd have to translate them for me, of course.'

'Let's hope there'll be some *good* news.'

A grunt. 'My guess is there won't be.'

'You think Port Arthur'll soon fall?'

He'd glanced round – made sure Egorov wasn't hearing this. Shrugging. 'If it does, a likely outcome is that the admiral will be in no hurry to get there. Since the only destination we could have then would be Vladivostok – and no use getting there in winter when it's iced-up.'

'So we'd mark time.'

'If we had the news by then, perhaps in Madagascar.'

'God help us. Mosquitoes the size of sparrows. D'you think we'd get through to Vladivostok anyway?'

'Having waited for the ice to melt, fight our way past Togo, you mean? Or trick our way past him somehow. There's a choice of approaches, of course. But – in battle, how would *you* rate our chances?'

'With the squadron composed as it is – frankly, not very highly.'

'There you are, then. But since you're giving frank answers this morning, Mikhail Ivan'ich, here's a different kind of question.' Michael looked at him, waiting for it, lowering his glasses halfway and guessing – from that preamble, the lowered tone of voice and the quick glance round – at the sort of question it might be. Had guessed right, too – Zakharov asking him quietly, 'Do you expect Natasha Igorovna – knowing her as you do – would you say she'll reconcile herself to the prospect of becoming my wife?'

'You think she'll *need* to "reconcile" herself to it?'

'You know damn well she will. At any rate, if we – if I – get out of this alive, she will!'

Glasses up again – for cover, as it were. And one was, after all, supposed to be on watch. He said diffidently, 'I suppose having it sprung on her like that it would have come as a shock.'

'Again, you *know* it. You were there – and you and she *are* very close – plainly were at that time too. What's more – oh, that pantomime next morning, the excuse that she couldn't be disturbed!'

'You mentioned it. But as it happened, I was leaving too—'

'And didn't see her – say goodbye to her? Or hear from her afterwards? Haven't heard from her since?'

You'd have thought from the penetrative quality of that

stare he'd have been seeing or guessing right through to the truth. Which in fact he wasn't anywhere near, it was still Michael's 'big brotherly' opinion he was on about. Michael shaking his head: 'I'd have thought that by this time – good Lord, it was *two months* ago we were at Injhavino – she'd have had ample time to – your word, Nikolai Timofey'ich – *reconcile*—'

'No.' Brusque shake of the head: and putting *his* glasses up. 'You're not being frank at all.'

By the 26th, approaching a distant haze of land – French Equatorial Africa – the swell had miraculously subsided. Prayer was reckoned to have had something to do with it, most likely the intervention of Saint Seraphim of Sarof, a saint canonized only quite recently and therefore fashionable, certainly much esteemed by Myakishev. Anyway – glassy surface, no wind at all, steamy heat reaching from the jungle to enfold them as they came nosing in. By six p.m. the squadron had anchored between three and three and a half miles offshore, in a slight declivity of the coastline that could hardly be called a bay, was to all intents and purposes open sea.

Not a collier in sight. And even through telescopes and binoculars, not a building visible against that greenish smear of coastline. Not even a mud hut. Michael remarked to Radzianko – when he'd finished in the chart-room – 'The settlement's right at the river mouth, isn't it? Just inside it.' 'Settlement' meaning Gabon: Libreville, which was the capital but itself not exactly a metropolis, was a few miles higher up the river. Michael engaging Radzianko in conversation now as a matter of policy – healing the breach, and not wanting to be included in the group who seemed rather to hound him. Having in any case – touch wood – as it were drawn his teeth over the Prostnyekova girl's titbit of information: over which incidentally he'd seemed willing to meet him halfway: his first and only reference to her since that episode had been to murmur, 'She really is a stunner, that little Nadia.'

'Nadia?'

'Nadyejhda Prostnyekova. The one I mentioned.' A shrug of the heavy shoulders. 'Perhaps should not have.'

Michael had stuck up for him in a wardroom dispute the day after the starsight business. Radzianko at first showing surprise, even suspicion, but then seemingly accepting the olive branch. Challenged later by Murayev, Michael had explained that he felt sorry for him in that he seemed to have no friends at all – except for Padre Myakishev – and that with months of this tortoise-like progress and God only knew what else ahead of them, things could only get worse if there was no positive effort to improve them – an effort which he as an outsider might be best placed to make. Murayev had agreed it might be as well: Radzianko *seemed* to have a skin like a rhinoceros's but on the other hand he might be suffering inside it – in which case he'd be likely to get worse, not better. So – all right, he'd ease off a little too.

Because the water even three miles out was so shallow and could have even shallower patches in it, Rojhestvensky had had the battleships hoist out their boats to steam in ahead of the squadron taking soundings and marking out the anchorage with flagged buoys. Somehow as a result of this, the hospital-ship had anchored on *Ryazan*'s quarter instead of on her beam, was thus not as isolated from the rest of the squadron as she had been elsewhere. Radzianko flipped a hand towards her. They'd strolled on to the flag deck – abaft the bridge but at that same level – and had a clear view from here of that elegant white quarter-profile.

'Rather less under mother's wing this time. Oh, thanks . . .' Lighting cigarettes: and glancing at the cruisers anchored on their other – starboard – side. The *Donskoi* at the line's tail end was really not far at all from the *Orel*, and more or less abeam of her. 'But from us here, Mikhail Ivan'ich –' nodding towards her, perhaps restraining himself from putting his glasses on her – 'it's again quite easy swimming distance.'

'If you were crazy enough to try it. Probably teeming with sharks.'

'Perhaps worth risking, though? Especially if they only caught me on the way *back*?'

That amused him a lot. Chuckling – and putting his glasses up now. 'On the way *back*, Mikhail Ivan'ich – after a really successful visit? Which I *would* have – Nadia'd welcome me, I'm sure of it!'

'She would, eh?'

'With open arms!'

'Discuss it with her, did you?'

'Oh, not – you know, in so many words, but—'

'Excuse me, your honours.' Travkov, the chief yeoman of signals. Pointing shoreward, northeastward: 'Launch coming off . . .'

As it turned out, it was the governor, calling on the admiral in a barge full of flowers, baskets of fruit and a crate of champagne. Michael heard this from Sollogub and Narumov when he met them ashore next day – Sunday – permission having been given by Rojhestvensky for officers and men to land, at their captains' discretion. The colliers would be arriving on Monday and coaling would start then: wouldn't be much fun either, the Gabon river's latitude being zero degrees ten minutes north.

Michael attended Myakishev's morning service before going ashore. Radzianko landed with him, and *Michmen* Egorov, Rimsky and Count Provatorov tagged along. They looked around Gabon itself, of which there was practically nothing, and walked for a few miles along the beach, once or twice venturing inland along jungle tracks where monkeys gibbered at them from the trees. But it was too hot and humid to walk for more than an hour or so, after which they turned back and in the settlement met Sollogub and Narumov and a whole crowd of others in what called itself a restaurant – they'd seen it earlier – but had nothing to offer except fish, fruit and lemonade. Sollogub asked Michael, when they'd got over their surprise, made introductions, shaken hands all round and gulped down some lemonade, 'You haven't yet made your number with the king, then?'

'King?'

'*We* paid him a visit!'

Narumov nodded, looking up from a wad of the paper on which he'd just finished off the sentence or paragraph he'd been busy on when their arrival had interrupted him. 'I'm telling my wife about him. The king, that is. First one I've ever met, tell you the truth. We were there this morning – quite a few of us. But you see, there's a steamer leaving for England tomorrow and they've agreed to take our mail, so I thought I'd –' tapping his letter – 'bring this with me and add a last page or two while I have the chance.'

'You've been ashore some while, then?'

'Landed at eight. You'd have still been snoring.' Nodding to Radzianko: 'My *God,* he snores. I shared a cabin with him, I should know . . . Yes, the fish is quite good, you could do a lot worse. And the fruit. Mind you, we've pineapples on board now – and bananas and mangoes – the governor brought them last evening. I was saying – landed at eight from the *Rus* – took us right into the river-mouth. A lot of our sailors landed too: their main interest seems to be the purchase of parrots and baby monkeys. The ships'll be fairly crawling with them. Wait now, Mikhail Ivan'ich, I'll read you what I've written. Don't worry, nothing about the damned English in this one. Listen: "Three nights ago a rat bit the first lieutenant on his foot, and last night gnawed off one of his corns. Must have liked the taste and come back for more! What do you think of that?"

'But that's just the end of what I'd already written. What trivia one comes down to, writing as I do nearly every day! Anyway—'

'You said some steamer's taking mail for England tomorrow?'

'Yes. Convenient for you, I suppose. And ours will be trans-shipped in England – if they don't steal it. But – yes, Mikhail Ivan'ich, there'll be a boat collecting it from all round the squadron, I'm sure – a boat from whichever's the duty battleship. I got this from Selyeznov, incidentally.

So if you finish off your own tonight, you'll be all right. I came prepared to finish mine here on shore because once I'm back on board they'll all start screaming for me – this ship, that ship, one after the other, ever since we dropped our hook I've been on the go like a water-beetle. With the major problem that we can't survey leaky hulls because we can't send divers down, on account of the sharks. Anyway – listen to this:

' "There are only a few hundred Europeans here. The rest are negroes, and amongst them are cannibals who in recent months have eaten two Europeans. On board the *Alexander III* they accidentally carried off a negro from Dakar, whom they have now landed, much against his will; he swears that the local people eat their dead, since other meat is so dear. Before they eat them they cut off the hands and feet and put them in a bog to swell, so that they become more palatable." '

Radzianko broke in: 'You're writing this to your *wife*?'

'Why, yes. It'll amuse her. So should this next bit. Listen:

' "I and the party of officers who came ashore with me in the tug this morning called on the king of this place. He received us in an English naval uniform complete with cocked hat. Some of my companions were photographed with him and his wives – one of them arm-in-arm with the queen-dowager, who never ceased to shout for money. She and other court ladies were drunk. It is two days since the king, who is seventy-two, and certainly looks no younger, succeeded his brother on the throne. Margarita, the eldest lady-in-waiting, staggers about stark naked; but as for that, the inhabitants in general do not trouble about completeness of costume. It is supposed to be a monarchy, under the protection of France, but in reality of course is a colony. Tomorrow there is to be some kind of coronation ceremony. The dead king is at present in a box under lock and key. One of our officers unwittingly sat on it, to the consternation of the new king and his prime minister – the latter also wearing cocked hat, with a necktie round his bare neck, and a sword belted on over a frock-coat, but without linen or trousers . . ."'

Glancing up again: 'Look, this is the truth, I swear to you!'

Michael finished his letter to Tasha after supper in the wardroom, and wrote one to Jane with all he could remember of Narumov's local-colour stuff in it. Jane would love it: he really wished it wasn't so late and he had time to spin it out a bit. His longer effort to Tasha was somewhat stilted, he thought, but it was too late to make a fresh start; the shore excursion plus the stifling heat had him drooping with exhaustion. He stripped, dragged his mattress and a sheet up on deck, found a space on the port side of the after control position, and slept heavily enough to miss the excitement which enlivened *Michman* Dukhonin's watch at some time around three a.m.

To start with a searchlight from the *Suvarov*, sweeping the anchorage in the course of some practice alarm which Rojhestvensky had ordered – as like as not warding off an attack by Japanese torpedo-boats – had picked up a skiff that was being rowed towards the *Orel* from the direction of the *Dmitry Donskoi.* Contact by boat between any of the ships during the dark hours was forbidden except with the express permission of the admiral, so the guard-boat, a steam-pinnace from the *Borodino,* was sent speeding to intercept the skiff, in which – Dukhonin told them at breakfast – there'd been two oarsmen, one person at the tiller and another in the bow; held in the searchlight beam they'd been only silhouettes, even with his telescope he hadn't been able to make out any detail beyond the fact that having been illuminated they'd begun rowing frantically – the great silver beam still holding them, but obviously desperate to reach the hospital-ship before the pinnace got to them. In which, of course, they failed, the pinnace running in alongside and a sailor springing over with a line, the officer of the guard then arresting them and taking the skiff in tow back to the battleship anchorage. It had since emerged that the boat's occupants had been Lieutenant Vaselago and *michmen* Varzar and Selitrenikov from the *Donskoi*, with a young volunteer-nurse whom they'd been smuggling back to the *Orel*.

Galikovsky had murmured, 'Poor devils. What *frightfully* bad luck.' Burmin fortunately didn't hear him: he'd been listening with his eyes fairly bulging at Dukhonin: growling then, 'My God! My God! What *next*!' Radzianko and Michael glancing at each other, both probably speculating as to whether the girl might have been Nadyejhda Prostnyekova. No reason it should have been, of course; although she'd have been a likely starter, amongst a hundred of them, cooped up like hens in a superheated barn, there'd surely be a few others of 'similar disposition' (Radzianko's way of putting it, later on). There were other areas of speculation too, around the breakfast table: how might those three have got her to the *Donskoi* in the first place, was one. In disguise? In the bottom of a boat with a tarpaulin over her? What about the *Orel*'s own gangway watch? Bribed, perhaps? For how long might they have had her on board? Might the whole wardroom have been in on it, or only those three? Or Lieutenant Vaselago alone, persuading the two *michmen* to act as his boat's crew? Had anyone ever met this Vaselago?

Radzianko muttered afterwards, 'Some actually *do* it, you see, put their ideas into action. While I just *think* about it. I'll tell you, Mikhail Ivan'ich – when I started my morning bathes in Dakar, it was in the hope that an opportunity might crop up for a somewhat longer swim – I thought it might seem I'd only been having my customary dip. If I'd got over there the evening before, you see. In fact if that collier had only stayed alongside one more day—'

'The odds are that a shark *would* have had you, over that distance.'

'Well – as I believe I said—'

'Worth it, you said, as long as it was on your way back. But it might *not* have been – uh?'

'Well.' A hand on Michael's elbow, and lowering his voice. 'We're going to our deaths in any case. Jokes apart. So what the deuce – a shark, a ten-inch shell?'

Later in the forenoon, by which time all the ironclads were coaling, Rojhestvensky issued Order of the Day number 158, referring to 'three dissolute officers' and 'an act of extreme depravity'. The three were in the flagship's punishment cells – which were well below the waterline, airless and cramped to a degree describable as torture – and were to be returned to Russia for court-martial. Nothing was said about the girl. A sequel to this, though, was that a day or two later Michael found Radzianko at the rail outside the chartroom with his glasses yet again on the *Orel*. Glancing round, and pointing: 'She's rigged a boom. Two boats at it – see? Fact is, these merchantmen don't usually, do they? They let boats cluster at the gangways in a way we wouldn't tolerate. But that'd be how they did it – uh?'

'What are you talking about?'

'Those three with the girl. We were wondering how they'd have got her past the gangway watch. Well, watches, plural – at the *Orel* and like as not the *Donskoi* too. She'd have only to nip out along a boom and drop down a ladder: anyone could've shown her how. Cast off then, drift away a bit before you touched an oar. Dark night that was, too. Moonless period. Eh?'

'You've a one-track mind, Viktor.'

'On the contrary – *enquiring* mind, dear fellow!'

16

The squadron weighed anchor and set off southwards for Great Fish Bay – which the Portuguese were calling Lobito Bay, and was close to the town and port of Benguela – in the late afternoon of December 1st. Calm weather had continued throughout the coaling, but within twenty-four hours of departure was beginning to go to pot: overcast sky at dawn on the 2nd, and by evening – after all the ships had enjoyed their Line-crossing ceremonies – a swell was mounting, rolling up-coast with a southeaster behind it. Wind and swell were thus luckily on the squadron's bow – the course after rounding the Gabon bulge being south ten degrees east – so that the grossly overloaded ships were pitching hard but not rolling all that much. They had more coal in them than they'd had on departure from Dakar; if Great Fish should happen to be barred to them they'd be able, at a pinch, to reach Angra Pequena – same distance, roughly, as the Dakar–Gabon stretch. Whether the Portuguese would try to prevent the squadron coaling – Zakharov's opinion, this – would depend on whether they had the backing of their British allies; chances were that if they knew or guessed Rojhestvensky was coming they'd have called for help from the Royal Navy's base at Simonstown, at the Cape.

Though why *anyone* should object . . .

'We're pariahs, is what it comes to. Thanks to –' Burmin

glancing at Michael – 'the monkeys' allies, shall I say?'

Michael in fact agreed. He was thinking to some extent in Russian by this time. The fact that he was in a well-commanded and reasonably well-officered ship, with a ship's company who quite surprisingly – since these *were* Russians – weren't noticeably abused or ill-treated and either knew their jobs or were doing their best to learn them, did make it seem almost like home. Not that he had any criticism of his own service; the Royal Navy only did what it was told, served its political masters of the day, would also, of course, be justifiably indignant over the Dogger Bank affair – but taking a broader view he felt that while the Anglo-Japanese alliance was probably good politics in terms of the Far East – Manchuria, China, Korea etc. – its extension to home waters mightn't be in Britain's own best interests. The real enemy, ultimately, was Germany and the fleet the Kaiser was building, beyond any doubt aimed at challenging the Royal Navy: so in European waters it would surely make sense not to estrange potential allies.

On the subject of personnel and training, and the abysmal performance of the rest of the squadron, Zakharov had admitted that having a leavening of Black Sea Fleet petty officers and other senior ratings in his crew had given him a considerable advantage. 'My good luck, of course, that I was in a position to get them. It's not only that they're experienced men whom I know and who know what I expect of them – and bear in mind it only takes a few in key positions to influence the rest – the fact is our Black Sea training's always been streets ahead of the Baltic fleet's. Simple reason – down there we're sea-going all year round, training's thus continuous, whereas with the Baltic frozen solid for months on end they're just twiddling their thumbs and talking revolution!'

No thumb-twiddling *here*. There were internal exercises and practices every day, often lasting six hours at a stretch. Not only in the *Ryazan* apparently: Rojhestvensky's Orders of the Day were largely concerned with battle exercises, at this stage. Battle damage and emergencies, primarily: coping with casualties among key personnel, weaponry and communications failure, shifting to emergency controls, improvising. Schemes were to be laid out on paper in every detail, and the objects of the exercises understood 'not only by the officers but also by all lower ranks'. Michael thought it should hardly have been necessary to mention this. While major disadvantages were that in their unstable condition, the ships couldn't safely indulge in mock attacks or other such manoeuvres, and that needing to safeguard ammunition there was none to waste on practice firings. Not that ships' gunnery officers would have called it 'waste'. As Murayev complained, 'What's the use of having even unlimited amounts if you can't land any of it on the enemy?'

Bad weather continued throughout the 4th, 5th and 6th. Chaplain Myakishev had no doubt at all that the splendidly calm weather they *had* been blessed with was due entirely to the intercession of Nicholas the Just, patron saint of sailors, to whom he'd made frequent approaches. 'Bear this in mind, my sons – that when we were sorely in need of it, couldn't have done without it—'

'Seems to have shot his bolt now though, doesn't he.' Galikovsky, the cynic with hooded eyes. 'Why not put old Seraphim back on the job?'

It was cooler now. South of the equator, one had the south-east trades coming up all the way from the Antarctic. Michael had written in his Narumov-style long-running letter,

> They're grumbling now at the fact it's cold enough at night to need a blanket. Having of course been roasted for the past three weeks or so. Tasha, darling, I'm praying that I'll have at any rate *one* letter from you at this next coaling stop – and that it'll tell me you're safe and well and – please God – of the same mind as when I last held you in my arms . . .

On the 6th the squadron made its landfall twelve and a half degrees south of the equator and steamed in to anchor in the wide entrance to Great Fish Bay. It wasn't much of a place to look at: one shore high with jagged, sand-coloured cliffs, the other low and also sandy; and a few small houses visible on that low-lying part. To all intents and purposes, desolation – miles and miles of sand surrounding a vast stretch of water. Only a few colliers were lying at anchor waiting for them, but there was also a diminutive Portuguese gunboat, which it transpired had been harassing the colliers and had driven some of them away by threatening to open fire. It was a ship of only about three hundred tons, with a single 9-pounder on its foc'sl. In fact the colliers were very soon re-assembling, from wherever they'd been marking time and no doubt watching the Russian smoke-cloud's slow approach; on entering the bay the first ones ran directly alongside the battleships. The gunboat, bustling out towards the flagship, threading its way through the crowded anchorage and colliers still on the move, passed close enough to the *Ryazan* for its name to be made out as *Limpopo.* Nick Sollogub described later how the resplendently attired Portuguese C.O., who was received at the flagship's gangway with all due formality, requested the admiral to leave at once. Rojhestvensky, towering over him, pointed out to him amiably enough – in fact his manner had suggested that he might be about to pat him on the head – that his ships were more than three miles from any Portuguese-owned coastline, *were* thus outside territorial waters. The Portuguese snapped back, 'But you're anchored in the bay! That's the point!'

'In that respect – ' Rojhestvensky explained, still beaming down at him – 'we can only thank the Lord that he made the entrance of the bay more than six miles wide, and that between the inshore stretches of Portuguese territorial waters – the neutrality of which is, of course, sacred to me – he has placed this piece of sea, open and accessible to all. What's more, as you can see, we've started coaling. So, appreciative as I am of the courtesy of your visit . . .'

From the gangway head he'd waved the man goodbye, and as it went chuffing off down the line of battleships – the *Alexander*, *Oryol*, *Borodino* and *Oslyabya* – the little ship was jeered on its way, making about ten knots in the direction of Benguela.

Coaling was completed by noon on the 7th, and by dusk the squadron was reformed and on its way to Angra Pequena – alias Luderitz Bay – German territory where Rojhestvensky was sure of a warm welcome. The weather on the other hand was less certain, varying day by day from calm and clear to rough and windy, wind directions shifting constantly; by the time the squadron reached latitude twenty-seven south and turned in to close the land a force eight gale was blowing from the south-south-west, with a heavy sea pounding straight into the bay. The battleships none the less clawed their way in and anchored. They'd had a hard time of it, especially when turning for the run inshore, having in the course of it to turn beam-on to wind and sea, unstable to start with and in those fraught minutes rolling really dangerously; then with their sterns into the force of it, every few minutes being 'pooped' – seas sweeping over them from astern to rush for'ard white and heavy, smashing and pluming up against obstructions such as ventilators, funnels and the bridge superstructure. The *Ryazan* in her turn had been pretty well over on her ear; bridge staff clinging to stanchions or other fittings, Michael himself wondering at each really bad roll whether she'd roll back again. Mental images of loose coal shifting, smashing the flimsy, temporary barriers to pile massively on one side or the other and weigh her over. All you'd need . . . Clinging on with that picture in mind – a calamity that *could* strike at any minute – and not a damn thing anyone could do about it: Michael grinning ruefully at the *michmen*'s taut faces and wide eyes, conveying to them that it wasn't all *that* unusual – scary, of course, but nothing one hadn't been through a dozen times before.

The battleships were inside, anyway – not that with the

wind where it was they'd be getting much shelter in there, wouldn't be able to lower any boats for instance – but cruisers and transports were to remain outside, anchor and ride it out. With limited room inside – in the western part the harbour being divided by a spur of rock which hid this end from the eastern part where the German settlement was located – and the colliers in there already, while in conditions like these the hazards of manoeuvring in restricted spaces were obvious – well, it made sense. Of a kind, anyway, since one had to economize on precious coal, although in more normal circumstances the seaman-like option would have been to stay out at sea rather than anchor this close off a lee shore. Steam had to be kept up anyway, in case of anchor-dragging – which *Ryazan* seemed to be doing her best to achieve, wrenching and tugging at her cable, bucking like a frightened horse. She was the farthest out, with Enqvist's *Nachimov*, *Donskoi* and *Aurora* astern of her. Quite distant from the shore therefore, and stuck here as long as the gale lasted. The *Orel* had left them, incidentally, continuing on course for Cape Town where as a hospital-ship she couldn't be classified as a belligerent and the girls would be given a welcome break from seafaring. She'd be rejoining the squadron later. The rest of the transports were anchored quite randomly half a mile south of the cruisers; they looked from here like abandoned, storm-swept wrecks.

At about seven in the evening Michael was in the bridge – watches were being kept as they were at sea except that one didn't need assistant OOWs – when a signal was made by the admiral to all captains, telling them that (1) there was no intention of trying to coal until the gale had blown itself out, (2) the squadron had been welcomed by this territory's German governor, who had no objection to their remaining as long as might be necessary, and (3) a consignment of mail which had been brought up from Cape Town would be delivered to ships when it had been sorted and distribution was physically possible.

Zakharov came from his cabin to show the signal to

Michael. He was having a copy sent down to the wardroom and another put on the notice-board outside the ship's office.

'You'll be getting your letter from England, perhaps. Those newspaper cuttings.'

'If any of it could have got to Cape Town . . .'

'If it had been sent via the agency in Odessa, it could. There are regular passenger services with which Gunsburg would be familiar, and plenty of steamers returning northward calling at all these places.'

'Do you make use of Gunsburg?'

'For private correspondence, yes.'

'From Moscow?'

'How did you know my family home's in Moscow?'

'Prince Igor must have mentioned it. In fact he did, didn't he, in his speech introducing you – mentioned your father's bank – or banks . . .'

'You're quite right.' Expressionless sideways glance. He was in oilskins, as Michael was – protection against the spray that burst up several times a minute from the *Ryazan*'s plunging bow and lashed over even at this height, at times quite heavily. Zakharov nodded. 'He made a big issue of my family's business interests, didn't he. Referred to my father as "one of Moscow's most eminent merchant princes".' A snort. 'How was that for condescension? Well – it's the truth, but the way he said it – nobody could have missed the point that he was admitting to his own people that mine are *kupechestvi*.'

Kupechestvo meaning merchant class. One grade up from *merchantsvi* – shopkeepers and artisans. Every passport carried such a designation. Minor government officials and junior officers were *chinovniki,* and the nobility were the *dvorianstvo.* Michael said, 'It's not a system I've grown up with as all of you have. But incidentally, Prince Igor did make a point of telling me that your father – and grandfather, am I right? – were highly successful and extremely rich.'

'It's his sole interest in having me marry his daughter,

that's why. After that explanation he'd have expected you to approve, that's why he told you. Explaining the whole business. Didn't you realize that?'

'The way I heard it, you came to Prince Ivan's attention on the strength of your service in the Black Sea.' Michael ducked – they both did – avoiding a bathful of flying green sea. It had to be gusting force ten now, he guessed. Straightening, spitting salt down-wind . . . 'Prince Ivan, surely—'

'I served under him – and achieved some success, yes – but I'd been eligible for promotion for quite some time and I wasn't about to get it then either. In fact I doubt very much whether if I'd not been the only son of this quote merchant prince unquote – as well as seeing which side of my bread had butter on it, for God's sake – after Prince Ivan had of course suggested me to his uncle as a candidate for princely favour – huh?'

'You're being very frank, Nikolai Timofey'ich.'

'I *can* be – can't I?' That hard stare: glittering eyes in deep holes in the wooden face running wet. 'With impunity?'

'If you mean I'd respect your confidence – of course.'

'None of it's news to you, in any case. Or to anyone else – least of all Natasha Igorovna. Correct?'

'I suppose she'd have guessed—'

'Damn right she would have!' Gritting this through his teeth. 'And her mother, and the rest of 'em! Man has no background, only a pot of gold – or *will* have – and what more do we want than *that*, we Volodnyakovs!'

'Two comments, Nikolai Timofey'ich. One, Tasha herself would never think that way. Two, on your own two feet you must have great prospects in the navy – irrespective of—'

'Wrong. Without the Volodnyakov influence I was a satisfactory work-horse, nothing more – and I'd be that again, believe me!' Hugging the binnacle, gazing at the end-on, tossing shapes of the cruisers astern of them, and farther beyond them the backdrop of seething white, the ocean spouting where it flung itself against sand and rock. Back to Michael then: 'When did you last check the anchor-bearings?'

He wrote to Tasha, in the wardroom after breakfast:

> I have my fingers crossed that within a few hours of writing this I may have a letter from you. Or even two or three! We're anchored outside a bay in German Southwest Africa; the big ships have gone inside but we've stayed out here because it's blowing hard and manoeuvring in that confined and crowded space would be difficult. The purpose of stopping here is once more to fill up with coal, but again, while the wind's this strong the colliers couldn't berth alongside; so we have just to sit it out. And meanwhile we've been told by signal that there's a quantity of mail on shore, brought here in a steamer coming north from Cape Town; and the highly frustrating thing is that until the weather improves no mail or anything else can be brought out to us. All I can say is that I'm trying not to bite my nails. It can't blow like this for ever, though, and when mail *can* be brought out it can also be landed – this dull letter with it – so I'll add to it from time to time and append some sort of reply to whatever I get from you. Please God there'll be *something*!

This was December 12th. It blew hard all day and throughout the night, but by dawn on the 13th was easing up, and at five a.m. the battleships began coaling by means of launches under tow from steam pinnaces and cutters. A slow, tedious and back-breaking business, with the boats always in danger of being crushed alongside the ships. But the *Rus* managed to come out during the forenoon with the promised mail; each of the cruisers in turn gave her a lee by using their screws to swing, still anchored, across the direction of wind and sea, the tug then closing in on the sheltered side to pass a line and then a taut wire for setting-up between jackstays, the mail sacks then being hauled across. The wire was backed-up by hand, at this end passing through a snatch-block on the jackstay, three or four seamen maintaining and/or relaxing the tension on it as ship and tug both rolled. It had to be done just right or you'd be in trouble: snap the wire or let a sack dip into the sea – huge strain then on the wire as well as the mail soaked, maybe lost. Michael watched the sacks come over: with considerable relief as each was received in the cruiser's waist. The wire then being cast off and hauled in and the tug as it were spinning on her heel, dancing out of that partial shelter and heading for the transports, fighting like a gamefish over and through the sea's white-sheeting ridges.

Half an hour later he had two letters in his hands, both addressed to him – by Jane – in care of the Gunsburg agency. Posting dates smudged, illegible: so open them, then take them in date order. But on second thoughts, not in here, in the crowded wardroom: glancing round it, his eyes lingering on the sick-looking parrot which a *michman* had brought on board at Gabon. Might have done worse, at that: there were parakeets and monkeys on the messdecks, even a snake or two, and in the *Oryol* apparently a small herd of goats. He told Radzianko, 'Going up to read these in the chartroom.'

'Good idea.' A shrewd glance at the letters in Michael's hands. He had a few of his own, had just ripped one open. 'I might join you.'

Jane had written in mid-November, in a letter that had no enclosure from Tasha in it:

> I think you and your princess must be writing to each other behind my back. I've had nothing from her for ages and I'm sure she can't have fallen completely silent. I had the one you wrote from Spain – in which you told me you were writing directly to her – but by now I'd have thought there'd have been one or two from her. Entirely your own business, I just want you to know I'm not neglecting my duties here, anything

that does come in *will* go out! Yes, I'll also send you any cuttings relating to the crazy enterprise you're engaged in, but so far I've collected only this small snippet which doesn't concern you directly but does suggest all is not exactly tickety-boo back there on the home front. In fact if they're getting down to their peasant rioting again one can only hope that your beloved is safe wherever she is. As regards newspaper reports in general though

He broke off to read the cutting:

Troop Moves Spark Riots In Moscow. The call-up and treatment of reservists has led to trouble in several Russian cities. The worst incidents appear to have taken place in Moscow when a detachment of over a thousand reservists were passing through the city on board a train. Most of the men were more or less drunk. They left the station and tried to break into the state liquor shops and restaurants. Police were called out and some shots fired.

On the back of the cutting was a report from the USA headlined *Roosevelt Romps Back To Power* and continuing,

President Roosevelt won a full four-year lease on the White House today, carrying most of the northern and western states in the presidential elections. Democrat Alton B. Parker, his challenger, sent the president a telegram, congratulating him on his overwhelming victory. In a statement issued from

Finish. Back to Jane:

newspaper reports in general though, my difficulty is that I can't cut great swathes out of *The Times* before your esteemed brother has finished with it, and quite often he peruses it in fits and starts over a period of several days and it then disappears. So I've had a brainwave of which I hope you'll approve when the results start coming in. My nephew William has a project going at school which concerns the Russo-Jap war and I'm getting him to hang on to whatever bits and pieces might be relevant. For his background information – they have to write essays and so forth – he's mainly using the *Daily Telegraph* – but anyway it's up to him. As you know he's hoping to become a naval cadet in about a year's time – which I suppose is why he chose this subject out of several alternatives – he admires *you* tremendously and is apparently only too pleased to have been asked to do this. Whatever he sends me that makes sense I'll forward to you right away – oh, and Mary says she'll arrange to get the *Telegraph* as well as *The Times* so that he can carry on with it during the Christmas holiday. She thinks it's probably good for him to have something like this to keep him out of mischief.

I wonder where you've got to now, where this will reach you. I do hope the outlook for Rogersvosky isn't as bad as most people seem to think. Because we really do want you back here with us one of these days, dear Mick – with, let us hope (for your sake), your princess. Incidentally, having recruited young William, I've had to tell George and your mother (to whom you really *should* have written by this time!) that you and I are in touch. I had a note from you giving this Gunsburg as a forwarding address and asking for any newspaper reports etc. I sent it on to William so as to make clear what was wanted, and William now says it wasn't enclosed with my letter – so it's lost and gone for ever, just like my darling Clementine.

He thought, having finished that one and slid it back into its envelope, what amazingly competent liars some women were. All right when such arts were employed in one's own good cause – in fact splendid – but that couldn't always be the case, and by God one should remember it, keep a weather eye lifting and one's wits about one. This dodge of Jane's, for instance – neither Mama nor brother George would doubt her for a moment, she simply knew at the drop of a hat how to be disarmingly convincing . . . He glanced over her slightly later communication – a note with which she'd enclosed this one from Tasha – and was about to switch to Tasha's when Radzianko arrived, squeezing in sideways through the narrow doorway.

'All well at home, I trust?'

'Not at *your* home, it isn't.' Pointing at the clipping about rioting reservists: and keeping Tasha's letter folded so that his deceptively casual gaze wouldn't pick up the Cyrillic script. Radzianko had picked up the slip of newsprint though.

'What calumny is this?'

Michael gave him a paraphrased Russian version. Radzianko, dumping himself at the other end of the couch, grimaced. 'Destroy it, don't you think?'

'When I've shown it to the skipper. He's asked to see any such items. I hope to be getting quite a lot, eventually – anything about ourselves and Port Arthur and so on. But excuse me . . .'

Tasha had written,

> We have just returned from a visit to St Petersburg, which was made as a concession to my father; Mama thought it would be tactful to spend a week or two up there with him. Michael darling, before we left I had the letter you wrote from that Spanish port; didn't have time to reply to it but was overjoyed at getting it, kissed it so often that it almost fell apart. I like to imagine that I can smell you, taste you, on your letters – your skin, *your* kisses. Oh yes, it's just as bad as it ever was! And having returned yesterday from Petersburg, I have the letter from Morocco which tells me that you were then on board the *Ryazan* so I can no longer write to you directly but only through Jane in England. Darling, I

do so hope you're well and not too sad and lonely and that you'll manage to get along with Z. It's really an extraordinary situation, isn't it? I'm dying to hear what he says to you and what you say to him about me and his dealings with my father – who I must tell you questioned me more than once about my feelings for you, emphasizing that I had no option but to accept Z and therefore must suppress and reject such other inclinations, which would amount to no more than howling at the moon. Hello, lovely moon! I had to be cagey of course; although I admitted that I love you and only you. He knows it, so I would be stupid not to admit it. He knows what happened that night too – despite your attempt to 'brazen it out', as he chose to phrase it. He challenged me with 'When Nikolai Timofey'ich returns, having played his part in securing victory over those damn monkeys—' and I interrupted with 'Who can say with certainty they won't defeat *us*?' Because I may as well tell you, people are saying that the war out there is already more than half lost. Port Arthur won't hold out and your ships, having no base, will be forced to turn back. And for you and me, what could be better? I don't want you to risk being killed out there, my darling! You *won't* be, God wouldn't be so cruel, it's only a nightmare one has to put out of mind whenever, in the small hours of the morning, it creeps in and one wakes in terror. I replace it, smother it – let me tell you this too – with thoughts of you in the most totally physical sense – the feel of you, closeness of you, what it does to me – and your hands, my darling lover – not mine, *yours*! About my father, though – he was furious at what I'd said, shouted at me, 'Zakharov will return in a blaze of glory and you'll marry him whether or not your pipsqueak Englishman also survives! You'll simply do as you're told, my girl!'

All I could do was keep silent and bow my head. I hate him. I'm sorry to say it but it's true, I hate my father. Just come back, my lover, and we'll beat him! *That* will be the blaze of glory!

* * *

'Why not concentrate on your *own* mail, Viktor Vasil'ich?'

Glancing up, he'd caught the flat brown eyes fixed on the letter which he hadn't quite finished reading but now turned face-down. Radzianko's gentle smile accompanying a shake of the pomaded head: somehow he managed never to look embarrassed. 'One would have to be an eagle – ' pointing – 'to read anything at that distance. All that caught my notice was the Cyrillic hand – whereas your envelopes—'

'You'd checked them first, had you? Well, my mother is Russian, Viktor Vasil'ich. But neither she nor my sister-in-law would be so idiotic as to address envelopes in Russian when they're to be handled by British postmen.'

Not bad, he thought – even by Jane's standards. He got up, went outside to finish this last page of the letter on the flag deck, in a degree of shelter as well as out of those constantly prying eyes.

> I have to tell you there's a great deal of unrest in the country now – riots and other unpleasantness – and in Petersburg one really felt the undercurrents of it. Mama and I used this finally as our excuse to return to Yalta, where things do seem to be fairly normal still. And here we are, thank heavens. But one other scrap of news before I close this: do you remember the Derevyenko family? You met the father – Count Andrei – here at the house when he came visiting with his two daughters, Nadia and Aksana. Their brother Pavel, younger than them, was then at the military academy, just finishing and expecting to join a regiment of hussars – the girls talked on and on about him, I remember. Well – we met him, in Petersburg! He's a lieutenant, although on the point of becoming a civilian; he was serving in Manchuria as an ensign, was promoted and decorated on the field of battle and only a week later severely wounded – in a continuation of the same battle, on the banks of a river called the Sha Ho – and lost his left arm,

poor boy. He was cared for in some military hospital out there before being sent home to the hospital in Petersburg, which in fact he seemed to be using as a hotel while getting his final discharge. He's still only just 22 – imagine it . . . But to come to the point, Mama and I were taken to lunch at Kontants – by none other than Ivan, who I must say has been very kind to us – and there at almost the next table was this boy with medals and an empty sleeve – Pavel Derevyenko, whom I wouldn't have recognized but Mama did immediately; and before one had had time to blink he was at our table, Ivan ordering champagne!

He's not here yet, but coming I believe quite soon, to his father's and sisters' great excitement – and this evening it's with them that Mama and I are dining! Which is why I must close this now – having run on for so long. Oh Michael, my precious darling . . .

Leaning on the rail, looking out across the wilderness of leaping, rushing sea. Rollers still racing shoreward, their tops flying like hail. No sign of it easing. He'd crumpled her letter in his hand, thinking then, why not get rid of it – Jane's too – all of it, straight away? There was nothing one needed to remember or comment on: and with Radzianko snuffling round like a pig after truffles – why keep it? Just as I told her not to keep mine, but burn them. Except for the scrap of newsprint, of course – otherwise, here goes! Ripping up the flimsy paper, letting the wind have it like confetti – gulls in full screech, swooping and soaring, some actually catching scraps, disgustedly letting them fly again.

The weather stayed as it was for the next two days, the battleships coaling when they could – a laborious and dangerous business with the boats, having to break off and hoist them inboard when things got worse again. Then, on the night of the 15th–16th, wind and sea dropped enough for the colliers to risk berthing alongside again, and by dawn it was clear the risk had been well justified – flat calm and fog. The big ships completed their coaling; according to Zakharov they'd each had about nine hundred tons remaining and had embarked another fourteen hundred, so for the long haul round the Cape to Madagascar they'd have more on board than they'd ever had. With Cape rollers to contend with, a lot more than was anything *like* safe. Colliers emerged from the bay while the battleships were washing-down, and berthed on the cruisers; others went out to the transports. Zakharov had been lunching in the flagship, came back aboard in the late afternoon when coaling was at its height. Michael had done his few hours at it, dragging sackfuls to the chutes, but he'd cleaned himself up since then and was on the flag-deck, out of the way of everything except the dust, when Zakharov on the way up to his sea-cabin with Burmin in company saw him and beckoned him to join them.

'You might as well hear this, Mikhail Ivan'ich. As a purveyor of bad news yourself . . .'

It was a very small cabin. A high bunk with drawers under it, a table fixed to the for'ard bulkhead and a few hooks for such things as oilskins and binoculars. The only time Michael had been in here had been when he'd knocked on the door to tell him about that report of reservists rioting – what Zakharov had meant just then about purveying bad news. Dumping some paperwork on the desk now, then turning back to tell Michael and Burmin, 'News of Port Arthur. Our admiral has twice had the so-called governor on board – a major in the German army – and apparently the steamer that came in during that lull a few days ago, bringing troops to fight some insurrection they've got on their hands, also brought news that the Japanese besieging Port Arthur have taken what's known as 203 Metre Hill. Well, there's a Captain Second Rank Selyeznov on the staff – you know him, Mikhail Ivan'ich—'

'Yes.'

'He was in the First Squadron, knows Port Arthur intimately. Has another name for that hill, as it happens – seems our own people call it Vissokaya. Don't ask me why. Its importance is that it commands the whole tactical area, including strong-points – forts – and the town itself *and* the inner harbour. Selyeznov says that even if they can only use it as a spotting platform – that's to say if they can't haul guns to the summit – its capture must mark the beginning of the end. For one thing, if any of the First Squadron were still afloat in the harbour when they captured it, by now they'll have been shelled to pieces. So there you are. If it looked bad before, it's worse now. First point, therefore – Mikhail Ivan'ich, would you like to be landed here?'

'No, thank you – sir.'

A shrug. 'Don't say you didn't have the offer. Second point, Pyotr Fedor'ich – when we get the news that Port Arthur's gone – which does seem inevitable – we say too bad, it's a setback, but all it means for this squadron is that our base, when we get out there, will be Vladivostok. No despair, no panic. Right?'

17

Ryazan, scouting ahead of the squadron, sighted Cape Sainte Marie on Madagascar shortly before sunset on December 26th. Rojhestvensky had sent Zakharov ahead in the expectation of meeting the hospital-ship, with whom a rendezvous at this time and place had tentatively been arranged; they should in fact have met her earlier in the day and hadn't, and with the short range of the German wireless equipment plus darkness and land close at hand it had been sensible to make some sort of reconnaissance. Result: Madagascar was there all right, but the *Orel* was not: had either pressed on ahead of them or delayed her departure from Cape Town until the gales that had been raging down there had eased off.

The squadron had made the trip from Angra Pequena in much better time than had been allowed for, not so much despite the foul conditions as with their help – a following wind practically all the way – and mercifully few breakdowns. There'd been a bunker fire in *Suvarov* – extinguished by injecting steam to smother it – and it seemed probable that the poor old *Malay* had foundered. She'd broken down at the height of the gale on December 21st, when the waves' height had been estimated as sixty feet and from *Ryazan*'s bridge Michael at one stage had had an astonishing gull's-eye view of the *Aurora* as she climbed a near-vertical wall of sea – stern more or less submerged, ram high out of water pointing at the low-flying clouds: in those seconds her entire plan view had been exposed to him. The day before – 20th – when they'd rounded Cape Agulhas and entered the Indian Ocean, it had been bad enough, but this stronger blow was from the west-southwest, pretty well dead astern, and the pitching was ferocious. At Zakharov's prompting Burmin had had men shoring bulkheads and rigging strongbacks under hatches that might otherwise have given way to the weight and power of seas crashing down on them; all the ships were dipping bows-under, *Ryazan*'s screws at times racing as they came up out of water – inviting serious, even irreparable damage to screws, shafts and bearings.

This was when the *Malay* developed engine trouble and began to fall astern. The squadron's practice had been to stop while any temporarily immobilized ship put itself to rights, but to stop in these conditions was out of the question, so Zakharov, as tail-end Charlie, took the initiative of standing by her – turned back to circle her, signalling the admiral that he'd keep her company and bring her along when repairs had been completed. The emergency had developed very suddenly, and Michael, who'd had the watch, had moved to the telegraphs when the skipper had taken over. Anyway, Rojhestvensky wasn't having it, ordered Zakharov to resume his station astern of the other cruisers. With which, of course, he complied – in another hair-raising turn across the full force of the storm. It had been more storm than gale by then. What was likely to remain one of Michael's lifelong memories was the sight of the old transport, former ocean liner, rolling like a harpooned whale, beam-on to wind and sea, with men crabbing around her canting, wave-swept decks struggling to set small jury sails in the hope of bringing her head down-wind again – knowing that beam-on she wouldn't last. While the rest of them carried on eastward in their own battering, staggering way – *Ryazan* from minute to minute with her snout deep in it, shaking like a great black dog with a rat in its jaws. It was dusk by then and one had had the sickening feeling of deserting friends. Envisaging how it might happen when it did – a cargo-hatch smashed in, that hold filling, and – curtains. Zakharov gave orders for a searchlight to be trained astern to flash the stricken ship's pendant numbers at ten-minute intervals throughout the night.

Not that that would save her. Only provide guidance and maybe encouragement if by her own efforts she did survive, if any of her company were alive to catch glimpses of it even half an hour after that last sight of her. Speculating then – the mind wandering on other levels as it tended to in night watches – as to whether Pavel Derevyenko would have got home to Yalta yet. Visualizing candlelit dinners and cab-rides back from that Oreanda restaurant, for instance. Winter now, but the Yalta climate was mild enough, so they'd all claimed. They'd be wrapped in their furs anyway if it wasn't. But a war hero and a count, and a family that was obviously well off. Empty sleeve or not, mightn't he be as good an alternative candidate, in Anna Feodorovna's calculating mind, as some Englishman on his way to be drowned in the Yellow Sea?

The squadron anchored at eight a.m. on December 29th in the channel between Madagascar and the island of Sainte Marie. Same name but no connection with the cape at Madagascar's southern extremity; Sainte Marie island was a French-administered penal colony which they used as an overflow from Devil's Island. As soon as they'd anchored and a boat had been lowered Zakharov had himself rowed over to the flagship, where he failed to see the admiral – who was said to be unwell – but talked with Clapier de Colongue and others, elicited that while the squadron's intended destination had been Diego Suarez – an excellent, spacious harbour with modern communication facilities, i.e. a telegraph station – British pressure on the French and Paris's ostensible surrender to it had led to the squadron *officially* being barred from it, and the General Staff in Petersburg had lacked the guts to argue the point, although the French would almost certainly have turned blind eyes.

This had infuriated the admiral who, according to the doctor, Nyedozorov, was suffering mainly from exhaustion. He wasn't a young man and he'd been on his flagship's bridge, they said, for ten days and nights without a break. He'd doubtless be back on his feet in a day or two, but for the time being wasn't seeing anyone except de Colongue and his flag lieutenant, Serebriakov.

Michael asked Zakharov over lunch in the wardroom, 'So what's our programme now?'

'There isn't one. We're stuck in this highly insalubrious place with damn little shelter. Coaling will start tomorrow – so let's pray the wind doesn't get up. Although in some ways I wouldn't mind a few clean breaths of it, the place stinks of fever, doesn't it?' Turning to Dr Baranov: 'How are your stocks of quinine?'

'Very little remaining, I'm sorry to say. At Gabon for instance—'

'Better see where you can cadge some. *Orel* for instance – can't be more than a day or so behind us.' Back to Michael and the others: 'For the staff the worst is they've no news of Felkerzam and his division. But since there's no telegraph except in Diego Suarez – three hundred miles north, and we aren't allowed in there anyway – and Tamatave about a hundred south – well, they're sending the *Rus* to Tamatave tomorrow – leaving at first light. Your friend Selyeznov's going in her.'

At four p.m. the hospital-ship arrived, looking as immaculate as ever, and anchored close to the *Ryazan*. She'd brought despatches, mail and newspapers from the Cape. They'd already sorted the mail, and ships were invited to send their boats for it; *Ryazan*'s cutter was already at the boom with steam up, and was on its way over within five minutes of that message being received. Being the first there, however, its coxswain was given the honour of delivering the admiral's despatches, and while they were at it the *Suvarov*'s mailbags as well. Anxious watchers on *Ryazan*'s decks were surprised when it set off towards the flagship instead of coming straight back, and by the time it did, word had already flown round – having been picked up from exchanges of semaphore messages between the *Orel* and other ships – that the First Pacific Squadron had been annihilated in the harbour at Port Arthur.

Michael now had his own despatches, enclosed in a rather bulky letter from Jane and by courtesy of her nephew William. In the same packet was a letter from Tasha which he slid into a pocket to read later.

Jane had written,

> William's come up trumps, as you'll see from the enclosures. Also, I'm sure far more exciting, a letter from T at last. Do wish *I* could read Russian! I've had one from you meanwhile from darkest Africa and will reply shortly at greater length but it's only a few days since I wrote and the important thing is to get this off to you prontissimo. *Look after yourself!* Love

Young William's contributions included a cutting from the *Daily Telegraph* listing the ships of this squadron and those under Felkerzam *en route* via the Red Sea, and 'third section' under Admiral Botrovosky – of whom one had never heard – consisting of the cruisers *Oleg* and *Izumrud*, eight torpedo boats and 'several transports'. Felkerzam's group having split up, presumably – unless the paper was mistaken, and God only knew where this Botrovosky had sprung from.

Next came what read like an essay – perhaps mostly because of the boyish handwriting – in two parts, the first headed 'Northern Theatre of War':

> The Russians are using all their resources to reinforce and reorganize their army and it would be inviting another defeat were they to attempt to move until their troops were again fully equipped and ready to advance. On the other hand the Japanese have every reason for

> not making any hasty move. The further they advance north the longer does their line of communications become and the greater the need of caution. It is probable that they have hopes of shortly releasing, by the capture of Port Arthur, a large number of seasoned troops for the reinforcement of Marshal Oyama's army and are therefore wisely biding their time until they can attack in such numbers that they will be certain of success. In any case the battle when it comes will be unsurpassed in fierceness, and should the Russians, if beaten, be unable to again draw off in the masterly way they have hitherto, it might result in a crushing and completely disorganising defeat for them.
>
> The other piece began:
>
> The Baltic Squadron is making slow though sure progress on its journey out to the Far East. On 28th November the division under Admiral Rojhestvensky had arrived off Swakopmund (wrong, by four hundred miles) and on the 25th the other division consisting of the *Sissoy Veliky* (etc., ships all listed) entered the Suez Canal. Botrovosky's squadron was reported in the English Channel on the 28th.

Half a page followed about untrained men and the coaling problem that faced Rojhestvensky: all true, but it doesn't tell *us* anything, William. Except that if the British press know that much about us, so do the Japanese. Skipping, therefore, and picking it up again lower down:

> Should Port Arthur fall before the spring, as seems probable, the Japanese fleet will be at once relieved from its blockade duties and with luck may have time before the Baltic fleet reaches eastern waters for some, at any rate, of the Japanese ships to undergo refit, although it is probable that many of them have already

> been sent home for that purpose and are even now ready to engage the Russians once more, whose ships will most certainly be in want of refitting after so long a voyage under such disadvantageous conditions.

Damn right, William. Except for that unfortunate 'with luck'. Stand in the corner for half an hour, boy, for that . . . But now the last item: a *Telegraph* cutting with no date on it:

> The officers of a French steamer report having sighted the *Mikasa* near Sasebo and the *Asahi* forty miles south of the Shan Tung promontory, both battleships looking as if they had been refitted. Reuter reports in connection with this that the refitting and repair of the Japanese fleet has been progressing secretly since August last.

None of it was exactly reassuring: certainly not stuff that the collapsed and – according to Baranov (who'd got it from Nyedozorov) – mentally as well as physically overwrought Rojhestvensky would want to hear. Michael, re-assembling the package, saw Radzianko looking flummoxed or at any rate less suave than usual, having had no mail himself in this delivery. Arkoleyev was ribbing him about it but most of them were poring over their own letters. Michael went up on deck and found peace and solitude in the after control position in which to read Tasha's letter, but paused to fill and light a pipe first, to keep the mosquitoes off. Zakharov was probably right, one could imagine malarial infection being rife here – whole clouds of the damn things, not *quite* as big as sparrows but a lot more dangerous.

Ridiculous, really. Humid air – humidity not far short of say ninety per cent – and tobacco so dry it crackled.

> Michael, my precious darling, it's only a few days since I wrote, but here I go again. I'm *frightened* for you – because of all we're hearing and reading – and what's

tormenting me especially is that you're where you are, obviously facing great danger very soon if not already, only because of *me.* Well – my father – but that *is* because of me. I want to ask you – beg you – when you're stopping at some place to embark coal, couldn't you find some ship that's leaving for Europe and come home on it? You're not in the Russian navy, Michael, you've really no business to be there at all! Some are saying the squadron will have to turn back – and that would be all right – but others who are in the know say Admiral Rojhestvensky is the sort of man who'd *never* turn back – even if he knows full well that he and his ships and all those thousands of men are heading for certain destruction he'd still press on regardless! But Michael darling – if a disastrous outcome *is* certain or so probable that people are talking and writing in newspapers the way they are – darling, even if Rojhestvensky and others see glory in it there's none at all for you, it's *not your war or business,* there's no reason you should link your fate with theirs – with Z's for instance. *Especially* with Z's! Do you understand what I'm telling you, my love? Do I deserve to lose you? Can that be the judgement of Fate? You who are not only my lover but my life. Even if your own life is of so little value to yourself, save it for *me* – leave them, get back here to me somehow. To England, or Paris – as you said before, isn't it the answer not only to this present danger but to all our recent prayers?

The dry tobacco was burning his tongue. Might dampen it with a sprinkling of brandy this evening, he thought. In the *real* navy one would have used rum. It was quite plain what Tasha was getting at: let Zakharov drown, if that was what was in store for him, but why on earth drown with him?

Or taking it one stage of the concept further: *with luck* he'll drown, so leave him to it.

So much for Pavel Derevyenko, anyway. Or any others, for

that matter. Shaming what separation, isolation, could do to you. On the other hand, if it didn't how cold-blooded – or arrogant – would that make you? What would the passionate love amount to?

At four p.m., to the delight of the entire squadron, the *Malay* came limping into the anchorage and dropped her hook among the other transports. Ships' crews massed on their upper decks to cheer her, sirens hooted, Rojhestvensky semaphored congratulations, and a pinnace which Michael suspected might have had Narumov in it chuffed over to her from the *Suvarov.* After so much bad news it was a fine display of high spirits by the ships' companies – of which there was a further indication that evening by Shikhin, Michael's sailor-servant. As he was intending to sleep on deck West African style, mosquitoes or no mosquitoes, Shikhin was taking his mattress up, part of the job being to beat the coal-dust out of it in the open air; he paused in the companionway to ask, 'Permission to ask your honour a question?'

'Of course. What is it?'

'Does your honour believe we'll have much chance of beating the Japs when we come up against 'em?'

'I'd say a very *good* chance. Why shouldn't we?'

'Hah!' Nodding with what looked like a calm certainty, and approval. 'That's what a lot of 'em's saying now. Me too, your honour! With our man Admiral Rojhestvensky leading us – that's what counts with the likes of me!'

'Think well of him, do you?'

'Brought us this far, hasn't he? And he'll have a trick or two yet up his sleeve, is my guess. Like they was saying down for'ard this evening – wouldn't bring us half round the world for *nothing*, would he?'

Awake soon after dawn, woken by the whine of mosquitoes in his ears, Michael saw the *Rus* leave on her mission to Tamatave. December 30th, this. Colliers were supposed to arrive today. Lying back again with the sheet over his head, wondering whether Radzianko would be taking his early-morning swim. In the wardroom last night they'd been encouraging him to do so – Galikovsky, Murayev, Skalinin, Lyalin – the latter insisting straight-facedly that although there certainly were sharks in these waters, they congregated mainly on the other side, in the Mocambique Channel.

Burmin had growled, 'What are you trying to do, get him killed?'

'Lord, *no,* Pyotr Fedor'ich.' Galikovsky winked at the others. 'Thinking of his own best interests, really. If he got just a bit of a nip, he might wind up on board the *Orel* – in all *manner* of comfort! Eh, Viktor?'

'Depends on what the shark bit off, surely!' Murayev had mimed it, leaping up, clasping himself and uttering a loud scream. Radzianko had smirked while the others guffawed, and said airily that he'd think about it; Michael wondered whether he might not actually have meant it, whether he wasn't so concerned to build a reputation as a daredevil – *molodyets* – that he might be crazy enough to risk it.

As it turned out, he didn't: and sharks were sighted on and off throughout the day; through the clear water they were easy to see from the upper deck and even easier from the superstructure. Coaling started during the forenoon. In the *Ural* – auxiliary cruiser, another former German liner – it was brought to a halt that evening when the traveller of a Temperley carried away and smashed into the two young officers who were operating it: one had his chest crushed and spine snapped, dying instantly, and the other was stunned by a blow on the head; the latest news of him, from the *Orel,* was that it was hoped he might pull through.

Ryazan finished her coaling by noon on the 31st, and was washing-down when the *Rus* came chugging into the anchorage, back from Tamatave, bringing the news that Admiral Felkerzam's division was lying at anchor at Nossi-Bé, a large indentation in the coast in Madagascar's extreme north-west – near the top of the Mocambique Channel, in fact – and that most of the colliers who were here to serve the squadron were in Diego Suarez. It was a muddled situation which perhaps nobody but Rojhestvensky fully understood – if in fact even *he* did. Zakharov, who'd talked with the staff, told Michael it looked as if St Petersburg had been sending instructions direct to Felkerzam, Rojhestvensky's subordinate, instead of through Rojhestvensky himself as commander-in-chief: which would account for the latter's almost unbridled fury, which he was said to be venting on everyone right, left and centre, not least on poor Clapier de Colongue. The *Rus* was despatched to Tamatave again, and Admiral Enqvist with the *Nachimov*, *Donskoi* and *Aurora* was sent to escort a group of colliers to Nossi-Bé and to transmit to Felkerzam, when in wireless range of him, orders to join Rojhestvensky in this Sainte Marie anchorage forthwith: actually not at Sainte Marie, but in Tan-Tan Bay just three miles further north where they were now moving because there was better shelter there. Enqvist sailed on January 5th at five a.m., but at noon a collier from Diego Suarez arrived bringing a report from Felkerzam to the effect that (1) he had no knowledge of the whereabouts of the cruisers *Oleg* and *Izumrud* and two destroyers who'd been with them – under the command, Michael guessed, remembering young William's despatches, of the mysterious Admiral Botrovsky – and (2) he, Felkerzam, had indeed been ordered by the General Staff in Petersburg to lie-up at Nossi-Bé and put in hand as complete a refit of all his ships as could be managed or improvised with the limited facilities at his disposal. All his ships had therefore been 'opened up' and would be incapable of moving for at least a fortnight. It was almost unbelievable that St Petersburg could have acted in this way, and apparently Rojhestvensky, still in poor health, was literally shaking and screaming with rage. Anyway on the evening of the 5th – Rojhestvensky on the principle of Mahommed going to the mountain having given orders for the squadron to sail next day, the Russian Christmas Eve, for Nossi-Bé – Zakharov invited Michael to join him for a drink in his sea-cabin – his day-cabin down aft being full of coal again – to tell him about these and certain other developments which he didn't, at this stage, want to discuss in front of others. He could talk to Michael, he'd explained, who was at one and the same time an outsider and '*almost* family', as he couldn't to anyone else; and Michael being his guest on board it was only right and proper for them to have a vodka or two together, from time to time.

The situation by and large was verging on the impossible, he admitted, after the first four-fingers shot of vodka had been poured, tumblers clinked, a toast proposed to the health of the Tsar and the liquor tossed back in a single gulp – *do dnya,* 'to the bottom'. Certainly unprecedented – the conduct of the General Staff and of Felkerzam, the appalling condition of the ships and incompetence of their officers and crews, and the desperate situation of Port Arthur – as well as a number of lesser factors, or symptoms, maybe. There'd been mutinous outbreaks for instance amongst the civilian crews of some of the transports – several, all the way from Gabon southward. Better not to talk about this elsewhere – one had to guard against such infections spreading, especially in view of the poor quality of the ironclads' crews *and* the revolutionary element among them. 'This is the point – I can talk to you, Mikhail Ivan'ich, in the certainty my confidence will be respected. We know each other well enough by now, and you're a good man, you've been pulling your weight as I hoped you would – and on top of that you're a free agent, you can speak your mind to me – in private – on any subject you choose . . .' Those mutinies had been quelled, he added, by Rojhestvensky signalling to the ships' captains that men who refused to obey orders were to be put into ships' boats and set adrift. Preferably at night, so that no one would see it happening. A chuckle, a shake of the head: 'They caved in, all right. It's well known that Zenovy Petrovich doesn't issue threats unless he's ready to carry them out. Although as I was saying, when I saw him yesterday I was horrified. In a month he's aged twenty years. Keeps it all to himself, you see, doesn't share any of the strain. And there's worse to come now. Look, you're closer to that bottle, Mikhail – put a fair wind behind it, will you?'

The vodka bottle was on the writing table. Michael was sitting on the only chair, Zakharov perched on the foot end of his bunk. Reaching for the bottle, Michael had a close-up of a framed portrait which he'd seen before but which had previously lain flat, was now propped upright. Portrait of a female – not bad looking, but no raving beauty, thirty or thirty-five perhaps. Rather dressy.

An actress, possibly.

'Help yourself, then pass it over.'

'You're an excellent host, Nikolai Timofey'ich.' He'd half-filled his tumbler, passed the bottle up uncorked. 'I mean it, you've been extremely hospitable right from the start. Considering that I was wished on you by Prince Igor – very decent, much appreciated. But you said a minute ago – worse to come?'

'D'you know who I mean by Klado?'

'Klado.' He remembered. On *Suvarov*'s bridge during the action against the fishing boats: that tall, rather stupid-looking captain of the second rank, who'd been swearing that the *Aurora*, at whom they'd been shooting at the time, was Japanese; and what Sollogub had said about him afterwards. The man who'd wanted to encumber Rojhestvensky with even more ancient ships than they'd lumbered him with already, and who'd been landed at Vigo to attend the Dogger Bank inquiry, Rojhestvensky grabbing at the chance to get rid of him. Michael nodded. 'Writes articles on naval matters, doesn't he? I was told he commands the respect of the General Staff, even of the Tsar.'

'Incredibly enough, that is the case. Respects *himself* even more, though – regards himself as an equivalent of the Americans' Captain Mahan. Which he certainly is not – he's a fool and a poseur. Compared to Mahan – well, he does *not* compare. But now it seems he's won. They're putting together something they're calling the Third Squadron – old coastal defence vessels, anything they can find that floats – and sending it out to us under the command of a rear-admiral by name of Nyebogatov. I don't know him but Selyeznov tells me he's a short, tubby man, very easy-going so he's quite well liked. But you see, it's lunacy . . .'

'Will we wait for them here?'

'At Nossi-Bé, you mean. Not if our admiral can help it. He's planning to sail east on January fourteenth. That's giving Felkerzam the fortnight he says he needs, d'you see. If Zenovy Petrovich *can* get away then, leaving Nyebogatov and lame ducks behind, he will.'

'But with Port Arthur likely to have gone by then, and Vladivostok iced-up—'

'Hole-up somewhere on the Indo-China coast maybe, then make a dash for it when Togo isn't looking. Or fight him. God knows – I'm only repeating what the staff are guessing. Let's have another?'

'No – thank you, but—'

'Drink to Zenovy Petrovich outwitting those fat swine in Petersburg *and* the monkeys?'

'Oh. Well . . .'

'You're impressed by Irina, I notice.'

'Irina?'

'A very old friend.' Nodding towards the photograph in its silver frame. 'Don't worry – I told you I wouldn't let Natasha Igorovna down, and I won't. They won't cross each other's paths, I'll see to it they don't.'

In the small hours of the morning the *Rus* got back from her second visit to Tamatave, bringing the news that General Stossel had surrendered Port Arthur to the Japanese.

18

The reunited Second Squadron sailed from Nossi-Bé not on January 14th as Rojhestvensky had planned, but on March 16th. After the seemingly interminable delay, he'd made up his mind only the night before – and was not informing St Petersburg of his decision. He'd received intelligence from the local French naval commander that day – the 15th – that Nyebogatov had coaled his Third Squadron in Crete and by this time would be either approaching the Canal or on his way through it, which meant that the 'self-sinkers' – Rojhestvensky's term for the reinforcements – might be arriving here in as little as two weeks; it was time therefore to disappear, and quickly. He'd spent an hour or two in his cabin chewing it over, then summoned Clapier de Colongue, shouted at him, 'General signal immediately! Squadron to raise steam and weigh anchors at noon!'

'Destination, sir?'

'Where d'you think, you damn fool?'

It wasn't as obvious as it might have been. Since his own recovery, and then his furious incredulity at what he'd found had been going on ashore while he'd been laid up – his men blind drunk a lot of the time, some of them actually moving between bars, brothels and gambling hells on all fours, finding that this could sometimes be easier than attempting it on their feet – having stopped all shore leave except for approved personnel only on Sundays and Saints' Days, he'd been driving the squadron hard, sending groups and divisions of ships to sea almost daily on manoeuvres, battle exercises and gunnery and torpedo practice. This could have been another outing of that kind; but de Colongue took a chance, gave the admiral his invariably courteous smile and enquired, 'Sea of Japan, sir?'

He – de Colongue – in passing that order to prepare for sea, had been shocked to the core of his being, according to Selyeznov, with whom Zakharov had conferred on board the flagship at breakfast-time this morning. There'd been no sleep for anyone from the time of that signal being made: ships raising steam and otherwise preparing for sea, boats between ironclads and transports embarking top-ups of essential stores, and so forth. (A last mail had been landed, with brief notes to Tasha and Jane in it.) But for Rojhestvensky to be openly defying the Naval General Staff, who'd given him direct and explicit orders to wait in Nossi-Bé for Nyebogatov to join him, was mind-boggling. Admittedly on receiving that order to wait for the Third Squadron he'd been so enraged that he'd seized an armchair in his cabin and smashed it up, but that didn't alter the fact it *was* an order, and still in force – from the highest in the land, those closest to and most trusted by His Imperial Majesty.

Zakharov to Michael, low-voiced, in *Ryazan*'s chartroom while bugle-calls were sending the ships' companies to their stations for leaving harbour: 'They could hang him for this.'

'But in all the circumstances – and his own judgement—'

'You mean thank God we're at last getting out of this hell-hole.'

'That, yes. But it's a case of either go on or go back, isn't it?'

'And if we were to go back, we'd have lost the war. All right, may have lost it already – but there's still a chance, Mikhail Ivan'ich. Given an ounce of the luck the Japanese have had so far—'

'Do you really believe that?'

A glance downward, at a chart of the whole Indian Ocean. 'Given half a pound of luck then. Including the gunlayers learning even the rudiments of their job!'

The recent exercises, in which some of the squadron's precious live ammunition had been fired, had not been much of a success. In particular the gunners hadn't yet come to terms with their new Barr and Stroud range-finders; with an actual range of twenty-four cables (forty-eight hundred yards) they'd made it six – twelve hundred yards. Ammunition hoists had jammed. The new telescopic sights had the layers and trainers baffled. From Rojhestvensky's Order of the Day number 42 of January 27th for instance: *The expensive 12-inch shell were fired without showing anything like the proportion of hits as guns of other calibres . . . Practice with the 12-pounder Q.F.* (quick-firing) *guns was very bad . . . As regards the firing of the 6-pounder Q.F. guns, which are intended to repel torpedo attacks, one really feels ashamed to speak of it. We keep men at these guns every night for that express purpose, and by day the entire squadron did not score* one single hit *on the targets which represented the torpedo boats, although these targets differed from the Japanese torpedo boats to our advantage, inasmuch as they were stationary.*

(As a sequel to this – the expenditure of ammunition – the transport *Irtysh*, which had been expected to bring replenishments of shells of all calibres from Odessa, had arrived on March 2nd – from Djibouti – with twelve thousand pairs of boots and a consignment of fur-lined overcoats. No shot or shell at all.)

Zakharov glanced round as Radzianko pushed in. The navigator hadn't lost any weight – as many had, in this debilitating climate. Civilians ashore, living mostly in small white houses around the aptly named settlement of Hellville – named in fact after the French Admiral Hell who half a century earlier had taken possession of the place – reckoned that life-expectation here for a white man was three years – if he stayed that long. The killers were malaria, dysentery, boils, infections of many kinds, mental breakdown often leading to suicide, poisonous spiders and snakes, flies by the hundred million ... Radzianko pulled off his cap and mopped his forehead, on which the dark hair had begun noticeably to recede: 'Do we know yet which way we're going, sir?'

'We'll be told when we get outside, I dare say.'

The course set by the admiral would make it obvious anyway. Although one did naturally want to know where one was and where one was going. In case of separation through breakdown or foul weather for instance. In the present case, to get past Singapore into the Pacific meant passing through either the Sunda or the Malacca Strait – round either the bottom or the top end of Sumatra, in fact, which right from the start would mean a difference in course of twenty or twenty-five degrees. Sunda, the narrow passage between Sumatra and Java, would be the shortest route, but might seem to the Japanese to be the obvious way for the squadron to go and therefore where they'd lay mines. Not that Malacca would be much less dangerous. Zakharov asked Michael, 'Which way would you go?'

'Sunda. Because it's the most direct. I don't believe the Japs will bother to meet us halfway. I still think they'll wait for us to come to them.'

'By which time we'll have worn ourselves out a bit more.'

He nodded to Radzianko. 'Staying close to their own ports, too. Refitted. Clean bottoms. Whereas ours, by this time ...'

Foul with weed and barnacles. You didn't have to say it. With no dry dock within a thousand miles and the difficulty and danger of sending divers down in shark-infested water, even in netting enclosures – for the little they might achieve in any case, except in repairing specific damage to rudders or propellers for instance. But another thing one didn't need to mention was that Togo's refitted and well-found ships would be manned by officers and crews who were seasoned, battle-experienced and self-confident.

Zakharov must have been thinking along similar lines.

'You should have taken up my suggestion, Mikhail Ivan'ich. You'd have been well on your way home by now.'

In the old *Malay*, who'd been sent home to the Black Sea in company with another old tub which had had more or less constant engine trouble, the *Knyaz Gortchakov*. When Zakharov had made the suggestion Michael had thought of Tasha's letter, that impassioned plea, and of the convenience of being landed probably in Odessa: contacting her from comparatively close range and within three or four weeks, say, getting her to England with him either overland or by sea. Imagining her happiness: and the thrill of it – give or take a few minor hurdles here and there, a classic happy ending!

A pipe-dream, though. For some reason. Such as *belonging* here now? Having to see it through? He'd done his best to rationalize it, in more than one of the four or five letters he'd sent from this place. Had not mentioned the *Malay* – who, in any case, a fortnight before she'd been due to leave had had a mutiny on board, which had been serious enough for the *Suvarov* to train her guns on her and send over an armed boarding party. Part of the cause of the mutiny, anyway a factor in it, had been that they'd been filling her with homebound passengers who didn't have much to lose – prisoners being sent home to face courts-martial, malcontents regarded as bad influences on the messdecks, quite a few who'd gone mad, including some officers; and other incurably sick – incurably here, in this climate, in the opinion of the *Orel*'s doctors – as well as an unspecified number of men who'd contracted diseases ashore in Hellville which were regarded as inappropriate for the young volunteer nurses to have anything to do with or even hear about.

But all right, the mutiny had been dealt with, as had another in the *Nachimov* – where sailors had been demanding fresh bread – one *could* have taken passage home in the *Malay* – or in the *Gortchakov*, for that matter.

Hadn't – that was all.

Burmin pushed in, reporting to Zakharov that the ship's company were at their stations for leaving harbour, cable party on the foc'sl, ready to weigh anchor. Radzianko followed him and the skipper out on to the bridge, and Michael on his way to the flagdeck stopped to light a cigarette – a German variety called Elmas. They weren't bad. Narumov had bought a thousand from one of the colliers' captains for a hundred roubles, and sold half of them to Michael for the same amount, telling him what the original cost had been only after their transaction had been completed. The German collier skipper had been scraping up cash to settle gambling debts; stakes in the Hellville gambling shacks – literally shacks, native-built huts with signboards over their doorways, one reading *Café de Paris* – where the game was usually macao, had been frighteningly high, as had the cost of liquor and the prices charged by whores of a dozen different nationalities who'd come flocking to the easy pickings – a seller's market, ten thousand Russians half out of their minds, spending money like water having as an excuse the fact they couldn't send any home to Russia even if they'd wanted to.

Michael had explained to Tasha, in a letter in early January replying to the one she'd written in something like panic – or to wake him up to this being their great chance, if he could get back to her now – all that – he'd told her that whatever she'd been hearing or reading, defeat of this squadron by the Japanese was no means a foregone conclusion. She was right in saying that Rojhestvensky was not a man to turn back from his avowed purpose: the only difference now was that purpose was to fight his way through to Vladivostok.

> As far as my own position is concerned, I embarked on this with the encouragement of my own naval superiors, and my strong inclination is to see the task through to its conclusion. If I left the squadron now – yes, I *could* – I'd be failing in my task, and no matter what anyone else thought about it *I'd* feel I'd run away. I wouldn't want

> to have such a thing on my mind or record. I suspect that in the course of time you'd come to wish I hadn't; it would mean I was not the man with whom you fell in love, only a creature determined not to take risks with his own life. The truth is that I *will* return to you, my sweet darling, but please God by way of Vladivostok and the trans-Siberian railway; and you *will* receive that telegram begging you to meet me – as you say, in Paris or in London. Just remember that your father won't be slow to react and is far from ineffectual; you (and your mother if she's so inclined, as I very much hope she will be) should move quickly and secretly to whatever rendezvous we'll have arranged – ultimately of course to Wiltshire.

In a more recent letter he'd told her that he was as worried for her safety as she was for his. Russian newspapers received on board during the past month had reported growing unrest all over the country – including a general strike of workers in Sevastopol, a lot too close to Yalta for one's peace of mind. Newspapers and journals which arrived in February on board the formerly 'missing' cruisers *Oleg* and *Izumrud* – also the destroyers *Gromky* and *Grozhny* and auxiliaries *Riona* and *Dniepr*, a detachment commanded not by the *Daily Telegraph*'s mythical Rear-Admiral Botrovosky but by a Captain Dobrotvorsky – had included accounts of the terrible events of January 22nd, the Winter Palace Massacre. A peaceful demonstration by two hundred thousand men, women and children, led by a priest and carrying ikons and portraits of Tsar Nicholas, the young priest also bearing a Loyal Address for presentation to His Imperial Majesty, imploring him to institute reforms in many areas including the working people's starvation wages and crippling taxation, lack of civil rights or political expression: *We come to you, Sire, seeking truth, justice and protection. We have been made beggars; we are oppressed, we are near to death.*

Nearer than they'd anticipated. In the snow-covered square in front of the Winter Palace – the Tsar himself had been spirited away to Tsarskoye Selo – troops opened fire, and within minutes hundreds lay dead. Three thousand were wounded. January 22nd had become known across the empire as Bloody Sunday, and the Tsar was no longer seen as the people's 'little father'. It hadn't done much to improve morale in the Second Pacific Squadron either.

The sun was a blow-torch boring its way through the smoke-laden fug: except for the smoke it was the same swelter they'd lived in for the past two months – and now longed to get out of. As far as *Ryazan* was concerned, they were having to be patient, with the anchorage only very slowly clearing. The first division of battleships had gone on out and the second division (Felkerzam's) was now on the move – not all of them seemingly in the same direction – and the transports as usual drifting around, somehow just managing not to collide with each other. There were more transports than they'd brought here with them, several of which had arrived quite recently. Cruisers – Enqvist's now fairly substantial body of them – were farther out there, in no clear formation at this moment but all moving seaward, while *Ryazan* with the hospital-ship on her port quarter was simply holding her position. She'd be following astern again, as the *Orel*'s close escort.

Strains of music came thinly across the flat blue water. Michael put his glasses up, in the direction of the *Suvarov*s – and at the same time recognizing the tune as the *Marseillaise*. The flagship's band, for sure – but the tune suggesting a presence of French warships . . . Which he saw now – two white-painted torpedo-boat destroyers, which one had seen around here from time to time and which were now escorting the admiral and his first division out to sea. And the colliers were under way now – ten of them. They'd be steaming in a separate group but in company with the squadron. Rojhestvensky had chanced his arm in that area too – in a big way, at that. The Hamburg-Amerika Line had notified him that they were breaking the terms of their contract, wouldn't send their ships any closer than this to the war zone, and St Petersburg when he called on them for help had failed to respond in any effective way. Nick Sollogub's guess, which he'd mentioned in an undertone one day when he and Michael had been ashore together – playing vint, Russian whist, as it happened, in the *Café de Paris* – was that it might have suited the Naval General Staff to have Rojhestvensky immobilized here at least until Nyebogatov joined him. If that was the case it would mean they'd anticipated some show of independence from Zenovy Petrovich: in fact they'd have been stupid if they hadn't, knowing how he felt about Klado and his crazy theories and the so-called Third Squadron. In any case Rojhestvensky had out-manoeuvred them, negotiated a deal with the German supercargo – the top dog with the collier fleet here on the spot – contracting to *buy* these ten colliers, fully laden, on behalf of the Russian government, and as part of the deal arranging to charter another four – an additional thirty thousand tons – who'd rendezvous with the squadron at Saigon.

Might make them a bit peevish back in St Petersburg, but there they were. They weren't dealing with any simpleton or lickspittle but with a *wild* man – yes, and by now they'd know it. Coaling, anyway, would take place at sea, every four or five days.

Travkov, the grey-headed chief yeoman, paused beside Michael. He was a pleasant fellow and good at his job, exercising a quiet but extremely effective control over his numerous signal staff. One of Zakharov's Black Sea people, he had a wife and three children at Nikolayev and had had a letter from her in every mail that had so far been received on board.

'All right, Chief?'

A nod. 'If I may say so, your honour, it's good that you're still with us. When you don't have to be. An experienced officer, they say, knows a thing or two – must reckon we got a chance.'

'Let's hope he's right.'

A tight smile. 'I'm sure he is, sir.' A moment later Michael heard him reporting to Zakharov, 'Message passed to *Orel*, sir.' Warning her, by semaphore no doubt, that they'd be moving shortly. Michael put his glasses on her, saw that her foc'sl was clear, bridge manned. Still and pretty, her whiteness reflected in the glassy surface. One tended when looking at her and wondering about the girls on board, how they were standing up to the ghastly climate and other hardships, homesickness etc., to think also of Radzianko and his obsessive interest in them: and here and now, of Burmin's recent shark demonstration, which in a way was connected – although not in Burmin's thinking, which would have related only to Radzianko's foolhardy early-morning dips. The circumstances anyway had been that a lot of meat had been going rotten and had had to be ditched, largely because of breakdowns of refrigeration machinery in the transport *Espérance*, and when a whole beef carcase was about to be put over the side, Burmin had sent a message to Radzianko to come up on deck. He – Burmin – obviously recalling exchanges in the wardroom when Galikovsky had been trying to persuade the navigator that there was very little danger, why *not* go swimming; Michael remembered Burmin having intervened in some way, and it must have stuck in his mind so that he made a point of having him up there with him when the stinking mess of a carcase was dragged to the side and levered over by several men with planks. It splashed in, and within seconds sharks were tearing at it, others coming from all directions, dorsal fins scything the surface – and the sea alongside boiling into a red froth, the carcase rolling and jerking this way and that as the frenzied monsters tore hunks and streamers from it.

Burmin had glared at Radzianko. 'Don't ever be such a damn fool again – eh?'

'No.' Radzianko's face filmed with sweat. 'No. My God . . .'

A really huge shark struck then. The size and power of a train-engine – ferocious impact – right alongside, you actually *felt* it – and for a few seconds the enormous creature was half out of water; then submerging in another burst of extraordinary power, taking about a ton of food down with it.

Gone: leaving only the stain and the violently disturbed sea settling. Burmin telling a petty officer, 'Get this deck and the side hosed down, Kostin.'

First night out, the 16th, the squadron was in no sort of formation: a disorganized pack covering a vast area of sea, floundering northward to clear first Cape St Sebastian and then Cape Ambre, the island's northernmost point. Distance to round that point about a hundred and fifty miles; *Ryazan* and the hospital-ship hanging back well astern of the confusion which the admiral must have spent the whole night trying to sort out. Michael had the middle watch, midnight to 0400, Zakharov with him most of the time, as was *Michman* Dukhonin. It was pleasantly cool, after the clammy heat of Nossi-Bé, and there were several heavy downpours of rain which left the ship's iron decks steaming and might eventually have a cooling effect below. Between the rain-spells, a half-moon lit the sea ahead and the squadron's constantly changing shape: ships sometimes dropping back, sometimes closing up and bunching, necessitating quick avoiding-action. There'd been breakdowns right from the start, sometimes total stoppages, sometimes periods of a few hours at five knots or less.

Despite which they were out of the Mocambique Channel by 0800, and the flagship led round to a course of about northeast by east. To pass south of the Seychelles therefore, but north of Peras Banhas, northernmost of the Chagos Archipelago. Which suggested eventually passing around the top of Sumatra into the Malacca Straits. Three thousand miles to that point, say, and then another six hundred or so to Singapore and into the South China Sea.

By two p.m. Madagascar was out of sight. Wind light from the northeast. The squadron gradually acquiring a recognizable formation. What it amounted to – or would amount to when it was completed – was the first division of battleships, the four *Suvarovs*, in line ahead in the van, then the transports with the destroyers on their flanks, and the second ironclad division – *Oslyabya, Sissoy Veliky, Navarin, Nikolai I* and *Admiral Nachimov* – followed by a still shifting pattern of cruisers and auxiliaries. The little that had been committed to paper by Rojhestvensky or his staff indicated that the 'scouting division' – *Svetlana, Kuban, Terek* and *Ural* – would at night take station ahead, with *Zemchug* and *Izumrud* on either beam, and although *Ryazan*'s allotted position was here astern, she'd be detached to investigate any sightings of 'suspicious' vessels coming up astern or from anywhere abaft the beam. It seemed to both Michael and Zakharov that the 'scouting division' was really a screening force; and that much as one might admire Rojhestvensky's strength, willpower, driving force and even fearlessness, his disposition of ships and divisions wasn't all that impressive. Neither was the almost total lack of communication in regard to his intentions, aims and tactics. Even the sketchy orders for deployment for action: battleships in single line ahead with destroyers on either quarter, transports including *Orel* to fall back with auxiliaries as escorts ahead and on the beams, *Ryazan* as division leader with *Oleg* and *Aurora* to take station as scouting/striking force on disengaged side abeam of flagship. That last bit was all right in principle and pleased Zakharov well enough, and there was more stuff about Enqvist's cruisers, but it was all vague – no detail for instance as to the actual methods of re-deployment, which would almost certainly lead to confusion amongst captains who weren't privy to the thinking behind any of it – or much good at handling their ships either.

At 0600 on the 18th orders were given for the destroyers to be taken in tow by the auxiliaries. The primary object was to save fuel: coaling the little destroyers at sea was virtually impossible. Passing the tows took an hour and a half, while all ships lay stopped, and soon after going ahead again –

at about 0900, by which time the formation had gone to pot – the towing hawser of the *Irtysh* parted. Another stop: duration this time, one hour. By mid-forenoon then, having worked up to eight knots, the *Sissoy Veliky*'s steering engine broke down and she sheered out of the line. The squadron lay stopped for an hour, then went ahead again at five knots. Zakharov remarked quietly to Burmin, 'And Nyebogatov's bringing us really *old* ships. Thank God we *are* running away from him.'

Michael began keeping a diary at this stage. With no great amount of detail in it, only notes as memory-aids for use when he came to write his report of proceedings for the Admiralty. Until now it hadn't seemed necessary, especially as the squadron's movements were being tracked by the world's newspapers as well as by the Royal Navy, but as one approached the periphery of the war zone the condition of ships and men might be expected to have some bearing on whatever was to follow.

Typical entries were:

> March 19, forenoon: General Quarters: battle-damage exercises and gunnery training. To be a daily routine from now on. The gunnery exercise is for layers and trainers to familiarize themselves with the telescopic sights, and for control-position personnel to get the hang of the Barr & Strouds. For their benefit the *Aurora, Donskoi, Zemchug, Izumrud, Dniepr* and *Rion* are to manoeuvre on both sides of the battleship divisions, frequently altering course, speed and distance-off. No target practice is possible, since ammo replenishments didn't come, but practice of this kind must be better than nothing. At least, that's what we're all saying.
>
> March 20: Only one stop – when destroyer *Blestyashtchy*'s tow parted. More rotten cordage probably. But a whole day without engine breakdowns! Distance made good

over 24 hours (fixes from one's own stars) 187 miles, giving average 7.8 knots.

March 21: Coaling, using boats. Swell too pronounced for colliers to lie alongside. Always will be in this ocean. Coaling started 0545 and was halted by signal at 1600. Including the time spent rigging gear, squadron was stopped for 13½ hours.

March 24: Various false alarms – false sightings.

And so forth: sketchy record of an armada of dirty, unseaworthy ships fouling sky and sea in its slow crawl northeastward. They coaled again on the 28th with better results – taking only half the time to rig cranes and Temperleys and then achieving a much faster rate of intake. Coaling again 29th. On the 30th, crossing the Line, the wind came up force five from the northwest.

April 5: At 0600, in my watch, *Suvarov*'s lookouts sighted Great Nicobar. Course then altered by 3 degrees to approach Malacca Straits between Great Nic and Rondo and Brasse islands. Entered straits soon after noon.

You could smell the land, and both temperature and humidity rose considerably. A change in formation was ordered, for the passage of the strait, not only for the obvious reason – its narrowness – but also because of the same old fears of ambush by Japanese torpedo boats. Cruisers *Zemchug* and *Izumrud* became the vanguard, with the destroyers – under their own power now – close astern of them. Auxiliaries and transports were sandwiched in the middle in two columns with the battleship divisions on either side and cruisers also in two columns bringing up the rear. Michael, who'd been here before, guessed that the battleships and transports forming the thick midriff of the procession were going to have to thin themselves out fairly drastically when they got to the really narrow stretch lower down. Even up here in the funnel-shaped entrance, in the Sumatran inshore waters whole groves of fishermen's stakes were proof that those weren't so much shallows as mudflats; the shallows extended between here and there.

Diary again . . .

April 7: Calm, foggy night. Phony reports of torpedo boats, submarines, God knows what. *Balloons* even! The dangerous nervousness that led to the Dogger Bank fiasco. Passed the One Fathom Bank at 0200.

April 8: Squadron got through the bottleneck between Malacca town and Pulan Rupat with a considerable squeeze and some temporary confusion. Facing even narrower waters 12 hours later though – the Singapore Strait, with Bulang Besar and then Batam Islands to starboard. At 1400 passing Raffles Island with the lighthouse on it. Singapore glittering in the sunlight, open to our view ahead and to port, and the ships ahead of us all listing by a degree or so to port from the weight of their companies all lining the rails on that side. Two British cruisers at anchor in the roads: Z asked me what they were and I was able to tell him *Drake* class – 14,000 tons, main armament of 9-inch plus ten or twelve 6-inch.

Zakharov holding his glasses on them. Radzianko was conning the ship: alert particularly for those ahead suddenly slowing or even stopping, without signal – as had been known to happen often enough. In such narrow waters at this breakneck speed of almost nine knots you needed to react quickly: and what a place this would be for a thorough-going Second Squadron-type mêlée – under the eyes of thousands on shore and especially of those British cruisers. Their bridges and upperworks would be packed, dozens of telescopes and pairs of binoculars trained on the passing armada. Wireless operators would be filling the ether with stuttering Morse, giving the world its first news of the squadron since its departure from Madagascar.

Zakharov muttered, with his glasses still on those cruisers, 'What's in *their* minds, I wonder.'

'Astonishment, probably. I'd guess a modicum of admiration too. No small achievement to have brought a fleet of this size and shape this far. Especially with the coaling problem – which, of course, they all know about.'

'Won't they be laying bets? Ten to one on Togo?'

'A bit of that, I dare say.' You'd get enormous odds if you backed *this* lot, he thought. Training his glasses slowly right, taking in the whole exquisite panorama which they were fouling with their smoke – glittering blue water with a few sampans fishing inshore, rocky headlands, and the heatwaves shimmering. He stopped abruptly: 'Small steamer coming out – steering to intercept—'

'Yes.' A glance round. 'Yeoman—'

'Aye, sir.' Travkov pointed forward. 'But they've seen him.'

A destroyer was moving out at twenty or twenty-five knots to intercept the would-be interceptor. No alert from the rearguard therefore necessary. Travkov had his telescope trained on the steamer – little tug-sized vessel with a high bridge and foc'sl. 'Flying Russian colours, sir!'

He was right. The mercantile ensign – three horizontal bars, white over blue over red, with some sort of badge in one corner.

'What's—'

'Consular flag, sir. Bringing despatches, likely.'

The destroyer was stopping for the consul, if that was who it was, to run alongside her. Or close alongside, for transfer of whatever this was. Despatches telegraphed from St Petersburg, perhaps.

The Japanese consulate would be telegraphing Tokyo, no doubt of *that.*

'Destroyer's the *Byedovy*, sir.' Travkov had made out her pendant numbers. Michael put his glasses back on her, saw her gathering way. Slim, black, two widely spaced funnels, the bridge (or 'compass platform') literally a platform with just a single rail around it, so that the three men on it were visible from head to foot – and in any kind of sea would surely be *soaked* from head to foot. She was returning towards the flagship. *Byedovy* meant 'mischievous'; all the destroyers' names were adjectives.

'Fellow's making for *us* now, sir!'

Radzianko, pointing at the consul's steamboat. Having been stopped for several minutes, lost that much ground, she hadn't a hope of catching up enough to get anywhere near the flagship – which one might guess would have been the consular intention – but might on her present course make it to within hailing distance of the *Ryazan* here at the procession's tail – if that was what was in the man's mind.

'No guns, no torpedo tube . . .'

'*Byedovy* had a much closer look anyway. And *he* wasn't worried.'

'No. All right.' Zakharov glanced astern at the hospital-ship: she was in station, as always. Back then to this consular craft, its tall funnel emitting perfect smoke-rings as it came puttering in on the beam. Zakharov moving over to that side, the bridge wing; *Michman* Egorov passed him the megaphone. The little steamboat had put her helm over now, was swinging parallel to *Ryazan*'s own course: there was someone with a megaphone in her bridge wing too. Tall man wearing a white topee – and having to hold on hard with his free hand, legs straddled, as the little ship bounced over the Second Squadron's combined outspreading wakes.

'Do you hear me?'

Zakharov yelled back an affirmative. 'Hear you well!'

'Pass a message to Admiral Rojhestvensky, please?'

'Certainly!'

'I am the consul-general here. I've given despatches to that destroyer captain, also newspapers. But in case of mishap to them, here's the gist of the latest important news. Ready?'

'Yes.' Glancing at Travkov, who had a pencil poised over his clipboard. Back to the consul-general then: 'Go on!'

'Mukden has fallen! Huge losses of men and material. Kuropatkin has resigned. Listen, now – *most* important –

Japanese cruiser squadron, Admiral Kanimura, was here three days ago, is now we hear *en route* Northern Borneo; and a force of twenty-two Jap ironclads is said to be at Labuan. Finally – still hearing me? – Admiral Nyebogatov's Third Squadron has left Djibouti to join with yours. Sorry to give the terrible news of Mukden, but you'll change our country's fortunes for us now, I'm sure. Good luck to you, and God's blessing!'

Zakharov waved again, and told Travkov, 'By wireless to the admiral. Let me see your draft before you send it.'

'Aye, sir!'

'Gavril Ivan'ich – a word with you.'

Michman Egorov: who was looking sick. His father the colonel of engineers might well have been in the thick of it at Mukden – where Kuropatkin had had his general headquarters. Very likely would have been; but might well not have been among the casualties. After all, he was on the staff, and if Kuropatkin had resigned *he* presumably was alive. Radzianko commented later in the chartroom – in the South China Sea by this time, course northeast by north, and the hook-nosed Tselinyev having relieved him at the binnacle – 'So Mukden's gone. They'll be laying siege to Vladivostok next.'

19

'Four thousand five hundred miles, sir!'

Radzianko to Zakharov – proudly, as if it were *his* achievement. April 14th, 1130; *Ryazan* had just anchored, in Kamranh Bay on the Cochin China Coast. Zakharov's wooden face and hard eyes on Radzianko for a moment: 'Is that the distance since weighing at Nossi-Bé?'

'Just so, sir.' Slightly ingratiating smile: but it was simply the way he *did* smile – was how it seemed to Michael, anyway. Seemed to most people, probably. If not ingratiating, self-satisfied. *Some* quality that irritated: irritation against which one had to guard. Self-conscious might be nearer the mark. Adding now, 'Must be a record, wouldn't you say, for a fleet of this size and composition?'

Zakharov had turned away though, was talking to Chief Yeoman Travkov; Radzianko promptly transferring his gaze to Michael. 'Wouldn't you say?'

In fact it was tragic that they were here at all. Although it had been their official destination, as ordered by St Petersburg in the despatches received off Singapore six days ago, and that particular item conveyed to the rest of them by general signal after Rojhestvensky had had time to digest his various instructions, most of which he would as usual keep to himself. When he'd sprung his surprise on the 12th, stopping to coal in the open sea only sixty miles short of this Kamranh place, it had been evident that he'd decided once again to defy his lords and masters – from that point, after coaling, striking off directly for Vladivostok, surprising not only the Naval General Staff but also Togo. The intention had been fairly obvious: why coal slowly and arduously at sea when you could do it far more quickly and easily a day or two later in harbour – *if* you'd intended going there?

Or waiting for Nyebogatov either. The admiral's resolve was in fact made all the plainer when in the course of coaling he'd initiated a succession of flag signals starting with *Are boilers and machinery in good order for a long passage?* and followed by the crucial *Report exact tonnages of coal on board.*

In *Ryazan*'s wardroom, Murayev had commented, after downing a third jam-jar of *kvass* – he'd been humping sacks of coal around – 'Making direct for Vladivostok, aren't we?'

Galikovsky had nodded cheerfully. 'Does look like it.'

Arkoleyev then, scratching his ginger head: 'Best chance we've got – grab it, is what I say. Eh, Padre?'

Myakishev looked startled: like a boy at the back of the classroom who hadn't been attending. Spaniel's eyes rolling upward to the deckhead: 'Into thy hands, oh Lord . . .'

'Catch Togo at *his* prayers, that's the thing. By the time he's off his knees – *wham*, we're showing him forty clean pairs of heels!'

'Hardly *clean* . . .'

Burmin had come in then – arriving down from the bridge. He'd listened for a moment, then shaken his head.

'Forget it. We're going to Kamranh. The *Alexander*'s short by three hundred tons. Four hundred less than she's been claiming in her morning reports lately.'

When he was giving bad news, or discussing anything of which he disapproved, Burmin had a flat, take-it-or-leave-it way of speaking. He'd added, slamming the words down like dominoes, 'That's taking into account this top-up. But to embark another three hundred tons now, at sea – the devil, two or three days lying stopped here on Togo's doorstep?' He jerked a chair back, dumped himself on it. 'Simply not possible!'

How *im*possible was demonstrated early that afternoon when wireless signals were picked up that didn't conform to any English or Russian code and were coming from a ship or ships that were approaching. An operator could tell that much at once because of the Doppler effect – frequency rising during approach, falling when range was opening. This – or these – was clearly coming towards. Coaling had ceased, boats hosed-out and hoisted, and the squadron got under way, on course for this bay, ships hosing-down *en route.*

Michael wrote in his diary that evening:

> Must be a terrible blow to Rojhestvensky. That might well have been his great chance and brought success – got us past Togo and into Vladivostok. Maybe a scrap on the way, maybe not. Chance lost through one small clerical error at some earlier stage resulting in its repetition in the *Alexander*'s morning reports – routine 0800 signals of fuel and fresh water remaining, number of hands sick and in cells, magazine temperatures and so on. Must have been wrong in all her reports since the last coaling at least, as any sudden discrepancy would have been noticed. For Rojhestvensky, who must be only too painfully aware of having only 4 sound battleships (*more or less* sound) in his squadron, there could be no question of leaving one behind: it must be bitterly disappointing.
>
> The hospital-ship is no longer with us, has been sent into Saigon to replenish stores and will rejoin later.
>
> April 13: Stopped at 0700 off the Pandaran Light. Destroyers sent into Kamranh to search for mines, and picket-boats to mark out the anchorage with buoys.
>
> April 14: 1100, entered Kamranh and anchored. Distance run from Nossi-Bé 4,560 miles, from Kronstadt 16,628. 4 colliers arrived from Saigon – summoned presumably by W/T so wireless silence thereby broken and our presence here known to the world including St P and Togo. Cruisers *Zemchug* and *Izumrud* stationed

at entrance to this bay with searchlights beamed across it throughout the dark hours, destroyers patrolling outside and picket-boats inside. Battleships have rigged anti-torpedo nets.

The colliers had brought mail, which was collected and sorted in the flagship and then delivered around the fleet in steam pinnaces from several of the battleships. Michael had a letter from his mother and one from Jane enclosing news-cuttings collected by William and a letter from Tasha – as always, to be kept to the last and read in private. Mama's, first: expressing concern for his safety, a review of the past weeks' weather, news of George and of his and Jane's children (Johnny, Andrew and Thomas) and of Michael's sister Emma's children (Harriet and Percy) and chat about various friends and neighbours. Death of a second cousin: and more about the danger he was in, his silliness in ignoring her earlier advice not to go to sea with that extraordinary Rojhestvensky person. What Igor could have been thinking of, to have issued such an invitation . . . Jane's now:

As you will see from the enclosures, William has been doing his best despite being on Christmas holidays now – hunting like mad, also shooting rather well, so Mary tells us – so his days must be quite full. The surrender of Port Arthur is very bad news for you, I imagine – obviously, must be. We scan *The Times* daily for news of your squadron and Rogersvosky, who by all accounts has been making great (surprising?) progress – but to what end, eventually? Prophets and pundits here are to a man utterly depressing on that score. Why don't you jump ship somewhere, Michael? Is that the right expression? Very seriously, though – and I may say George and your mother agree with me, I've told them I'm writing to you and they both say *please* get ashore at the first opportunity, even if you have to *swim* home! Seriously, Michael dear – we are *so* worried for you. Can it be that you're the only living person who doesn't realize how fraught with danger the whole thing is? Well, perhaps you *are* ashore somewhere by now, or in some ship coming home – we pray to God that you may be – but if not, I *implore* you

News cuttings:

Tsar (spelt for some reason 'Czar') Offers Liberalizing Reforms but Warns that Strikes and Riots Must Stop (December 26th).

Fall of Port Arthur. Japanese Conditions Accepted. Forts and Ships Blown Up (*The Times*, January 3rd).

Bloody Sunday: Tsar's Troops Kill 500 (January 22nd).

Grand Duke Killed by Bomb Dropped in his Lap (February 17th).

200,000 Russians Routed at Mukden (March 10th).

That was the latest. The bulk of the enclosures were about Port Arthur. There was an excellent map from the *Daily Telegraph* and a mass of detail, mostly quoting Japanese military sources. The 'Bloody Sunday' item included a photograph – troops in foreground and the crowd in background, scattering; it must have been taken from an upstairs window in the Winter Palace. The Grand Duke was – had been – Sergei, an uncle of the Tsar's, and the assassination had taken place in Moscow as his carriage was passing through the Kremlin gates. The bomb, filled with nails, had torn the Grand Duke into 'unrecognisable pieces of flesh' and parts of the carriage were found two hundred yards away. The Tsar, when told of it in his Winter Palace in St Petersburg, went white and bowed his head in silence for some moments; exclaimed finally 'But how can that be? Everything is so quiet – the strikes are ceasing, the excitement is subsiding. Whatever do they want?'

Tasha had written from Yalta on March 5th – Michael read it in the heads:

Michael, my precious love – I've received your letter

in which you insist you have to 'see it through' and while there's nothing I can do other than accept that this is what you *will* do I must admit that what you are inflicting on me is the worst imaginable ordeal. I love you, my darling, you are *everything* to me, and in taking this decision you seem to spurn that devotion. The news is so bad from everywhere; the loss of Port Arthur for instance, then that horrible business in St Petersburg in front of the Winter Palace, more recently the murder of Grand Duke Sergei – and the continuing students' and peasants' riots everywhere. While what the newspapers say is the bloodiest battle ever is being fought at Mukden – to the south of Vladivostok which is where *you* are going – or so you tell me! Such a catalogue of woes, and it's so frightening! Mama says it was ever so – in respect of your decision not to leave the squadron, this is – as you admit you *could* do quite easily – she says men's minds are invariably set on winning honour and glory in the cannon's mouth, and that this blinds them to the hideous consequences of defeat – which their women have then to endure alone in far more sustained and bitter suffering, while the men have gone happily to blazes – 'so many little dancing flames snuffed out and knowing no more about it'. Mama is of course still afflicted by the tragedy of losing the man *she* loved; she perhaps over-emphasizes a little, but please, darling Mikhail, save *me* from that fate. Think again, change your mind? It would be no dishonour – it's neither your war nor your navy! Today is Sunday and we've just returned from mass; I don't have to tell you the subject of my prayers, whether in church or here at home. Oh, my love, I suspect you won't yield to any of my entreaties, so what I'm really praying for is a miracle – that a day will come when I *do* receive your telegram. – I'll *fly*.

'This paragraph here, for instance.' Showing it to Zakharov, with all the other cuttings, although there was nothing much in any of them that was really news; it was only that Zakharov had said he'd like to see whatever Jane sent him. Michael had translated some bits – samples – and Zakharov had had to tell him he'd had virtually all of it before this, from his own family's letters. This was on the evening of the arrival of the mail.

'What's that one about, then?'

It was one of the cuttings about the surrender of Port Arthur and its aftermath. Michael read from *The Times* of January 14th: '"Our Correspondent with General Nogi. There are no signs of privation in Port Arthur. There was food sufficient for two months, and the surrender is inexplicable. It is attributed to want of ammunition, loss of the warships, the death of the real defender of the fortress – General Kondrachenko, who was killed on December 18th – the severity of the Japanese artillery fire, and the difficulty of maintaining order among the workmen in the fortress. The Japanese casualties—"'

Zakharov stopped him. 'Rations for two months. *And* knowing we were on our way. I take the point about the *real* defender. Meaning that Stossel was *not.* Another of the same, Mikhail Ivan'ich?'

'Well – thank you . . .'

'The same' being vodka, one hundred per cent proof. Again, under the calm and candid gaze of Irina in her silver frame. 'But there's this little report too – for what it's worth. *The Times* again, but quoting the New York *Evening Sun* as saying: "But for the connivance of French colonial administrations and contributory negligence or worse by the French government, Rojhestvensky would not be in any position to offer battle to the Japanese. Our own naval authorities are inclined to the belief however that Admiral Togo will relieve US naval commanders on the spot of all responsibility".'

'For the protection of the Philippine Islands' territorial waters, I suppose they mean.' Zakharov shrugged. 'In which we're hardly likely to intrude in any case. They're backing Togo anyway.'

'That's how I read it.'

'But who *isn't*. We're entirely on our own, aren't we? Look, help yourself, Mikhail. Here – mine too, if you would. The French have done very nicely out of us, of course. Everything we've eaten or drunk, just about – including all the squadron's wardrooms' brandy and champagne. While also seeming to toe your English line by forbidding us their harbours. Clever swine – eh?'

'And the Germans – how many millions of roubles' worth of rotten coal?'

'Indeed. And the damn students all over Russia demanding an end to the war. We *are* on our own. You got a few letters as well with these cuttings, did you?'

A nod: busy with the vodka. 'As you did yourself, I see.' On the desk, a scattering of them. He passed Zakharov his refilled tumbler. In the wardroom so many glasses had been broken – in rough weather, but in boisterous, glass-smashing toasts as well – that they were drinking mainly out of jam-jars and caviar-pots. 'Your health, Nikolai Timofey'ich.'

'And yours. Did you hear from Natasha Igorovna, by any chance?'

'What? When?'

'I withdraw the question. One should not embarrass one's guests. You don't want to be put in the position of having to tell me how much she abhors the prospect of becoming my wife. But I would like to write to her. She and her mother were going to Yalta, I remember Prince Igor told me – while *he* couldn't afford to spend any longer away from Petersburg, was wishing he'd made everyone else go there instead of to Injhavino – for which, of course, the reason was that Injhavino is what in his mind and Prince Ivan's the whole business was about. But now with the riots there've been in that part of the country, I doubt he'd have countenanced their return to Injhavino – the women's, I mean. I could write to her in care of *him*, I suppose—'

'I know the address of Anna Feodorovna's house in Yalta. I spent a holiday there once.'

'Might be better. Yes . . . Something about Prince Igor deters me. Despite his generosity, the power of his influence—'

'I thought he was counting on *your* generosity.'

'Ah. That's the other side of the coin, isn't it? But she *is* in Yalta – is she?'

Face not wood, but granite. Eyes like chips of glass. Michael nodded. 'Where they were going, certainly. If you addressed a letter there it would find her, anyway. But I was reflecting on what you didn't *quite* say about her father. Personally I wouldn't trust him further than I could spit.'

'But *I*, you see, am already in his debt – for this command and my promotion.'

'We've had a conversation before very much like this one, haven't we? Outside Angra Pequena, one evening.'

A nod: 'But you're in his debt too. We touched on that as well – to the extent that you were prepared to go into it, which wasn't very far. But I've given thought to it since, and my conclusion is that being aware of your closeness to his daughter and disapproval of our betrothal, he might have wanted to be rid of your influence on her during my own absence. How does that strike you as a theory?'

'It's – possible. He's wily enough to have known I wouldn't turn such an offer down. Although I'd have been returning right away to my own naval service, wouldn't have been – hanging around, exactly . . .'

A long stare. He'd relaxed a bit, though. Granite reverting to wood, eyes less harsh. A small jerk of the head: 'Actually – in the short term anyway – the least of our worries – eh?'

'I suppose . . .'

'But I'd like to – as it were – make myself known to her. And *not* through her father. That's all. After all, the situation facing us here and now – well . . .'

'Not good, is it?'

'Not *good* at all. Although, as I remember we were saying before, luck *can* change. And Zenovy Petrovich—'

'I was going to ask – is he not receiving visitors?'

'Apparently not. I had a personal message from the chief of staff, together with some official stuff. The admiral is holed up, licking his wounds. That was a savage blow to him, the *Alexander* business. We'd have been well on our way now.'

'Two thousand six hundred miles.'

'To Vladivostok?'

'The shortest route – through the Korea Strait.'

'And if we'd taken Togo by surprise – as we might have done, seeing he must know we've been ordered to wait here – well, imagine it! Sudden appearance of Rojhestvensky's squadron off Vladivostok!'

'And the war *not* lost. Through the initiative of one man – Zenovic Petrovich Rojhestvensky. Is it too late for him to make that move now, d'you think?'

'A bit late, yes. By this time Togo will have deployed his fleet as far as possible to ensure we don't slip past him. He knows he's *got* to stop us. If we did make Vladivostok, everything could change dramatically in our favour. Offensive operations, putting him on the defensive; and they're not a great or rich nation, you know, as we are; our resources are infinitely greater. Now – come on, one more. Tell me, though – when you were last up here and I introduced you to –' a nod towards the portrait, as he reached over with his empty glass – 'Irina there – I had the impression you were shocked?'

'Surprised.'

'So. Another question. As big brother to Natasha—'

'Tasha.' Clink of the neck of the bottle on his host's glass. 'All her close friends – which should include her fiancé—'

'The point is it doesn't. I'd like to *make* friends with her. While there's time – so we'd have known each other just a little . . . My question to you – big brother – would you expect me, at the age of forty-four – in fact rising forty-five – to have had no previous romantic involvements?'

'Of course not.'

'Well, I'm glad to hear it.'

'Here.'

'Thank you.'

'It's your vodka. No – certainly not, you wouldn't be fit to know!'

'That's true, I wouldn't. Of course, a *bride* should be a virgin . . .'

On the 15th the *Orel* rejoined, after her visit to Saigon. The squadron had begun coaling early that morning, and there was speculation as to whether Rojhestvensky might make his move when it was concluded. Nothing had been seen or heard of him since they'd anchored, but Selyeznov had told Zakharov of a terse exchange of signals with St Petersburg, opening with Rojhestvensky reporting *Have arrived Kamranh Bay, awaiting orders,* the Naval Staff then replying *Remain until arrival of Third Squadron and please keep informed of movements* – which when you thought about it amounted to a rebuke – to which the admiral had riposted *I will not telegraph again before the battle. If I am beaten, Togo will inform you. If I beat him, I will let you know.*

Which seemed to leave it open: he *might* make an early move. But also on the 15th, a French cruiser, the *Descartes,* arrived with a Rear-Admiral de Jonquières on board, and Rojhestvensky interrupted what seemed to have been a brief hibernation in order to receive him. The visit was entirely amicable, apparently; the French were delighted to have their Russian friends here and would gladly supply them with whatever they might need. The *Descartes* left after only a few hours, returning to her base at Nhatrang Bay, twenty miles north of Kamranh.

Ryazan's collier berthed on her at dawn on the 16th and coaling was completed by nightfall, the collier moving from her to the *Orel,* who was again her nearest neighbour. On the same day a steamer, the *Eridan,* arrived from Saigon with a cargo of fresh provisions, mainly cabbage, enabling the ships' companies to return to their standard diet of cabbage soup. There were quite a few supply ships coming in.

Michael's diary entries at this stage included:

April 18: Battleships and *Aurora* to sea, to swing compasses and cover departure of empty colliers to Saigon where they are to embark Cardiff coal. They are escorted by *Kuban*, *Terek* and *Ural*. To protect them from Jap cruisers who are rumoured to be cruising in the vicinity, keeping watch on us or looking out for Nyebogatov. Nothing more than rumour though. In any case the Japanese know where we are and will most likely be informed by the local telegraph station (run by an Annamese) when we do make any substantial move.

April 19: Scraping ship's waterline from boats – whaler, gig and skiff, using all kinds of implements including coal shovels. Some but not all other ships doing the same, having seen or heard of us doing it. There's a fresh breeze but inside here it's flat.

April 20: Battleships and others including the 3 auxiliaries who went to Saigon are back and coaling. They left the colliers at Saigon and saw nothing of the enemy.

April 21: Return of de Jonquières, announcing sadly that French govt demand immediate departure of Russian ships from French territorial waters. Rojhestvensky has 24 hours in which to remove himself. Comment by Zakharov: 'If Kuropatkin had given General Oyama a hiding at Mukden, rather than the other way about, the frogs'd be singing a very different tune!'

Working-parties at it all night shifting stores out of transports *Tambov* and *Mercury* and other steamers who've brought provisions recently from Saigon.

April 22: 24 hours' notice expired 1300. All ironclads weighed and left harbour. Auxiliaries and *Orel* left in their berths – by agreement with de Jonquières presumably.

There has been a meeting of flag and commanding officers on board *Suvarov* and copies of various Orders of the Day were lent to me by Zakharov on his return. They detail at some length Rojhestvensky's plans for action offshore and inshore in the event of our being attacked here at Kamranh either by surface vessels or submarines. The orders are not very clear: in fact are pretty well certain to lead to a high degree of confusion if any attempt is made to put them into effect . There's a lot about inshore defence: picket-boats (steam pinnaces and cutters) being armed with torpedoes – 'in order to attack in the entrance of the bay, not revealing their presence until the last moment'. *What* last moment? And how become invisible?

NB Statement by Rojhestvensky at the meeting, as quoted by Zakharov from his own notes: 'My orders are to wait for Nyebogatov. I shall wait. I will endeavour to maintain telegraphic communication with St Petersburg through Saigon. I shall wait until we have just enough coal left to take us to Vladivostok. If Nyebogatov has not arrived by then, we go on without him. Forward! Always forward!'

Rojhestvensky took the squadron to sea on April 22nd, but as soon as de Jonquières in the *Descartes* was out of sight he turned north and entered another commodious bay, Van Phong. Unfortunately a little steamer which called there only once a month did so that same day, so the secret was out and the *administrateur* from Nahtrang arrived on May 2nd, having trekked overland to deliver notice to quit. Meanwhile Easter had been celebrated, on the 30th – services in all ships, eggs and cakes and a splendid evening meal at which Narumov and Sollogub were present on board *Ryazan* as Michael's guests.

Michael's diary read:

May 3: Sailed from Van Phong. De Jonquières present

in cruiser *Guichen* – bigger than the *Descartes.* Warned that he'd be cruising down-coast to ensure departure was final and permanent.

May 4: Re-entered Kamranh. Anchored in previous berth. Semaphore from *Orel* 'Welcome back'. Comment by Radzianko, 'No sharks here, either.' Smirking, but no one taking notice. Sole purpose of the remark being to remind us all what an intrepid fellow he is. The tug *Rus* with Selyeznov in command is being sent with flagship's assistant navigator (Nikolai Sollogub?) to investigate alternative bays (a) large enough to accommodate the squadron, (b) having no telegraph facility, (c) in which ships at anchor not visible from seaward. As they certainly are here. Defensive measures are as before – searchlights illuminating the entrance, destroyers patrolling outside (despite typhoon warning) and armed pinnaces/cutters patrolling inside. Reasonable: the whole world knows we're here, Japs might well try sneak attack.

May 6: Selyeznov returned, allegedly recommending Port Dayotte as suitable in all respects except not fully surveyed or charted.

May 8: News by telegraph via Saigon that Nyebogatov passed Singapore 0400/5th. *Rion, Zemchug, Dniepr* and *Izumrud* despatched to meet him.

Burmin argued in the wardroom that evening that it was a waste of coal. 'Why meet him? Find his way here, can't he?'

'You have a point.' Zakharov was dining with them. There was a French red wine, a Burgundy, which even out of jam-jars wasn't bad. The trouble with reds, of course, was that in shipboard conditions they never got the rest they needed. 'But if it's going to take him a day or two to get here, and this Frenchman kicks us out again before that – might need the wireless link.'

'It's humiliating.' Burmin again. 'Harried from pillar to damn post!'

'Petersburg's doing, not ours. The admiral's carrying out his orders as best he can, that's all. If you want to fulminate at anyone, Pyotr Fedor'ich, revile Klado – and those members of the Naval Staff who've listened to him.'

'They *all* must have, surely.'

'I dare say. Toadying to—' He'd checked, shaken his head. 'Never mind.'

Meaning, Michael realized, toadying to the Tsar – who, according to Sollogub, was one of Klado's admirers.

'When Nyebogatov does get here – ' this was Murayev – 'd'you anticipate we'll sail immediately, sir?'

A shrug. 'Can't see what would keep us here. Except he'll need to coal his ships and perhaps make repairs.' Zakharov drained his glass. 'I'm for my bunk. No – no brandy. Talking too much as it is. Goodnight, Pyotr Fedor'ich. Mikhail Ivan'ich . . .' On their feet, moving together towards the door, Michael said quietly, 'Prince Ivan must be one of those who've backed Klado.'

'Don't I know it. Don't I *know* it.' Voice up again: 'Goodnight, gentlemen . . .'

Radzianko was saying to Murayev: 'So we'll be off quite soon. At last – getting on with it!'

'As you say – at last.' Engineer Lieutenant Arkoleyev put down his jar. 'Long enough bloody *contemplating* it, let's get it over with!'

'All bets placed.' Paymaster Lyalin – ignoring the engineer's mime of the cutting of his own throat. Shrugging his thin shoulders: thin-voiced too. '*Rien ne va plus* – huh?'

'Reminds me. ' Burmin was trimming a cigar. 'Who's for baccarat?'

Michael, sleeping on deck – the flagdeck, a longer haul for Shikhin with his mattress, and under a blanket because even this close to the equator, twelve degrees north of it, the nights were still cool – was woken in the small hours by what he took to be the explosion of a signal rocket: which would have meant a 'for exercise' night alarm, such as the admiral had been fond of initiating, in earlier stages. One rocket meaning 'for exercise', a practice, two meaning the real thing, an attack on the ships in harbour. But what in the moment of waking seemed like that second *crack* of the alarm was in fact the start of a whole fusillade of rifle-fire. Shouts as well as shots were carrying across the slightly choppy water of the anchorage, and the outfall from searchlights was blinding, while nearer the bay's entrance – astern, beyond the other cruisers, but close enough, in this location one was helping to shield the battleships from say torpedo-boat attack – a quick-firing gun had opened up. Four-pounder maybe: but only three, four rounds, then finished. Whatever it was was much closer at hand – and not easy to get a view, or even move, flagdeck and bridge filling rapidly with others blundering around straight out of sleep and shouting questions, as uninformed as he was. Zakharov too, bursting out of his cabin – in pyjamas, whereas Michael was in a singlet and once-white drill trousers – and Burmin leaping from his mattress in the forefront of the bridge, a quite startling apparition in a long nightshirt and a nightcap with a tassle on it.

Michael had some sort of view of what had to be the scene of action now, from the starboard rail of the flag-deck; the *Orel*'s port side brightly though indirectly lit by searchlight beams reflected off the water, one could see men moving on her promenade deck: it had nothing to do with her though – something in the water between here and there – small boat? Didn't seem to be any attack in progress, anyway. Hard to make out in all that dazzle – here, and from the barrage of light across the entrance. There was a boat of some kind, though – stopped now but must have come from – well, seaward. *Ryazan* and *Orel* and all the others were lying with their sterns towards the entrance: the way the ebbing tide had swung them. That boat – weighted over by a body humped over its gunwale on this side, closer to its bow than stern, and one oar cocked blade-up, the rower having collapsed across the loom of it.

One could see much more clearly now the searchlight beams had shifted. The boat slowly turning – effect of wind on its up-slanting stern – as well as being carried seaward on the tide. And now – leaning out and looking to his left where a signalman was pointing, shouting in some language that wasn't Russian – one of the guard-boats, steam pinnace, in sight fine on *Ryazan*'s bow. Having crossed it from port to starboard about half a cable's length ahead? Under helm, and at about full speed, half a dozen men on its forepart crouching with rifles half up as if ready to fire again. You could visualize it now: as they'd cleared *Ryazan*'s bow they'd have spotted the boat coming apparently from seaward, the bay's entrance; might have hailed it, might not – depending on what they'd thought it was – before opening fire. At sea-level there'd have been some dazzle-effect, in otherwise total darkness, from that searchlight barrier – low down there, could have been quite blinding. There was another boat in sight now though – steam-cutter – maybe *Ryazan*'s own, from her boom which was on the port side aft, not visible from here. It had rounded the stern and would get there before the other did. Would have been called away by the officer of the watch: duty boat on stand-by. Michael's glasses were in the chartroom, hanging with Radzianko's. Turning to go quickly for them, he came face to face with Burmin – the broad, heavily whiskered face under that silly-looking nightcap – protection of bald head from mosquitoes, maybe, although mosquitoes hadn't been much in evidence in this place. Burmin glaring, wide-eyed: rasping, 'God almighty, you don't think—'

Telepathy. One's mind instantly jumping to the same – not conclusion, *possibility*. Resisting it just as instantly: that fat lump would be in there, snoring – on the couch he'd slept on in enviable comfort ever since Dakar. Please God, he would . . . Wrenching at the door and shoving it open with a shoulder – it had always stuck a bit. Insisting or pleading – the words in one's brain, maybe on one's lips – he *must* be . . .

Was not, though. As maybe for the last two or three seconds one had *known* he wouldn't be. Burmin was there for a moment; then cursing, blundering back out, roaring, 'Radzianko? Anyone seen Lieutenant *Radzianko*?'

20

Ryazan's steam cutter had got to the skiff well ahead of the *Borodino*'s pinnace – from which the shots had been fired, killing Radzianko stone dead and splintering the washstrake and gunwale at the boat's stem. The cutter's crew had recognized the dead man and brought him back – in the skiff still, under tow – while the pinnace lay off until called alongside, for its coxswain to come on board and give his version of the events of the previous ten or fifteen minutes. Radzianko's body had been carried into the quartermaster's lobby and there inspected by Surgeon Lieutenant Baranov, who'd formally pronounced him dead – from a bullet in the back of his skull – while Padre Myakishev crouched beside him imploring the Lord to have mercy on his soul.

Zakharov conducted an inquiry there and then, in the ship's office. *Ryazan*'s steam cutter meanwhile taking over the guardboat duty. It was now two-forty, on the morning of May 9th. What was established first was that the skiff was *Ryazan*'s, had been secured at the boom from where Radzianko must have taken it without attracting the notice either of the officer of the watch (*Michman* Vortzin) and his gangway staff or of the sentry on the foc'sl, a seaman by name of Umnov – who admittedly had been some distance away, *Ryazan*'s length being four hundred and thirty-six feet. The sixteen-foot skiff was one of the boats that had been in sporadic use scraping the ship's waterline; it was a sailing skiff but had no mast shipped or any other gear – even rudder – other than a pair of oars and two shovels. Radzianko, in shirt and trousers, barefoot, must have crept out along the flat-topped boom, climbed down the dangling white-painted wooden-runged rope ladder, cast off and allowed the tide to take the boat clear of the ship's stern before he took up oars and started rowing. Whether he'd got to the *Orel* or not – to her boom, which was aft on her starboard side, would have meant pulling across the strong tide and then turning up into it after rounding her stern, or whether he'd only got out to some point between the two ships where he'd been combatting the tide, or trying to, when the guardboat crossing *Ryazan*'s bow had come in sight of him – mistaking the skiff for a torpedo-boat or surfaced submarine coming in from outside – with that curtain of light behind it, to the pinnace's crew it would have been no more than a dark *something* powering in, having to pass through the cruiser anchorage to reach the battleships, which would have been any incursor's first choice of target . . .

'Were you able to see which way it was moving – left to right, or right to left?'

The guardboat's coxswain, a Petty Officer Mrakvintsev from the *Borodino*, shook his close-shaven head. 'Bashing straight in, your honour. Stern to the searchlights at the entrance. None of us doubted that's where it come from.'

'Don't you think it would have been spotted in that lighted entrance?'

'Could've been a submarine, your honour, surfaced when it was inside like.'

'Yes. It could. But as we now know, wasn't. The question is whether he'd come from this ship or from the *Orel*.'

'Does it matter, sir?'

Michael, quietly: Zakharov glancing at him – in surprise at first, then getting the point. He'd asked Michael to be present as one who'd spent a lot of time with Radzianko, especially in the bridge and chartroom.

'Perhaps not. Indeed. Since there was no alarm given from

– any other ship. And no complaint laid now – so presumably no sort of incident on board. No – I dare say it may not.'

There was a degree of urgency in any case. First, a signal from *Suvarov* asking what the shooting and searchlight display had been about, and second, some unintelligible signal had been intercepted at midnight addressed to the *Nikolai I* from the *Vladimir Monomakh*, both of them belonging to Nyebogatov's contingent. The *Nikolai* was in fact Nyebogatov's flagship, and the *Monomakh* an armoured cruiser which had started life under sail. The message had been unreadable because of poor reception by the Slaby-Arco W/T gear, but still suggested they couldn't be all that far distant – although nothing had been heard from the four ships who'd been sent out to meet them.

Zakharov was going to have to report on this Radzianko affair to Rojhestvensky in any case; and since it looked as if they'd be weighing anchor not long after first light, the sooner the inquiry was concluded the better.

'So what we have is this.' Zakharov was making a pencil sketch of it on a signal-pad. '*Ryazan* here. *Orel* here on her quarter. Radzianko must have taken the skiff from the boom here – for whatever reason, which is not established – found the ebb carrying him away as soon as he cast off, and it was more than he could cope with. He was not in very good condition – would you say?'

Baranov concurred. 'Overweight, sir. I believe *you* told him to eat less or take more exercise – he mentioned it when I made a similar observation. Which was when he started his morning dips, as he called them, in shark-infested waters.'

'In any case, he wasn't up to it. He was stemming the tide, very likely pulling as hard as he could, when you – Mrakvintsev – crossed our bows and spotted what you thought was an enemy infiltrating from seaward and at speed – which in the tideway I concede it would have looked like – and you opened fire. In accordance with your orders, and incidentally with impressive accuracy.'

'Couple of them lads, Sprokin and Kollyayev, is real marksmen, your honour.'

Radzianko's good luck, Michael thought. Far better dead than wounded – than unharmed, even. Radzianko in one of the *Suvarov*'s punishment cells would have been neither a pretty sight nor a happy man. Zakharov, who'd been sitting on the paymaster's desk, was on his feet, pocketing the pencil sketch.

'All right. Deeply regrettable as it is, the circumstances are clear enough. Despite the tragic outcome, Mrakvintsev, I'll recommend that your prompt and effective action should be recognized. If it *had* been an enemy, as you had reason to believe, you'd have scuppered him.'

'Very much obliged, your honour. But I'm very, *very* sorry—'

'He should not have been where he was. A somewhat eccentric character, of course. But that's all there is to it.' A nod. 'Your pinnace is lying-off, isn't it, so – carry on, please. Pyotr Fedor'ich, wait a minute. You too, Mikhail Ivan'ich. Padre . . .'

'Yes . . .'

'You had something to tell us.'

'To tell *you*, sir. A matter very personal to the deceased.'

'These two officers can hear it. Both have concerned themselves with him, to some extent. As I have – and if I'm to write to his father – as I must—'

'That's very much the point, captain.' Sad brown eyes wandered from face to face: then glanced at the door, and Burmin moved to push it shut. Myakishev thanked him with an inclination of the head, told them, 'Viktor Vasil'ich confided to me some weeks ago that he had become estranged from his family. Some misdemeanour which had been attributed to him – unjustly, I do believe.' A sniff. Dabbing at his nose and eyes with a dirty-looking cloth from his sleeve. 'His father had forbidden him the house and was taking steps to disinherit him. This was when he volunteered – indeed, made determined efforts to join the squadron. He managed to get an introduction to Captain Clapier de Colongue, who at first regretted there was no vacancy for a navigator, then—'

'Passed him on to me when my own choice of navigator got himself crippled by a horse. Padre, this explains a great deal. Thank you.'

'Burial—'

'Probably at sea. I'll let you know. Today even, or tomorrow. But in the circumstances as you describe them I shall *not* write to his family. Since we're virtually certain to be going into battle very soon now.' A glance at Burmin, who nodded. Zakharov looked at Michael. 'However it turns out, we're not likely to get off scot-free. Could be dozens of fathers and mothers to write to. That is, for *someone* to write to. Uh?'

Narumov came on board before it was fully light. There'd been a collision the evening before between two of the destroyers, the *Bezuprechny* and the *Grozhny*, both of which had put into Port Dayotte, and another destroyer currently outside on defensive patrol was going to take him there to assess the degree of damage and organize repairs. *Ryazan* was handy for him as a stopover while waiting for this other one to come in, and he and Michael shared an early breakfast in the otherwise empty wardroom. Zakharov had already gone over to the flagship: and Narumov was eager to know about the shooting in the early hours. It might in fact have been what he'd come for, he could just as easily have waited on board *Suvarov* – and Michael told him it had been nothing, a trigger-happy guardboat shooting at – 'God knows, Pavel Vasil'ich. The moon, perhaps.'

'The moon set early last night. Midnight or not long after.'

'Nonsense. You're fabricating. There was cloud-cover for an hour or two, but—'

'There was no moon on the night those others were engaged in funny business with one of the young ladies from the *Orel*, either – when we were off Gabon.'

'You think that's in some way relevant?'

A snort. Reaching for the bowl of sour cream. 'If it's not, where's your friend Radzianko?'

'Why? D'you want to see him?'

'Cagey swine. They say, don't they, when an Englishman's taking pains to look sincere, watch your back?'

'*Who* says that?'

'Why, everyone! Throughout history!'

'Have you been overworking, Pavel?'

'Certainly I have. I work twice as hard as anyone else in *Suvarov,* I can tell you!' He shrugged. 'Except perhaps for the admiral – at certain times, when he hardly eats or sleeps – and our captain. He's magnificent – you know?'

'Ignatzius. In what way? I like him, certainly – jolly sort of fellow, but—'

'No "but" about it. He lives life to the full and he believes implicitly in Almighty God and all the saints. How is this all to end? he asks. For me personally – or for any or all of us – what, a shell, torpedo, poison gases, wounds, suffocation, drowning? We'll do our duty, that's all, the rest is in *His* hands, he says. And *laughs* – you know? While on one thing he's deadly serious, insists absolutely – when he's telling his second-in-command and senior lieutenants who'll succeed to the command when he himself is killed, he says, "If this ship's going to sink, so be it, *let* her damn well sink but before she does just see to it the admiral's moved elsewhere. Without him, we'd be lost, he's the one who'll get us through all this – our mainspring, huh? So you lads look after him, *cherish* him, eh?" And he means it – doesn't even crack a smile!'

'I do remember he laughed a lot.'

'He's a man who loves life and through his faith does not fear death. That's his secret.'

'Do you fear death, Pavel?'

'I don't have time to think about it. I suppose if I did have, I would . . . What about you, though – who don't need to be here at all? Why *are* you? An Englishman, God's sake!'

'I *am* here, that's all. *Was* here, and – stayed on. Tell me – how's Flagmansky?'

'Well, that's another thing – he's very much the captain's dog, now. Follows him everywhere – even stays with him on the bridge! Infuriates the admiral when he parks his great turds up there – they have to keep a shovel handy, follow him around. Skipper just about splits his sides whenever it happens – when the admiral's anywhere near he has to stuff his handkerchief into his mouth to stifle it. I hear these things from Nikolai Sergei'ich, I might say.'

'Sollogub.'

'Sollogub, indeed. Our good friend the count. Spends most of his waking life on the bridge – keeps his ear to the wind too. Have you heard yet, by the way, that Admiral Felkerzam has had a stroke, they aren't sure he'll recover?'

'No. I'm sorry. Not that I've ever met him.'

'Keep *this* to yourself, Mikhail Ivan'ich. If he dies, Zenovy Petrovich has decreed that his flag in the *Oslyabya* is not to be struck. His spirit will sail on. Nikolai Sergei'ich has a suspicion that it may be because the next senior in succession would be Nyebogatov – whom as a matter of principle our Zenovy detests, of course.'

'Command would pass to a dead man, then?'

A shrug. 'Could be in worse hands, couldn't it?'

Narumov wasn't on board for long; the torpedo-boat *Bodry* which had been detailed to take him to Port Dayotte came in from sea at about six, lay between *Ryazan* and *Orel* while he was transferred to her by whaler, then backed out, turned and headed for the entrance at about twenty-five knots, fortunately well enough over to starboard to avoid collision with the *Guichen* which, under an enormous French ensign and with Rear-Admiral de Jonquières on board, came forging in at the same time, pitching over the rollers created in the entrance by the speeding destroyer's bow-wave. The Frenchman was anchored close to *Suvarov* by six-thirty, and within a few minutes *Suvarov* diplomatically – or pusillanimously, some might have said – hoisted the signal to weigh anchor. Cables were already being shortened-in when *Ryazan*'s steam cutter left the flagship and chuffed under the *Guichen*'s stern on its way back to drop Zakharov at his own gangway, the boat then being swung aboard on the main derrick, which under Burmin's direction had been trained out ready and waiting for it. The whaler was simultaneously being hoisted, other boats including the damaged skiff already inboard in their respective davits. The cable's rhythmic clanking ceased as Zakharov reached the quarterdeck and Burmin saluted him, taking his cue from that cessation of sound: 'Shortened-in, sir, cable's up and down.'

'Very well. Weigh anchor.'

He went straight up to the bridge. From that wooden face of his you couldn't tell how it had gone between him and the admiral. Burmin went on up after him, having sent a messenger running for'ard with that order to Vetrov. The capstan began turning again, cable links crashing as regularly as drumbeats over the rim of the hawse. Michael was on the bridge, ready to perform any of Radzianko's functions if he should be called upon to do so. To be going on with, he had the chart of this stretch of coast ready on the bridge chart-table, with all essential adjuncts. Meeting Nyebogatov was obviously to be the primary objective, but then what? Back to Kamranh, or to one of the other bays, while the new arrivals fuelled?

Zakharov, arriving in the bridge, looked round for Michael – beckoned to him; Burmin arriving at the same time, moving to the forefront, megaphone in hand, to glare down over the glass screen at the cable party on the foc'sl. Zakharov telling Michael quietly, 'The admiral offered me a replacement for Radzianko from one of the three navigating officers he has on his staff. He said he'd be delighted to get rid of one. I told him I already had one. Was I right?'

'I'm honoured, sir.'

'Good. I was taking a bit of a chance, but – ' a nod – 'yes, good.'

'Want me to take her out, sir?'

'No, I'll do it. But – thank you. I hope you won't regret it.'

'I'm sure I won't, sir.'

'Anchor's aweigh!'

Burmin looked back, checking that his skipper had heard that. And now the next report in natural sequence: '*Clear* anchor!'

'Slow ahead port. Port five.'

Telegraphs clanging, quartermaster reporting via the voice-pipe, 'Five of port wheel on, sir!' Zakharov telling Burmin, 'Burial at sea this forenoon. On our own – we'll be leaving the squadron while we do it. In the circumstances as he chooses to see them, the admiral does not favour gun salutes or half-masting ensigns – which *we*'ll do of course, also turn out the guard and band. Pass the word to Myakishev, will you – and to the bosun – and Murayev and Warrant Officer Lodchikov.'

For the guard and band, presumably: and for Bosun Feklenko to put the sailmaker to work – if he hadn't already – sewing Radzianko's body up in canvas with a weight of iron in it to make sure it sank. Sharks might get him after all, Michael thought – if they were attracted and hungry enough to bite through canvas on the sea-bed. Which they wouldn't if they didn't get a good whiff of blood. Might depend on where you dropped him, into what depth of water. But while this wasn't anything like the Mocambique Channel or Gabon, there'd surely be a few around. He asked Zakharov, 'All right if I go and square things off in the chartroom, sir?'

A nod. 'If I want you I'll yell for you.'

Since it was his job now, he'd have it organized his way. Charts from here to Vladivostok to be ready to hand, others that were only cluttering the place up to be replaced in their folios. Check through the East Coast of China folio in case any were missing – if so, they might be replaced from one of the transports, or *Suvarov*, or – wherever. There were various routes to Vladivostok anyway: Rojhestvensky might choose to keep clear of the Korea Strait, pass instead through either the Tsugaru – between Nippon and Yezo – or through La Perouse between Yezo and Sagalien. Michael hadn't studied the charts, had only heard Zakharov and Radzianko discussing the alternatives. He did know, of course, that the Korea Strait was the shortest, most direct route, also the one most likely – even virtually certain – to be blocked by Togo's fleet. Or mined. Or both . . . On his way to the chartroom, he saw the chief yeoman whip his telescope up to his eye, bawling after a few seconds, 'Signal from Flag to us, sir – our pendants – *Proceed in accordance with previous orders.*' He broke off, shouting to his team on the flagdeck, 'Answering pendant close-up!' Zakharov had stooped to the pipe again: 'Midships the wheel.' Straightening then, telling the young seaman at the telegraphs, 'Half ahead together.'

You could forget Tsugara. Too narrow by far, especially for this armada. And checking in the sailing directions, a swift and dangerous tidal stream. Meaning it would be liable to reverse its direction at the drop of a hat, so captains and navigators would need to be very much on their toes. You'd also by then have steamed right round Japan – around Kiushiu and Honda, by the grace of God undetected – and would have had to stop and coal somewhere; which might pose its own problems. Much the same applied to La Perouse, a fairly tricky passage – or it would be at any rate for Second Squadron-type ship-handlers – between Capes Krilon and Soya – *after* getting through the Kuriles, incidentally, with a particularly hazardous pinnacle of rock smack in the middle and steep-to so you'd get no warning from soundings: and this in an area notorious for thick fogs clamping down unexpectedly 'especially in Spring'.

Korea Strait, therefore, or Tsushima Strait – the difference between which was only a matter of whether you passed east or west of Tsushima Island. Unless Rojhestvensky was right out of his mind, this – either/or – would be his choice. Despite its being where Togo would expect him: despite also the proximity of Japanese naval bases. Sasebo being virtually *on* the Tsushima Strait, and Nagasaki only a few miles further south. Kure and Kobé on the so-called 'inland sea' would be construction and refitting bases mainly, he wouldn't have any of his fighting squadrons cooped up in there now.

But on the other side – the Korean side – Masampo, and Fusan. And only slightly further north, on the Japanese coast, Matsuru.

Maybe one *was* a damn fool to be here? Not – until now – seeing wood for trees, or vice versa? Ladies in Wiltshire and Yalta having a clearer overall view of the odds against?

What he'd come into the chartroom for, anyway – five minutes was all it took. Making sure everything was where he wanted it – that if Zakharov called for a certain chart for instance, he'd be able to produce it instantly. And dividers, parallel rule, sharpened pencils all handy in the rack. Sextant clean and dry, star-globe in its box, chronometer and deckwatch making sense and synchronized, navigational log up to date – at least, up to sunset yesterday. Poor, sad bastard: and *that* was a point which had sprung to mind earlier – what Myakishev had said about his being alienated from his family: remembering that he'd said he was writing to the father of the young man – Nelidov – who'd dropped dead while coaling at Dakar. A shot at wedging his fat knees under *that* table?

The Second Squadron's smoke was a spreading stain in the sky to the southeast when *Ryazan* hove-to for the committal of her former navigator to the deep. Lieutenant Vetrov had been left on the bridge as officer of the watch; down aft here were Myakishev in his robes, officers and men in their Number One white uniforms – officers wearing swords – an honour guard of a dozen men with rifles, and the six-man band with its highly polished instruments. Zakharov had told his officers in the wardroom, 'I don't want gossip passing around the squadron. Some of you may think you know what was in Viktor Vasil'ich's mind, but all we know for certain is he unwisely cast off in the skiff with no idea of the tide's strength and found himself in trouble. He did not visit any other ship; whether it was in his mind to do so – as I say, we don't *know,* therefore have no reason to assume it. My own belief is that he was acting on my own as well as Dr Baranov's suggestion that he should take more exercise; and since he knew we'd be sailing at first light or thereabouts, with probably no further chance of shore leave – well, his judgement was certainly at fault, he may have had more brandy than he should have.' A shrug. 'End of story.'

Burmin had asked him while the ship's company were assembling, 'Is that what you told the admiral, sir?'

'What else *could* I have told him?'

'But he wasn't swallowing it?'

'He has much larger problems facing him. *There's* the immediate one.' Pointing southeast, where to the right – south – of the squadron's smoke there was another, smaller stain on the horizon.

'Nyebogatov . . .'

'As you say. But *this* business he's left to me. *Ryazan* business, not squadron business.'

Burmin called the ship's company to attention and told them what they were here for. Then – at ease and off caps; and Zakharov to Myakishev: 'Carry on, Padre.' The canvas-wrapped body was on a plank right aft with four *michmen* standing by it. Myakishev intoned the customary prayers and delivered a brief homily on the virtues of our dear brother here departed. A psalm then, and another prayer, a certain amount of chanting and a sprinkling of holy water as the guard of honour was called first to attention and then to 'Port – arms!' Murayev pausing for a moment, seeing the *michmen* getting a hold on the plank, raising its inboard end. Zakharov nodded to his gunnery lieutenant, who ordered 'Fire!' Ripple of blank-cartridge shots, and the band of six seamen-musicians struck up *Kol Slaven* while the plank was angled slowly upwards until the canvas-wrapped bundle began its slide. Over the ship's port quarter – not the stern, where it might have fouled one of *Ryazan*'s twin screws and been sliced up when the engines were put ahead. *Splash.* Tears glistened on Myakishev's pale, whiskered cheeks: there were other damp eyes too, the individual mattering less than the fact he'd been a shipmate; Michael, remembering that he hadn't always been kind to Radzianko, and reflecting that death was sad enough even when it came to a *happy* man – as that one most certainly had *not* been. Later, when Murayev asked him whether he thought Viktor Vasil'ich had been some kind of sex maniac, he told him no, he was pretty sure – had thought of it on some previous occasion in fact – that his motivation had been ninety per cent bravado.

'Stop both engines.' Closing up from astern to where the Second Squadron's battleships were already lying stopped – in line astern of their flagship, with the other cruisers on both quarters and the auxiliaries tucked in between them. While half a mile or so ahead a trail of black smoke drifted eastward behind Nyebogatov's approaching 'self-sinkers'. Michael had conned *Ryazan* up into her customary tail-end station. No *Orel*, he'd noticed: she and the transports must have been left in the bay – ten or twelve miles astern, the coast a greyish smear edging the blue heave of ocean and indented by the bays of Kamranh, Van Phong, Vung-Ro and Port Dayotte – where Narumov would by this time be sorting out the damage to those destroyers and where Zakharov had said he thought the admiral would send Nyebogatov to coal. There was too much of a swell out here, for sure, and in any case they'd be bound to want a few days for maintenance and repairs.

The *Dniepr* had met Nyebogatov and led him in, had come on ahead of him now to park herself between the *Ural* and the *Kuban*. Like their sisters *Riona* and *Terek*, having a capability of nineteen knots the former passenger liners were of some use as scouts, although being armed only with pop-guns that was about the limit of it. From a distance, of course – for instance when passing Durban or Singapore –

being roughly the size of battleships they'd *look* impressive, to the untrained eye.

Now for Nyebogatov's contribution. You could already hear cheering from ships' companies massed on the battleships' upper decks. Understandable, at that – Russians greeting Russians on the far side of the world – effectively *defying* the world . . . The first cheers were for the flagship, the battleship *Nikolai I* with the rear-admiral's flag fluttering at her foremast-head. Michael, focussing his glasses on her, was surprised to hear Burmin telling him, '*Imperator Nikolai Pervhy*. Displacement's about ten thousand. Launched in the late eighties. Two twelve-inch in the for'ard turret, and twelve six-inch. That's since they've re-gunned her – which must have been done in the devil of a hurry!'

'The twin twelve-inch, I suppose.'

'Exactly. And the old ducks paddling astern of her are what we call flat-irons. Don't ask me which is which, but the three of them are the *Admiral Graf Apraksin*, and the Admirals – untitled, poor creatures – *Ushakov* and *Seniavin*. They're rated as coast service ships – shallow draught, about seventeen feet is all. Flat bottoms, hence "flat-irons". And you'll see in a minute how *short* they are – not much more than half our length. Main armament of nine-inch guns in twin turrets fore and aft. No – wait – the *Apraksin* has ten-inch, but only three, a twin turret for'ard and a single aft. Yes, that's it, and that's her leading the other two – see those ten-inch turrets, uh?'

'Yes.' With his glasses on them still. 'Yes, I can.' Could also see the old cruiser *Vladimir Monomakh* bringing up the rear. Short, stubby, twin-funnelled. Not unlike the *Donskoi*, but shorter. Both of them had been sailing-ships, in their youth. The volume of cheering was tremendous. Ships' sirens too: and flag-signals fluttering up to yard-arms. The usual sort of thing, of course – welcome, congratulation: despite Rojhestvensky having done his best over a period of several months to avoid their getting anywhere near him. Travkov had a signalman in the spotting-top who'd report over either voicepipe or telephone if any signal from *Suvarov* should call for a response from *Ryazan*, because otherwise with such a mass of ships between them you wouldn't see it – unless it was repeated to her from one of the cruisers out there on the beam, and you couldn't count on that: not with *this* lot, you couldn't. Lowering his glasses to check the ship's head and whether she still had steerage-way on her, he was thinking that even without having been addressed, Burmin had spoken more words to him in the last few minutes than he probably had in the whole of the six months they'd known each other.

Signifying acceptance? That in his view one did now *belong*?

21

Four days, Nyebogatov had needed, to coal, water and store his ships and carry out necessary maintenance and repairs in preparation for the long haul to Vladivostok. May 14th now, 0630; calm and warm, would be hot when the sun had burnt the sea-mist off in an hour or so. Michael was on the bridge, as were Zakharov and others, watching the 'flat-irons' filing out of Port Dayotte behind their flagship; the rest of the squadron waiting for them here three miles out – more or less where they'd been all the time, except for once creeping into Van Phong to coal during a temporary absence at Natrangh of Rear-Admiral de Jonquières.

He was here now in the *Guichen*, cruising slowly about a mile offshore, no doubt highly relieved at finally speeding his unwanted guests on their way to either glory or perdition.

There'd been two letters from Tasha, both forwarded by Jane; they'd come in the *Kostroma*, Nyebogatov's hospital-ship, which having called in at Saigon had arrived at Van Phong on the 11th. In the first of them she was quite bitterly critical of his disregard of her earlier pleas, and again despairing of the squadron's chances – she'd had the news of Mukden of course, which when she'd last written had been in the balance – and in the second she'd soft-pedalled on the war situation and his obduracy but described an evening spent at the Derevyenkos, their neighbours in Yalta – of whom he hadn't particularly wanted to be reminded.

There'd also been two brief covering notes from Jane – with the line in one of them *I suppose you must believe you know what you're doing, but has it occurred to you to wonder what you might be doing to that poor girl?* – and at last one from brother George, oddly enough not mentioning Igor's letter about Tasha; just country chat, culminating in his own version of what had become the popular refrain – *Look here, old chap, you really had better get yourself on to* terra firma *pretty deuced quick – seeing as in your present company and circumstances it seems to be universally agreed you're on a hiding to nothing* . . . And some hand-written 'despatches' from William that weren't now of much interest. A report of Nyebogatov having sailed from Djibouti for instance, a lot of post-mortem reportage on the crushing defeat at Mukden, and a story from Vienna – *Vienna?* – that a commission of inquiry into the surrender of Port Arthur had unanimously sentenced General Stossel to be shot.

Zakharov had been interested in that one. Having his own personal worries too though, asking Michael diffidently, 'Any communiqué from Natasha Igorovna, may I enquire?'

He'd shown surprise, then smiled: conveying that he wouldn't have *expected* to hear from her. 'Have you written your letter to her yet?'

'I've been making attempts at it. One difficulty is my slight confusion over the events of that night at Injhavino. How she'd see it – *did* see it. Whether I shouldn't have paid court to her instead of conversing – and I'll admit, to some extent carousing – with Princes Igor and Ivan. The truth is, Mikhail Ivan'ich – it embarrasses me to tell you this – that in relation to Natasha I was in a state of – what's the word, confusion. My age, of course – and knowing only too well I'm no Adonis – and in contrast her own extreme youth and beauty. I felt like a – a lecher. *Buying* her . . . In fact, as you know, buying Volodnyakov influence – but through her, *using* her – taking such *advantage* . . . Well, I'd agreed to it – oh, months before, when Prince Ivan put it to me as suddenly as if it were some wild notion that had just occurred to him. I admit, I jumped at it—'

'He and his uncle would have discussed every detail before as much as a hint of it was dropped to you.'

'Of course. But *did* I behave in a manner that offended her, that night?'

'Not that I know of. What must have stunned her was that her father hadn't seen fit to say a word to her about it – ask her how she'd feel or—'

'And she'd have seen me as part of that.'

This conversation had taken place on *Ryazan*'s bridge in the fading evening light of the 11th or 12th. After the *Kostroma*'s mail had been distributed, anyway – that was what had been in his mind, those two letters and their apparent indications. Trying to convince himself that she'd only have been writing about those people in order to fill a letter *without* whole pages of remonstration. Zakharov meanwhile droning on, explaining *his* problem – 'If in more ordinary circumstances, one had – oh, come to ask a man for his daughter's hand in marriage, then with his assent to propose to her – well, in the loftiest of romantic tradition one might have been down on one knee to her, but even without that at least making efforts to present oneself as favourably as possible. Instead of which – a foregone conclusion, and Prince Igor and his nephew lavish with their hospitality – in which in some degree of personal embarrassment *vis-à-vis* this beautiful young lady, I was perhaps in a way taking refuge—'

'May I make a suggestion?'

'Please do.'

'Put it all on paper to her. Clearly and frankly. It makes perfect sense to me. How *she*'d take it – well, one can't tell, can one. Only way to find out, though – eh? You might tell her that if – *when* – we get back from Vladivostok you hope she'd receive you, allow you to – say, make her acquaintance in a more normal way. And add—'

He'd paused, thinking about it.

'Add what?'

'That if after that she felt disinclined to – continue with the betrothal—'

'But my agreement with her father—'

'Agree with *her* is what we're talking about. Irrespective of what dowry arrangement you've made with him.'

'Speaking as her big brother – huh?'

'If you like.'

'And as opposed to the betrothal as I suspect *she* must be?'

In the two or three days since then nothing more had been said. In his sea-cabin Zakharov would no doubt have been struggling with his letter. There'd be a coaling stop before they reached Tsushima, and mail would no doubt be sent off in the coal ships – the *Tambov* and the *Mercury,* who when empty were to be sent into Saigon. Might be an even later opportunity when other transports and auxiliaries were detached when off Shanghai. As well as his old ironclads and the hospital-ship, Nyebogatov had brought with him several transports, a water-tanker and a repair ship, the *Keenia.* Most were being sent home from here, stores of any value trans-shipped from them to the *Anadyr, Irtysh* and *Korea,* who being the least unreliable of the old brigade would be staying with the fleet right through to Vladivostok. As were the *Sibir* – whose cargo of field-guns intended originally for Port Arthur would no doubt be very thankfully received by the army now preparing to defend Vladivostok – and the crazy old *Kamchatka.* The best of the machine-tools, materials, and spare parts in the *Keenia* were to have been transferred to her, space being made for it by moving less useful gear from her to the *Keenia.* Engineer-Constructor Narumov's province of course – deciding what should be kept and what discarded. Really a *very* important personage now, was P.V. Narumov. But also staying with the fleet were the tugs *Rus* and (Nyebogatov's) *Svir*; personnel had been exchanged too, between those ships coming and those leaving, civilian crews and workmen who were averse to confronting Togo being sent home, so that those staying on should all be volunteers.

Loonies?

A notice on the board outside the ship's office read: Following the tragic demise of Senior Lieutenant V.V. Radzianko, the responsibilities of navigating officer have been assumed voluntarily by Senior Lieutenant M.I. Genderson, who will be assisted by Michman G.I. Egorov . Signed: N.T. Zakharov, Captain.

Chief loony, this M.I. Genderson?

But as he'd mentioned in one of his letters to Tasha, there was nothing pre-ordained, i.e. suicidal about it. All right, these ships had come halfway round the world, were foul-bottomed and in poor mechanical condition, most of them cranky and out-dated and manned by crews who were still no more than half-trained; but (a) despite the narrowness of the Tsushima Strait, the East China Sea and Sea of Japan were vast expanses of open water – respectively four hundred and eighty thousand and four hundred and five thousand square miles – and given anything like suitable conditions, evading Togo shouldn't be by any means impossible; (b) despite the handicaps imposed by having Nyebogatov's old relics dragging along behind – lack of speed, and even more of a tendency to break down – it was a fact that ship for ship and gun for gun they did probably have the edge on Togo's battlefleet.

As navigator, he didn't keep watches: spent most of his days and nights on the bridge or in the chartroom. For his own satisfaction he was keeping the ship's position fixed by taking morning and evening stars – having been lucky so far with clear skies – and encouraging young Egorov to do the same, showing him how to do it better.

Thinking pretty well constantly about Tasha, meanwhile. Perhaps the worst contingency would be if the bitterness of the first letter and the hint in the second of ever-closer friendship with the Derevyenkos had been – *was being* –

initiated/orchestrated by Anna Feodorovna, who for all her charm and elegance was hard-headed, decisive, he guessed quite ruthless. If she'd decided that Tasha should – well, *disengage* . . .

Thoughts merged into dreams – senseless but also bad ones, from which one had to force oneself awake, sit up – on the late Radzianko's couch – reach for a cigarette . . .

Derevyenko – father Andrei, *Graf* Andrei – meaning count – one-armed son Count Pavel. But getting her next letter after that one – the one she'd written after her visit to St Petersburg and which he'd read when they'd been at anchor outside Angra Pequena – he remembered having felt ashamed – of jealousy sparked by distance and impotence. Felt the same now too: recognizing also that it was mostly his own damn fault – in *her* eyes, her view of his obduracy being perfectly understandable. Although – rasp of the match, the Russian cigarette's cardboard tube squashed almost flat so it'd draw better – as things were now there wasn't a damn thing he could do about it.

Didn't help, of course, that there was no chance at all of hearing from her now – between here and Vladivostok. Touching wood for that – eventual arrival at Vladivostok: which incidentally should settle all *that* in Tasha's mind. Apart from the fact that one would be around, extant. Touching the polished mahogany of the chart-table, over which a dim light glowed – pulled right down on its flexible, telescopic deckhead mounting so as to reduce the spillage of light from it. The fleet was steaming without masthead or navigation lights, with shaded stern-lights only. Even smoking on the upper decks was prohibited. Throb of *Ryazan*'s engines, the creaking and groaning of her iron frame and plates, rattling of loose fittings, seesaw motion as she rode the low swell and smashed through the rolling wakes of the forty-odd ships ahead. (Almost forty: down from fifty-two, since the shedding of those transports.) Thinking back to Zakharov's admission that at Injhavino he'd been out of his depth, overawed by Prince Igor's effusive hospitality.

He'd have been more than half-seas over too, probably – he certainly enjoyed his drink, which loosened his tongue though not his facial muscles. And was obviously well aware of that face of his: which in fact one got used to, but a young girl wouldn't, certainly not on first acquaintance. They *had* been sloshing the drink around that evening; there was a punch for instance with a kick like a mule's, and when Michael had mentioned this, Prince Stepan – Ivan's older son, who had a club foot and with his younger brother Pyotr (physically strong but mentally less so) worked on the estate, Stepan calling himself the overseer but both of them actually labouring like peasants – Stepan had joked that a mule might have provided some of the content of the punch as well. Zakharov had, of course, been a stranger to everyone in the house except Prince Ivan, yet was guest of honour and at any rate to start with too shy to have done much more than mumble a few pleasantries at Tasha and at her mother and then retreat, hide his face and dull his sensitivities. And that had been long before the speech by Igor which must have embarrassed him all over again – that heavy over-emphasis on his father being one of Moscow's foremost *merchant* princes.

(Not exactly one of us, my friends: *but* . . .)

A snapshot flickering into mind then of Tasha in her mother's arms, on a great tasselled sofa with a rip in its red-and-white satin covering, the two dark heads together, Tasha in tears and her mother's lips moving, murmuring 'There now, my darling, but stop it now, don't let them see you in such a state, you know how the wretches gossip. We'll see to it, put it right, I *swear* we will. Please, darling . . .'

Waving *him* away then. Probably wisely, at that. Prince Ivan a minute later throwing an arm round his shoulders and leading him over to clink glasses with this dog-faced, moneyed stranger; and a neighbour of the Volodnyakovs, a Count Selander who had Swedish blood and an enormous brood of children – fat, soft-faced Swede with a cigar about two feet long and a brandy glass so full he kept slopping it over his white hand and wrist. Ivan and a young woman who was staying in the house but seemed to be related to the Swede's wife had something going between them, Michael had thought; Ivan having left his own arthritic wife Ilyana in Petersburg, as she hadn't felt up to making such a long journey just for a day or two. No positive reason to disbelieve him, it was simply how it had looked and felt, as one remembered it – in memory one image imposing itself on another, the last in that particular sequence being of Tasha and her mother slipping out of the room together, quietly and swiftly, leaving behind the roar of conversation punctuated by bursts of merriment and, in the quieter moments, music coming from several rooms away, much of the time inaudible.

He'd gone up after them and knocked on her bedroom door. Her door or her mother's – they had interleading rooms, on the first floor in the front of the house where the corridors were wider, rooms and windows larger. They were together in there anyway: Tasha had thrown herself face-down on the bed and her mother had come to the door and opened it: 'Micky . . .'

'What can I do?'

'Nothing.' She – Anna – with her guard down, looking utterly *distraite.* 'But come in – quickly, just for a moment . . . Nothing we can do *immediately*, I meant. We left it too late – *I* left it too late. With you away in any case – God, you might as well have stayed away, spared yourself this—'

'Tasha?'

Tear-stained: sitting, then standing, dabbing at her eyes. 'Nothing you could have done even if you *had* been within a thousand miles. He must have guessed what Mama was intending, waiting for – otherwise why all the secrecy, and this cruel *suddenness* . . .'

'We can still beat him.'

'How?'

Her mother had asked that question: and he couldn't answer it. Shaking his head: 'It's inconceivable that they can do such a thing to her. Although you were right, Anna Feodorovna, you did anticipate some such—'

'It was always in his mind.'

'In any case, I –' gazing at Tasha – 'and Tasha, you too, I hope . . .' Tongue-tied, though, over this: letters were one thing, a declaration face-to-face and in the presence of a third party, and with the awful feeling that one might effectively be ham-strung – and couldn't *allow* oneself to be . . . 'Anna Feodorovna – would I have your approval – help – if Tasha and I were simply to run away together?'

'No! – I mean – oh, let's calm down a bit . . . Micky, the answer in principle is "yes", but it would *not* be at all "simple" – and in any case there's no need to – oh, stampede . . . Time's on our side – the only thing that *is*, but it's the most important. My brain's *beginning* to work again – thank heaven. You see – if this Zakharov's to go with the Second Pacific Squadron – I wasn't listening to all that, but he is, isn't he? – he'll be away for months. Months and *months* . . . Of course, Igor will be watching like a hawk: in fact if he had any reason to suspect . . .'

She'd dried up: brain at work but running into problems. 'Micky, let's talk in the morning. You'd better go – really, we must be very careful. In any case, so I can get this child to bed—'

'May I kiss the child goodnight?'

A pause, looking from him to her. Then: 'Child would probably insist in any case.'

He'd kissed her cheek when he'd arrived, earlier in the day: under everyone's eyes in a general toing and froing, servants dragging trunks up the stairs and along the passages, new arrivals discovering who'd been allotted which room, and so forth – the allotting and supervising of it all being done by old Princess Olga, Igor's spinster sister. But other than that necessarily chaste, cousinly greeting it was more than three years since he'd seen her, let alone touched or kissed her. Whispering now – her mother having tactfully drifted into the adjoining room – 'I love you.'

'And I love you.'

Her eyes huge under his; lips and tongues in contact and sweet-tasting between murmurs. Back to Yalta: might have been no more than *weeks* ago. 'Never stopped loving you, wanting you. Don't intend stopping now – or ever—'

'Ever. No – you mustn't!'

'*Will* beat them – I swear—'

'I know how.'

'*How?*'

'Don't lock your door.' *Tiny* whisper: into his mouth first, then – when he might have heard it but hardly dared believe he had, his expression therefore questioning – a repetition with her lips close to his ear. Down off her toes then, inching back, with a glance at the door to the other bedroom and speaking in a normal if slightly breathless tone: 'Goodnight, my darling.' Anna Feodorovna's voice then before she actually came through, by which time they were bodily apart although facing each other, holding hands. Anna asking him, 'Will you go back down there now, Micky?'

'Might be – diplomatic.'

'I agree. You should. If Igor asks, tell him Tasha and I were both exhausted.'

'All right. I'll spend say half an hour down there. Then back up to my little corner room.'

'Sleep well in it. And we'll talk tomorrow.'

'Yes. Goodnight.' He kissed *her* cheek. 'You sleep well too.'

He freshened up a bit before returning to the party, chatted to various people in his far-from-perfect Russian, accepted another glass of brandy, made sure Prince Igor saw him, and discussed with Admiral Prince Ivan the Second Pacific Squadron's prospects. Ivan assuring him – with his arm round the hour-glass waist of the Swede's wife's sister – if that was what she was – 'We'll teach your Jap allies a lesson they won't forget. They had the devil's own luck at Round Island and now they think they're world-beaters. They *would,* you see, being bone-headed monkeys. The "little learning" syndrome, isn't it – teach a peasant the ABC and he's a damn professor – uh? Well, the world will see, Mikhail Ivan'ich!'

People were leaving, carriages scrunching up and some of their owners being helped out to them, Michael went out on the steps to see a group of them off – was complimented on his Russian – which needed all the practice it could get – and on his way back inside told the hobbling Prince Stepan, 'I'm for bed. Whacked. Daren't take another sip.'

'I did warn you about the punch . . .'

He couldn't have locked the door even if he'd wanted to. There wasn't a key. When he'd got himself ready for bed he left one candle burning – there was no electricity on this upper floor – lay down in his dressing-gown and wondered if she'd come. Or have fallen asleep by this time: or changed her mind. Or be unable to make a move because of her mother's proximity and sharp ears.

But would her mother give a damn now?

Creaky old house, gradually falling quiet. Michael hardly breathing and not stirring, listening intently. Hearing over and over that thrilling whisper – promise – *Don't lock your—*

Its hinges squeaked. First sound he'd heard. He was on his feet as it squeaked shut. Telling her softly – because she was fumbling for it – 'There's no key.' She was in his arms then: her gown open, slipping away over those incredibly lovely shoulders and his palms following it, caressing them, continuing over and down to the warm, astonishingly soft hollow of her back, the sculptured swell of hips. Up from there to cup her breasts: 'Tasha, you beautiful, *beautiful—*'

'*This* is how we'll beat them!'

That and the next few hours had been the glory of it: had been and still was, always would be: astonishingly, mind-stunningly *wonderful.* While the sequel hadn't at that stage been – imaginable. Starting with her whisper half-waking him, her silhouette discernible between him and dawn's glimmer in the small, half-open window with its rotten frame. Her whisper: 'Better go now, Mikhail darling, lover . . .'

'Uh?'

Still so dazed that for a moment he'd thought she was telling him *he'd* better go. Go where? Then catching on as she slid across him: catching *her*. 'Tasha—'

'No. Getting *light*, my darling!'

He realized she was right. Recalling Anna Feodorovna's *Must be very careful*. Which this already didn't *quite* measure up to: but as far as he was concerned – well, there was nothing he *wouldn't* do to steal her. *Be* hard up, incur the displeasure of Their Lordships of the bloody Admiralty – as well as Igor's and all the other Volodnyakovs' . . . 'I'll come with you – as far as your door and—'

'I'll be quieter on my own—'

'I can be going to the lavatory.' Scooping up her gown, holding it for her while she slipped her arms in. Holding *her* again then. 'Tasha, you sweet, *lovely*—'

'Come on.' With the door slightly open though, turning to kiss him again: his hands on the outside of the flimsy gown now, and even from that contact almost irresistibly inclined to pull her back inside, shut the door again—

'*Christ!*'

Like the sudden rush – escape – of some large rat – outside, along the passage. Shocked, stock-still in each other's arms: hearing it reach the stairs and slither – patter – down. Human, bare-footed?

No sound now.

'What on *earth*—'

Her fingers on his mouth. Stable-door treatment, in fact. At least, as far as one might guess, the horse had bolted: *some* horse, to *some* purpose. Tasha's whisper: 'Old Dmitry – sneaks around, tells my father whatever – oh, Christ almighty . . .'

'Why'd he spy on *us*?'

'On *me*, I suppose. He'll go straight to him – at least, as soon as he wakes. Oh, Mikhail—'

'I'm on my way to the lavatory, came out of my room for that purpose. You aren't here, *weren't* here, never left your room. He can't *know* you were here – unless he has ears like—'

'Probably followed me up here. Oh, *God*!'

'Come on now. It'll be all right – you'll see . . .'

A bugle-call sent the hands to action stations before dawn. Some guns and turrets were manned all night but this was a general and customary stand-to, dawn like dusk being a favourite time for surprise attacks. Michael was in the bridge with Zakharov and others, Burmin on his usual roving commission springing surprises on the unwary if he found any, Galikovsky at the torpedo-control position in the conning tower – access to which was by way of a narrow flight of iron steps curving down from the side of the forebridge – and Murayev in the spotting-top, alternatively the conning tower or visiting the turrets. Michael with his Heath binoculars trained on the lumbering herd ahead while it did its unimpressive best to transform itself from a random mass into a fleet in cruising formation. The onset of daylight might help, he supposed; but there'd been a good moon last night – only three days short of a full one – so darkness was hardly an excuse.

He'd taken his morning stars; Egorov was in the chartroom working them out for him. He was a pleasant lad, grimly silent with anxiety for his father and seemingly glad to be kept busy.

'It's a mess again.'

Zakharov, beside him. Adding, 'The breakdowns won't have helped.'

There'd been two during the night: the transport *Tambov* first and then the battleship *Oryol* – the latter while Michael had been asleep. A steering-engine failure, Milyukov who'd had that watch had told him. The squadron had started off in reasonably good style yesterday, making nine knots, but if stoppages and slowing-downs continued at that rate you'd be doing well to cover one hundred and fifty miles a day. Two hundred would have been slow enough – with two and a half thousand miles to go, two thousand to Tsushima and another five or six hundred then to Vladivostok.

Nyebogatov's captains and watchkeepers had had no practice at working with Rojhestvensky's squadron – the only practice they'd get was what they were getting now. Perhaps more worrying, though – as Narumov had told them when he'd dined on board in Van Phong – was that Rojhestvensky had had Nyebogatov on board the *Suvarov* for no more than thirty minutes on the evening of the 9th – when the 'self-sinkers' had first arrived – and in that half-hour not a word had been said about tactics or battle-plans or even the route to be taken to Vladivostok. The towering but now apparently gaunt, sick-looking vice-admiral had met the short and tubby rear-admiral at the head of the flagship's gangway, and they'd embraced, then paced the deck together exchanging only small-talk, and although during his few days in Port Dayotte Nyebogatov had been expecting to be called to some sort of conference, nothing of the kind had happened.

It was already quite light: the sky in the east flushed with pink and gold and the sun's first rays gilding the hospital-ships' white hulls, the sea around them blue-black and glittering, swirl and suds of broken water reflecting the pink flush overhead. To port the land, if one could have seen it, was still the bulge of French Indo-China, while to starboard at a range of about five hundred miles were the Philippines. Steering northeast as they were – aiming to pass around Formosa, to the east of it – by this time tomorrow the nearest land would be Luzon, at the top end of the Philippines. They'd pass roughly a hundred miles off Negra Point: nothing like close enough to upset the Americans, even though whatever ships they had based there would surely be on the lookout for them.

Burmin came back up into the bridge. Zakharov checked the time, and nodded. 'You can send the hands to breakfast.'

'Aye, sir!' Turning, yelling: 'Bugler!'

Zakharov told Michael, 'I completed the letter we were discussing. Very much as you advised. Not taking it as far as you proposed, but – a level-headed approach, I think.'

'Good.'

'Is she likely to communicate it to her father?'

'I don't know. Truly, no idea.'

'I feel better for having written it, in any case. Should have months ago. I'd rather she didn't show it to him, but if she did – well, nothing in it he could reasonably object to.'

'If you consider him a *reasonable* man.'

'You don't?'

'We've spoken about him before, haven't we. You expressed reservations, and I agreed with you. He and I are not the best of friends.'

'Which leaves at least one question unanswered.' A shrug. 'Anyway, I'm obliged to you for the advice you gave me.'

The unanswered question, of course, would be the one he'd asked on Michael's first night on board, in Tangier: 'Only to satisfy my curiosity, Mikhail Ivan'ich – why did Prince Igor want me to bring you along with us?'

The answer to which he'd somehow fudged. Could hardly have told him 'Because he knew I'd slept with his daughter and this was easier for him – in fact he might have thought it was cleverer – than having my throat cut or putting her in a nunnery – or both.'

Igor hadn't sent for him that morning; doubtless would have, but Michael had anticipated any such summons by asking for a private interview. It had taken place in mid-forenoon in the park behind the house: there was an orangery with a lot of its glass broken, a lake, an orchard and a birch avenue. A lot of space, but everything in it noticeably run-down. The avenue led to a chapel that was actually in ruins.

Igor had told him, 'We have plans for this estate. My great-nephew Stepan is overflowing with ideas. Mostly it's to do with the latest kinds of agricultural machinery, not only for the working of our own land but for hiring out to neighbours. It calls for heavy investment, of course, but I am advised would lead to substantial profits. Before I die I should like to see the place not only commercially successful but looking as beautiful as it did when I was a boy . . . You wanted to speak to me?'

'About Tasha, sir.'

'Well?'

He knew, all right. Eyes like a snake's, in his Roman Emperor-type face.

'I'm told that Captain Zakharov has already left. But I'm not taking advantage of that, to raise this behind his back. If he was here I'd be more than ready to tell him what's on my mind.'

'If I'm guessing correctly it concerns the betrothal – on which as far as I'm aware you had no comment to make last night.'

'I've had a night to sleep on it since then.'

'*Sleep* on—'

He'd checked himself: probably in some vulgarity. Checked physical movement too; facing each other, the snake's eyes vicious. 'Well, *what*?'

'I'd like to ask you for your daughter's hand in marriage, sir.'

'Although she's formally betrothed to Captain Zakharov?'

'She was given no choice in the matter, sir. She *detests* the thought of marrying him.'

'Wants to marry *you*?'

'I've loved her for a long time. I was only waiting for her to be older before I approached you on the subject. While she was so young – right up to the time I had to take up this last appointment – it would have been – premature, if not improper—'

'Concerned with what's "proper" or "improper", are you?'

'I don't—'

'In Russia – even in England, I believe – it's generally

accepted that a father is entitled to protect his daughter's honour with a horse-whip!'

'I'm at least as concerned for your daughter's honour as you are yourself. I'm asking for her hand. If you think her honour or her happiness is better protected by selling her to a man she's never met—'

'She is formally betrothed to him, Mikhail Ivan'ich. That is a fact and can't be changed. As far as *you* are concerned – and I'd advise you to watch your tongue – I've an idea which is a lot more than you deserve and which I feel sure will appeal to you. I've sent a telegram on the subject and should have a reply within hours. I'll tell you this, meanwhile – the only reason your hide may be left intact and your naval career un-ruined is that I'm averse to the creation of a scandal that would besmirch my daughter's reputation and with it the honour of my family.'

He'd turned away. 'When I have an answer to the telegram I'll send for you.'

Egorov had pencilled a neat intersection of the three stars' bearings on the chart; he stood back, making room for Michael to take a look.

'Mikhail Ivan'ich?'

'Huh?'

'Looks good. Must 've got all the figures right, for once!'

Still staring: remembering Tasha's incredulity when he'd told her what had been said. 'You asked to *marry* me – when he already *knew* we'd—'

'I'm *going* to marry you! But I had to get in first, make the point there was nothing casual or—'

'What can he mean about a telegram?'

'God only knows!'

Dragging himself out of it: but with her expression of alarm hanging on in memory, only very slowly fading . . . Right back to earth then – to Egorov, Gavril Ivan'ich, who was looking at him curiously. Couldn't blame him, either. A shake of the head as he leant over the chart: 'Sorry. Mind wandering. Yes, *does* look like a good one. Well done. Want my job?'

A smile: 'Glad to understudy you, Mikhail Ivan'ich.'

'Which you're doing very well. Take evening stars yourself tonight, will you?'

22

At daybreak on the 18th in a flat calm the squadron stopped to coal from the *Tambov* and the *Mercury*. Nyebogatov's ships, having had little or no practice at open-sea coaling using boats, were slow at it, but fortunately didn't need much coal and the evolution was completed by three in the afternoon. Mail from all the ships had been put on board the *Mercury*; she and the *Tambov* now riding light, finished with, destined for Saigon. The destroyer which the latter had been towing was to be taken in tow by the *Livonia*, who made such a hash of it that it was an hour and a half before the squadron could get under way.

Michael had written to Tasha:

> May 17: We are at sea now on our way to Vladivostok, and mail is being sent ashore, probably for the last time, in an emptied transport which is going into Saigon. In the same mail there must be a letter to you from Z, which you'll have received before this reaches you since he's writing directly to the Yalta address. I could do the same, but I still fear interception by agents of your father; although I suppose it's just as likely that they'd intercept letters from England. In fact I *will* send this directly to you: Z has some notion that I write to you, and/or hear from you – although I have not admitted it – and what the hell, I can't see that at this stage it

would matter if he did know. I am still, as far as he knows, a 'big brother' to you.

Anyway – I gave him your address in Yalta, and advised him to write. He's been worrying for months now about the scant attention he paid you at Injhavino, and how to get to know you and have you know him etc. I advised him to write and explain his feelings as best he can; also to ask whether on his return to Russia you would receive him and discuss it all. I suggested that after you'd got to know each other to some extent he should be prepared to accept your decision as regards ending or continuing the betrothal; but I think he may have dug his heels in on that issue. Having made his deal with your father he's loath to go back on it: he's buying Volodnyakov support, and knows of course that if he made *enemies* of your father and Ivan – which he surely would if he went back on the agreement – he could kiss his career goodbye, they could break him as easily as make him.

That's the situation as far as Z and my advice to him are concerned. I've explained it in this much detail because you might otherwise be puzzled, getting his letter and perhaps some reference in it to his having discussed it with me.

Tasha my darling, I do hope you're all right, and not as fed up with me as you seemed to be in at any rate one of your comparatively recent letters. I received two when we were on the coast of Indo-China. I know you'll be thinking I'm a pig-headed swine for not having taken your advice and disembarked at one of our ports of call, and perhaps I am, but there's more than one angle on it, including the fact – as I mentioned before – that my superiors in London *will* be expecting me to see the business through. Irresolution is not a quality they favour – and now with 'Jackie' Fisher at the top this will apply even more strongly. Conversely, if I do see it through and produce a paper on it that might contribute to decisions on future strategy, my career prospects can only be enhanced. I happen to know this, was actually told they would be; and I have a secret dream of which I'll tell you now – in absolute confidence, don't please ever mention it to anyone at all, because in the cold light of day it may seem over-ambitious – it's of having you at my side eventually as *Lady* Henderson.

Obviously that's looking ahead quite a few years. And simply having you at my side in any case is all I truly crave. I love you so much, my darling, so entirely, that if I were to die I would do so far less unhappily for having had the huge fulfilment, sheer joy of knowing and loving you and – amazingly – being loved by you. To live without you would now be inconceivable. No matter what happens, please remember this: I swear to you it's the truth and nothing but the truth.

Now all you need do is wait for my telegram. I love you, darling Tasha, and I always will.

Less than an hour after getting under way, the *Livonia*'s towing hawser parted. There was another stop therefore, while the tug *Svir* took over the towing of that destroyer. On again – the squadron slowly shaping itself into something resembling the ordered cruising formation, but still basically a rabble. Then at eight p.m. a steamer was spotted coming up from astern, and *Ryazan* was sent to investigate. It was, after all, on course for Japan, war materials were being shipped to them from all over the world and Russian war vessels were fully entitled to stop, search and seize or destroy such cargoes.

At close quarters it was still light enough to see that the ship was flying a Red Ensign: which for Michael was a touch embarrassing – or would have been if he'd allowed himself to be personally involved and she was found to be carrying munitions. Despite which, on Zakharov's instructions he put the first questions to her, using a signal-lamp and Morse code, eliciting that she was the *Oldhamia*, registered in Liverpool and bound from New York to Nagasaki with a cargo allegedly of petroleum.

Zakharov looked up at the darkening sky. He'd already taken the precaution of training *Ryazan*'s for'ard 6-inch turret on the steamer; the guns weren't loaded yet but Murayev was in the conning-tower with the telephone-line open to that turret and the turret-officer, Tselinyev, awaiting orders. Zakharov told Michael, 'Make to him, *You are to remain in company with us and will be boarded and searched at daylight.*'

Michael called the ship up again and passed that message, phrasing it in translation as *Regret to inconvenience but you will have to remain in company in order to be boarded.* Both ships got under way, and Zakharov drafted a signal to be passed to the flagship in Tabulevich over the foreyard signal lights. He asked Michael, 'Will you go over with the boarding party in the morning?'

'No, sir. Sorry.'

A shrug. 'Would have eliminated any language problem, that's all. But naturally . . .'

At 0200 on the 19th the 'flat-iron' *Apraksin* developed engine trouble. Speed was reduced to six knots while repairs were carried out. Michael passed the speed alteration by light to the *Oldhamia* – whose skipper might well have been impressed by the fluency in English of Russian signalmen. The *Apraksin* had estimated that repairs might take as long as twenty-four hours, but in any case after falling out from dawn action stations the whole squadron stopped engines while the *Oldhamia* was boarded by a party from the *Suvarov*, then moved up to lie close abeam of the flagship while she was searched. Meanwhile *Ryazan* was sent to intercept and examine another ship which seemed to have been giving the squadron a suspiciously wide berth, but which turned out to be Norwegian and in ballast, southbound from Shanghai to Singapore.

From Michael's diary – continuing the entry for May 19:

At 1130 proceeded, at revs for 9 knots. Negra Point on Luzon somewhere abaft the beam to starboard, Hong Kong 400 miles WNW. The *Oldhamia* is being simultaneously towed and coaled from the *Livonia* and searched by the flagship's boarding party, German crew members having alleged that guns and shells are in her lower holds under the cased petrol. This is supported by discrepancy between her draught marks and cargo as declared, *Suvarov*'s problem now, not ours. Searching is difficult owing to the haphazard way the cased petrol has been stowed. Captain and mate are being obstreperous, apparently, and an engineer tried to sink her by opening a flood-valve in the engine-room, which a Russian warrant engineer officer happened to see in time and shut. Typically bloody-minded attitude from British Merchant Navy stalwarts, delights the heart to hear of it, but unfortunately also rather gives the game away – she *must* have war material in her.

During the stoppage this morning a new General Order was distributed around the squadron by boat. Order No 240 of May 19, 'Night Cruising Formation while Passing Japanese Islands'. Have studied and absorbed it. One problem is the difficulty these chaps have of getting themselves into *any* formation, even in broad daylight.

May 20, 0500: Wind has come up a bit, from the East. Fresh, cooler air most welcome. Sea is up too, scale 2 to 3. To starboard Batan, to port Sabtan: small alteration was necessary to pass through Bashi Channel, returning then to previous course to head up east of Formosa approx 100 miles offshore.

May 21: The *Oldhamia* with prize crew on board commanded by a senior lieutenant from *Suvarov* (actually Russian mercantile marine reserve officer) is being sent on her own to Vladivostok via La Perouse Strait. Explains the coaling – without it she wouldn't have had enough to get there. Searching lower holds at sea has proved impracticable: need to have her alongside a quay with cranes. Her British captain and four officers have been put on board the *Orel* – in the circumstances, quite decent treatment.

May 22: Cool, misty night. At 0800 altered course to N 20 West to pass between Miyoko and Liu-Kiu. Overcast, with patchy fog, sea scale 3, wind NNE. Fog raises hopes of more to come – dv. Have already benefited by not being visible from either Miyoko or Liu-Kiu. But if we could have a good old pea-souper – and rather less wind than at present . . . Why shouldn't we? Up to now there's no doubt Togo *has* had all the luck!

Kuban and *Terek* have been sent to cruise off the east coast of Japan with orders to be seen – *en route* they might for instance be spotted from Okinawa and/or Amami, perhaps then Tanega – as a diversion aimed at making Japs think squadron could be making for Tsugaru or La Perouse. Marvellous if it came off – draw Togo's main strength northward from the Tsushima area.

Wind has backed to NW.

May 23: 0530, stopped to coal. The last time, for sure. Officers in ships' boats alongside the *Livonia* during coaling heard from *Oslyabya* people that Adml Felkerzam is on point of death.

May 24: Weather deteriorating. Padre Myakishev has convinced himself and others that Saints Seraphim and Nikolai the Just have intervened to fix it for us. There's no doubt there *is* a certain amount of optimism around – in this ship anyway. Extraordinary, but true. In *Ryazan* of course, the spirit has been good right from the start.

May 25: Showers, and grey overcast. No stars last night or this morning. DR position reliable enough however, puts us about 100 miles off Shanghai. Auxiliaries together with *Dniepr* and *Rion* detached. They (*D* and *R*) will escort auxiliaries to the Yangtse then carry out cruiser operations off the west coast of Japan.

Vis is down to 2 or 3 miles, despite wind. Short, choppy sea. ETA Tsushima Strait, early 27th.

Zakharov had asked him, while drinking a glass of tea in the chartroom on the Wednesday – 24th – 'Any letters to send, Mikhail Ivan'ich?'

'In the *Livonia*, you mean?'

'Have you?'

'No.' He'd said about all there was to say to Tasha in the last one, which by now would have been landed and posted in Saigon. There'd be nothing worth adding, since nothing had changed. In any case, long before she got it – got even that other one – he'd either be in Vladivostok or – or not, and the whole world would know it. He'd asked Zakharov, 'How about you?'

'Same applies. In that last mail I sent letters to my family, as well as the one you know of.'

Valedictory letters. They didn't look at each other, but were both conscious of it. Those who got the letters would know it too: but there again, before receiving them their newspapers would have had telegraphed communiqués from Vladivostok, Shanghai, Tokyo. They'd know much more than the senders had when writing them.

'And to Irina?'

A grunt: pushing a pack of cigarettes to him across the chart-table. '*Importantly*, to Irina. Don't bother to look so clever, I don't mind your knowing, it makes no difference to anything else. But that question was only the first of two. The second one is this: would *you* care to take passage into Shanghai in the *Livonia*?'

'Then read in some news-sheet of your triumphant arrival in Vladivostok? No thank you. Sooner arrive there with you. Share the glory – uh? But why – d'you want to get shot of me?'

'Far from it.' A sucking noise as Zakharov drained the glass. 'Only thought you might have come to your senses.'

Actually there was another element in his thinking now,

he realized: a reluctance to have it construed that at the last moment his nerve had cracked.

In the early hours of the 26th Japanese wireless transmissions were picked up, apparently emanating from shore stations. The squadron was now – at 0800 – just over one full day's steaming from the Tsushima/Korea Strait, with the island of Cheju Do sixty miles on the port bow and Nagasaki a hundred and sixty to starboard, broader on the bow. Slightly astern of schedule as compared to yesterday, through the flat-iron *Senyavin* having developed engine trouble during the night; ETA Tsushima was now noon tomorrow, 27th. The wireless intercepts were apparently routine transmissions, all of about the same duration and being exchanged at regular intervals, with no suggestion of alarm or excitement. A report had been made by light to the flagship, who'd confirmed that her telegraphists ('torpedomen') were listening to them too; it was a reasonable assumption, from the uniform nature of the transmissions, that as yet the squadron had not been sighted or reported.

As the forenoon wore on the cloud-cover was breaking up, but mist still hung in banks restricting visibility to a maximum of about three thousand yards and often only half that. Pretty short range in fact at which to run into a battlefleet – or more likely scouting cruisers. Eyes were skinned, voices lowered, concentration and alertness probably greater than they had been since the Skaw and the Dogger Bank. Cruising formation since parting with the auxiliaries off Shanghai had been – was now, in essence – the scout division consisting of *Svetlana, Almaz* and *Ural* in the lead in arrow formation, then the battlefleet in two columns comprising – to starboard – *Suvarov, Alexander, Borodino, Oryol, Oslyabya, Sissoy Veliky, Navarin* and *Nakhimov*, and to port *Nikolai I, Senyavin, Apraksin, Ushakov*, and for good measure the cruisers *Oleg, Aurora, Donskoi* and *Monomakh*. On the port beam the *Zemchug* had two destroyers with her and to starboard the *Izumrud* had another pair. They were the guardians of their respective sides; while astern of the 'battleship' columns in single line were the transports *Anadyr, Irtysh, Korea, Sibir* and *Kamchatka* with the tugs *Rus* and *Svir* to give them a hand if necessary, and the other five torpedo-boat destroyers. Astern of them in line abreast came the two graceful-looking, high-prowed hospital-ships, with *Ryazan* to defend them as well as act as rearguard, with freedom to move out to either quarter if there was reason to – to ward off out-flanking attempts by torpedo-boats, for instance. Similarly the scout division, prior to commencement of battle, were to fall back on the disengaged side and conduct the transports to some safe distance, while the *Zemchug* and *Izumrud* with their four destroyers would take station wherever on the disengaged side they could best counter encircling movements by enemy cruisers or destroyers.

The basic premise, in Russian intentions anyway, was that the heavyweights with their big guns would win (or lose) the battle, cruisers and destroyers then administering *coups de grâce* and cleaning up the lesser fry. Alternatively of course being cleaned-up themselves.

Michael added to his diary entry in the afternoon:

> Forenoon spent exercising re-disposition into order of battle. In nutshell: scouts and others hauling out to starboard, auxiliaries ditto, while 'battleships' form single line: starboard column – *Suvarov* plus 7 – increasing revs and altering together 2 points to port, Nyebogatov's column then forming line astern on them as they (*Suvarov*s and co) resume previous course. At third attempt this was executed to Rojhestvensky's satisfaction.
>
> NB The *Oslyabya* is now flying a dead man's flag.

Japanese wireless transmissions continued throughout the day and into the night, in the same pattern of routine communications. Michael snoozed on the chartroom couch during the late afternoon/early evening, aware that there might be little chance of sleep in the days and nights ahead, and woke *knowing* that Anna Feodorovna would have been the influence behind Tasha's apparently changing attitude – if indeed there had been any such change, not merely his own over-sensitivity to the combination of those two letters, their sequence first recrimination, then 'By the way, we're seeing a lot of the Derevyenkos'.

Euphemism for '*I* am seeing a lot of *Pavel* Derevyenko'?

Almost certainly would have been Mama's influence. As she'd said that day in Yalta, *We're close – as you'll have realized, she takes notice.* Meaning, *Does what I tell her.* Although that might not be quite as much the case now as she – Anna – thought it was; in Paris, Tasha had *not* been so compliant – bless her . . . He'd arrived from England to join them for two days at old Tatiana's magnificent hotel on the Place des Vosges, expecting – partly out of wishful thinking maybe, but since this Paris rendezvous had been Anna Feodorovna's idea, to mollify Tasha, who'd been in despair at the imminence of his departure as well as traumatized by the betrothal business – that in the circumstances Anna's blind eye would be discreetly turned. But not a bit of it. That may have been in her mind when they'd left Injhavino, but if it had been she'd had second thoughts since then, had taken a room for him in a pension a few hundred yards away. She'd murmured to him when they'd been alone and he'd made some comment on it, 'Did you think I'd want her left *enceinte*?'

'Why, no, of *course*—'

'At Injhavino, did you take precautions?'

'No, because—'

'So let's hope to God—'

'I didn't *have* any – precautions!'

'But now you do have, you're going to tell me. It's beside the point. Nothing's certain in this world, and I will not risk – my God, Micky, the situation you'd leave us in – may even have done already! Can you *imagine* what would be her father's reactions to such a scandal – and you'd expect me actually to connive at my own daughter's—'

'I suppose I just didn't *think*.'

'Was I wrong when I said in Yalta you're a man of honour, wouldn't risk such appalling—'

'At Injhavino it was entirely different. You know it was. It was – cataclysmic. As for being a man of honour, I'd marry her *today*!'

'When she's betrothed to someone else and you're leaving for Port Arthur the day after tomorrow?'

'Well – there might be some way . . . Except it would put you in – a somewhat invidious position . . .'

She agreed – it would have put her in an absolutely frightful position. As would permitting him to stay in the house with them: and the servants knowing. Servants got to know *everything* . . . 'I'm astounded you haven't learnt *that* lesson, Micky!' But Tasha had written him a note which she'd had inside her glove and slipped to him next morning when the three of them went out for a stroll together. He'd read – later:

> If you can extend your stay by one day, on Wednesday afternoon we could have the use of a friend's apartment. I'm supposed to be visiting a dentist and then taking tea with other people. You might contrive some pre-arrangement of your own for that afternoon.

He'd told them he had to keep an appointment at the British embassy on Wednesday, was therefore extending his visit by one day – might cut it a bit fine in getting to Libau, but couldn't help that, could only trust to luck. Looking at Tasha: 'I'd have that morning free, anyway – and the evening—'

'Wednesday – I've promised the de Carentans – it's the afternoon we're—'

'You shouldn't let them down, Tasha. You're seeing the dentist too – and *that* you mustn't miss. But the three of us might dine together. A farewell dinner. What time is the embassy meeting, Micky?'

'Early afternoon – if this man arrives on time –' glancing at Tasha – 'and I dare say a few hours—'

'You'd be free to join us for the evening, anyway.'

'But –' to Tasha – 'you will see me off on Thursday at the Gare du Nord?'

'Of course I will! I wouldn't dream of letting you set off on your own!'

Her mother had shrugged. 'I'll let you do that on your own. Friday, you realize, we leave for Yalta?'

Tasha's shining eyes and subdued inner smile then: telling him while not letting her mother see it *Wednesday – the hell with Friday!* Wednesday at 2.30, Rue des Poiriers, deuxième étage: she must have been waiting with her ear against the door, he'd been about to tap on it when it had opened as if by magic and she'd pulled him in: Tasha lovelier than ever in a green-striped *peignoir* borrowed from her friend Elise.

Rojhestvensky made a general signal that evening – the 26th – *Tomorrow at Colours battle ensigns are to be hoisted and ships cleared for action.*

Colours was the ensign-hoisting ritual invariably performed at 0800. Dawn action stations would be at 0500, falling out after about an hour – depending on visibility and whether there were indications of enemy ships nearby – and the ship's company would then be sent to breakfast. By 0800 – subject to breakdowns between now and then – the squadron would still be about four hours short of Tsushima.

Zakharov came into the chartroom, where Michael was bringing the navigational log up to date. This morning there'd been a few stars visible, but thanks to the fog, no horizon. He was still relying on dead reckoning therefore – course steered and distance run by log. The flagship – Captain Sidorenko, assisted by Nick Sollogub – would have been doing the same, one might assume getting near-identical results.

Michael pointed at the signal-file. 'Battle ensigns at eight.'

'Yes. I saw it.' Zakharov leaning with his fists on the table's edge, eyes following the pencilled track passing east of Tsushima, midway between it and the Honshu mainland coast. 'He's not trying to persuade us we'll get through without a fight.'

'Doesn't have much faith in his own deception gambit, then.'

'Having had time to think about it, nor do I. Togo wouldn't either – that's what counts. Who in his right mind would elect to steam an extra fifteen hundred miles – needing coaling stops – at least one – in the open sea, which might be rough the whole damn way?'

'A gambler might. Counting on conditions being right for one coaling – and, as you say, on Togo's certainty that's where he *wouldn't* be.'

'He'd be a madman. Because he wouldn't achieve surprise in any case. An interval of eight to ten days, say – and no sign of us – where else might we have gone?' Abrupt shake of the head. 'We're in for a scrap, and Zenovy Petrovich knows it.'

'I'm sure you're right.' Opening his cigarette case. 'Smoke?'

'Thank you.'

'One point, Nikolai Timofeyevich. No – two.' Stooping to the match. 'Thanks. The first is I can't really serve as your navigator when we're in action. On the bridge as your right hand, so to speak – and me an ally of your enemies?'

'Originally you were going to assist Baranov.'

'That's the second thing. My purpose in being here, as you know, is to report on battle tactics and so forth – and if I'm below decks, shuffling stretchers around—'

'You'd see nothing. You need to be up here. Yes, all right.'

'I'll explain to Baranov.'

'And will you answer one hypothetical question – while we have the time and opportunity?'

'Of course.'

'If I should be killed in this battle, Mikhail Ivan'ich, and you survive it—'

'*Very* hypothetical.'

'The question is, what would you say about me to Tasha?'

'Oh.' He took a drag at his cigarette. 'I'd tell her she was well out of it. That you were a terrible bad hat, with girls in every town in Russia.'

'Seriously, please.'

'You want me to pay you compliments?'

'To tell me the truth.'

'Well – that *would* be paying compliments.'

'That's my answer, then. Thank you. Despite the arrangement concluded with her father, I get a clean bill of health, so to speak. I'm glad. But now let's imagine it the other way about. If you were killed – which could happen; a ten-inch *chemodan* is no respecter of individuals or nationalities, you know.'

'Isn't a *chemodan* a suitcase – piece of luggage—'

'It's a slang word for a type of enormous shell they use. We heard of them from survivors of Round Island. From that fellow Selyeznov, for one. Shells about four feet long, they turn in the air like a stick you throw for a dog, and – a huge explosion, apparently. Anyway – want to know what *I* would say to Tasha?'

'I can see you want to tell me.'

'I'd tell her that you were in love with her.'

'In love . . .' In the circumstances it wasn't difficult to show surprise. 'That *I*—'

'Would it surprise her?'

'My dear Nikolai—'

'Does she return your affection, is what I'm asking. This is not in any way accusatory, Mikhail Ivan'ich. I'm only telling you something that's been obvious to me for some time. At any mention of her, I see it. Your reaction to *me*, in respect of her, was at first hostile, but more latterly has become merely guarded. But there's also a look, and a tone of voice. I'm quite certain you *are* in love with her.'

'Well.' Pressing out the cigarette. 'If you're certain – not much point in my protesting – commenting, even.'

'Not even on whether she returns the affection?'

'In the sense that you're putting it – no. I do have a

warm regard for her – which you might choose to call love—'

'Is it reciprocated?'

'– but since she was a child, you see. Yes, I'd say there *is* a mutual affection. Which I value very highly. Putting it in proportion though, when I saw her this last time at Injhavino it was the first time since she was fifteen!'

'Beautiful even then, I imagine.'

'Oh.' A shrug. 'Yes – she *was* – a very pretty child. She's her mother's daughter, after all – and Anna Feodorovna—'

'Is an exceptionally good-looking woman. But tell me this—'

'I'll tell you *this*. The first time I set eyes on Tasha— '

'You have that look again. And the way you pronounce her name—'

'– the first time, she was a babe in arms!'

'At Injhavino, was that?'

'Yes. My mother and I had been on a visit to her family estate – to celebrate her father's seventy-fifth birthday – after which we spent a few days at Injhavino. I was – oh, eleven—'

'What I was about to ask you, Mikhail—'

'I'm not sure I like your questions.'

'Well – that tells me something—'

'To be extremely fond of someone is not necessarily to be *in love* with them, Nikolai.'

'Not necessarily – no. But I'll still ask you this. Returning to the hypothetical: if I were killed tomorrow and you survived—'

'I'd tell her you weren't a bad fellow at all, except for your habit of asking embarrassingly personal questions.'

'Would you marry her?'

Staring at him. Reaching for another cigarette – but Zakharov got in first with his. Michael asking himself, why not admit it – steering clear, of course, of the least hint of kiss-and-tell? He gestured, helplessly: 'I suppose that is – conceivable, but—'

'But?'

'For one thing, if I did find myself in that position and state of mind – *she'd* have to – be of the same mind. Unlike your own approach, Nikolai—'

'Yes, get *that* in!'

'Part and parcel of the answer, that's all. Part one, yes, I could envisage much crueller fates; part two, how *she* might feel about it I've absolutely no idea. And that's the subject finally disposed of, uh?' He touched the chart. 'I hadn't realized until now that Tsushima is actually two islands. Or that *shima* means "island". So for "Tsushima", if one was being pedantic, read Shimo Shima and Kami Shima. Did you know that?'

'As it happens, yes. Caught on to it when discussing alternative routes and so forth with the late lamented Viktor Vasil'ich Radzianko. Here,' striking another of his matches. 'My apologies for interrogating you on so personal a subject, Mikhail Ivan'ich.'

23

He was in the bridge long before dawn. The wind had come up a bit, *Ryazan* slamming through a three-foot head-sea, kicking up spray that lashed back salting her black sides, but the fog seemed impervious to it. Two-thirty now: Konyev had the watch with Denisov as his assistant, the signal yeoman of the watch was Putilin, bosun's mate Drachin. The bridge messenger, Sokolov, asked Michael if his honour would like a jar of tea, and he thanked him, said yes, he would.

He did belong. It was amazing, really, but he *did*. Born, what was more, of having fallen in love with a schoolgirl a few years ago. Prince Igor might claim responsibility but that was where this had begun.

'Tea, your honour.'

'Thank you, my friend.' He took it to the bridge chart-table, let the canvas hood down, pushed his head and shoulders inside and switched on the light; taking care, with the ship's lurching movement, not to slop tea over the chart – which was the same as the one in the chartroom. He checked the log reading – distance run since midnight when the ship's position had last been updated – and marked it on as 0230.

Eighty-five miles to go, to the Tsushima Strait. At nine knots, just under ten hours. ETA at the southern end of Shimo Shima a little after noon, therefore. Or maybe noon or as near as dammit, the current according to a note in the sailing directions being stronger northbound than it was when southerly, in the alternating tides. He switched the light off and backed out, took his tea with him to the starboard fore-corner of the bridge.

'Up to schedule, aren't we?'

Konyev: a large young man with a full beard and slitted eyes. About twenty-five, and engaged to a girl who wrote to him on heavily scented paper. He was from Moscow but had served in the Black Sea under Zakharov.

Michael said yes, barring breakdowns they'd be entering the Tsushima Strait at about midday.

'Needn't interfere with our celebratory breakfast anyway.'

'Ah – no, I suppose . . .'

Today, May 27th – by the old calendar May 14th – was the ninth anniversary of the coronation of the Tsar and Tsarina. Also, of course, of the dreadful stampede by his loyal subjects on the Khodyinka Field: but that one did *not* celebrate.

Or mention.

He finished his tea, put the jar down on the step on the other side where bridge messengers had a plug for their electric kettle, returned to his position in that fore-corner and unslung his binoculars.

Should have tried to sleep on, maybe. Might not be any rest at all from here. Denisov was asking Konyev, 'Champagne for breakfast, huh?'

'That's the tradition. But don't count on it.'

'No . . .'

'Just keep your eyes peeled.'

The more pairs of eyes the better. There were two lookouts in bays like iron nesting-boxes on each side of the bridge, and another two in the spotting-top – up there on the foremast, a black smudge against the fog-laden overhead, halfway to the foreyard. Michael added his own contribution now, having wiped his binoculars' front lenses clean and temporarily dry.

In Togo's boots – or slippers – wouldn't one lie in ambush either in or above the straits?

With one's main force, surely, well to the north of them. Maybe a cruiser squadron or two further south; as likely as not a few scouts on the prowl down here. If one was guessing right, that was what one should be looking out for now – primarily in order to know when/if the squadron was spotted. Although it was likely that when that happened the telegraphists would know in any case – the airwaves quivering with excitement and reports to Togo.

For *Ryazan* meanwhile, stuck here as rearguard to about thirty-nine other ships, the only useful lookout was from the beams to right astern, for enemies either cutting it fine across the squadron's stern, or overhauling.

Only the hospital-ships were in sight. Thirty degrees on either bow, Konyev adjusting revs slightly from time to time to maintain his distance-astern of two cables or four hundred yards. With their light-coloured paintwork though, you'd see them at three times that distance. Training right now, slowly, years of practice keeping the glasses steady against the ship's jolting pitch and roll. Reminding himself that warpaint on Japanese ships was grey: in peacetime their hulls were black and upperworks grey, but in war all grey.

As well to have in mind what you were looking for. Reactions tended to be faster.

Lights were winking ahead – red and white Tabulevich – as he swung back to begin another sweep. A shout from P.O. Putilin then: 'Signal to us from Flag, your honour!'

Konyev to the messenger: 'Shake the captain.'

'From Flag, sir –' Putilin reading it aloud word by word as it was passed on to them by the rearmost of the starboard column – mental effort telling Michael that that would be the *Nakhimov* – '*Investigate vessel on reciprocal course on beam to port approx fifteen cables* – end of message!'

'Starboard fifteen.' Zakharov had heard it as he came bounding from his cabin. Ordering three hundred and eighty revs then – for twenty knots – and Denisov jumping to a telephone. 'All quarters alert.' Zakharov, over the open line to the turrets: 'Lieutenant Murayev to the conning-tower.'

Since the guns were already manned and turret and barbette crews had now been alerted there was no need to go to action stations: nothing might come of this, 'vessel' could mean anything, and attack by torpedo-craft was hardly to be expected. *Ryazan* heeling under port rudder, vibration matching the increased revs, wind on the beam as she swung away. Zakharov's voice again: 'Midships.' Easing the fifteen degrees of rudder off her. Michael on his way meanwhile to the chartroom to snatch up a blank plotting-diagram – an item like a chart but with nothing on it except the compass roses – and bring it to the table on the bridge. Back-dating the time of turning by one minute and noting the log-reading; their course *had* been north forty east, was now northwest. He laid off the squadron's continuing northeasterly progress at nine knots: a mile every six and a half minutes would be close enough, with *Ryazan* diverging at say an average of fifteen knots working up to twenty if this jaunt lasted long enough. At *some* point Zakharov would want a course on which to rejoin the squadron, and this plot would provide it.

'Ship red one-zero, sir!'

A lookout's hail, high like a seabird's screech. Konyev's bellow then as he got on to it too: 'Moving right to left, high speed. Cruiser, I think—'

'Starboard ten.'

'Starboard ten, sir . . .'

Bringing her further round to port, to put the enemy to starboard and stay with him on a converging track. 'Steer southwest. Yeoman – make to Flag, *Enemy cruiser steering south at high speed* – distance, Konyev?'

Konyev told him, 'Mile, mile and a quarter.'

'*Distance about ten cables. Shall I pursue?*'

'Midships!'

'Midships, sir—'

'Steer south eighty west.'

Ryazan was probably making her twenty knots by now. Both hospital-ships already lost to sight. That signal was flickering from the foreyard and if the Jap was on his toes he'd see it: might not, though, and the real question was whether he'd spotted the squadron – the battle squadron itself or the *Zemchug* out to port of it – or was sweeping south in search of them and hadn't. If he was on a scouting foray he might well be one of a group of others, as like as not in line abreast.

'From Flag, sir – *Negative, resume station*!'

Made sense, too. Zakharov's real question had been, Do you want action here now, or to continue trying to get through and on to the Vladivostok side of him? *Him* meaning Togo. Michael ducked back in to his plotting diagram, brought it up to date: time, distance run at this speed and to all intents and purposes circling slightly south of west, squadron continuing on north forty degrees east at nine knots . . .

'Pilot?'

'Sir?'

'A course to rejoin?'

'North forty-seven east at fifteen knots would do it, sir.'

'The devil it would.' A snort of amusement. 'Port fifteen.' Reduction in revs, then: down to three hundred and twenty. Murayev's voice: 'Shame to have to let the bugger go, sir.' Murayev must have come up when Michael had been in the chartroom or busy under that hood. Zakharov calling down the tube, 'Steer north forty-seven east.' He answered Murayev, as *Ryazan* butted her stem through north, smashing the waves into flying white sheets and streams again, 'Unless he hadn't spotted any of us. Don't want to tell 'em we're here, do we? Might as well relax your gunners.'

'Aye, sir . . .'

'Mikhail Ivan'ich – I thought you'd resigned the office of navigator?'

'Happened to be here, sir . . .'

There was still no excitement on the air-waves, only the same exchange of incomprehensible but routine-sounding messages. Suggesting that that cruiser's watchkeepers had *not* been on their toes. *Ryazan* was back in station astern of the hospital-ships by 0300, and Michael retired to the chartroom to put his feet up and smoke a pipe, Egorov joining him there with jars of tea for them both; Michael explained the plot to him, the relative velocities involved, and left it to him to clean the diagram off so it could be used again. At 0400 the watch changed, Pepelyayev taking over from Konyev and Dukhonin from Denisov. Michael had in fact nodded off to sleep a few minutes before the bugle-call sounded for dawn action stations at 0430: he jerked awake, complaining to Egorov who was still there, 'Hear that bloody row in Nagasaki!' He guessed that Zakharov might have told Egorov to be ready to take over as acting navigator when he himself threw his hand in: he had the feeling that he was waiting for it, for his big moment. And why not? But there was also a feeling that this was the longest, slowest coming of dawn in history. Light *was* growing, spreading through the enshrouding mist, but only very gradually. Of which one should be glad, maybe – if one could have believed in it lasting. On the bridge again, leaning against the side of the chart-table and sucking an empty pipe while the crew were settling down at their action stations, reports being passed via voicepipes and telephones; he realized that this wasn't just the dampness of fog: while he'd been inside a fine drizzle had set in. Further reduction in visibility . . . Burmin paused beside him, commenting, 'If this could *last* we might get away with it . . .'

'Signal from Flag, sir!'

Travkov, chief yeoman. His caboose was on the starboard side of the bridge, opposite this navigational position; a signalman had read the ripple of Tabulevich from the spotting-top and passed it down to him by voicepipe. 'Flag has enemy in sight starboard, sir!'

'Port fifteen.'

Moving her out to starboard: crossing the wake of the *Orel*, to be in a position to put himself between her and whatever – *wherever*—

'Captain, sir.' Travkov had moved quickly into the fore-bridge. 'Spotted it from aloft, your honour – auxiliary cruiser, Morozov reckoned. Come an' gone though – fog lifted an' he put his helm over smartish like!'

'Come and gone'. Meaning the Jap had had the surprise of his life and nipped back into the murk. A scout, who'd blundered into what he was looking for. In which case—

'What's W/T doing now, chief yeoman?' Wooden face dipping to the wheelhouse voicepipe again: 'Midships and meet her.' Putting on opposite rudder to check the swing to starboard. Since the Jap had made off so smartly, and knowing that Rojhestvensky wouldn't want to disperse his forces chasing individual specimens into the wild blue yonder: at this stage, most certainly would not. Burmin – materializing from nowhere – growled, 'By midday we'll be at it hammer and tongs, you'll see,' and vanished down the steps into the conning-tower – probably to use one of the telephones. Travkov, meanwhile, had got his report from the wireless-room: 'Jap W/T's going mad, sir!'

'I believe you, chief.' It was just about light now, lances of watery-silvery sunrise penetrating the haze of mist and drizzle; the wetness glistening like polish on that face devoid of all expression as it turned glancing back at the chief yeoman. A mutter to Burmin then as the second-in-command came back up on to the bridge: 'They're telling Togo where we are.'

Might be an end to the squadron's strict wireless silence too – since its position (and approximate course and speed) were known. And sure enough, the first signal came from the flagship within minutes: *Almaz*, *Svetlana* and *Ural* to haul out to starboard and fall back to become rearguard a mile astern of the hospital-ships, and *Ryazan* to take station ten cables' lengths on the flagship's starboard bow.

To discourage any further approach by that auxiliary cruiser – which might be keeping station on them somewhere out on that bearing, Michael guessed. Could be waiting there for others to join it. The transports wouldn't be any better protected by those three so-called scouts with their light weaponry than they had been up to now by *Ryazan.* The *Svetlana* did have a main armament of 6-inch, but the other two were only lightly armed, 3-pounders or somesuch – the *Almaz* more like a yacht than a warship, and the *Ural* formerly the liner *Kaiserin Maria Theresa.* Between them, of course, they'd cover a wider area than *Ryazan* could have done on her own, if Rojhestvensky had reason to expect an attack on the transports from astern – to which, making only nine knots, and the enemy most likely having a superiority in cruisers, they certainly would be vulnerable.

Zakharov's low-voiced explanation was 'Paying us a compliment. Wants us where he can shift us quickly into the way of trouble.' *Ryazan* making about twenty knots again at this time, legging it up the squadron's starboard side, men in the bridge exchanging waves with those on the *Izumrud*'s as she ploughed past her. Wind and sea had risen during the past hour and it was a pounding, thrusting progress; the destroyers with *Izumrud* were having a hard time of it.

Michael noted in his diary:

In new station at 0600. Signal to Flag from *Ural* 0620 that 4 ships, indistinguishable owing to poor visibility, were crossing from east to west two miles astern of her. One might guess, cruisers. They seem to be all over the place. Enemy W/T still very active. The squadron back there on our quarter under its pall of smoke looks like a forbiddingly powerful fleet – if it could shoot straight perhaps it would be. The enemy won't lose us now, having found us: we're no needle and the straits ahead of us are no haystack, and our lack of speed, especially now that we're further slowed by Nyebogatov's flat-irons is another major handicap.

He'd told Tasha more than once that there was nothing

predictable about the outcome of a battle, if there should be one. *Wasn't* there? Or was it just that as one got closer to the proof of the pudding one became somewhat queasy?

Diary again:

> 0645, ship on starboard beam. Z proposed intercepting with *Ryazan* but flagship vetoed this. Z sounding sour about it then. I would too: we could at least make a move to drive her off. She's staying with us, converging very gradually, doubtless noting and passing on every detail – and being allowed to get away with it.

'Mikhail Ivan'ich – chartroom, a minute?'

To look this Jap up in the Russian-language edition of *Jane's Fighting Ships.* Michael got it out of the cupboard of reference books and opened it at the Japanese section.

'Armoured cruiser – right?'

A nod from wooden-face. 'Three tall, narrow funnels.'

'Here, perhaps?'

'Battleship, that.'

'Well . . .' Two pages on: 'How about this?'

'Looks right. Eight-inch. Has the range of us, therefore. Either the *Idzumo* or the *Iwate.*'

A quick look at cruisers on the next few pages confirmed it: on all others with three funnels the funnels were squatter, thicker. Zakharov admitted, 'For eight-inch guns I don't mind remaining in station. Might clear the range if necessary for *Suvarov* to try with her twelve-inch.'

'Think we'd *need* to clear the range?'

'Trust *Suvarov*'s gun-trainers to that extent, would you?'

They didn't need to shift out of the way, in fact. At about eight, by which time the range had come down to less than ten thousand yards, when the flagship's 12-inch turrets swung out to the beam and the massive barrels lifted, the Jap's length diminished within seconds as she turned away.

Having seen and reported all she'd been told to report on, no doubt.

Diary entry at 0812:

On port bow suddenly clear of mist, Japs identified as *Chin Yen* (old battleship), *Matsushima* (old cruiser, but has 12-inch guns), *Itsukushima* (similar), *Hashidate* (same again) and *Akitsushu* (smaller, with 6-inch) appeared on parallel course but soon drew away northward.

We are closing up towards Tsushima. At this stage it's only a hump of land intermittently visible when mist thins or parts. By and large the mist probably *is* dissipating to some extent.

10 a.m.: on port beam, light cruisers *Chitose, Kasagi, Niitaka* and *Otawa,* these again steaming on parallel course, but staying there. Not much doubt of the identifications, young Egorov has a keen eye for it.

Arkoleyev, the engineer, at Zakarov's invitation came up for a look. Burmin pointed out the line of enemy cruisers, which were then at something like fifteen thousand yards. 'Studying us and noting what each captain's had for breakfast, uh?'

'Or measuring us for our coffins?'

Surprisingly, several of the bridge staff laughed. Rojhestvensky on the other hand must have decided it was time to do something about such blatant provocation; he ran up the signal for the squadron to assume battle formation.

'Showing willing.' Burmin, with his glasses up. 'Telling 'em he's as eager for the fray as they are. Good idea. And there we go – signal's coming down!'

Hauling a flag signal down meant 'execute'. First and second divisions increasing speed and turning twenty-two and a half degrees to port, third division (Nyebogatov's) tagging on astern; one single line of battle, therefore. Cruisers shifting meanwhile to station themselves around the transports – except for those three remaining as rearguard and *Ryazan* staying put until otherwise ordered.

1120: *Oryol* fired one shot from her for'ard 12-inch and immediately semaphored that she'd done so by mistake, but others mistook it for the admiral setting an example which they should follow. The entire line opened fire, enemy cruisers turned away at the same time, replying with a few shots of their own. Flagship then signalled *Cease fire* and *Ammunition not to be wasted.*

Midday: Ko Saki, southernmost cape on Shimo Shima, abeam to port. Course altered to N. 23 degs E. – course for Vladivostok. Signal from flagship, ships' companies to be sent to dinner.

To drink to the health of the Tsar and Tsarina the sailors would get tots of vodka with their 'dinner', but in the wardroom it was called 'breakfast' – a Coronation Day tradition, normally a sumptuous meal with admirals and captains attending, but in this instance more a spread of *zakuski* than a proper meal; and Zakharov, of course, wouldn't leave the bridge. Champagne was served though, and Burmin proposed the royal toasts: 'On this anniversary of the coronation of their Highnesses, may God help us to serve with honour our beloved country! To the health of the Emperor! The health of the Empress! To Russia!'

They cheered, and proposed more toasts – including the health and strength of Zenovy Petrovich Rojhestvensky. Michael, having seen that young Egorov had only begun to croak 'Emperor, Empress' and had then given up, choking and with tears in his eyes, told him, 'Keep your hopes up, Gavril Ivan'ich. Awful not getting news, but the odds are he's alive and well.' The cheers were fading: Karasyov swilling the champagne down and shouting, 'What's this we're eating – fried monkey?' and Arkoleyev proposing cynically to Burmin, 'With so much to celebrate, why don't we all dance the Kamarinsky?'

'Well, look here, Pyotr Davidovich—'

'But why *don't* we?' *Michman* Count Provatorov springing up, sending his chair crashing over. 'Thundering good idea, *I'd* say!'

'Hey—'

Alarm buzzer: penetrative, insistent: then, overlapping it, a bugle-call Michael hadn't heard before but which Burmin told him meant 'Clear for action'.

The reason for cutting short the celebrations was that a force of cruisers had reappeared on the flagship's port bow, seemingly with the intention of crossing ahead of the squadron, more than likely to lay mines; to thwart this, Rojhestvensky had led his ships of the first division round to starboard, to open their broadsides to the cruisers and thus deter them from any such attempt. Michael recorded it in his notes: in terms of battle tactics it was a first move in what amounted to preliminary sparring, would indeed have been commendable as a quick and effective response to that threat if the *Suvarov* division hadn't bungled it, some turning 'in succession' and others 'together' – course alterations which in the Royal Navy were referred to as either 'red' or 'blue' turns. The result of the mix-up was that the first division finished up in a column of its own, parallel to and slightly ahead of the others.

Ryazan was under helm, Zakharov having turned similarly in order to maintain his distance – as previously ordered, ten cables – on the flagship's bow; he was now turning back. The Japanese cruiser force had in any case taken the hint and hauled away to port – so the purpose of the manoeuvre had been achieved – and the cruiser admiral would no doubt be telling Togo that the Russian battle-squadrons were now disposed in two columns instead of one. Togo and *his* battlefleet being at this moment anything from say five to fifty miles away. More likely five or ten, in view of the number of lesser units in the immediate area. Michael was jotting all this down in his notebook. There were logs kept in the bridge (on the signal desk) and in the wheelhouse (three decks lower, directly below the forefront of the bridge and conning-tower) and when the time came (touch wood) to draw up his report he hoped he might prevail upon

Zakharov to allow him access to them; but in the meantime *Ryazan* might be sunk, in which case he'd have his own notes in his pocket.

All right – probably so much papier mâché in his pocket. But you could only hope for the best. Time now: 1310. Rojhestvensky had got his four battleships in line and back on course and had signalled for divisions two and three to take station astern of him, i.e. for the *Oslyabya* to close up into station astern of the *Oryol*. Michael had his glasses on them, saw that the line was pretty well as it had been, except for a noticeable gap in it at that point. It would be in the *Oslyabya*'s own best interests to close up, he thought; in her present position you wouldn't doubt she was the leader of the rear divisions, and as such she'd get special attention from the Japanese gunners, once it started. *Suvarov* would certainly receive the lion's share, since to knock out flagships and admirals was always a primary endeavour. Togo wasn't to know that the admiral in *Oslyabya*, Felkerzam, was already dead, that Rojhestvensky's second in command was now Nyebogatov in his old *Nikolai I*. After all, Nyebogatov himself didn't know it.

'Ship cleared for action, sir.'

Burmin. Zakharov gave him a nod. They'd started on those preparations much earlier in the day, and on receipt of the order from the admiral would only have had to complete the job, throwing over the side all non-essential combustible objects – including chairs, so that from now on in the wardroom, if you ate at all you'd do it on your feet. Before that, teams of sailors had been making 'sandbags' out of old cordage soaked and parcelled in tarpaulin, hammocks also soaked, sailcloth bundles, coal-sacks, mattresses, all of it drenched from hoses which would now be left connected in order to keep the decks running with salt water. The 'sandbagging' would surround locations that were particularly vulnerable to shell-splinters: the small-calibre guns at all levels of the ship's upperworks, for instance.

One would be a lot safer on *this* bridge than on the

flagship's. No doubt at all, she'd take the brunt of it. Michael had his glasses focussed on her – steadying himself against the ship's quite violent pitching plus a bit of a corkscrew roll now resulting from the weather being on her port bow instead of from right ahead – with thoughts in mind of the jovial Ignatzius and others: including Nick Sollogub with his recollection of having been a page at Anna Feodorovna's wedding to Prince Igor: and Narumov, a lot of whose hard, expert work was likely to be blown to smithereens in the course of the next few hours.

'Excuse me, Mikhail Ivan'ich—'

Padre Myakishev: robed and hatted, sprinkling holy water from the fingertips of his right hand, a jug of it in the crook of the other arm and a carved ebony cross in that left hand.

'Bless you, my son.'

'And bless *you*, Padré.'

'Well . . .' A small smile as he moved on, muttering his benedictions. Perhaps he didn't ordinarily come in for much blessing – being the bless*er*. He'd left the chart unsprinkled, thank heavens: would have sprinkled every gun, turret and barbette though before coming up this far; was on his way down into the conning-tower now.

'Bridge!'

A hail from the spotting-top. Murayev staring up, hands funnel-shaped at his beard: 'Yes? What?'

Disdaining telephone or voicepipe: there were both, allowing for either to be shot away. You could see the spotter's pointing arm as with the mast and yards he swung in an arc, black against grey sky, pointing ahead or maybe fine to starboard. Michael put up his own glasses to sweep across that bearing. All drizzly mist still: the low visibility they'd prayed for but which hadn't done anyone much good – as evinced by this yell from the spotting-top, a strident 'Battleships, sir! Crossing from starboard to port! Four – no, *five*—'

'Chief yeoman – make to the admiral, *Enemy battleships in sight ahead, crossing bow right to left.*'

'Six of 'em, sir!'

As it turned out – when identification by silhouettes became possible – Egorov's frantic efforts again – they were the *Mikasa* – Togo's flagship – the *Shikishima, Fuji, Asahi, Kasuga* and *Nisshin.* Right ahead now: grey miniatures, toys, objects in a magic-lantern show – unreal perhaps because one had had them in mind, imagination, for so long. Breaking off to wipe the lenses dry again, then quickly back up, re-focussing . . . Then – three, four minutes later, in a further thinning of the mist – six more, converging to join that first group from a more northerly direction, and proving after further research to be the *Idzumo, Yakumo, Asama, Azuma, Tokiwa, Iwate* . . .

24

Battle ensigns quivering in the wind, ships' companies all at action stations: if the guns weren't loaded yet they soon would be. In these minutes before two o'clock in the afternoon the Japanese were steering south twenty-three west and the Russians north twenty-three east; opposite courses which if all concerned held on to them would have them passing each other at a range of about – oh, eight thousand yards, but at any rate well inside big-gun range of each other, making whatever they could of it and ending with the Russians on the right side – north – of Togo and on course for Vladivostok.

Rojhestvensky's *hope*, no doubt. Unlikely to be Togo's choice.

In fact there it was, the *Mikasa* had put her helm over: and a howl from the spotting-top was delivering the same news. Not strictly necessary, since from this bridge level one had a clear enough view of them, on a line of sight well ahead of the leader of the pack, the *Suvarov*; and the *Mikasa* was undoubtedly under helm – turning inwards, towards, and on the bow of the Russian battle line. In the longer run though, reversing course, in so doing closing the range and intending then to steam more or less parallel to the Russians. The *Mikasa*'s range from the *Suvarov* at this moment being about seven thousand yards, six thousand five hundred perhaps; the striking thing about it being that in making an 'in succession' turn – each of the twelve Japanese turning successively on the same spot – well, it was either a colossal blunder by Togo or a demonstration of his utter contempt for the Russian gunners, who if they were up to snuff would only have to keep dropping shells into that one patch of water to have them raining down on ship after ship as each reached that point and turned in the swirling wake of its next-ahead. The *Mikasa* at this moment bow-on, about halfway round: high time in fact that the Russian gunners – or rather the admiral, captains, gunnery officers—

Had opened fire. The *Suvarov* had loosed-off with her 12-inch and the others who'd have been waiting for that lead were joining in. A growing thunder: and the sea around the Japanese turning-point spouting whitened pillars. Shells falling, by the look of it from here, surprisingly close. Possibly even hitting: on the *Mikasa* then for sure, a flash and a streak of flame up the side of her bridge superstructure as she bore round.

Maybe Nyebogatov had brought gunners with him who knew their jobs?

The second Japanese was turning now. Range after turning maybe less than six thousand yards. And the *Mikasa* even before steadying on her new course was shooting back. Had certainly been hit that once, in the opening squall of surprisingly accurate shellfire. Number two was in it now – coming out of the turn on what was definitely a converging course and with all her guns firing – while number three was hit in the moment she began to turn, the flash of a shell bursting on her port side but any result lost to sight seconds later, in the turn. Egorov shouted through some cheering, 'That's the *Fuji* was hit!' Splashes were lifting all around her: at least, how it *looked*. You could only know for certain whether fall-of-shot was short or over when it fell in line, on your own line of sight: which was why in directing a shoot you went for line before bothering too much about range: if you got it right, so much the better, but otherwise line first, *then* range. The *Fuji* in any case was ploughing on out through the splashes, hadn't been hit again: which meant that Nyebogatov's gunners, after that false promise at the start, were no better than Rojhestvensky's. Catching at that moment in his glasses a soaring, rapidly expanding speck that was the end-over-end path of a *chemodan* (or 'suitcase') lobbing towards *Suvarov,* who was already smothered in dark smoke that wasn't of her own making, with – inside it – the flashes of exploding shells, and was now, as the *chemodan* vanished down into it, totally obliterated in a huge gush of the same dark (actually greenish-black) filth mushrooming to funnel-height before blowing clear. The *chemodans* weren't fuzed, burst on impact even with the sea's surface, Selyeznov had told him in one instalment of the continuing saga of Round Island; whereas fuzed shell didn't of course, it simply splashed in.

Back to the thought that had been in his head a moment ago: that he was watching the opening stages of a massacre. Having assured Tasha twice, *Nothing pre-ordained* . . .

Unless Rojhestvensky hauled round to port, led his ships across the Japanese line's tail end, as it were crossing the bottom of Togo's 'T' at close enough range for even his gunners to really hammer it, regain the initiative, draw *Japanese* blood?

Suvarov was in a very bad way, though. He – Rojhestvensky – might even be dead, or out of action. It was the Russian line that was being hammered, the sea around them boiling with near-misses, and *Suvarov* and *Oslyabya* both on fire. The range had closed significantly, in a very short space of time: that was only the fourth of the enemy coming out of its turn now. Michael – of a sudden, disbelieving a new phenomenon which he'd thought he'd just seen through his glasses – yelled to Travkov, 'Lend me your telescope, chief yeoman.' Because the magnification would be greater: and what he'd just spotted – *dreamt* he had—

'Only for a moment . . .' Couldn't give him his binoculars in temporary exchange – being on their strap around his neck and his hands busy focussing the telescope . . .

It *was* him. Even the name sprang to mind – from that

briefing in the Admiralty by Captain White ... Glancing sideways at Egorov for a moment: 'Jap that just turned – fourth in line – *Asahi*?'

Egorov consulting his scrawled list: '*Asahi* – yes. Three-funnelled battleship, sister-ship of the *Shikishima*. Yes, she's—'

Asahi. In which was serving Captain W.C. Pakenham, Royal Navy, their Lordships' chief observer and liaison officer with the Japanese. Very tall and spruce and always (White had said) immaculately turned out: 'A character with a capital C by *any* standards, Henderson!' It couldn't be anyone but him – on the *Asahi*'s quarterdeck, in a deck-chair. It *had* to be: *Asahi* being the ship in which he'd served throughout this Russian war. In any case, what Japanese would sit and watch a major fleet action from a deck-chair on a battleship's otherwise bare and empty quarterdeck?

'Thanks.' Returning the telescope to Travkov. Still hardly believing ... Pakenham and Togo held each other in great respect, White had told him. Oh, and he wore a monocle. That had *not* been visible, but one had seen that he was as tall – or long – as a praying mantis. Seen, or had the impression, imagined, deduced ... No deductive powers being needed to see that the poor *Suvarov* had been hit again, or that the *Oslyabya* was still catching it hot and strong – as were all the rest of them. Togo's men could shoot. While here the *Ryazan* was untouched, unscratched, merely spectating: not that that would last for very long, he guessed. In any case she had a function here, watching out ahead and to starboard for cruisers and/or destroyers working their way up on this blind side of the action – where admittedly if they went in close enough they'd be running the gauntlet of their own battleships' fall of shot – so you could take it that they would not, would be more likely to move in well astern of the main action as it shifted northward and northeastward; but Zakharov and his bridge staff would also be looking out for developments on the quarter, southeastward, where at some considerable distance now the *Oleg*, *Aurora*, *Donskoi* and others would still be nursing the transports and hospital-ships

– who you could bet wouldn't be left alone for ever and to whose assistance *Ryazan* might well be called upon to divert. There were, after all, cruiser squadrons on the loose, in or around this strait, and when the battleships and flat-irons had been disposed of – which could happen even before the light went . . .

Michael turned back to where this battle, which they'd come eighteen thousand miles to fight, was clearly being thrown away, undoubtedly at huge expense of Russian lives. The Japanese *might* be suffering too; it wasn't easy to tell whether many of the flashes sparking from the enemy ships were the flashes of their own guns firing or of Russian shells hitting. Russian shells being filled with Pyroxylene, which was smokeless, gunners thus deprived of the morale-strengthening effect of seeing their shells burst when/if they did score hits. That was the last of the Japanese turning now. They weren't by any means all battleships, several were armoured cruisers, but none had guns that were less than 8-inch and they were all modern ships capable of twenty knots or more: and none of them were showing any signs of having suffered serious damage. W.C. Pakenham no doubt still at ease in his deck-chair, monocle in place and high wing collar freshly starched: jotting down an occasional note with surely nothing other than a *gold* propelling pencil?

Suvarov back there was a smoking junk-hcap: and still taking punishment. Also – astoundingly – still shooting back, with her 12-pounders, or a few of them. Shooting at what, though? Her main armament had all been smashed – turrets breached, gun-barrels sticking out at all angles . . . Oh, *God* – explosion just *then,* under her fore-turret. The enemy perhaps using armour-piercing shells now instead of high-explosive. Or that might have resulted from internal fires. *Oslyabya* was also still afloat – just – and still burning internally, leaking smoke and intermittently jets of flame from her many wounds. A big, high-sided ship, she was low in the sea, listing heavily to port and down by the bow; you could imagine the inferno inside her, and the rising flood.

And the *Alexander* had hauled out of the line. The line in fact – as far as it still existed – two flat-irons – only *two*? – and the *Navarin, Sissoy, Nikolai* – was bending, developing a curve to starboard, Togo as it were shouldering them round, away from any northward course, above all away from Vladivostok, forcing them round to starboard, and the range down to – oh, hard to see, but two thousand yards? *Suvarov* was quite on her own and still taking hits; *Oslyabya* practically on her side; the *Alexander* with both funnels and most of her bridge shot away, also holed for'ard and down by the bow; *Borodino* with flames licking from shell-holes extending from stem to stern, and the *Oryol* also on fire; effectively there was *no* Russian line of battle.

Tsushima, he thought. *This* was the picture that name would conjure – in one's memory and in the history books. For 'battle', read 'rout', read 'annihilation'. 'And what did you do while it was going on, Grandfather?' 'Oh, I *watched* it, my dear. Safely out of range, mind you . . .'

'Mikhail Ivan'ich!'

A hand on his arm. In the same moment he felt the change in the ship's motion: revs increasing and helm over, heeling as she altered course as well as picked up speed. This was Egorov shouting across the wind and general racket, 'Captain says better move into the conning-tower!'

'All right.' He had his glasses up again though: it looked as if the battle lines were separating, the Japanese altering away to port. And closer at hand the *Oslyabya* was going, dipping that side right under, rolling belly-up and bow-down, men like ants tumbling down the steep, black-painted weed-smothered iron slope of her: bow-down and stern lifting then, she'd begun to slide. Had gone. Taking her dead admiral with her – as well as a few hundred others.

Zakharov had steadied *Ryazan* on course for the burning *Suvarov*. Or anyway for the smoke covering that area. Making about twenty knots now, with – if that was where he was taking her – about four thousand yards to go. Six minutes, therefore. A destroyer – Russian – was moving in to pick up *Oslyabya* survivors: not that there'd be many. Egorov was shouting something about a wireless message from another destroyer – the *Buiny*, 'buiny' meaning 'furious' – who'd been asked to try to get in alongside the flagship's remains and take off the admiral.

'Take *off*—'

'Some geezer semaphored to 'em, your honour.' Travkov, coming up against a stanchion on the chart-table's other side as the ship rolled, catching him off-balance. 'His Excellency's hurt bad and the staff want him off, so—'

You'd hardly believe anyone could be alive in that burning wreck. Except one or two guns somewhere near her stern *had* still been firing a short while ago: which meant there had to be attackers too, a target for them to have been shooting at, whoever/whatever was still making a target of *her*. So much smoke though – and not only hers . . . The idea of getting the admiral out of his floating bonfire of a flagship meanwhile rang a bell: Narumov describing V.V. Ignatzius's insistence on his admiral being saved: *He's our mainspring, without him we'd be lost . . .*

The *Buiny* wouldn't get in on *Suvarov*'s lee side. Even from here you could see that the flames and smoke were blowing out horizontally a good hundred yards down-wind. You'd be burnt to a frazzle, as well as choked and blinded. She'd have to do it from windward – dangerous enough even without whatever sporadic bombardment was still in progress; and to give her a chance of getting away with it, *Ryazan* would have to put herself – hold herself – where she'd provide some degree of shelter from shot and shell as well as weather, the wind tending to smash the little torpedo-boat against that hulk.

'Conning-tower, Mikhail Ivan'ich!'

'But you're staying up here?'

'For the moment only. Until I can see into the damn smoke. Destroyers in there somewhere—'

'You mean *Buiny*—'

'I mean *enemy. Suvarov*'s been holding 'em off this far, but—'

'Guns on her stern?'

'Gun, singular – one three-inch in her lower stern battery. Which they're still trying to knock out, obviously to get in then with torpedoes.'

'I'd take that gun's crew off and give 'em medals!'

'Hear, hear.' Ducking to the voicepipe: 'Steer five degrees to starboard.' Glancing at Burmin then, who was shouting into a telephone – to Murayev in the conning-tower – 'No, no target yet. I'll warn you, when—'

'Want me to do that?'

Point being that the view from inside the conning-tower was so limited, although it was where Murayev had to be to control the guns, and Galikovsky his torpedoes. Once targets were picked it was all right, but as it was – smoke creating virtual darkness and with only a slit to look through in that 5-inch armour, no idea yet what your enemy was or where – and the second-in-command having about fifty other things to do . . .

'All right.' Thrusting the telephone at him. 'Torpedo-boat destroyers we're looking for – right?'

He'd nodded. And been thrown one hard glance from Zakharov. He was on the step then with his glasses up, the telephone held with them, in one hand. Gunfire still more or less continuous but most of it from four or five miles away, in this vicinity definitely sporadic. Here – ahead – *Suvarov*'s smouldering hulk glowed through her own and others' smoke: *Ryazan* entering it like a train rushing into a tunnel.

'Here's *Buiny*.' Emerging from the smoke with them, a cable's length to port: Zakharov must have seen her before, known where she was: hence that recent small alteration to starboard, maybe. Gun-flash on the bow: Jap destroyer. Turning away but had been *very* quick off the mark, the splash of that shell lifting only just short of the *Buiny*'s foc'sl. Michael told Murayev, 'Thirty degrees on the bow to starboard – second one just beyond it – no, that's a light cruiser!'

'*Right!*'

Light cruiser wreathed in its own smoke, on fire aft and listing but with some guns – probably four-sevens – still manned: maybe by reduced crews, hence the slowness . . .

Ryazan slowing, interposing herself between the *Buiny* and their enemies. Zakharov was putting on starboard helm now, port rudder, to leave as narrow a gap as possible between this ship and the flagship's wallowing, burning hulk, while still allowing *Buiny* room for manoeuvre. Ear-slamming impact of *Ryazan*'s for'ard 6-inch: more of it as she swung and brought her starboard broadside to bear. A spurt of flame then and a different but equally deafening explosion seemingly just abaft the bridge: 12-pounder shell – or a four-seven – bursting on either the foremost funnel or a ventilator, metal fragments whirring overhead. But it was a case of tit for tat, the destroyer had been hit and hit hard, cheers just audible through the continuing barrage. As she was lying now, five of *Ryazan*'s twelve 6-inch were in action, and the Black Sea influence – guns' crews who knew what they were doing – was making itself felt. She'd been hit again though – starboard side aft. Michael trying to get rid of the telephone he'd found himself stuck with, Egorov obligingly taking it from him: he'd moved to the other side to watch the *Buiny* making her dangerous approach, when a torpedo from *Ryazan* blew the cruiser's bow off. There was cheering over the gunfire and general racket: that was one enemy done for, leaving only the destroyer to be dealt with. And *Buiny* was in there now, lifting and falling on this lively sea, her skipper working his screws and helm to manoeuvre her in closer without getting skewered on the bent and twisted barrels of smashed guns projecting at all angles from their ports. Coming up against any of them his ship's thin plating wouldn't have stood a chance.

The focus of the whole endeavour was an embrasure standing open in *Suvarov*'s shell-scarred, ripped and punctured side, near her bow, with men moving in silhouette inside it waiting for them, no doubt the admiral amongst them – presumably *not* on his feet. How they hoped to make the transfer . . . Well, at the top of the three hundred and fifty ton destroyer's upward swoop, obviously – slinging him over *somehow.* Difficult enough even with a normal, man-sized body, but that huge one . . .

The rate of fire from *Ryazan*'s guns had risen again, but less 6-inch now than 12-pounders blasting away: a new target presumably, maybe that destroyer chancing its arm again – or another one. One of its torpedoes was all you'd need – for a one-way ticket to Kingdom Come, a transfer which hundreds or even a few thousand had already made in the course of this now darkening afternoon. Not darkening, quite, but the light definitely fading: and a sudden blossoming of *rosy* light out there! He was in time to see the source of it – the destroyer or *a* destroyer, steel plating opening like the petals of a flower and from the brilliance inside a shower of burning debris—

'Scrambling-net's in place port side, sir!'

Burmin, hauling himself off the ladder into the bridge, reporting it to Zakharov – who after all had *not* transferred himself to the conning-tower. A scrambling-net was a large area of rope netting whose upper edge could be lashed to ship's-side stanchions so that it covered the side down to the waterline – for use by survivors, swimmers, in this case *Suvarov*'s – if there were any. *Buiny* was now clear of her side, they must somehow have got the admiral on board and she was coming out of it stern-first, backing out around *Ryazan*'s stern.

Waiting now for men who'd jump – and have only to flounder about thirty yards to find sailors climbing down on the net to help them.

No one yet. Plenty of gunports standing open: and that embrasure as it had been, but untenanted. *All* such points untenanted.

'Give 'em five minutes.' Zakharov, shouting across the bridge to Burmin. 'Before the big boys come back and finish us.'

Gunfire was all distant, none close by at all. And still no

jumpers. Where they might come from anyway: there were none in sight anywhere. Maybe the men who'd brought the admiral down to that level through the internal furnace had gone over into the *Buiny* with him. Would have – dragging him over with them. Watching, waiting. Michael was thinking of Narumov and of Sollogub, or V.V. Ignatzius, maybe with Flagmansky in his arms.

No such luck.

Dark, now. On course south forty east at twenty-two knots, looking for the *Dmitry Donskoi,* who'd wirelessed in code *Under attack by two light cruisers, holding them while* Sibir *runs for it on course Shanghai. My position midway Wakamiya Shima and Okino Shima. Have sustained considerable damage and heavy casualties, support would be welcome.*

Gunfire at that time had been like distant thunder from – they'd *thought* – the south, which was the way they'd been steering anyway, at more moderate speed, looking for the transports and Enqvist's cruisers – amongst whom *had* been the *Donskoi.* On the basis of the position she'd given, however, they'd altered course to southeast and increased to their maximum four hundred and forty revs. At the same time Zakharov had wirelessed *Joining you from northwesterly direction. Where is Enqvist?* Paymaster Lyalin and *Michman* Rimsky had coded it up and the signal would have gone out just minutes ago.

Michael, wearing Radzianko's oilskins, was in the front of the bridge with Zakharov, Burmin and Murayev, other bridge staff behind them. Wind and sea were on the quarter, there'd been some flurries of drizzle and there was a lot of movement on the ship – a lot of sea, ship and weather noise as well. Depending on the accuracy of the position given by *Donskoi,* one might see her at any time – especially if she was in action and had suffered damage, quite probably including fires: and *Ryazan* having had only fourteen miles to cover, at a rate of slightly more than a mile every three minutes. Although another factor was that a position given as midway between one island and another didn't sound like needle-point accuracy, could have been a fairly wild and hurried approximation.

The battle astern had fizzled out at sundown. All they'd heard between then and the sound of action which had been reverberating more recently from this southerly direction had been – heard from below decks – what Engineer Arkoleyev had reckoned were torpedoes exploding a long way astern: one had guessed at *coup de grâce* by Japanese destroyers.

The *Alexander*, *Oryol* and *Borodino* would have been likely recipients of those, he guessed. Even *Suvarov* herself, if she hadn't gone down before that.

'Reply to your signal, sir!'

Egorov. It struck Michael at about the same moment that the gunfire had ceased. There was only weather noise now, and *Ryazan*'s own, a lot of it from the action damage aft; and now Zakharov's shout of 'Saying what?'

'To *Ryazan* from *Donskoi*: *I do not know the whereabouts of Enqvist. He ran away. Regret you are too late but thank you for trying.* End of message, sir.'

End of *Dmitry Donskoi.*

'Damnation . . .'

Burmin's growl: 'If we'd had his call a bit sooner—'

'We're looking for two enemy light cruisers now. Tell the lookouts.'

'Aye, sir . . .'

'She *might* still be afloat.'

Murayev. No one argued with him but it seemed unlikely. That old *Donskoi* had been through a lot of trouble, Michael reflected. Innumerable breakdowns, problems in station-keeping, the incident with the girl from the *Orel*, and a spot of mutiny at Nossi-Bé. Vintage early eighties, converted from sail to steam near the end of the century: and by the sound of it, died fighting like a lion.

While Admiral Enqvist with the fast modern cruisers *Oleg*, *Aurora* and *Zemchug* had run away?

Zakharov had cut *Ryazan*'s speed to fifteen knots.

'Mikhail Ivan'ich, it's the *Sibir* those cruisers will be after now. Give me a course she might have taken for Shanghai.'

'Offhand, sir – west-southwest. But I'll check.'

From the chart, he heard him putting on starboard rudder. And for the time being southwest would be as good a course as any. At daylight there'd be plenty of land-features to fix on, one would adjust again then. Might with luck have picked up the *Sibir* before that, in any case: *if* she – and *Ryazan* – were allowed a clear run out through the strait, if those two cruisers weren't about to make a meal of her . . . He switched the light off and withdrew his head and shoulders from under the hood.

'West-southwest'll do until daylight, sir.'

'Good.' Steadying on that course: wind and sea on the starboard side now. 'It's the way she would have run, I suppose.'

'What about Enqvist?' Burmin, pivoting slowly, sweeping across the bow. She was rolling quite hard now as well as pitching. 'Where'd *he* skedaddle to?'

'They must have got separated somehow. He had the two hospital-ships to look after too, didn't he? *And*, oh, *Anadyr*, and—'

'He could have been miles away before those cruisers caught the *Donskoi*—'

'Who stood by the *Sibir* – or held them off while she – why, yes, if Enqvist started running soon enough, and—' Burmin caught his breath. 'Ship forty on the bow!'

'Christ, *yes*!'

A lookout had shouted too. And Michael was on it, and Zakharov . . .

'*Sibir*. Beyond doubt. All-round search for anything else, please. Chief yeoman!' Ducking to the pipe: 'Port ten. Egorov – revs for twelve knots. Chief yeoman – by light to the *Sibir* – she's *there*, see her?'

'On her, sir.'

'Identify ourselves, then make *I will escort you to territorial waters off Shanghai*.'

'Aye, sir.'

'Captain, sir.'

Michael, moving up beside him. 'If you'd delay that a moment—'

'Hold on, chief yeoman. Yes – what?'

'Why Shanghai, sir? Why not Vladivostok?'

'Vladivostok?'

'Six hundred miles on a direct course, but detouring around the battle area, say eight. Wide detour, well east of Okino Shima to start with. *Sibir*'s holds are full of field-guns and ammunition, Vladivostok'll be the prize now and after their losses at Mukden your army'll be desperate for a cargo like this one. Worth some risk, Nikolai Timofey'ich – don't you think?'

Face like a block of wood with a couple of chips of glass in it. He'd seen it like this before – about as expressive as it ever got. A grunt then: and looking back to Travkov: 'Chief yeoman . . .'

Dawn of the 28th came up in a fiery glow which within half an hour slid up behind a horizontal edging of black cloud. No mist or drizzle though, wind and sea about the same and visibility unfortunately not bad. The *Sibir* had said she could make fourteen knots (and yes, had coal for eight hundred miles) but they'd averaged better than fourteen over the past eight hours, more like fourteen and a half. In discussion with Zakharov over the chart last night, they'd settled on making this drastically eastward leg, passing between islands called Mino Shima and Taka Shima – Mino would be abeam to port (but not in sight) in about an hour, Taka similarly out of visibility range to starboard two hours later. Then on longitude one hundred and thirty-two east they'd alter to north by east, which would (a) make the whole transit less than seven hundred miles, (b) skirt widely around the area of yesterday's action – which no doubt would be resumed this morning – and (c) once past the approaches to Matsuru, take them well clear of any Japanese fleet bases.

The approaches to Matsuru were potentially dangerous now and would be all day, if any damaged enemies were making for it from the scene of action, for instance. Lookouts were being changed hourly, to keep fresh eyes and alert brains on the job, both at this level and aloft. Zakharov and Michael had been on the bridge all night, as well as officers of the watch who were changing over every two hours. Guns' crews were sleeping at their weapons, and Burmin had organized a system of action messing, with men from each station collecting rations including tea for their own parts-of-ship from the galley.

Daylight was established now, the pink flush all gone, replaced by a steely brightness under the dark cap of cloud. Zakharov was sipping at a glass of tea: it might have been the first time in about six hours that he'd had binoculars away from his eyes for more than seconds. All of that time he'd been on his high stool near the binnacle, but he was leaning in the port fore-corner now with his eyes on the *Sibir* plugging along a cable's length on the quarter.

'If we get through to sunset, Mikhail Ivan'ich . . .'

'Then we'll make it. We'll make it anyway.' Michael reached sideways to touch wood, the polished side panels of the binnacle. He added, 'ETA Vladivostok dawn day after tomorrow.'

In late forenoon they passed, at a distance, a small south-bound steamer; she was Japanese, and *Ryazan* hoisted the Rising Sun, *Sibir* then following suit. Fortunately her skipper wasn't disposed to exchange identities or news, soon faded far enough astern for Zakharov to tell Signal Yeoman Putilin, 'Have 'em pull that foul thing down now.'

'Hoist our own colours, sir?'

'No. Just keep that one handy.' To Michael then: 'How long before we alter?'

'Another hour. Unless you'd like to cut the corner?'

Shake of the head. 'Stick to what we planned.'

At noon, soup with bread and cheese was brought up for

the bridge staff, and Zakharov and Michael had the same. The soup came up in two buckets, with bowls and a metal ladle. Shikhin, Michael's servant, was one of the ration party who brought it up. Galikovsky, who was taking over the watch, had already had his meal, and Milyukov would get his in the wardroom; you could bet it wouldn't be cabbage soup down there, not even with the refinement of lumps of cheese in it, and they'd both looked askance at Michael's and the skipper's rations. Zakharov had in fact asked Michael whether he wouldn't rather have his down below, and Michael had surprised him by opting to remain. His main reason for it, privately, was that he had something he was anxious to discuss with Zakharov, and this might have been a good time for it; but it wasn't for Galikovsky's ears – not even for those of *the* V.A. Galikovsky, whose torpedo had sunk a Jap cruiser – and murmuring in corners didn't have much appeal. So he left it: in any case there was plenty of time. Having finished his soup he went into the chartroom to get his pipe, then checked the log-reading and told Zakharov, 'Better come round, sir – or we'll be getting a bit close to Oki Shima.'

'All right. Yeoman – by semaphore to *Sibir*, *Altering to north five east.*'

'Aye aye, sir.'

Five degrees east of due north because there were other islands to be passed on the long haul north – Take Shima, for instance, about a hundred and twenty miles north from here – and this with slight adjustments later would take them clear. Burmin came up when Galikovsky was steadying her on the new course; he glanced at the compass, and nodded. 'Course for Vladivostok, eh? My God, when we steam into Zolotoi harbour, skipper, delivering this lot here –' a nod towards the *Sibir*, who'd just put her helm over – 'why, they'll be ringing the church bells; you'll be the hero of the hour!'

Zakharov pointed at Michael. '*He* should be. I'd have escorted her to internment in Shanghai.'

'No, sir.' He was quick on it. 'Nothing to do with me at all. I'm English: we're allies of the Japanese. I've been acting purely as an observer, nothing else *at all*—'

Burmin chuckling, pointing at him: 'The monkeys' uncle – eh?'

'Seriously – you may have thought of Shanghai – since it was mentioned in the *Donskoi*'s signal – but then you had second thoughts. Please – leave me out of it.'

'Hero of the hour's our skipper then – as I said. Like it or lump it, Nikolai Timofey'ich! Steaming through into Zolotoi, all the ships' sirens screaming – why, glory to God—'

'Very amusing, Pyotr Fedor'ich. In any case, we have to get there first, let me remind you.'

He'd turned away, seemed truly not to like it, but Michael raised the subject again that evening when they were on their own in the chartroom for a few minutes, refreshing themselves against another night of it and a rising wind with a tot of Zakharov's vodka.

'Just one won't hurt us.'

'I'm sure it won't.' They'd each had a few hours' sleep during the day, while Burmin plus officers of the watch had held the fort, and there'd been no alarms. Nothing intelligible had come over the air-waves either, only streams of Japanese – Togo doubtless reporting to Tokyo, and Tokyo telling the world – a world in which Tasha would no doubt be holding her sweet breath. Michael began, watching Zakharov pour about two inches of vodka into each tumbler, 'On the subject of your being the hero of the hour, Nikolai—'

'Oh, come off it. Here . . .'

'Thanks, but – bear with me . . . You played a big part in getting Rojhestvensky out of *Suvarov*. Whatever may come of that. But also you finished off that cruiser and sank a torpedo-boat. Then you went to the aid of the *Donskoi* – too late, but it wasn't your fault – and, most importantly, you'll have brought this absolutely vital cargo through to the army defending Vladivostok. No exaggeration in any of that, it's plain fact. Has it struck you what it adds up to?'

'You tell me.'

'That you don't need any Volodnyakov influence now. D'you think the Tsar won't hear of it? Or that any of those politicos in Petersburg can stop you now? Isn't it what you really want – to get to the top on your own merits?'

'So what are you—'

'You don't need the Volodnyakovs, so you don't need Tasha. I *do*.'

'Ah. I was right.'

'Of course – and what's more—'

'No, let's cut the cackle. How might we handle this?'

'No question of back-tracking on your deal, there'll *be* no deal. She'll be gone. You'll simply accept it as a *fait accompli*.'

'You'll take her to England?'

'Yes – but the less you know – in detail anyway—'

'Agreed. As a matter of fact it's a weight off my mind. And I dare say you're right, his Majesty *might* see this as some – accomplishment—'

'Of course he will. And with colossal failure everywhere else he looks . . . You'll be an admiral in two shakes.'

'Well – let's not go mad. But I'll drink to that. *Tomorrow* we'll drink to that. This one's to *you*, Mikhail Ivan'ich!'

'Think we might make it to absent friends?'

'Oh.' Motionless, except for a necessary and natural balancing against his ship's motion. '*Suvarov*s, you're thinking of.'

'Quite a few of them, as it happens.'

A nod. 'To the bottom, then. Absent friends.'

One might, he thought, back in a corner of the bridge with his glasses up, have drunk more usefully to a safe arrival in Vladivostok.

But they *would* get there. In fact, with the weather easing, would probably have to reduce speed by a knot or two tomorrow evening so as to arrive in daylight – Tuesday's first light – rather than in the dark hours and be mistaken for Japanese. Although if one was in *very* good time one might use the Slaby-Arco from about thirty miles offshore. Give them time to roll the red carpets out.

Play it by ear. Then while Zakharov was enjoying the applause, and as likely as not receiving a telegram from the Tsar, nip ashore to the telegraph office and send the message one had drafted in one's mind at least a hundred times; and count on Nikolai Timofey'ich's new fame and influence to get one an immediate reservation on the Trans-Siberian to Moscow, thence to Paris.

Cable Jane as well. *Arriving home in about ten days probably not alone. Will wire again from Paris.* That would do it. Leave the rest to her discretion. There'd be hurdles to negotiate on the home front, her help would be invaluable and she'd be a great support to Tasha. Training right with his glasses, sweeping slowly and carefully down the starboard side, thinking *Tasha darling, you've got news coming. You may at this stage be biting your nails and losing sleep, but – oh, my love, I hope you'll think it's good news, howl with joy and rush to tell Mamasha, both of you start packing like two wild things . . .*

Vetrov, who had the watch, had just increased to revs for fifteen knots. Wind and sea still easing, Michael realized, and the *Sibir* out to do her best, treading on their heels. He went to the chart to make a note of the increase in speed, time and position by D.R. And while he was at it, checking the time by his own watch – Anna Feodorovna's gift – against the ship's chronometer. Correct – absolutely to the minute – despite having been banged around a bit. And thinking then, as he measured the distance still to be covered – his mind for a moment off Tasha, or at any rate half off her – *please,* no prowling armoured cruisers in the next – oh, say sixteen, eighteen hours?

Factual Note

The Floating Madhouse is a novel, not a history, but – for the record . . .

Rojhestvensky, with Clapier de Colongue and Semenov (on whom the character Selyeznov is based) and two other members of his staff, was transferred that same night from the *Buiny* to another destroyer, the *Byedovy*, which was undamaged and had enough coal to reach Vladivostok. The admiral was, however, very severely wounded – amongst other injuries he had a cracked skull and a splinter of it embedded in his brain – and since the little TBD's violent motion would have killed him, Clapier de Colongue decided to surrender the ship, so that his admiral could be taken to a hospital in Japan. Where in fact – in the naval hospital in Sasebo – he was well cared for and eventually returned to Russia.

Most of the second and third squadrons who had not been sunk were surrendering in any case that morning. Admiral Nyebogatov did most of it – to the surprise of the Japanese, who at that time did not have the word 'surrender' in their dictionaries. Two of those who hoisted white flags, the *Vladimir Monomakh* and *Sissoy Veliky*, hadn't fired a shot. In contrast, before she sank, the old *Dmitry Donskoi* had severely mauled four Japanese light cruisers and sunk two torpedo-boats – while Admiral Enqvist, who'd deserted her, ran with the *Oleg*, *Aurora* and *Zemchug* for the Philippines, was met and escorted into internment by ships of the U.S. Navy, which at first he mistook for Japanese and got the wind up all over again. He then reported by telegraph to the Tsar that the conduct in battle of all ranks had been 'beyond all praise', and the Tsar was graciously pleased to take his word for it.

By way of contrast, one might quote here a Japanese account of the last moments of the *Suvarov*:

> In the dusk, when our cruisers were driving the enemy northwards, they came upon the *Suvarov* alone, at some distance from the fight, listing heavily and enveloped in flames and smoke. The division of torpedo-boats which was with our cruisers was at once sent to attack her. Although much burned and still on fire – having been subjected to so many attacks, shot at by all the fleet – although she had only one serviceable gun she still opened fire, showing her determination to defend herself to the last moment of her existence. At length – at about seven p.m. – after our torpedo-boats had twice more attacked her, she went to the bottom.

Taking with her, amongst nearly a thousand others, *Michman* Werner von Kursel, who single-handed – the rest of its crew having been killed – had kept that last gun firing. Earlier (while cracking jokes and handing out cigars) he had played a leading part in the difficult business of getting the admiral through the blazing ship and over to the *Buiny*, but had then refused to transfer to the destroyer with him and those others.